Acclaim for Gemma O'Connor

Time to Remember

'A complex, atmospheric and gripping story that keeps you guessing until the very end.'
Mail on Sunday

'Cleverly woven . . . The author skilfully builds the tension and produces a surprising resolution'
Sunday Telegraph

Farewell to the Flesh

'A complex, intelligent story, with lashings of atmosphere and tension and a clever climax'
The Times

'Gemma O'Connor has produced another gripping murder mystery'
Irish Post (Book of the Week)

Falls the Shadow

'A gripping tale of moral rottenness and manipulated innocence in which the reader becomes increasingly entangled'
Irish Independent

'This page-turner mystery is written with the author's usual verve and energy – fans won't be disappointed'
Belfast Telegraph

Sins of Omission

'Grimly convincing . . . compulsively readable'
Daily Telegraph

'Written with great verve and brio'
Irish Times

www.**booksattransworld**.co.uk

Walking on Water

GEMMA O'CONNOR

BANTAM PRESS

LONDON · NEW YORK · TORONTO · SYDNEY · AUCKLAND

TRANSWORLD PUBLISHERS
61–63 Uxbridge Road, London W5 5SA
a division of The Random House Group Ltd

RANDOM HOUSE AUSTRALIA (PTY) LTD
20 Alfred Street, Milsons Point, Sydney
New South Wales 2061, Australia

RANDOM HOUSE NEW ZEALAND
18 Poland Road, Glenfield, Auckland 10, New Zealand

RANDOM HOUSE SOUTH AFRICA (PTY) LTD
Endulini, 5a Jubilee Road, Parktown 2193, South Africa

Published 2001 by Bantam Press
a division of Transworld Publishers

A catalogue record for this book is available from the British Library.
ISBN 0593 047192

Typeset in 11½/14pt Bembo by Falcon Oast Graphic Art

Printed in Great Britain
by Mackays of Chatham plc, Chatham, Kent

1 3 5 7 9 10 8 6 4 2

In affectionate memory of Kate Cruise O'Brien

Author's Note

All the characters in this book are fictitious, as is the plot, and any resemblance to actual persons, living or dead, is purely coincidental. The geography, too, is imagined. The Glár River and its estuary bear more resemblance to a certain bay in Connemara than anything along the coast of Cork, and although the county boasts a Passage West and Waterford a Passage East, Passage South is my own invention, as are Duncreagh, Trianach and Daingean.

The place names are mainly from the Gaelic: Daingean = citadel; Glár = silt; Trianach = ternary (habitat of terns). Daingean is also the Irish for Dingle in Kerry, which added a pleasing (to me) link with Recaldo.

Acknowledgements

This book could not have been written without the loving support of my husband John, my children and children-in-law and grandchildren, who are always a source of joy and strength but most particularly so over the past eighteen months. I give them all my love and thanks.

I am indebted to the Master and fellows of St Peter's College, Oxford, for their hospitality while I wrote the first draft of *Walking on Water*. I would also like to thank my friends in Ireland: Gardaí Ciaran Smyth, Pat Flaherty and Ted O'Driscoll. In Oxford: Jane Jones of the Audiology unit at the Radcliffe Infirmary, lawyers Shelley Cranshaw and Dorothy Flood, and yachtsman Tim Goodfellow all gave me technical advice and help. While thanking them, I should say that any mistakes of interpretation or fact are mine and mine alone. I am particularly grateful to Cole Moreton for suggesting Recaldo's name.

Police – or Garda Siochana – procedure has been manipulated by the author to serve the purposes of the story. My advisors, therefore, should not feel responsible or embarrassed and I trust I will be forgiven by those to whom verisimilitude or exactitude matters. The same necessarily applies to medical problems which are written about from the patient's rather than the physician's point of view.

Finally, my warm thanks to Ruth for her unwavering support, my editor Francesca and my agent Chris for their constant help and support.

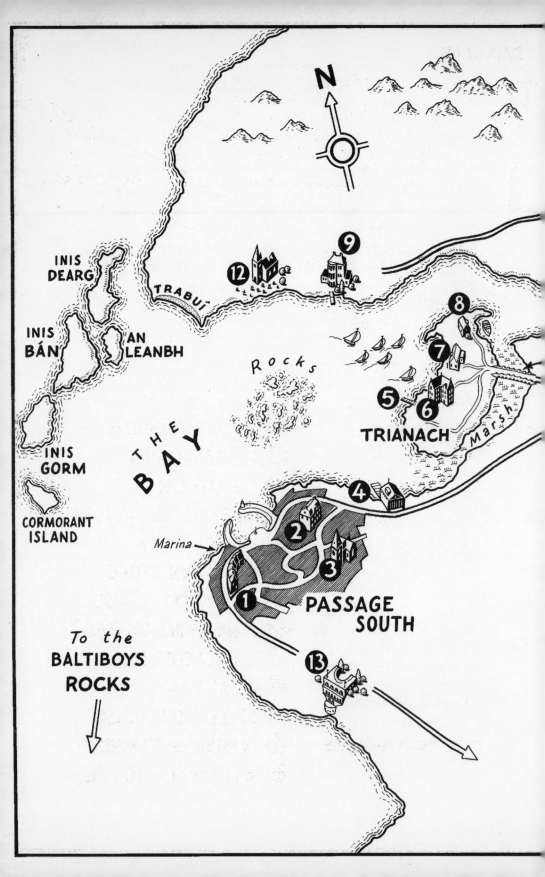

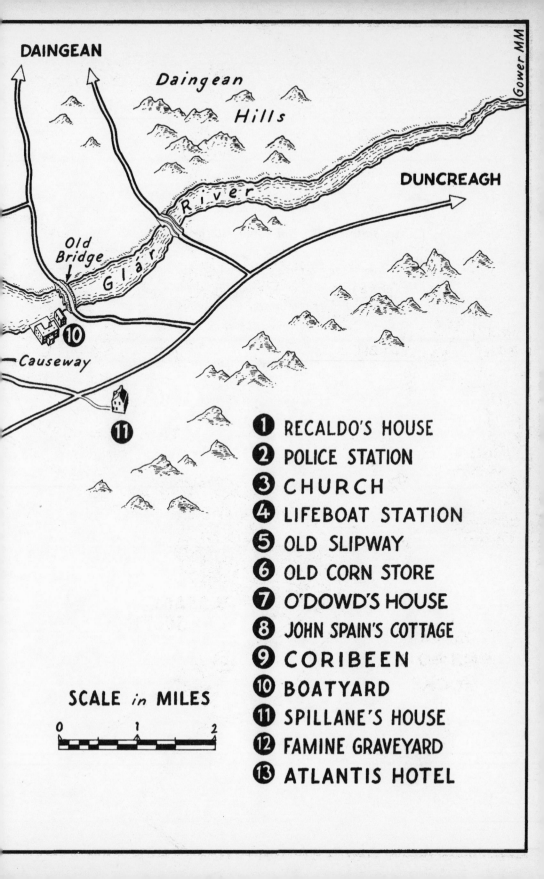

DAINGEAN

Daingean

Hills

Gower MM

DUNCREAGH

River

Old
Bridge

Glár

⑩

Causeway

⑪

SCALE *in* MILES

0   1   2

① RECALDO'S HOUSE
② POLICE STATION
③ CHURCH
④ LIFEBOAT STATION
⑤ OLD SLIPWAY
⑥ OLD CORN STORE
⑦ O'DOWD'S HOUSE
⑧ JOHN SPAIN'S COTTAGE
⑨ CORIBEEN
⑩ BOATYARD
⑪ SPILLANE'S HOUSE
⑫ FAMINE GRAVEYARD
⑬ ATLANTIS HOTEL

Non sum qualis eram bonae sub regno Cynarae

Last night, ah yesternight, betwixt her lips and mine
There fell thy shadow, Cynara! thy breath was shed
Upon my soul between the kisses and the wine;
And I was desolate and sick of an old passion,
Yea, I was desolate and bowed my head:
I have been faithful to thee, Cynara! in my fashion.

Ernest Dowson 1867–1900

Prologue

'I NOTICED HER WHEN I WAS COMING IN LAST NIGHT,' JOHN SPAIN said, 'but I didn't pay much heed. I often see her, of an evening, specially when the tide is low, standing down there by that stunted oak.'

Sometimes the American woman leaned against the tree, silently watching the water while she smoked, languid and elegant as a balle-rina. There was something about the way she presented herself – not merely as a beautiful face, a lithe body; the overall picture pleased his eye. His was the long romantic view of presbyopia; he perceived her through a kindly blur. Her extravagant, whimsical way of dressing merely added to his enchantment. Long, floating, diaphanous dresses. Pale colours, plain, never patterned; blues, greens, white sometimes.

'She often wore a shawl draped around her head,' he said suddenly. 'I suppose it was just for protection against the damp . . . the sea breeze.' The old man stopped for a moment and nervously massaged his neck with his splayed hand. 'Maybe the light had me confused but it didn't dawn on me. . .' He lapsed into a sort of trance and when, eventually, he continued his story, he sounded as though he was trying to convince himself of what he'd seen.

'I was out a bit earlier than usual. The early-morning fog hadn't quite cleared when I spotted her. She was like something from a pic-ture book, a film . . .' He waggled his head sadly. 'Breathtaking, beautiful, in that strange, mysterious pink light.' He looked at the policeman balefully, as if ashamed of his poetic lapse. Sergeant Recaldo remained oppressively silent, waiting for him to continue.

'I'd cut back the engine, slowed down and let the current carry the boat along, while I lit my pipe and sat back enjoying the dawn. You don't get many days like that, so you're inclined to make the best of them.' He closed his eyes and took a deep breath. 'It was as I rounded the turn here,' his outstretched arm described the contour of the point, 'that I saw her. She was all lit up, rising out of the swirling mist. It was all around her. At first I couldn't believe my eyes, for God forgive me, I thought she was walking on the water.'

Tuesday

Chapter One

WHERE THE BROAD GLÁR RIVER OPENED OUT TO EMBRACE THE SEA, at the coastal village of Passage South, it was almost three-quarters of a mile wide. There, where the water curled playfully around a cluster of craggy rocks, the fishing was best and the lobster markers stuck out of the sea like so many miniature flagpoles, dancing through the waves with their tattered ensigns fluttering, horse-tailed, from the constant buffeting of the wind. The young weekend sailors used them as a sort of marine slalom course, dodging the sleek little Lasers between the sticks like frenzied bats.

It was mid-September. After several days of rain and almost every variation of autumnal squall short of hurricane, Tuesday morning dawned bright and sunny, a perfect if chilly day which, by some miracle, was still holding at noon. On the cliff top overlooking the bay, Garda-Sergeant Francis Xavier Recaldo, resident one-man police force of Passage South, amateur musician and occasional travel writer, stood looking out over the sea, his neat and powerful binoculars trained on a blue-painted fishing vessel which was playing hide and seek between the islands on the far side of the bay.

After a few minutes his radiophone began to crackle. He lifted the receiver to his ear and listened. 'He's playing us for sport,' he replied. 'But he should come into your sights just about . . . now. See him? He's going around the head of Cormorant Island. You've spotted him? Right then, I'll see you later, as arranged.' He retracted the aerial and rehitched the receiver on his belt.

Recaldo – Frank to his friends and FX to those who assumed they were – was over six foot four, with the picturesque looks of his Spanish forebears. His abundant hair was blue-black, his eyes hooded, dark-lashed, deep blue. Aquiline nose and sensuous mouth. He was reserved in manner, with a curious air of stillness about him. Unusually formal, extremely courteous; his good manners rarely slipped, but he found small talk difficult and was not gifted at making easy friendships. In the main, women found him attractive; men less so since he had little interest in being one of the gang. Discretion was a desirable trait in a country officer of the law, and Recaldo was nothing if not discreet. Whatever information came his way he kept strictly to himself. He was good at his job, approachable if not overfriendly.

It was getting on for noon. He had been on surveillance since dawn and was feeling somewhat drained. He hoisted himself up on a large smooth rock and held his face to the sun. Three years before, at the age of thirty-eight, he'd had a coronary immediately after a vigorous game of squash. Just dropped like a stone. Bang. Stress and sixty cigarettes a day were among the suggested causes. And genes, since his father had died of a heart attack at fifty-five. The bypass operation was successful, though his illness had effectively spelt the end of his high-flying career at Garda Headquarters in Dublin. It also ended his marriage, though this had been on the rocks for some time.

The irony was that when, against his own expectations, he began to recover, he came to the realization that what he most wanted was to step off the career conveyor belt and completely change his lifestyle. So strong was this impulse that he immediately put in for early retirement. And neatly demonstrating just how out of touch he was, he did not consult his wife. Not unnaturally, this proved the last straw as far as Sheila was concerned. Theirs was one of the first homegrown divorces under the new legislation. They agreed to part before he realized that fifty per cent of the marital spoils wouldn't buy even a retirement cottage, much less the house he had dreamed of building on his family plot near Dingle. The scheme didn't seem to be a viable proposition until a mate tipped him off about the job in Passage South. It wasn't his beloved Kerry but, being in Cork, the next county, near enough.

It took considerable powers of persuasion to talk his superiors into appointing him – the force did not like to demote its officers – but eventually he prevailed. He arrived at Passage South allegedly cured, but with his emotional life in tatters. His worldly goods comprised a newly acquired eight-year-old ex-army Jeep, two suitcases of clothes,

4

a large trunk of paperbacks, a disgusting-looking ghetto blaster and an extensive CD collection.

His two teenage sons resolutely refused to visit him 'in the sticks', but by sheer persistence he was somehow managing to build a reasonable relationship with them. His visits to Dublin were at their convenience, and he'd learned to take their ages and tastes into account.

Being a musician helped. To his own amusement, he'd developed an active interest in the current music scene – though, he had to admit, inevitably trailing light years behind his sons.

Oddly enough, music also helped to make him accepted in Passage South – though perhaps it was his dogged attempts at learning to sail which proved the bigger ice-breaker. The sight of that tall elegant figure shoehorned into his little dinghy caused the more lavishly accommodated much merriment.

And it was in his boat that Recaldo longed to be that morning, as he scrambled down from his lookout. He walked restlessly to the cliff edge and surveyed the scene below. The sparkling sea looked tempting beyond measure, with its islands scattered like jewels in the sunlight. There were several small craft scudding across the bay as fishermen and sailors made the most of what might well be the last good day of the season; amongst them he spotted his friend John Spain in his sturdy wooden boat. Most mornings saw the old man putputting the couple of miles down the estuary from his cottage to spend three or four pensive hours fishing, catching bait, or checking his five lobster pots. Sometimes, in good weather, he spent all day in the small open craft, switching off the outboard motor and rowing as soon as he came within range of his chosen ground.

From his vantage point Recaldo could just about make out the golden sands of Trabuí Strand on the other side of the bay where, later that day, he'd arranged to meet Cressida Sweeney whom he'd been wooing for some months. Illicitly, of course, with all the awkwardness, secrecy and inconvenience that implied. And frustration. Because he'd spent Saturday and Sunday with his sons in Dublin, he hadn't seen her since the previous Friday. He had much to tell her – for there was at last some hope of persuading her to leave her ghastly husband. Getting together. The thought of her filled him with deep longing, as it always did. He regarded her as a kind of miracle, for love had found him when he least expected it and startled him with joy.

5

Trabuí beckoned. Or perhaps it was the thought of Cressie that fired his imagination and made him decide to take the afternoon off and sail across the bay to meet her. A romantic gesture to mark a turn in their fortunes. The day before, he'd signed a modest contract for his first collection of travel pieces and his ex-wife, who was about to remarry, had, without any prompting from him, suggested they sell the family house and split the proceeds. He stretched out his arms and cried: 'Thank you, thank you, God, or whoever is looking out for me.' Then he whistled for his dog.

It was several minutes before the unruly half-Labrador, Barker, came hurtling towards him, barking his head off. Recaldo grabbed his collar and held him firmly for the five minutes it took to get home. As they passed the Atlantis Hotel the old gardener called out a greeting. Recaldo waved but didn't stop for fear of being caught. He was rather wary of Finbarr Spillane, who was a dedicated gossip.

Home was a small modern house tagged to the end of a terrace of empty holiday-lets which clung to the side of the hill on the very outskirts of the village, close to the cliff walk. He barely took time for a quick sandwich before strolling down to the village which was half-asleep in the sunshine, with a peaceful, end-of-season atmosphere.

Passage South was much like any other seaside village the world over, except it had the advantage of a breathtakingly beautiful situation. True, the original compact little settlement had grown over the years and not always in sympathetic style, but on the whole it retained its age-old charm. The village fanned up a gentle hill from the small harbour at its heart; neatly bisected east to west by the main street which boasted six bed-and-breakfast establishments (*seomrí en suite*), a chandlery and general store, three pubs, a café and a gift shop. There were two good restaurants, one seasonal, the other open all year round.

A cobblestone road ran down to the pier where the ferries and fishing boats tied up. The sailing school and marina were off to the right. It had started with one small dock, but over time first one and then another had been flung outwards into the bay. As the number of pleasure craft grew, colourful little mooring buoys danced north-west to the cluster of rocky islets at the mouth of the estuary.

There was very little activity in the pre-dinner lull, just a couple of delivery vans outside the grocery shop and three or four people leaning against the harbour wall. The thousand-odd inhabitants of the village and hinterland could, and often did, increase threefold during the summer months but from the end of August slipped back to sleepy normality. It was then that the local sailors, Recaldo among them, came into their own, for September could be the most beautiful month of the year.

'Grand day, Frank.' Michael Hussey, landlord of the most popular bar in the village, greeted him as he walked by. Recaldo stopped to pass the time of day. 'Will it hold?'

'It might, then. Are you thinking of going out?'

'Maybe,' Recaldo conceded. 'Once I see what's waiting for me above.'

He continued his way up to the two-roomed garda station which was situated on the Duncreagh Road, just off Main Street, close to the church. Normally he spent as little time as possible at either. As luck would have it there were two or three people waiting for him, but in the end it only took just over an hour to sort out their various trivial complaints. It was a quarter to two when, at last, he switched the station phone to automatic, slipped his mobile in his pocket, got into his ancient Jeep and headed for the estuary.

Chapter Two

RECALDO KEPT HIS SMALL OPEN DINGHY, *PEIG*, OUT OF THE WATER, on the east bank of Trianach Island which was only a mile or so upriver from the mouth of the bay, but a good five miles by road. The island – or rather near-island – was reached by causeway from the road to Duncreagh, a bustling market town some seven or eight miles further inland. Trianach was triangular in shape with its longest side to the river, along which there were three or four extensive properties, all but one owned by non-residents. Indeed there was a large and growing number of incomers on both banks of the estuary. They were known locally as blow-ins.

The dinghy was sitting forlornly on a patch of wasteland between the two largest houses, a hundred yards or so from either. The most extensive properties on Trianach were built on the south side, facing the estuary. To his right there was a converted early nineteenth-century warehouse occupied by an American woman called Evangeline Walter. To his left, an appalling ranch-style holiday bungalow, built by a German couple, which was empty eleven-twelfths of the year.

The *Peig* was in a poor state after the weekend rain. The tarpaulin covering it had slipped off, leaving three or four inches of brackish water in the bottom of the dinghy. He undid the stern bungs and tilted the small craft upward to let it drain, then manoeuvred the trailer over the gravel and into the water. Once she was floated he tied her to a submerged boulder, then hauled the trailer laboriously back up the beach and secured it in its usual spot. As he recovered his breath he looked across the wide estuary to the opposite bank on which, a little further upstream, Cressie lived in a house called Coribeen, though at this distance it could not be seen with the naked eye.

There were perhaps a dozen yachts of varying shapes and sizes moored to floating buoys on either side of the river. The most opulent of these, a forty-four-foot ketch, belonged to Cressida's husband, V. J. Sweeney, once a successful businessman, now something of a lush. Amongst the others there were at least four or five which never seemed to be used from one end of the year to the other. Of the rest, most belonged to local residents. One, the *Cynara*, a smartly kept twenty-six-foot sloop owned by Mrs Walter, was moored a short distance from the bottom of her garden.

It was almost three o'clock when Recaldo clambered on board and rigged *Peig*'s sail, then, settling himself at the tiller, he pushed away from the shore. He looked rather comic, scissored into the small boat like an awkward black stork. A stiff breeze quickly caught the sail and carried him swiftly into midstream and he soon saw that he wasn't alone on the estuary. Boats which had looked forlorn and abandoned were beginning to show signs of life. One or two of their occupants raised their hands in greeting.

It was a glorious day to be on the water. 'Fine day,' John Spain called as he rowed past. 'Watch out if you're going upriver, Frank, there's a tree down by Whelan's yard – it's floating free.' Recaldo registered, with some surprise, that little Gil Sweeney, Cressida's son, was sitting upright in the prow, pointing at something in the water. The sun glinted on his curly blond hair as he turned his head. When he spotted Frank, he waved enthusiastically and shouted, 'Tank!' Recaldo waved back. He surmised they were off to watch the seals on the rocks at the mouth of the estuary, and marvelled, as he always did, that the old man had the strength to handle his small but heavy wooden boat. As he idly followed their progress, two thoughts lazily crossed his mind: first, he'd never before seen the child alone on John Spain's boat, and second, that Gil, who was deaf, was rarely far from his mother's side. Ergo, for once he and Cressie might actually have some time on their own. His spirits lifted as images of her settled comfortably into his thoughts. Instead of heading straight for Trabuí, Recaldo decided to go over to Coribeen, in the hope of catching her at home before she set out for the strand. Her husband had gone to London over the weekend and, with any luck, might still be away.

It was a moment of perfect contentment. I am happy, he thought, as his little boat skimmed the water. Today I am happy; everything is going right. Somehow things between him and Cressie would work out. They would make it. He had never been so sure of anything in his life. He began to hum a Corrs number he'd heard that weekend – 'What can I do to . . .' – which matched his mood exactly. Why was it, he wondered, that what the pop song described sounded like complete goo if he tried to say it?

While Recaldo was tacking across the estuary, out of sight of Trianach, Mrs Evangeline Walter came out of her house, the Old Corn Store, and strolled down through the garden to the water's edge, carrying a picnic basket in her right hand. She was about forty-five, of medium height, but being extremely thin looked rather taller. She was dressed in pale blue loose trousers and a long overblouse with a silky scarf wrapped around her head, its ends lifting in the breeze. When she reached the bank she set the basket down on the grass and lit a cigarette, then leaned against a stunted tree which overhung the water.

A powerful fibreglass motor boat came speeding downriver, its front end well clear of the water. The pulsating noise as it hit the surface was deafening. It weaved erratically between the moored yachts. Mrs Walter watched it approach then raised her left arm and called out, though the words were lost on the wind. As the engine was cut back the boat made a lazy half-circle and eased into the bank. Mrs Walter adroitly caught the rope that was thrown to her and tied it to the tree trunk. A well-preserved man, dressed in navy slacks, striped shirt and blazer, stepped nimbly off the boat onto the bank. He had curly greying hair, a fresh complexion and a dashing smile. Jeremiah O'Dowd, or Smiler, as he was habitually called, was her neighbour, an obliging man, though less appreciated by the locals than the incomers whom he beguiled with his ready charm, Mrs Walter chief among them.

'Hi, Jer,' she smiled. She was an attractive woman, with flawless skin and perfect teeth. 'All set?'

Jer O'Dowd put his arm around her shoulder. 'Are you sure about this?' he asked tenderly. 'Sure you're up to it?'

She shrugged him off but still smiled. 'Sure, I'm sure, honey. Trust me.'

He stood rolling back and forth on the balls of his small neat feet. 'Well, I think it's a mistake, Vangie,' he said quietly. 'You should leave well enough alone. Haven't you got him where you want him? The man is unpredictable, you don't want to rouse him. You'll only make trouble for yourself. Spoil things.'

'I know what I'm doing.' Her voice was steely. Then she smiled and her face softened. It was clear she was fond of him. 'Anyway I'll have you there to look after me. So what's to worry?'

'You're not going to gloat, are you, Vangie?'

'Don't worry, I won't rock the boat.' She smirked, pleased by the pun.

He cocked his head and grinned but didn't argue. They stood looking at each other until something caught his attention and he turned around to the house. A young woman, a girl, with long hair flying out behind her, jumped down from a rocky outcrop and came running down the garden towards them. She was dressed in jeans and a white sweater and was barefoot.

'Oh God, Vangie. *She's* not coming, is she?'

'Of course she is,' she said sweetly, as the girl came to her and clutched her arm. Mrs Walter touched O'Dowd's cheek with a long frosted-pink fingernail. 'So, what are we waiting for, Jer? Let's go, honey.'

'God alone knows what you're up to, Vangie, but I hope you know what you're doing, is all I can say. I thought you trusted me?' He tried, unsuccessfully, to hide his hurt and irritation.

'Sure, I trust you,' she protested. 'It's just a little treat for my baby.' She drew the girl closer to her and linked her arm. 'But I think you'll find it quite entertaining.' Her lizard smile belied the easy words.

He gave her a sideways look and huffed out his lips. '*That* doesn't make me feel any better,' he said uneasily. 'Listen to me, Vangie, you're not well . . .'

'Hell, Jer, you can be such an old woman. Will you just forget it? I know what I'm doing.'

O'Dowd looked at her sourly. 'Well don't blame me, if it goes wrong.'

'No, Jer, I won't blame you. That, at least, I can promise you.' She raised her eyebrows at him, mockingly. 'You've always benefited from my schemes, so why the sudden panic?'

'I don't want anything to go wrong with the sale, that's all.'

Her eyes narrowed. 'And why should it?'

He shrugged. 'I don't like to count my chickens . . .'

'Don't worry, they'll hatch.' She laughed. 'We'll wait until the last minute before mentioning it. I can't wait to see his face.'

'Are you out of your mind or what?' he said sharply. 'I'll stick a note through his letter-box tonight and let him have his tantrums in the privacy of his own home.'

'Only teasing.' She smiled enigmatically.

'I hope you are,' he said. She pecked his cheek then began to tease him archly, coaxing his ill humour away; and after a moment he grinned and helped her and the girl on board, untied the line and jumped nimbly in after them. He backed the boat slowly away from the shallows before opening up its powerful engine. The wake made a wide, swelling, inverse V, as the boat swept around in a great half-circle and set off across the estuary.

A few minutes later they pulled in on the near side of the Sweeneys' ketch. O'Dowd saw the two women safely aboard and waited until they were below decks and out of sight before he headed for the wooden dock below Coribeen, where he pulled in behind a hand-some motor launch and waited with the engine idling.

After about ten minutes or so a man came walking down the field from the large late-Georgian farmhouse, surrounded by a clump of trees, a couple of hundred feet up from the dock. He paused to light a cig-arette before stepping on board. He too was dressed in navy, with a white scarf knotted at his throat. He was carrying a soft skipper's cap. V. J. Sweeney was tall, middle-aged and fair-haired, a handsome, if dissi-pated-looking man. He grunted rather than spoke a greeting. O'Dowd pushed the engine into gear and backed the boat away from the dock.

'The weather should be good for a couple of hours. We'll motor out into the bay, then see how we get on,' Sweeney announced. He seemed unusually affable. 'We'll sail back.'

'I prefer not to sail today,' O'Dowd said. 'I need to get a bit more con-fidence with manoeuvring her first and I find it easier with the motor.'

'Oh? Do you now?' VJ raised his eyebrows. 'You'll never get any-where being chicken. We'll sail back,' he said firmly. 'And you'll bloody well do what I tell you, I don't want another fiasco like last week.' O'Dowd shuddered. The fiction was that Sweeney was teach-ing him to sail, though his irascibility made him a hopelessly overbearing instructor and Smiler a nervous pupil.

'Just watch what I do and follow instructions. Right?'

'Whatever you say.' O'Dowd sounded preoccupied. He said nothing more while they motored out to the ketch. He was not looking forward to the next few minutes. Luckily, there was no sign of the other two passengers. He clambered aboard first and held on to the line until Sweeney joined him on deck. O'Dowd secured the motor boat to the mooring buoy and remained at the front waiting for instructions to cast off. Sweeney took his time. Without bothering that he might be overlooked, he peed over the side of the boat before taking his place behind the wheel.

Recaldo didn't recognize who was behind the wheel of the motor boat until it pulled in at the Sweeneys' dock. He was idly wondering what O'Dowd was up to when V. J. Sweeney came strolling down the garden. 'Shit,' muttered Recaldo, hurriedly changing direction, and was immediately caught by a sudden squall which came rippling over the water. He threw himself forward as the *Peig* jibed, and barely missed being hit by the swinging boom. This distracted him for a while, and it was only when the *Peig* settled on an even keel that he looked over to the dock. O'Dowd's boat had gone. He glanced around in search of it and his heart almost stopped beating when he saw V. J. Sweeney standing in the cockpit of his yacht, shouting orders at . . . for a moment he couldn't see but then O'Dowd straightened up. Recaldo, now completely intrigued, eased the *Peig* on to an empty mooring buoy and grabbed hold. Sweeney, still barking instructions at his hapless companion, slowly and effortlessly circled around. As the stern came into view Recaldo saw that the ketch had recently been renamed. Hitherto known as *Azurra*, it was sporting *Halcyon* in newly painted, bold white letters on the blue transom. Then, as the yacht purred away, he had a further surprise: two women came up from below decks and joined Sweeney and O'Dowd. He instantly recognized Mrs Walter from her clothes. It was the other woman who arrested his attention. From that distance he couldn't see her clearly but in any case she had her back to him. It was the long fair hair that made him think it might be Cressida.

Cressida? It couldn't be, surely? Cressie was meeting him at Trabuí. They'd arranged it. Besides, she hated sailing and specially hated it with Sweeney shouting orders at her the whole time. *Cressie?* Doubt assailed him.

Chapter Three

RECALDO, ABANDONING HIS HASTILY COBBLED PLAN TO SURPRISE Cressie at Coribeen, sailed towards Trabuí with more hope than expectation. Even if the girl on the yacht wasn't Cressie, he knew there was very little chance of her turning up now that her husband was around. He kept an eye on the ketch until it was swallowed up in the bay. He was mildly puzzled by the name change and what it might possibly imply, though he was more concerned that VJ's sudden appearance might mean that he wouldn't be able to see Cressie – for days perhaps. This worried him. The last time he'd seen her she'd been sporting the latest in a recent series of unexplained injuries.

He'd been in the crowded supermarket in Duncreagh the previous Friday, trying to decide on a brand of coffee, when a bandaged hand shot out and picked up a bag of beans. 'Try this one,' she said, and grinned at his surprise. Gil was pushing a shopping trolley beside her. Frank took the package from her. 'What happened to your hand? Cressie?'

'Shush,' she said, glancing around her uneasily. 'It's nothing. Just a little burn.' She stuffed her hand in her cardigan pocket. 'Say hi to Frank, Gil.' She bent down to her son, and spoke slowly and clearly. Six-year-old Gil looked up with his ready smile. 'Hi.' He pushed the word out, losing the H somewhere, but it was still recognizably hi. 'Tank,' he added impishly and burst out laughing. Frank stretched out his hand and tousled the blond curls when all the time he wanted to touch Cressie, take her in his arms. 'Hi, Gil. How's the shopping going?' Gil held up a long list and silently pointed to the half-full trolley. He pushed it a little further on and began to select more items from the shelves, carefully consulting the list each time as well as checking for his mother's approval. He looked very pleased with himself.

'It's great to see you,' Frank said foolishly, feeling a hundred eyes on them.

'We're on our way back from getting Gil's hearing aid checked out,' Cressida said loudly, then whispered, 'Val's going away for a few days.'

'When?'

'He didn't say. Tomorrow, I think.'

'I can't believe this,' he said, frustrated. 'I'm on my way to a meeting at headquarters and after that I'm going straight to Dublin. My weekend with the kids. I won't be back until late Monday.' He leaned closer to her. 'That London publisher I was telling you about is coming to see me in Dublin. Blast. I'll put him off.'

'No,' she whispered urgently. 'No, no don't do that.' She bit her lip. 'I don't know when Val's going, much less coming back, could be any time.' She shrugged. 'Or not at all. You know what he's like. Just for heaven's sake don't ring. I'll get in touch when I can.'

'Have you time for a cup of coffee?' he asked. This was against all their self-imposed rules. A flicker of anxiety appeared in her eyes but her voice was gentle enough. 'No.' It would be noticed, she implied, and commented upon. 'If he's still away on Tuesday, we'll go out to Trabuí for a run,' she whispered. 'About four?' She smiled then glanced around and put her hand to her face. 'Watch out, Frank, that Walter cow has just come in. That's all we need.' She moved away from him. 'Goodbye then,' she called. 'I'd better go after Gil or he'll buy the shop.'

Recaldo navigated his way into a little cove close to Trabuí Strand, leapt ashore and pulled the *Peig* up on the sand. Remembrance of her closing remarks made him realize how unlikely it was that it could have been Cressie on the boat. She loathed Evangeline Walter.

He strolled along the sand for almost an hour before he gave up hope of seeing her. By the time he got back to his dinghy it had clouded over and the air had turned as damp and chilly as his mood. Fortunately, though, the wind was in the right direction and he made it across the estuary in record time. Before dragging his boat out of the water, he retrieved his mobile from his locked car and checked to see if Cressie had left a message. There was none; he dialled her home number but cut off when he got the answering machine. Her mobile appeared to be switched off, as it had been for some days.

His helplessness completely frustrated him. She couldn't stay with her bully of a husband. Soon, soon, soon, he vowed, things between them would resolve and they could get together. He thought about this for a moment, then scorned himself for a romantic fool.

On the way home he stopped to buy some provisions from the redoubtable Mrs Imelda Ryan, who ran Passage South post office which also served as a quasi-deli. Amongst other things, she made marvellous soup which she sold by the pint.

'You were out then, Frank? You caught a bit of the sun. Wasn't it well for you now, the weather forecast is for rain.'

'What? Tonight?'

'No, the long-range. Tomorrow or the next day. Desperate over the weekend, wasn't it?'

'It wasn't so bad in Dublin.'

'Yes, I heard you were there all right. How are your boys?'

'Teenagers,' he replied laconically. 'We saw a couple of good films.' With all the other semi-detatched dads, he thought guiltily. It had been a particularly gruesome visit, with the boys making demands he couldn't possibly afford and then comparing his generosity unfavourably with his ex-wife's new partner. Her letter, which was waiting for him on his return, had therefore come as a major surprise. He'd carried it around in his pocket all day, hoping to show Cressie. Now he touched it, superstitiously, while he searched for loose change.

'Are we ever going to see them here at all?' Mrs Ryan broke in on his thoughts.

Recaldo laughed. 'Well, once I manage to persuade them that life doesn't end south of O'Connell Street.'

'Did you hear Marilyn Donovan was taken bad last night?'

'No, I had business in Dublin yesterday, I only got back just before midnight.'

'Wisha God love her, she lost the baby. Mrs Sweeney drove her to the hospital. Isn't she a very obliging woman?'

He pricked up his ears. 'Mrs Sweeney? Why not Steve?'

'Wasn't he out on a job over Daingean way, he didn't get back until nine.' Mrs Ryan could be trusted to supply all the details.

'I'll take a quart of tomato soup and half a cooked chicken.' He appeared only vaguely interested. 'Oh. And a loaf of bread. Duncreagh hospital, is it?'

'No, then. Cork City. Mrs Sweeney took her all the way.'

'She back yet?' he asked casually.

'Who? Marilyn? No, they're keeping her in for a few days.' She paused knowingly, waiting for him to enquire about Cressie, but he didn't oblige. 'I heard Mrs Sweeney stayed with her the whole time. Isn't she great altogether?'

Of course. Her mobile would have to be switched off in the hospital. Recaldo's spirits were restored. Like every true lover he was enchanted to hear the name of his beloved mentioned, and Mrs Ryan had managed it three times in the space of a few minutes. And what she told him suggested that it couldn't have been Cressie on the boat. Now he realized why she wasn't answering her phone and why old John Spain was minding the child for her.

Mrs Ryan knitted her brows. 'At least I thought she wasn't back yet but funny enough, I thought I saw her out with a crowd on her husband's yacht earlier. But I was probably wrong, I always thought she didn't go in for the sailing.' Recaldo laid a tenner on the counter and picked up a copy of the *Irish Times*. He was uncertain again and didn't trust himself to say anything. He didn't need to, Mrs Ryan was hoeing a different furrow.

'I saw you had that old mongrel of yours out for a run this morning. You'll have a job training that fellow. Wouldn't you be better off with a decent pedigree dog, Frank? There's a card in the window from Mrs Reilly above at Kishaun kennels. Her red setter had a litter a few weeks back and she's offering two of the pups for sale.' Had she guessed that he'd only bought the blessed animal so he and Cressie could meet? Recaldo left her to her steamy speculation and went home.

He listened to the six-thirty news headlines as he stored his food in the fridge, had a quick bite to eat, then he headed off for John Spain's cottage to see if Gil was still there or if the old man could throw any light on Cressida's whereabouts. But John Spain wasn't at home.

Chapter Four

THE BOATING PARTY DID NOT GO WELL. WHEN THE WOMEN APPEARED on deck, Sweeney exploded and threatened to go home. O'Dowd took over the wheel and had some pleasure in telling him he could bloody well swim for it. Sweeney then rounded on Mrs Walter. A low-pitched slanging match broke out between them though, oddly, it was Mrs Walter who seemed to be calling most of the shots. In the middle of the battle, when O'Dowd went too close to another boat, Sweeney pushed him aside. O'Dowd retreated to the prow and remained there for the rest of the outing, thus missing a good deal of what went on at the back.

The girl seemed to be in a world of her own. She sat at the back of the boat raptly examining the bow wave and appeared utterly fascinated by the pattern it made, which was just as well, since nobody paid her any attention whatsoever. Once or twice when she inadvertently touched Sweeney he jerked away. They circled the bay a couple of times until, at around four, the sky clouded over and they turned for home. By then a sullen silence enveloped them. Smiler came aft and, living up to his nickname, tried desperately to cajole Mrs Walter into a better humour. She had turned very pale and sat listlessly beside the girl, who held her hand. O'Dowd went below and found a blanket for them.

The tide was in when they got back and Sweeney skilfully eased the ketch onto its moorings. He remained at the wheel while O'Dowd pulled the motor boat to the bow and climbed in. As he helped the two women off the yacht, some signal passed between O'Dowd and Mrs Walter.

'Don't,' he muttered, his hand over his mouth. Mrs Walter didn't answer.

'Say, Val,' she called. 'Thanks for the ride. Halcyon loved it.' She pulled the girl close. 'Didn't you, sweetheart?' Sweeney stared ahead, his face set. 'She's real tickled with the name. Too bad she's sold,' Mrs Walter continued.

'What are you talking about?'

'Oh, didn't Jer tell you?' she said airily. 'The *Halcyon*'s sold. Oh yes, the new owners will be here at the weekend.' She turned away, avoiding O'Dowd's eye. 'Better make sure everything is in order,' she added gaily.

Sweeney's face suffused with colour and his mouth slowly opened. 'Just like that?' His voice was a dull croak. 'What have you to do with it? My agreement's with O'Dowd.'

'Not just him and not any more. It's over. If you don't like it you can always sue me.'

'Stop, stop, you can't do that!'

'We already have,' O'Dowd chipped in and without a backward glance fired the engine.

Ten minutes later they disembarked at the Old Corn Store. 'Maybe I should have listened to you, after all,' Evangeline Walter said. She looked utterly washed out and was shivering with cold. O'Dowd took off his blazer and wrapped it around her. He held her shoulders as they walked slowly up to the house. The girl streeled in after them and switched on the television.

Mrs Walter threw herself down on the sofa and closed her eyes. For a few minutes she didn't move and appeared to lose consciousness.

'Are you all right? Vangie? Can you hear me?' Smiler slipped his arm under her shoulders and raised her head tenderly. Her eyes fluttered open.

'Sure,' she said softly. 'Sure, but I don't think I can manage her tonight.' Mrs Walter jerked her head at the girl. O'Dowd nodded. He helped her to her feet and brought her into the kitchen where they sat down on either side of the long refectory table. She looked across at him. 'Would you mind taking her back on your own? Please, Jer?'

O'Dowd didn't answer. He went to the fridge and poured them each a glass of white wine. 'Are you going to tell me what that was all about?'

'I fainted, that's all. I haven't eaten much today.'

'Don't give me that,' he protested angrily. 'You never eat much. Anyway you know full well that's not what I was talking about. Just what exactly was that play-acting on the yacht all about? I didn't know where to put myself. Vangie?' His voice rose dangerously. No sign now of the origins of his nickname.

'Oh Jer,' she said wearily. 'Not now. I really don't feel up to it.'

'And you know why, don't you? You should have stayed at home resting, like the doctor told you. The way I told you.' He fussed her like an overconcerned mother hen. Anxiety blocked out the anger on his face. 'Vangie, it was a mad caper and all you did was drive him wild. It's an ill turn you did yourself. Give it up. Whatever it is. Give it up. I told you I'd look after you. Why can't you trust me?'

She clutched his hand. 'Oh dear, dear Jer. You know you're the only one I do trust.' She looked at him bleakly. 'I didn't tell you the good news,' she said. 'Mure-Robertson is going to sell me his hotel shares.'

O'Dowd's eyes opened wide. 'You're serious? He's actually agreed? On paper?'

She hunched her shoulders carelessly. 'Not yet. We're meeting on Friday. He'll do it then.'

His smile faded. 'Almost but not quite, is that it?'

'It'll be fine, you know he's crazy about me.'

'There's many a slip,' he said heavily. 'I hope you're right.'

'Oh Jer, don't fuss. Have I ever messed up? Well, have I?'

'You went too far today,' he said slowly. 'Sweeney's not worth the effort. I wish you hadn't brought *her*.' He held her gaze.

She looked startled, but after a moment or two nodded her head. 'Yes, I guess you're right. I shouldn't have told him we'd sold the boat on, should I?'

'No.' O'Dowd gave a bark of hollow laughter. 'Amongst other things. Tell me, what did you hope to achieve? I mean, apart from annoying him?' When she didn't answer he said softly, 'It's all got too personal. And that's bad for business.'

Evangeline Walter smiled: a long, lazy, conspiratorial smile. It was a brave effort but he wasn't fooled. 'Will you take her back?' she asked.

'What, now? Tonight?' He looked alarmed.

She suddenly lost patience. 'Just do it, will you? Please? I can't stand another second. She never stops prowling around.'

'But isn't she supposed to be staying on to meet your cousin? That's why she's here, isn't it?'

She was angry now. 'Yeah, yeah, yeah, but as usual he's let me down. They're not coming till Friday. Some old pal of his is ill.' She raised her eyebrows at him and gave a bitter little laugh as she lapsed into a caricature drawl. ' "Oh, Evangeline honey, I don't know what to say, I just can't leave right now." ' She looked up at O'Dowd. 'Typical,' she said briskly. 'I wouldn't be in this mess except for him. That damn wife of his put him up to it.'

He sighed deeply. 'OK, I'll do it. Just this once, mind,' he warned. 'You better ring and say we're on our way.' He stood up. 'I'll get the boat back to my place and collect the car. I'll only be a few minutes, so get her ready. I don't want to have to stop halfway.'

'I've given her a tranquillizer. She'll go to sleep shortly,' she said when he returned. 'But even if she doesn't, it's only a couple of hours and you know how she loves your car. I promise she won't give you any trouble,' she wheedled.

'You won't come?'

'No, hon, d'you mind? I'm all tuckered out,' she said softly and smiled bravely.

'OK so, but you're to go to bed, Vangie. Rest, for pity's sake, you look awful.'

'Thanks very much,' she glared.

He stood over her and put his hands on her shoulders. 'Look, you know I think you're the most gorgeous woman in the world and the best friend a fellow could have. But I'm not haring around the country with that young one unless you do what I tell you.' He began to count his instructions on his fingers. 'Now listen to me. You're to ring the doctor, take some painkillers and then go to bed. For God's sake, woman, you're barely over a major operation. You shouldn't even be walking about.'

'I'll have a bath,' she decided when at last they had persuaded the girl away from the TV and into the car – the front seat, much against O'Dowd's wishes.

'You'll be all right, Vangie? I'll look in when I get back,' he told her, as he hitched his seat belt in position. 'OK?'

'Ring first. I'll probably take a sleeping pill.'

'Good idea. Promise you'll eat something.'

'I promise.' She leaned in the window and pecked him on the cheek. 'You're my dear, dear friend, Jer. I don't know what I'd do without you.'

'Maybe I'll drop in on Mr Mure-Robertson while I'm in the area?'

She considered this for a moment. 'I don't think that's a good idea,' she said dismissively, then smiled at the girl who smiled eagerly back. A sweet, innocent smile.

It was a quarter past six when he left Trianach. He noticed his fuel gauge was low as he went over the causeway and since he had a long way to go, he decided to stop for petrol in Duncreagh. He didn't notice the temporary sign on the way into the petrol station saying that the tanks were being filled, and got trapped behind a half-truck whose driver was nowhere to be seen. He sat fuming with irritation for a few minutes and was just about to back out when Cressida Sweeney's Range Rover came careering in behind him. Both bumpers made contact as she screeched to a halt. She jumped out, and Gil, who was sitting up front, scrambled out after her. She looked white and exhausted. O'Dowd opened his car door and glowered at her. There was no sign of his habitual smile as he pointedly examined the back of his two-year-old Mercedes.

'You should look where you're going, Mrs Sweeney.'

Cressie looked. 'I'm sorry,' she said. 'But it's only the bumper.'

'Yes it is, but it might have . . .'

Cressie was tired. 'I said I was sorry, Mr O'Dowd,' she retorted wearily. 'I'll pay for the damage, if there is any,' she added pointedly.

The girl sitting in the Mercedes started to wave and smile at Gil who laughed and waved back at her. With this encouragement, she got out of the car and went up to Gil and started pawing his face. She had a pretty, rather vacant face and though she looked about eighteen or more, she acted like a child. Gil was overwhelmed. He stepped back in alarm and looked pleadingly at his mother. O'Dowd, who was bent over his bumper looking in vain for damage, straightened up. He strode over to the girl, grabbed hold of her arm and tried to lead her away from Gil and into the back of the car. 'God in heaven,' he cried when she wouldn't budge.

By now, passers-by were stopping to gawp. Cressida went to her son and, after a moment's hesitation, placed her hand on the girl's shoulder. The girl immediately transferred her attention, throwing her arms awkwardly around Cressie and resting her head against her shoulder. Cressie began to stroke the long silken hair.

'Mama,' Gil protested jealously. 'Mama.' He pressed against his mother's side and held on to her. Cressida put her face down to his.

'Gil, my darling. Gil? Let's help Mr O'Dowd,' she said clearly. 'Come.' She put her arms around her son and the girl and edged them over to the Mercedes. O'Dowd, quick and nimble as the dancer he was, leapt forward to open the door. Cressie pulled a half-finished roll of mints from her pocket and gave a couple to the girl, who smiled and ran her hands over Cressie's face. 'Ma,' she said. 'Mama.' Gil, who had been watching all this, shook his head violently and grabbed Cressie's hand. 'My mama, mine,' he shouted. Then suddenly he laughed and pointed to himself. 'Gil, Gil.' He put his hand out to the girl. 'Ooo?' *Who?*

'That is Halcyon,' O'Dowd said quietly, his expression hard to read.

'What did you say?' Cressie asked curiously. At first he didn't answer and when he did, he spoke directly to Gil, though he must have known the little boy couldn't hear. 'Don't you know Halcyon, Gil?' he asked. Cressida looked mystified. 'Halcyon?' she repeated.

'Isn't that a strange thing, now, Gil?' he went on. 'Your daddy's just had us out on the boat. Pity you weren't there. We had great sport altogether.' He looked at Cressida for the first time. There was mischief in his smiling eyes. 'But Halcyon won't tell anyone, don't worry. She can't.' As he spoke, his gaze shifted to the little boy and his fingers pulled absently at his ear lobe. Cressie swallowed hard.

'Who did you say?' she croaked. But O'Dowd must have misunderstood. He spoke over his shoulder as he got back into the driving seat and waited for the half-truck driver, who'd just returned, to pull away. 'Your husband, and Mrs Walter and myself,' he said distractedly as he turned on the engine. He smiled at her through the open window.

Cressida stood, as if hypnotized, on the forecourt and watched him drive off. Gil, who must have sensed that something was wrong, got into the Range Rover without being told. It was some minutes before Cressida shook herself out of her trance and climbed in after him. She patted the little boy's cheek and checked that his seat belt was fastened. Usually she described every action for him but this time she didn't say a word. Her face was troubled as they drove home.

Chapter Five

CRESSIDA'S HEART WAS STILL POUNDING WHEN THEY REACHED Coribeen, and her anxiety intensified when she saw VJ's car parked outside the front door. She pulled into the garage and sat staring at the blank wall while Gil finished a bag of chips. The smell of the slightly rancid oil filled the air and nauseated her, but Gil was tucking into this rare treat with delight. 'Bath time,' she said when he finally crumpled the empty bag and handed it to her. She forced herself to be calm, to smile at her little son who tore at her heart strings whenever she looked at him.

He snuggled into her as she lifted him out. 'Bath time,' she said again. 'Then a story, then . . .'

'Bed,' he cried and made a face. Her fingers were trembling so much that she could hardly insert the key in the lock. Then she stood absolutely still for a few seconds, as she had begun to do whenever she stepped into her own house, waiting for the miasma of tension to envelop her. Sometimes she could smell the fear, hers and Gil's, which seemed to linger, in the hall, waiting for her. The child could feel it too, she could see it in his eyes and the way he moved, sluggishly, hesitantly, whenever Val was near. Did she transmit her own anxiety or could he, too, pick it up from the atmosphere? He had never witnessed their fights, never seen her husband strike her, yet he skirted around his father as if he was waiting for the axe to fall on his head.

She took Gil's hand and held it tightly as they went inside. VJ was standing in the hall talking on the phone. He put his hand over the mouthpiece and smiled. 'Won't be long,' he mouthed. Cressie felt weak with relief and began to breathe properly. Still clutching his hand, she took Gil into the kitchen for some milk. VJ was still on the phone as they went upstairs. From what Cressida overheard he was either buying or selling something. While Gil was playing in the bath, she tiptoed out on the landing and listened.

'. . . derisive . . . worth more than three . . .' VJ was saying. Three? Three hundred? Three thousand? Million? The land? The house? Oh God, she prayed, not that, not the house.

'. . . a majority has more value . . . I insist.' A short angry bark of laughter. Cressie shuddered.

'Five per share, Robertson . . .' he said. She put her hand to her mouth to prevent herself crying out. She knew who he was talking to now and what about. Mure-Robertson was one of the shareholders of the Atlantis Hotel. Val too. As far as she knew it was his last major holding, though she had no idea how many shares he owned or what they were worth. Val never discussed business with her. But she did know that he was desperate to be the major shareholder: he wanted to close the place up, develop the site and make a killing.

'Thursday? . . . Friday then. Liquid? All right,' he ended with a triumphalist shout. Cressida froze. Buying? What with? So, he must be selling. She put her hand to her forehead. The land? The house? He couldn't. The one thing he couldn't do, unless she agreed. She crept back to the bathroom when she heard him hanging up.

Half an hour later, Gil was tucked up and almost asleep. By now Cressida was dropping with tiredness and all she wanted was a long soak and an early night. It was as if she'd unconsciously made her momentous decision. Somewhere, sometime in the past hour or so, the iron had entered her soul. Her marriage was over; she had to start fending for herself.

She had no idea if O'Dowd had been winding her up, or where she figured on his agenda – if at all. But she had, for once, believed the evidence of her own eyes. And the fear in Gil's. The moment of truth had not been the awful terror that gripped her as she stepped into her house, but the humiliating relief when she saw her husband's smile. At that moment she would have sold her soul to please him. Or her house.

When had she slipped from merely ineffectual, complacent, to being his toerag? When had she learned to love her role as victim? Overlooked the danger Gil was in? She had turned away from the possibility of love, because of her fear of poverty. She closed her eyes in self-disgust. The world was full of single mothers managing to bring up and protect their children. She had allowed herself to believe that Gil's disability made them unique. Unique, yes, but not in the way she'd thought. Gil was special and their symbiosis was special, re-demptive. John Spain had taught her that. And Frank. Beloved, kind, gorgeous Frank. He was so *grown-up*.

She thought about him all the time, as he claimed to do about her. But she was determined not to be another burden on those already overloaded shoulders. She had known him by sight, more or less, ever since he'd arrived in Passage South and the gossip about him was rife. The mystery man he was called, or the Spaniard. The man with a past. There was much speculation about why he had been demoted from his job in the capital and buried himself in an insignificant seaside village, so it was something of a let-down when Mrs Ryan in the post office found out about his coronary bypass. Sometimes, when she and Gil walked Finnegan on the cliffs, he would be there, striding along, or else sitting on a rock scribbling in a tiny notebook. Then one day he appeared with that lunatic puppy of his and thereafter they walked together perhaps once a week; usually in companionable silence. Whatever his reasons for buying Barker, she had absolutely no thought of love, or the possibility of love. She was married and took it seriously, no matter how ghastly things were between her and Val. But then, just nine months before, on New Year's Eve, against all the odds, in a total *coup de foudre*, they had fallen instantly and bafflingly in love.

Frank had been playing his double bass with a jazz trio who occasionally jammed in Hussey's pub. As midnight approached a disco started in the small function room off the bar and people began dancing. Val, well tanked up, was all over a couple of German girls, insisting they both dance with him. He'd ignored her all evening and she was fed up and getting morosely drunk when Recaldo edged along the crowded bar to where she was sitting, elbows on the counter, resolutely trying to ignore her husband's antics.

'What'll you have?' he asked, surprising her.

'I'm not sure I ever want to see another drink, as long as I live,' she retorted. 'Anyway, I have one, thanks.' He looked at the half-empty glass of sad-looking red wine at her elbow, which was sporting a faint scum on the surface.

'That's disgusting,' he said, and nodded at the barman. 'A couple of glasses of Murphy's, Michael.'

They didn't speak while the drinks were being poured – hardly appeared to notice each other. But an awareness of his proximity slowly crept through her and she had difficulty resisting the temptation to draw even closer to him.

'Try that, Mrs Sweeney,' he said. He pushed one of the glasses towards her and raised his own. 'I wish you a happy New Year.'

'I've never tasted this stuff,' she said. As she sipped it gingerly, she looked directly at him for the first time. 'It's quite nice,' she said, surprised. He laughed. 'Cheers,' she said.

'Sláinte,' he replied and raised his glass to her again. She felt like weeping. Her husband was trying to get one of the German girls to strip. She turned away in embarrassment, feeling trapped and desperate. That may have been the moment when she knew for certain that her marriage was down the tubes.

'Are you all right, Mrs Sweeney?' he asked.

'Cressida.' She held out her hand tentatively as if she was introducing herself. 'Thank you for this.' She took another sip. He dipped his head down to her.

'Frank,' he said, and touched her hand with the tips of his long, slender fingers.

'I know,' she said with a watery smile. 'But I prefer Recaldo, it has more music.' And immediately felt a fool. Even to her own ears her voice sounded affected; worse, it was slurred. That was the moment. He reached out and traced the moustache of creamy foam on her upper lip, then stuck his finger in his mouth. She stared deep into his cobalt eyes.

'I'm sorry, I don't know what came over me,' he mumbled. Casting her eyes down, she noticed that his hand was inching along the counter towards hers. And without thinking what she was doing she leaned forward until her forehead was touching the counter and rested her cheek on the back of his hand. One of the tortoiseshell combs holding her hair in place had worked loose and for an instant he touched the silver bar at the top. 'Tiger hair,' he said softly, then drew his hand away as if he'd been scalded. Afterwards she wondered if she'd imagined the incident.

'I have to get home,' she said and jumped off the stool. 'I promised the childminder I'd be back before one.' Pulling her coat over her shoulders she pushed her way through the crowded bar and out into the cold night.

A fracas erupted shortly after she left. Val was thrown out of the pub and brought home in the early hours by Jer O'Dowd and Evangeline Walter. The three of them sat up drinking for hours and were still there when she and Gil went downstairs for breakfast the next morning. She cooked for them while Evangeline treated the chaps to her views on house-wives. She used the word pathetic several times. Val was highly diverted.

Cressida changed into a black sweater and jeans, brushed back her hair and fixed it behind her ears with the tortoiseshell combs. She patted her cheeks to give her some colour, put on some lipstick and, taking a deep breath, went downstairs. She told herself firmly not to cower, to walk in with her head held high, not to succumb to her husband's easy charm. O'Dowd had inadvertently handed her a weapon; she would use it. But at every step her feet grew heavier.

Sweeney was in the kitchen, looking out the window with a bottle in one hand and a glass in the other. 'D'you want something to eat?' she asked.

'What have you got?'

'Rashers and eggs?'

'Rashers? We *are* going native. Whatever happened to good old bacon and eggs?' He chucked her playfully under the chin. 'I'll get a bottle of Beaujolais.'

It was the first time for ages that they'd sat down together. At first he went out of his way to be civil, but he was restless and had diffi-culty keeping up any sort of conversation. She knew by his behaviour that he was working up to something, softening her up to do whatever he wanted. 'I need some housekeeping money,' she said and was sur-prised when he took out his wallet and gave her two hundred pounds. She slipped the wodge into the back pocket of her jeans. 'Thanks,' she said and was even more astonished when he promised to transfer some money to her account at the end of the week.

He pushed back his plate and refilled his glass. 'I've put an offer in on a flat in London,' he announced casually. 'I need to get out of this godforsaken hole and get back in business.'

Cressida froze. This was an old and familiar tune and she knew what was coming. He would try to browbeat her into selling the house. Wanted to make things so intolerable that she'd give in. They had been playing a game of attrition for ages, but the previous month or so had been a nightmare. Please God let him just go, she prayed silently. Let him disappear and leave us.

Unexpectedly he began to cajole her. 'Come on, Cress, you'd like the flat. It's in Victoria, really central; four bedrooms. I'll use one as an office until I can find something better.' A tingle of fear ran down her spine. He's dangerous, she thought, he'll stop at nothing to get what he wants. She took a deep breath.

'Go,' she said quietly. 'We're staying, Gil and me.'

'What'll you live on?' His voice was hard and the broken capillaries on his high cheeks suffused until a bright red patch glowed on either side of his nose. He used to be so beautiful, she thought sadly.

'I think you should go to London on your own,' she said bluntly. 'You don't need me. We should get a divorce.'

'A divorce? Don't make me laugh. You've cost me enough already. Fuck divorce. I'm not spending my life supporting you two and that's flat.'

'I don't want . . .' she was beginning, when Gil appeared at the door. He was clutching a battered teddy in one hand and his empty beaker in the other. He ran to her.

'Oh for fuck's sake,' Sweeney said under his breath. He got up and poured himself a large whiskey. 'That child should be in bed.'

Gil said, 'I saw the l-l-lady, Dada.' Cressida stared at her son in horror. Usually he couldn't manage the words but tonight he spoke really clearly, and she wished and wished that she had never taught him to speak. She put her arms around him protectively.

'Let's get you back to bed, darling,' she said and stood up.

'What did he say?'

'Nothing.'

'I saw the l-l-lady,' Gil repeated. 'L-l-lady.' He rolled the word, mightily pleased with it. 'L-l-lady.' He laughed.

'What was your child doing out in that old perve's boat today?' Sweeney shouted.

'What was *your* child and that Walter bitch doing on yours?' she screamed. A deadly hush descended.

'What did you say?'

Cressida swallowed hard. 'I said,' her voice wavered, 'you had a girl out on the boat . . .'

'And?'

'And, and, Mr O'Dowd said she was . . .'

'Mr O'Dowd? Mr Fucking O'Dowd said what exactly?'

'He didn't have to say anything,' she said quietly. 'I have eyes in my head.' She gave a hollow laugh. 'You must have very strong genes.'

Without any warning VJ lunged across the room and took a side swipe at Cressida. Gil cowered behind his mother and began to whimper. Sweeney pushed him aside and the child went flying across the slippery tiles. There was a sickening thud as his arm made contact with the floor. Cressie rushed to him and took him in her arms and crawled over to the door. Sweeney was there before her.

'Don't you move. I'm not finished with you yet. What do you know about genes? That idiot . . .' he choked on the word, 'is nothing to do with me. Halcyon Walter she's called. Did O'Dowd tell you that? *Walter.* Do I have to spell it out for you?'

'The boat . . .'

'Yeah. The bitch bought the boat, not Mr Fucking O'Dowd, and named it after her idiot kid. Now there's a bit of gossip for you. I'm surprised your pal Spain didn't tell you all about it.'

'John Spain?'

'God, don't you know anything? He can't keep away from her. Or you either.'

She thought she was beyond surprise, that she could follow the con-volutions of his addled brain, but what he said next took her beyond fear.

'Do you know what Evangeline Walter told me when she saw your son on that old bastard's boat? She said that if the Social Services found out that you left him alone with that pervert, he'd be taken into care. Away from you. The authorities are hot on that sort of thing. Specially if they think the old bastard's your lover.' This idea seemed to please him. He put his face down to hers. 'Just one little phone call is all it takes. And if you don't agree to the sale of the house that is exactly what I'll do.'

'Nobody would believe you.' *They would, they would.*

'What does that matter? All I have to do is say it. Then watch. She's a clever woman.'

Then, very casually, he reached down and pulled the wadge of notes he had given her from her pocket and, as he straightened, gave her a ferocious thump across the shoulders. Sickened with pain and fright,

Cressida pushed Gil out the door. 'Run, Gil,' she screamed. 'Go upstairs, go to bed.'

Sweeney pulled her to her feet and pinned her against the wall. 'No,' she screamed. 'No, don't hit me. I'll sign.'

'Of course you will,' he shouted. He waved the money in her face. 'No money, no escape. You stay put till I get back. Just remember what I said. One wrong move and you lose the kid and, of course, the house.' He balled his fist and smashed her eye. Cressida fell.

When she came to, he was gone. She ran to the window and spied the launch weaving across the river. 'Gil,' she sobbed. 'Gil, it's all right, baby.' She looked around for him – he wasn't there. She tore into the hall and up the stairs screaming his name. 'Gil, Gil, oh Gil.' He was lying under his bed, curled in a foetal position with his thumb in his mouth. The gash on his forehead was bleeding.

'Gil, darling, come out love,' she coaxed. But the child shrank back in fear. It took half an hour before she managed to persuade him to creep into her arms. She bathed his cuts, gave him a Disprin and held him until he fell asleep, then laid him gently on the bed and wrapped the duvet around him.

She went to her bedroom and looked out across the estuary for the launch but couldn't see it anywhere. He must be on the other side, at Trianach. At Evangeline Walter's place. If she had bought his yacht – why? why? – had she also made the offer on the house? In the early days when they'd been kind of friends she had once told Cressie that if they ever decided to sell, she'd like first refusal. Had he gone now to tell her the deal was on? Why? It was all too muddled. She felt paralysed and unable to think straight. Why had he gone out? Didn't he know she'd take Gil and run away? Or did he think she was too frightened? Too stupid? Gil's arm was badly swollen, and needed treatment.

She half ran, half fell down the stairs to the phone and dialled Recaldo's number. 'Be at home, Frank,' she prayed. 'Be there.' The answering service cut in after seven rings. She did not leave a message.

She went back upstairs again and picked up Gil as gently as she could. His injured arm felt hot and he whimpered in his sleep when she touched it lightly with her finger. She grabbed her bag from the hall and stumbled out to the Range Rover. She was halfway down the drive when she admitted there was no winning this one. Whether she ran away or not, Val would destroy John Spain's reputation. If she stayed he might attack Gil again, and she couldn't risk that. But, some-how, she had to warn Spain.

It took about fifteen minutes to cross to the other side of the estuary. John Spain was not at home. Thinking he might still be out on his boat, Cressida ran down the laneway to the water's edge, but the boat wasn't there. There was a spit of land between her and the bay so she couldn't see any distance downriver. She glanced at her watch. It was just on half past nine. She knew he always went out at the crack of dawn and was usually in bed by ten. He wouldn't be far. She went back to the Range Rover and waited for fifteen minutes. Gil stayed fast asleep. She started the engine and backed up the lane until she could turn. She knew there was a good lookout about half a mile downriver beyond the spit.

She saw Spain's boat as soon as she stepped out of the car. It was tied to a submerged boulder by the old slipway. She scrambled up on the bonnet of the car and stood upright. She spotted him immediately. He was walking across Evangeline Walter's garden, holding something in his hands.

Chapter Six

IT WAS NINE THIRTY-SIX WHEN SPAIN TIED UP. THE SEA TROUT WAS lying at the bottom of the boat, shining in the moonlight, bright silver against the dark green vine leaves. A noble offering, worthy of her beauty.

She emerged from the house and stood for a moment poised and still, her figure dark against lighted windows. She had one of her diaphanous gowns wrapped around her and he could see the full out-line of her naked figure beneath the silken material. As he looked she half turned away, as if she was watching something in the herbaceous border which nestled against the high sandstone outcrop off to her right. A light breeze played with the shawl around her head and shoulders, which rose and fell, like a child's breath. The hem of her gown fluttered gently against her bare feet. She said something, called out. He couldn't make out the words, just undulating, meaningless sounds. He held the fish in both hands, bearing it like an offering on a platter, but, uncertain of his welcome, hesitated a moment longer before starting up the garden. She turned slowly at his approach, then suddenly threw back her head and laughed.

'*Introibo ad altare Dei,*' she mocked. She stretched out her arms and twirled slowly around, inviting his admiration. As the gown fell open he stood quite still, labouring to control his breath. She was naked. A rush of blood suffused his face. She watched his struggle for a moment, then laughed harshly again.

'Welcome, Father,' she sang out, taunting him. Something rustled in the shadows by the rocks. She twirled slowly around again. Around and around like a young girl. An illusion of youth.

This was not why he came, yet he stumbled towards her, no longer able to restrain himself. The pain was startling in its intensity, humiliating for the way he embraced it, courting it rather than pushing it away, hoarding the exquisite pleasure of ancient, half-remembered delights. The surprise was that he should feel anything at all. For deep down he still believed, just as he had always believed, even in his far-off youth, that the pangs of – not love, nor lust – but of physical attraction were for the young. Yet he, of all people, could affirm that it continued. Not all the time, not often, but intermittently and unexpectedly.

Lust assailed him now. Passion. A fierce excitement tore through him as he lost the battle of sixteen years. Other times he had come secretly with his tributes, or let her call out to him, listened to her siren voice, covertly watched her from his boat, testing his control, his indifference. It was all gone now, her mocking smile told him she knew it, and knew the power she had over his rapacity.

She took the fish from his hands and dropped it casually on the ground and to his surprise took his hands in hers. She drew him towards her, standing so close that he could feel the rise and fall of her breasts through his rough shirt and overalls. For a moment her slim hands rested in his, then slowly and sensuously her fingers began to explore his, making sexual images as she toyed. Her body swayed dreamily, her eyes were closed. She required no response. She was turned inwards, an exercise in self-excitation, with no emotional investment. Assailing but not assailable. All she required was casual stimulation and his presence provided that. He realized, bitterly, that anyone would do. He was simply a human scratching-stone. It was a deadly lesson in humiliation.

She gave a long, low laugh and put her mouth to his ear. 'You see? When I need relief or entertainment I can conjure up – not your image but my own pleasure in your response. You never learn, do you, priest?' In one deft movement, she pulled the braces of his old overalls and dropped them, pinning his arms to his sides. Her eyes were still closed and a half-smile played on her lips as her clever fingers began to unbutton his shirt, slowly, effortlessly. The demons she awoke in him were of no consequence to her. They could be brushed aside. Controlled. He looked absurd and thought his sense of shame was complete, but it had just begun.

'Oh my.' She looked at his shaming, erect penis and laughed. 'Oh my, oh my.' And slithering to her knees, she took him in her mouth.

How often he'd dreamed of this, how often, watching her cavort with her various lovers, he had enacted just this scene. Her expert tongue teased as her small, sharp teeth chastised and stimulated his lasciviousness. He cried out then, the primeval, hoarse, despairing roar of something mortally wounded. And an uncontainable excitement rose in him as he thrust himself against her, pushing her backwards, trying to force her to the ground.

But it was he who fell forward, hobbled by the trousers around his ankles, while she skipped nimbly aside. 'Come,' she called. He rolled over, tugging at his crumpled garments, trying to cover himself. He wanted her now. Now he would have her. He lunged at her, half crouched like a centaur, more beast than man.

But again she disarmed him. Expertly, mockingly. 'You poor old thing,' she whispered, loosening the folds of her dress as she came towards him. He dragged it off her shoulders as she lifted her breasts and pressed them to his face. 'You don't have to take me. I want you,' she cooed, then raised her voice slightly and cried out, 'come, my lover.' They locked together as she manoeuvred him backwards until they were outlined against the brightly lit windows of the house. She stared into his eyes, then feeling his anger abate, slowly and sensuously raised one long elegant bare leg and wrapped it tightly around him. She waved her right hand above her head and with her left she eased him into her, as she pushed her salamander tongue into his mouth.

A tall, shadowy figure emerged from the house and for a moment was outlined against the lighted window before slipping into the shrubbery at the side of the house. Yet Spain did not notice, so engrossed was he, so taken over. He could not come, could not control the wild gyrations of his tortured body. She kept screaming out in ecstasy and he in wild despair. She goaded; he strove, not now interested in her or his shame but only in ending it, pushing himself beyond pain and way, way beyond desire.

It might have gone on for ever, that wild naked dance, but then the old man opened his eyes and saw the apparition. Cressida Sweeney was dressed completely in black so that all he saw was her shocked white face, which seemed to hover in mid-air halfway down the garden.

Spain let out a ferocious roar and pushed Evangeline from him. She fell back but recovered herself in an instant, stretching languidly. She threw her head back and grinned at Cressida. 'Well? Don't you see? I was right. Think he's had enough?' She got to her feet and turned to face the house.

'You bitch.' Cressida followed her eyes and saw the lights in the house doused. At the same time, Spain realized that he'd been duped, used as some sort of toy, weapon. He knew now that her desire had not been for him but an invitation to a spectator sport, and that the real object of her desire or revenge was close at hand.

Cressida lunged and pushed Evangeline to the ground. Her head hit the edge of the stone terrace with a muffled thud. She gave a little moan then lay still, arms outstretched. Spain was struggling into his overalls when Cressie picked up a bottle from the nearby garden table and went at her again, but he threw himself between them and pulled her off.

He armlocked Cressida and dragged her after him down the garden. When he got to the old slipway he saw the Range Rover abandoned beside it. Gil's white little face was staring out the window.

Wednesday

Chapter Seven

IN THE NORMAL COURSE OF EVENTS SERGEANT RECALDO RARELY wore uniform, since his day-to-day professional activities didn't call for such formality. But on Wednesday morning, when John Spain woke him out of his restless slumber at ten to six, he'd instinctively taken it from his wardrobe and found a freshly laundered shirt. The barely used uniform hung on him like a tailor's dummy and his tall, lean frame lent an air of distinction to the drab navy blue. He could have been dressing for a funeral.

The moment he walked through the side gate into Evangeline Walter's beautiful garden and saw her lifeless body lying at John Spain's feet, he knew that his time of innocence on the estuary was over. He also knew that Spain would, inevitably, fall under suspicion, not only because he'd found the body but also because of his unyielding temperament and checkered past.

The situation was awkward, to say the least. He felt uncomfortable and compromised. He knew and liked old Spain; there was a sympathy between them, perhaps because they were both outsiders. But then, he assured himself, he would feel the same about anyone from his patch in a similar position. Violence was unusual, almost unheard of, in that peaceful place. His outrage wasn't just on account of the dead woman: experience elsewhere had taught him that murder – and it looked very like murder – changed everything for everyone. It was an evil vortex into which the innocent as well as the guilty were easily sucked. He stared moodily into space, mentally going back over Spain's story, trying to make sense of it before the scene-of-crime unit arrived from headquarters. Recaldo flicked through his notebook and fervently hoped that when they took over he would no longer be required.

The local GP had been and gone. 'She was not my patient,' he explained, 'so the coroner will have to be notified.' Though invited to, Dr McCarthy wouldn't venture an opinion on the time of death, nor its immediate cause. He gently folded back the woman's dressing gown and examined a livid scar across her stomach. 'Recently been operated on. Very recently,' he murmured and looked up at Recaldo. 'And she's obviously haemorrhaged. Though why, specifically, is another matter.' Beyond that he would not go. 'I'll leave all that to the pathologist,' he said. 'I have little enough experience of this kind of thing, thank goodness.'

As soon as he left, Recaldo covered the body with a sheet of tarpaulin from the back of his Jeep. He led Spain up the garden to a bench on the terrace and sat him down.

'Now then,' Recaldo said sharply. 'I'm going to have to present a coherent report when the investigating team arrives and so far you haven't made much sense, have you? I know it's difficult, John, but could you just go over it again for me? Take it slowly this time. Leave nothing out.'

'I'll try.' Spain sighed wearily.

'Go back to when you first spotted her.'

Spain hesitated, as if marshalling his thoughts. He gazed down the garden to the prone body and beyond to the shimmering water. 'She was there when I was coming in last night,' he whispered.

'What time did you go out?' Recaldo interrupted, recalling that there had been no sign of Spain or his boat when he'd gone to the old man's cottage around seven the evening before. Or Gil for that matter.

'I had Gil with me in the afternoon. Cressida collected him at six or so, and I went out straight afterwards. I suppose it was about half eight or so when I got back. I'm not sure, it was coming on for dark but it was still mild. Very calm.'

'And you didn't go out again?'

The old man looked away. 'I'm always in bed by ten.'

'And you saw her in the garden on the way in?'

'Yes. She's often there of an evening, standing by the water's edge.' He used the present tense unconsciously as he recalled how the woman leaned against the stunted oak, silently watching the water while she smoked.

'You recognized her? Even in the dark?'

'It wasn't quite dark, there was light coming from the house.' He turned to the windows behind them, which were wide open with the lights inside still on.

'She had on that scarf thing she always wore,' Spain said dreamily. 'Like an Indian woman – I think they call it a sar-ee.' Spain looked at Recaldo earnestly. 'You see, I'd never seen her before in the early morning. That must be what arrested my attention. That and the dress.' He gnawed at his thumbnail.

'I thought . . . Maybe the mist had me confused but when I first saw her I thought she was wearing a patterned dress.' He shook his head disconsolately, as though this detail was the most troublesome of all. 'To tell the truth, at the time it didn't dawn on me . . .' he murmured. 'It was only when I got closer that I realized . . .'

'Hang on, John, you have me confused,' Recaldo said. 'Are we talking about last night or this morning?'

'This morning, this morning.' The old man became agitated and dangerously flushed. His voice rose. 'Haven't I told you twice already? I never before saw her in the morning. Not once.'

'So what happened then?' Recaldo spoke slowly, soothingly. He sensed the old man was obfuscating but knew it would be counter-productive to fuss him. 'In your own words, John, when you feel ready.'

When Spain eventually spoke, it was as if he was talking to himself rather than to the garda. His voice was so low, Recaldo had to strain to hear him.

'The reason I went out so early was on account of the spring tide; I wanted to catch it on the turn, let it do the work for me. The old out-board motor has been giving me a bit of gyp lately.' He grimaced and looked away, avoiding eye contact. 'As it turned out, I was a bit too early. The water was unusually high. When that happens the water rises up on the grassy bank,' he pointed, 'all along the shore. Floods the gardens sometimes.

'I didn't see her until I was well away from my mooring, out into midstream.' He pointed to the centre of the channel, where the water was deep and the flow swift. 'I let the boat drift along with the current, while I enjoyed a pipe.' He closed his eyes and took a deep breath.

'It was only as I rounded the spit that I spotted her.' He pointed. 'The light was strange, pink . . . red. She was rising out of the mist . . . glowing. She gave me a terrible start.'

He clamped his hand to his mouth, gagged, then bolted behind a bush while Recaldo tried to ignore the sound of retching. He emerged some minutes later clutching a filthy bloodstained handkerchief to his face.

'Sorry,' he murmured, 'delayed shock.' Recaldo noted, but didn't remark on the kerchief. He motioned Spain to continue. He did so hesitantly, confessing that he'd been enchanted by what he thought was an optical illusion so that at first it didn't occur to him that he'd never before seen her in the morning, but always as he was coming in in the late evening, after baiting his lobster pots.

'It was unusual for anyone else to be out at that hour, so I suppose I thought I'd go and pass the time of day – share the pleasure of the beautiful sunrise with her. I heard she'd been in hospital, I thought I'd ask how she was doing.'

He'd drifted slowly towards the shore, he said, enjoying the sight of the veiled woman whose limp clothes clung, revealingly, to her slender frame.

He didn't notice how chilly it was until he raised his hand to his pipe and compared his heavy oilskin with her flimsy garment. He did a double take then and almost overturned the boat as he jumped to his feet and shouted at her. She didn't answer. It was only as he drifted closer that he saw the tide had risen over the bank and spilled into the garden. Far from her standing on the water, it was lapping around her knees.

'You'll get your death of cold out here. Go in, go in,' he roared, before he realized that the colour from the dress was leaching into the water and spreading like a red whirlpool around her.

When he tried to increase his speed too suddenly, the outboard motor cut out and he panicked. He grabbed the oars, nearly dropping them overboard in his anxiety to push them into the locks, then pulled too hard; with a sickening crunch, the boat almost bottomed on the jagged remains of an ancient jetty, hidden just below the surface of the peaty water. There was nowhere to tie up except the old tree she was standing against, but he couldn't get close enough to grab hold of a branch. After several attempts, he pulled away from the bank and headed for the long-abandoned slipway a few hundred yards downstream from her property. 'Where you keep your boat, Frank,' he said. Recaldo nodded but said nothing.

'I remember wondering if I'd only imagined it, imagined seeing her . . .'

He dumped his cumbersome oilskin jacket in the boat and ran back along the bank, calling out as soon as he came within sight of her, and thought it very strange that she still gave no answer. 'There was about a foot or two of water at the edge of the garden. I had to wade the last few yards.'

He could feel the icy water through his rubber boots. The cold clutched at his heart, his breath coming in slow painful gasps. 'My foot got stuck in the mud and I fell over. I called out to her as I ran, kept shouting at her to go inside the house. But she didn't move or answer me. Or even turn. I stretched out my hand to her . . .' It was only then that he saw to his dismay that Evangeline Walter was dead. What made it even more horrifying was that she was propped against the tree, standing upright. 'As if she was alive. I thought she was alive . . .

'Her hair was plastered to her face and there was blood coming out of the side of her mouth.' Spain sank heavily to the ground and sat rocking backwards and forwards with his head in his hands.

'There's little enough blood there now,' Recaldo remarked with deadly calm.

'No,' Spain muttered. 'I wiped it off, I had to. I couldn't have her looking like that.' He stared up, aghast. 'The terrible thing is that I kept talking to her.' He urged her to rouse herself, to come back up to the house for a cup of hot tea. 'I couldn't comprehend she was dead. In my heart, I knew she was, but somehow I couldn't take it in.' He knew he shouldn't have wiped her face or laid her down, but how could he leave the poor creature like that with the blood flowing down her dress into the water, as if it was her very life, just seeping away? He wagged his head in disbelief and kept repeating, 'It was a pink dress.' He was strangely emphatic.

'More a dressing gown,' Recaldo murmured. 'What time was it?'
'What?'

'Have you any idea what time it was when you got here? When you moored at the slipway? Do you know? It's the first thing you'll be asked.' The old man swallowed hard and shook his head.

'Go back to when you first saw her. You live less than a quarter-mile up river, what time was it when you set out?' Recaldo urged gently. 'Oh come on now, you must have some idea what time it was when you got to her?'

Spain looked around in bewilderment; his hand began to tear at his ear. 'I,' he cleared his throat. 'I remember wondering as I got out of the boat if I'd imagined it all, because it was only just after half five.'

'Jesus. And how do you know that?' Recaldo blurted, 'all of a sudden?'

'My watch, of course. How else would I know?' Spain countered with dignity. The exchange was becoming surreal.

'Your watch? You looked at your watch?'

'Well, I must have, mustn't I?' The tired eyes were shuttered. 'It usually only takes fifteen minutes or so for me to get this far downriver. Even going as slow as I did, it wouldn't take above fifteen, twenty.' He spoke more to himself than to the other man. 'I was up before five and left the house shortly after. I didn't sleep much. I don't sleep much,' he added.

'Wasn't it still dark?'

'Not dark. Getting light.'

'How long d'you usually stay out?' Recaldo asked.

'Three or four hours.'

'And you intended being out that long this morning?'

'Why wouldn't I?'

'Just trying to build the picture,' Recaldo remarked mildly. 'So, half five at the slipway? Is that right?'

'Within a few minutes. Five or ten at most.'

Recaldo groaned. 'God save us, will you make up your mind. Was it five thirty or twenty to six? There is a difference, you know.'

'Half five.'

'You sure about that?'

'I'm sure.'

'So what was holding her to the tree, John?'

The old man looked around vaguely. 'I don't know. The scarf ? Or was it a rope? I don't know.'

God give me patience, Recaldo thought savagely, but somehow managed to keep his voice calm. 'Come with me.'

He caught Spain's arm and dragged him to his feet. 'You said she was standing against the tree. So come and show me.' His face was stony as they marched back down to where the body lay. Spain fell on his knees, bent double, and his shoulders began to shake as great raucous sobs tore out of him. 'I didn't say there was a rope. She just seemed to be lashed to the tree somehow,' he gasped. Recaldo let him be for a minute or so, then pulled him to his feet. 'In that case, for God's sake,' he said softly, 'let's not be hearing any more about ropes. D'you hear me? You're only confusing the issue. The body was leaning against the tree? Propped against the lower branches. Isn't that what you meant?'

Spain nodded in agreement. 'Yes, that would be it. She looked as though she was resting against it.'

'You ever see her standing like that before?'

'Oh yes, often. But only in the evening. She'd stand with her back to it, one foot resting against the trunk, facing the bay. Smoking usually.' *'Good luck, John Spain, I hope the fish are biting today,' she'd call, the laughter gurgling out of her. 'Fisherman Spain.' The sly reference seemed to amuse her hugely.*

'Did you say the blood was coming out of the side of her mouth?' Recaldo asked quietly. He looked at the elderly man intently as he waited for him to mull the thought over in his mind.

'*On.* On the side of her mouth, I think,' he mumbled, his head down. 'No, flowing down, though that may have been because of the spray.' He looked out over the water. 'It rained in the night. Maybe it was that, carrying it down her neck?' He shook his head. 'I don't know. Flowing, dribbling? What does it matter? All I know is she was dead.'

Recaldo threw his eyes upwards but kept his peace. He was uncomfortable with the situation. He was as close to John Spain as anyone was ever allowed to get – which, in truth, wasn't far. Spain the outsider, the blow-in, with a recognizable and shunned past, lived on the edge of the scattered rural community which, though it tolerated his presence, made little enough move to welcome or befriend him.

In his mid-seventies, he was a heavy set, burly man, somewhat above average height, and retained the massive shoulders of an athlete, though he was stooped and walked with a forward tilt as if he had, at some time, suffered a major back injury. His expression was closed and sad. He only rarely allowed himself to smile, and though the teeth were stained and too small for the wide mouth, it was a sweet, rather attractive smile in an attractive face. His skin was weathered a deep reddish-brown; greying sandy hair had thinned over the mottled dome. The slightly retroussé nose added a touch of the ridiculous, the clownish, and gave a clue to the self-deprecating manner but not to the sharp intelligence. The most notable thing about him was a kind of suppressed power, not quite masked by his habitual air of despondency.

Recaldo knew he must distance himself, discount all he knew of the man as well as the gossip. He, as investigator, needed to view him afresh, but he found it impossible to read the dark faded eyes. Was he in shock? Or genuinely confused?

So what had held her to the tree? If, that is, Spain's story was not a figment of his imagination. Recaldo looked at the long wrinkled scarf escaping from under the tarpaulin. Perhaps the scarf had got caught in the branches . . .

Spain must have known it was stupid to interfere with the scene of crime. Another thing, it wasn't just her extraordinary get-up which was splotched. There was blood on her hair and neck from a gash on the side of her head. He glared pointedly at Spain's jersey, which was also heavily stained. Were those new stains amid the dirt and the dried fish scales? It was impossible to tell. Aware of his scrutiny, the old man rubbed his chest nervously.

'Why did you take her down?' Recaldo was more insistent, curt.

'I didn't think.' John Spain's sad brown eyes looked into his, fathomless with deep, deep sorrow. Unknowable. He gnawed at the inside of his lower lip. 'I only wanted to help her. It was instinctive, I suppose . . .'

'I can't believe she's dead,' he said after a long silence. 'So beautiful, so young.'

Not that young, Recaldo thought sourly. Well into her forties, but certainly good-looking, exotic. He remembered her coming into the supermarket the previous Friday and the knowing look on her pale, drawn face when she saw Cressie talking to him.

'Who did she mix with?' he asked.

'How would I know?' Spain replied with deepening surliness.

'You live only a small way upriver.' Recaldo kept his voice cool, but he couldn't quite achieve the amiability he strove for. 'Come on, John, you passed the place every day. Who were her friends? Was there anyone with her last night, for instance?'

The hesitation was almost imperceptible. As Spain opened his mouth to say something the eyelids began to droop. He was spared by a call from the gate. Mr Jeremiah O'Dowd, more often known as Smiler, strode into the garden. 'Hello? Vangie?' he called. 'Are you there?'

He came down the garden towards them. He had a rolling gait and exuded confidence, from the fixed smile to the sparkling eyes. He was immaculately dressed, incongruously for early morning, in a navy blazer, white shirt open at the neck and buff chinos.

'What the hell's he doing here?' Recaldo muttered irritably under his breath as he watched O'Dowd approach. 'You can't come in here,' he called but Smiler paid no heed, he didn't miss a step. Instinctively Spain and Recaldo moved closer together to block his view so that he was almost upon them before he caught sight of the covered figure on the ground. He stopped short. 'What's that? What's going on?' The voice was uncertain, the eyes restively darting this way and that, the perennial smile fading.

'You have no business here, O'Dowd. You'll have to go,' Recaldo told him.

'Why?' O'Dowd asked pugnaciously.

Recaldo stepped to one side. Smiler's mouth opened in a startled O. 'Is that . . .? Is that Evang . . . Oh, Jesus God,' he shouted. 'What's happened to you at all?' He dropped to his knees beside the woman's body and stretched out his hand to pull back the cover.

'I wouldn't do that,' Recaldo warned. 'Get up, man.' He clamped his hands on Smiler's shoulder, firmly restraining him. 'What are you doing here, Mr O'Dowd?'

O'Dowd shrugged Recaldo's hand away. 'I just dropped by to see her. Vangie,' he mumbled. He remained crouched beside the body, but turned away from her, looking up at the two men.

'Vangie?'

'Evangeline. Mrs Walter.'

'At half seven in the morning?' Recaldo's eyebrows arched. 'Bit early, isn't it? For casual calls?'

'She's an early riser.' Smiler O'Dowd, all-Ireland step-dancing champion circa 1972, was still nimble on his feet. 'To tell you the truth, it was to apologize I came. I promised to check on her last night when I got back.' He cleared his throat. 'From Dublin, but I ran out of petrol; the fuel gauge was on the blink. Took me hours to sort out.' He stood up and rubbed the grass stains on his trouser knees. Sharp, cunning and quick-witted, it was obvious that his thoughts were racing; his flickering eyes took in the scene, noting everything. He clamped his lips together as if to prevent himself showing any emotion or sharing his distress, but the habitual self-satisfied smirk was etched into his tanned skin and impossible to disguise, much less switch off. After a moment's stand-off, Smiler's face sagged as if air was slowly leaking out of it. The effect was to suddenly make him look his age. As he struggled to rearrange his features, the distorted grimace he achieved was extraordinarily poignant; he looked now like a sad, lost child. 'When did she . . . she collapse?' he asked.

'Collapse? Was she ill?' Recaldo considered whether to tell O'Dowd that he'd seen him the day before, then decided to hold fire for the time being.

'That's why I came – to see was she all right. She's only out of hospital a couple of weeks.' His face twitched with distaste. 'She had an operation.'

'What for?' There was an awkward pause.

'Something to do with her stomach, I'm not sure . . . Poor Evangeline.' O'Dowd clearly assumed this was the cause of death. His eyes began to water.

'You were a good friend of hers?' Recaldo asked after a short pause.

O'Dowd didn't seem to notice the past tense. He turned his head. 'Yes, I'm her friend,' he mumbled indistinctly before bursting out, 'God almighty, is that all you can say?'

Recaldo was unmoved. 'Oddly enough, I was just asking Mr Spain about her friends, before you turned up.' His tone was sour.

O'Dowd bristled like a cock in a pit. 'What?' His face contorted. 'What?'

'It's simple enough. Who else did she know around here? Who else comes to visit her?'

O'Dowd's eyes narrowed. 'Why are you asking *me*?'

'It's normal,' Recaldo said blandly. 'When someone, er, dies in unusual circumstances.'

'Unusual circumstances?' O'Dowd echoed incredulously as if he didn't quite grasp what was being said. But in the following heavy silence, light dawned. 'What unusual circumstances?' he repeated. 'What are you telling me, man?'

'I'm not *telling* you anything. I was asking who she knows, knew, around here.'

O'Dowd's features knitted in confusion. 'For God's sake, are you saying someone *killed* her?'

'I didn't say anything of the sort. Just answer my questions, would you? We don't know what happened yet.'

O'Dowd pursed his lips. 'Finbarr Spillane works in the garden for her, Terry Whelan from the boatyard looks after her boat, Kevin Corkery as well. Michael Hussey – she's often in the bar, I'm sure you've seen her there. She knows a lot of people. But friends?' He shrugged. 'She doesn't socialize much around here.' It seemed to be a matter of some pride to him. 'The Sweeneys I suppose. She saw a lot of *her* at one time,' he added spitefully.

'What about *him*?'

O'Dowd didn't answer directly. He looked at Recaldo, slyly, under his lashes while he figured the angles. 'Oh no,' he said, too casually, 'she hadn't much time for him. It was *Mrs* Sweeney she was friendly with.'

'Oh.' Recaldo struggled to maintain a blank expression but the knowing glint in O'Dowd's eye gave an unmistakable signal that his own interest in Cressida Sweeney had been noted. God, he thought in exasperation, *this place*. Did anything happen that wasn't noticed? Commented on, gossiped about, picked over, talked to oblivion? But O'Dowd's urge to score a point was a mistake; it was a pointless lie and Recaldo was too canny to confront him before he checked out the details.

'Who else?' he asked grimly.

'Himself here.' O'Dowd whirled round to face John Spain. 'He's always hanging about,' he said savagely then glared at Recaldo. 'Why

49

are you leaving her like that? Why don't you get her into the house? Where's the feckin' doctor?' He looked ready to explode. 'What the hell is that fella doing here, anyway?' he shouted.

John Spain looked straight into those feverish eyes but said nothing. He eased himself to his full height and stood absolutely still, mono-lithic. His suppressed power was menacing. Recaldo, watching him, realized that despite his sturdiness it was *mental* rather than physical strength he exuded. A man so used to authority he could not, despite his best efforts, entirely conceal the fact.

The silent confrontation lasted no more than a few seconds before Spain turned and stomped off through the coarse wet grass.

'Hey, Mr Spain, where do you think you're off to? Get back here,' Recaldo shouted. 'You can't just go like that.'

Spain stopped. His arms hung loosely by his sides like a disconsolate baboon. He half turned and addressed himself to Recaldo. 'I can and I will,' he said fiercely. 'I'm old, I'm wet and I'm cold. I'm going home, Mr Recaldo. I have no doubt O'Dowd will know what's to be done.'

'Then make sure you stay there,' Recaldo warned. 'We'll be want-ing to talk to you.'

As they watched Spain stagger uncertainly towards his boat, Recaldo's mobile began to ring. He lifted it to his ear and listened for a minute or two, all the while keeping his eyes on O'Dowd. 'I'll have to ask you to leave now as well, Mr O'Dowd,' he said politely when he'd hitched the phone back on his belt.

'You're getting very formal all of a sudden, Frank,' O'Dowd started, then his hand went to his mouth. He looked at the figure lying on the grass and then at the garda. 'Can I see her?'

'I'm sorry,' he said quietly, 'but we have to leave things as they are.'

To his surprise, O'Dowd dropped to his knees and knelt beside the dead woman with his head bent. Recaldo watched him uncomfortably, aware that in a short time O'Dowd's apparent grief would be overwhelmed by the murder investigation. He was her nearest neighbour as well as – what? Her friend? Her lover? Whichever, his life would be minutely examined, his weak-nesses exposed, his privacy lost – perhaps for ever. O'Dowd, Spain, along with everyone else who had any contact with the dead

50

woman, however innocent. The gardener, the barman, the boys from the boatyard. Cressida Sweeney. Himself. They would all be grist to the mill.

O'Dowd broke into his thoughts. 'Can't we do something? Bring her inside out of the wet grass? Surely you're not intending to leave her just lying there like that? It's terrible. We've got to . . .'

'No, I'm sorry, but she has to be left where she is for the moment. You'll have to go now, I'm afraid. Someone will be along to see you shortly. Meantime, you're to stick to the house, if you don't mind, and you're not to even think of mentioning this to anyone. D'you hear me? I don't want any discussions down in Hussey's bar. I'm serious about this, mind.'

'I didn't hear you giving any such instructions to old Spain,' O'Dowd remarked sharply.

Recaldo was not drawn. 'Well, now,' he said in a conciliatory tone. 'If I thought there was any danger of *him* spreading the word, I'd have done so. But you know as well as I do that John Spain doesn't pass the time of day with anyone.'

'Nor them with him,' O'Dowd sneered.

'Indeed. So I'm sure you'll agree that you're a different matter entirely, Mr O'Dowd. I'd say you know more about the people around here than anyone.' Recaldo gave him one of his chillier smiles. 'More about Miss Walter too. Am I right?'

'Mrs,' O'Dowd murmured silkily. '*Mrs* Walter. She always insisted on her proper title.'

'Did she now? I wonder what I should make of that?' Recaldo put a firm hand under O'Dowd's elbow and headed him towards the side gate. When he was gone, the garda went straight to the flagged terrace at the back of the house. Something had caught his attention earlier, while he was talking to Spain. He'd glimpsed it reflecting a sudden flash of sunlight. He walked slowly, pace by pace, searching each inch of grass along the perimeter of the paving until he found what he was looking for.

His heart lurched as he picked it up and held it in his open palm. It was a small tortoiseshell comb, with a distinctive etched silver bar at the top. One of a pair Cressida Sweeney habitually wore to hold back her long hair.

He dialled her home number and let it ring a dozen or more times before he tried her mobile. It was switched off. He declined the invitation to leave a message. He slipped the comb in his pocket and sat down at the picnic table, waiting for the arrival of the crime unit. His face was troubled.

Chapter Eight

IT WAS A QUARTER TO NINE, AND RECALDO HAD BEGUN A CLOSE
search of the garden when the two officers from divisional headquarters banged on the side gate. They introduced themselves as
Superintendent Peter Coffey and Detective Inspector Phil McBride.

'Francis Xavier Recaldo?' McBride had a breezy manner. 'Bit of a
mouthful. What do they call you? FX?'

'No. Frank. Or just plain Recaldo.'

'Right.' McBride grinned cheerfully. Probably in his late thirties,
and about five foot eleven, he was well built. His receding, closely
shaved hair gave him a rather brutish wide-boy look, as did the black
leather jacket.

Coffey looked to be in his mid-fifties, three or four inches shorter
and almost as thin as Recaldo. His face was sharp-featured, foxy, his
expression humourless. He had restless eyes and an unhealthy sallow
complexion beneath thinning grey hair badly discoloured by tobacco.
His clothes – a rough tweed jacket and baggy grey trousers – looked
as though he'd slept in them.

'You made good time,' Recaldo remarked.

'Not bad,' Coffey replied. 'Phil here drives like Stirling Moss.' He
cleared his throat. 'We'd have got here sooner but we had a dickens
of a job finding this place, even with your directions. Just as well you
told us not to rely on signposts.'

Recaldo gave a little snort. 'Twisting them around is the local
sport – the district council has obviously got fed up repositioning
them.'

'That's an unusual name you have, sounds foreign,' Coffey

remarked predictably as they strode across the wet grass. Recaldo, who was rather proud of his Armada ancestry, sighed.

'About as foreign as de Valera, I suppose,' he replied laconically. 'Sir.'

'Huh?' Coffey looked mystified, then belatedly latched onto the reference to the Republic's late President. 'You from Clare then?'

'No, Kerry. The Dingle peninsula.'

'Oh well,' cut in McBride with a grin. He had a strong Dublin accent. 'That *is* foreign. As I well know,' he added, ignoring Coffey's glare. 'I'm a Dub, myself. And you can't get more foreign than that in Cork City, believe me.'

He turned back to look at the house. 'Quite a place,' he remarked. 'You'd want to be pretty rich to maintain it. What was it originally? Some kind of institution?'

'No, a nineteenth-century grain store – hence the name.'

'Huh?'

'The Old Corn Store,' Recaldo said, deadpan.

'Handsome. Great site as well,' McBride said, looking around. 'Has it been a house long?'

'I'm not sure, but I believe it was converted by the Swiss people who built the Atlantis Hotel in Passage South about twenty years or so ago.'

'We're not here for a lecture on architecture,' Coffey said shortly. 'So, let's get started. How was she found?'

'A passing fisherman, John Spain, found her just after half five this morning.'

'Spain? Queer names ye have around here,' Coffey remarked sourly and sniffed. He consulted his watch. 'We have only his word for the time? No other witnesses?' he asked. Recaldo shook his head.

'GP seen her?' McBride asked.

'Yes, I called Dr McCarthy as soon as I saw the woman was dead. He called in on his way to his surgery in Duncreagh. He lives close by, he got here at six fifty. He'll be at the surgery until he goes on his rounds at eleven, if you want to talk to him.' He handed Coffey a slip of paper with the doctor's number.

'Was the deceased on his list?' McBride asked.

'Apparently not. He's notified the coroner.'

'Good man. The pathologist is on her way from Cork – or will be after she's dropped her kids to school.' Coffey turned his mouth down, though whether in disapproval of a female pathologist or her domestic preoccupation was unclear. 'Ah well, at least we don't have to wait for the State Pathologist to come from Dublin – as we did in the old days. It's all women these days. The photographer and finger-print people are coming under their own steam, they'll probably get here first. Husband and wife team.'

The three officers were in the middle of taping off the area around the dead woman when there was a sharp rap at the side gate. Recaldo strode over to admit a thirty-something couple, carrying a large box-like black briefcase apiece.

'Louisa and Mark Duffy,' the young woman said by way of intro-duction. 'I'm prints, he does the snaps.'

Mark Duffy grinned. 'And she does the talking, I'm the strong silent type.' They walked down the garden and reported to Coffey. They listened without comment to his instructions and within a very few minutes were at work.

Coffey glanced around the garden. 'So where's the old fellow that found her?' He held his head on one side and jutted out his jaw. He looked like a terrier: aggressive and irritable.

Recaldo ran his finger around the stiff collar of his uniform jacket where the rough serge was chafing his skin. 'He went off home,' he admitted sheepishly. This was greeted with heavy silence. 'I'm sorry, sir, but it was the best I could do. He's an old man. He'd been hang-ing around for hours and was wet through. Anyway, once he'd decided he'd had enough there was little I could do to restrain him because, unfortunately, at that stage a neighbour called O'Dowd barged in and I was in a bit of a dilemma. I couldn't chase after Spain *and* guard the body at the same time, could I? Or leave O'Dowd with it on his own. Old Spain is reliable.'

'Unless he killed her, of course, but I suppose you'll have thought of that? Nobody is reliable in a murder investigation.' Coffey pursed his lips, obviously weighing the advantages and disadvantages of making an issue of the fact that the principal witness had been allowed to skedaddle before *his* arrival. He allowed his silence to continue long enough to labour the point, then asked, 'What time was it when you got here?'

'Just on twenty past six.'

Coffey's eyes narrowed. 'Almost an hour after the body was found? So, what time did Spain ring you?'

'He rang the station at five fifty-two. The call was transferred automatically – I live on the other side of Passage South. He just told me there'd been an accident, which is why I didn't ring headquarters immediately. It took me less than twenty minutes to get here, from the time of the phone call. I was at the front of the house,' he glanced at his notebook, 'at six fifteen. I banged on the side gate and Spain let me through – it has a Yale lock on this side. Once I checked Mrs Walter had no pulse, I contacted divisional headquarters.' He consulted his notebook. 'That was just on six twenty-five. I took Spain's statement before Dr McCarthy arrived. Then, after the doctor left, I went over it with him several times until O'Dowd barged in. A few minutes after that Spain went on home, I told him to wait there till we call on him. He lives only a short way upriver.' He held his notebook out to Coffey, who waved it aside.

'Why didn't you lock the garden gate?'

'I did.'

'You did? Then how did this O'Dowd "barge in" as you call it?'

Recaldo, caught on the hop, scratched his head. 'You know, I was so flabbergasted to see him, I didn't ask. I suppose he must have a key, he's a friend of hers.'

'Jay-sus,' said McBride succinctly. 'That'll be a bit of a problem, then. We better get that geezer back here, pronto. Don't you think?'

'We'll do that in a minute,' Coffey cut in. 'Let's get back to Spain for a minute. I'm puzzled. Why did it take him twenty minutes to call for help?'

'He says he panicked, couldn't think where to phone from – he doesn't have a mobile.'

'So, where *did* he phone from?'

'Inside the house, here. The lights were on and the French windows were open.'

'Janey,' McBride said, sotto voce. '*Inside the house?*'

Coffey glared. 'He went in the house? Alone? Footprints inside tally with that?'

Recaldo coughed. 'No footprints that I could see. I haven't been in myself, but it seemed all right from the window.' The other two stared at him in some amazement. 'He said he took his boots off,' Recaldo added.

'Did he, by the hokey?' Coffey turned on his heel, stalked up to the house and leaned in the open window. McBride was close behind.

'Why didn't you search the house?'

'I was unable to make two of myself,' Recaldo replied stolidly. 'Regulations demand that I stay beside the body. Which is what I did from the time I arrived till I frogmarched O'Dowd off.'

'Don't quote the rule book at me, boy,' Coffey said sniffily. He pronounced it 'bye'.

'Correct me if I'm wrong, FX,' McBride interjected coolly, 'but wasn't Spain alone here for at least forty minutes from the time he came across the body until you got here? That's one hell of a long time.'

'He's an elderly man, he moves slowly. Reacts slowly too, like we all do when we're in shock.'

'I suppose we have to assume he's telling the truth about the time he found her,' Coffey said.

'There's no way of knowing that, except for his word.' Recaldo bit back any sharper reply. 'There wasn't a soul out on the estuary even after I got here. The old fellow was in deep shock, though. That was plain to see and genuine.'

'And that makes him innocent, you think? Well, I'd say there could be many reasons for it. You shouldn't have let him go.'

'I know that, but as I've already explained, I hadn't much choice.'

'There's always choice. Always a right way and a wrong way. You should know that.' Coffey sighed. 'Let's hear your report.'

Recaldo leafed through his notebook while he described the scene that greeted him on his arrival, then he read out John Spain's description of finding the dead woman. After a few sentences Coffey held out his hand. 'Tell you what, why don't I read it myself while you continue your search of the grounds, back and front? Oh, and give your man Spain a ring and tell him to stay at home, that we'll be around soon. That should keep him fixed.' He checked his watch. 'We'll get him over here at, say, ten o'clock. But don't tell him that, I don't want him wandering off. And the other joker – O'Dowd was it? Get him first and give him the same message. We'll tackle him as soon as we get through the preliminaries here. Tell him to stay put and that we'll want those keys off him. I take it you have your mobile?' he added sarcastically.

'Yes I do,' Recaldo said. 'And I can certainly ring O'Dowd but John Spain isn't on the phone.'

'Christ,' exploded McBride. 'You're joking.'

'No I'm not,' Recaldo replied mildly. 'He's not very well off. When he wants to make a call he uses the public phone in Passage South. If you want to contact him you call around. He's not very sociable.'

'Anything else we need to know?' McBride asked sarcastically. 'Funny little ways you have around here.'

'I told him to stay put already but I can go around and get him if you like?'

'No,' Coffey said. 'You stay here. Call the other fellow though.'

Recaldo made the call while Mark the photographer was setting his equipment up and Louisa was doing her routine around the deceased. Superintendent Coffey and Inspector McBride crouched down on either side of the body, speaking to each other and the experts in a low murmur. It could have been that they were simply following an established modus operandi, showing no more than the standard contempt of the plain-clothes officer for the uniformed mule, but it felt more personal, as if they were demonstrating how things were properly done. Recaldo, who was already feeling touchy, went into a slow burn.

How the hell had he overlooked O'Dowd's bloody keys? God, what else had he missed? 'FX?' McBride called as if he was mind-reading. 'Have *you* a set of keys to the house?'

'No, as I already said, I didn't go in. They're probably still inside. Nothing's been disturbed since I got here.'

'*Since* could well be the operative word,' Coffey murmured sourly. 'Right then, we better spread out or we'll be at this all day. Phil, you go check the house while Mark is finishing up here. Have a thorough look around and find the keys. Make sure Louisa checks everything – light switches, door handles.' Behind him, McBride was silently mouthing, yeah, yeah, yeah. 'And check the phone for . . .'

'We'll work it out, boss,' McBride said jauntily and strode off.

'Oh, and see if you can manage a pot of coffee while you're at it

58

... Or tea. And make it strong, will ye? My head is cracking open.'
He turned to Recaldo. 'Now then, I wonder what's keeping that
pathologist? She's taking long enough. Probably lost her way. Why
don't you go on out to the road and keep an eye open for her. I'd say
she's going to have one heck of a job finding this place. And while
you're at it see what you can do about securing the entrance.
Otherwise we'll have a crowd of sightseers before we know it. Or
worse, the press, God help us.'

'I have a spare padlock and chain in the back of my car.'

'Good. You get on with that.'

Excluded. The pulse in Recaldo's temple quickened. So simply
done. Elegant. He almost admired Coffey, though he was filled with
resentment at the invasion of his territory. Used to being his own boss,
he didn't much care for his menial role or Coffey's offhand manner.

He collected the padlock and a small can of oil and strode swiftly
along the muddy driveway. The gates had obviously not been shut for
years and it took considerable effort, and oil, to get them moving. He
hung about for almost twenty minutes before the pathologist turned
up. The damp air was chilly. He stamped his feet to get the circulation
going, then walked a little way up the lane to see if there was any sign
of her, while he carefully went back over the previous few hours in
his head, trying to get things straight. He turned the little comb over
in his hand, wondering when exactly he had last seen Cressie wearing
it. Friday? Yes, certainly on Friday, in the supermarket. He was now
more than ever uncertain about the boat party and the girl's identity.
Was it Cressie? And if so, what was she doing? What were any of them
doing? The fact that O'Dowd didn't mention it also seemed highly
significant. O'Dowd was playing shtumm. But then, so was he. And
if he wasn't careful McBride would soon cotton on: he was sharp as a
knife.

After a little while, when there was still no sign of the pathologist,
he dialled the Sweeneys' number on his mobile. He let it ring fifteen,
twenty times and only gave up when he heard the roar of a car engine.

A maroon Volvo Estate came batting down the narrow road. When
Recaldo stepped out to flag it down it skidded then screeched to a
halt, barely missing him.

'Phew, you gave me an awful fright.' A friendly, rather matronly
face leaned out the window. 'Still, I'm glad you're here, I'd have gone

59

straight past.' She smiled and held out her hand. 'Joanna Morrow, I'm the pathologist. Are you Inspector McBride?'

'No, I'm the local, more lowly, force,' he replied with only the vaguest hint of irony. 'Frank Recaldo.' They shook hands. 'Come through, Dr Morrow, but take it slowly, the drive is like a bog. It's badly rutted. Superintendent Coffey and DI McBride are above at the house, waiting for you. Just follow the track, but watch out, it veers sharply to the left.' Dr Morrow held up her hand. 'Hop in, you can show me yourself.' He pushed the gates shut and padlocked them, then eased himself gingerly into the front seat beside her. The floor was ankle deep in debris: paper, toys, crisp packets.

'Have you enough room for those long legs? Shove the seat right back — the thingummy is at the side. Oh, and toss that stuff in the back, with the rest of the junk,' she said cheerfully. 'My kids reduce everything to a tip.' She laughed fondly. 'Besides keeping me up half the night. It's too much, at my age.'

About the same age as himself, Recaldo estimated. She did indeed look as though she'd been but recently roused from a deep sleep and was still in shock. Tired but comfortable, even on such slight acquaintance. He allowed himself a brief fantasy of snuggling up and having his brow soothed. He noticed, with some self-disgust, that his cravings were becoming more sad and desperate with emotional and sexual deprivation.

'How old are your children?' he asked politely.

'Five and three. I was a late starter.' She rolled her eyes as she pulled up beside the two police cars. 'What about yourself? Have you got a family?'

He was spared answering by McBride, who, at that moment, popped through the side gate with Mark and Louisa Duffy who were obviously on the point of leaving. He saw them to their van before strolling over to open the car door for the pathologist.

'Howya Doc,' he grinned, and took her heavy bag from her. Recaldo noted, and admired, the grace with which she thanked the younger man but at the same time slipped into professional mode. He followed them through to the river garden in silence.

'There's a hot pot of coffee on the stove,' McBride announced as he set the doctor's bag on the ground. 'Good coffee but there isn't a scrap of food in the place. No biscuits even.'

'I won't, thanks, I have to get on. Busy day.' Joanna Morrow put on thin rubber gloves. 'What was her name?' she asked.

'Evangeline Walter,' Recaldo told her.

'Fanciful. There's a Longfellow poem by that name, isn't there? Evangeline.' She rolled the sound enjoyably on her tongue. 'I like it. Do we know anything about her?'

'Very little. American. She lived alone.'

Dr Morrow fastened a tiny receiver to her lapel. 'Right then,' she said. 'Better get started.' She stood in silence, intently examining the scene where the body lay, and then she slowly got down on her knees. The three men grouped around her, in effect shielding her from the stiff sea breeze. 'Strangely peaceful, isn't she?' she remarked. 'Not often you see that.' She touched Evangeline's head and the fabric covering it fell away, exposing the shoulder-length unnaturally black hair which was a shocking contrast to the pallor of her skin. She brushed back the fringe and revealed hairline scars close to the scalp which, on closer inspection, also circumscribed her face.

'Plastic surgery, and plenty of it,' she murmured in amazement. 'Now isn't that extraordinary? I've never seen so much. Beautifully done though.'

'Expensive?' McBride asked.

'Very, I should say.' She touched the woman's eyelids and slightly tilted the chin. 'All over. She certainly kept the years at bay.' They looked at Evangeline's strange, rather beautiful, doll-like mask on which no lines or wrinkles hinted at her age or temperament. It was without expression of any kind: neither fear, nor anger. 'Lips blue, might be bruised. Gash on left temple, contused.' She ran a swab under the fingernails. 'Nails manicured, painted frosted pink and intact, no sign of struggle. Odd, that,' Dr Morrow murmured. 'Considering the gash. Could have fallen, of course.' She looked around. 'There's plenty of rocks about.' She lightly touched the neck beneath the chin on the left side, where there was a small red mark about the size of a penny.

'Love bite?' McBride asked.

Morrow ran the tip of her finger around its slightly raised contours then pressed it gently. 'No, a strawberry mark.' She grinned up at him. McBride asked if she could smell alcohol. Dr Morrow bent over the dead woman and sniffed. 'Yes, indeed,' she said decisively. 'Was she a drinker?'

'There's a half-empty wine bottle on the kitchen table,' McBride said. 'Napa Valley Chardonnay. White Rock Winery,' he elaborated as one who took an interest in such things.

Dr Morrow shook her head. 'No, smells like whiskey. I'll check it out later. In the lab,' she murmured. She unbuttoned the bodice of the fine cashmere robe and ran her finger lightly between the breasts. Recaldo had an immediate mental picture of a scalpel moving down the pale flesh. He glanced at his companions and saw that they too seemed mesmerized by the inert body. Beneath the delicate wool of the woman's robe her nipples pointed obscenely upwards, even in death defying gravity. Recaldo realized with a shock that the corpse vividly reminded him of Cher – that walking talking living doll – whose ubiquitous magazine photographs showed no sign of change from year to year, no expression beyond the Giaconda smile.

'Goodness, there's nothing of her,' Dr Morrow exclaimed. 'Middle-aged anorexic, silly woman.' She lifted the edges of the robe to expose the torso and her gloved hand traced the length of a six-inch puckered scar. 'Very recent. No more than a couple of weeks or so. Well, that'll teach me,' Dr Morrow murmured to herself. 'Not a diet, then.' As her finger gently prodded the stomach, Recaldo gasped. She glanced up sharply. 'Oh dear, you're not going to be sick are you, Mr Recaldo? Put your head between your knees, like a good man.' But he ignored her advice, judging it more prudent to stand absolutely still and wait for the wave of dizziness to pass.

'Was she an actress? A film star or something?' she asked. 'I'm told the ground is thick with them around here.'

'FX would be able to tell us that, wouldn't you, FX?' McBride suggested shrewdly.

Recaldo hunched his shoulders and shook his head as he fought off recurring spells of nausea. He swallowed hard. 'I believe she was an art expert of some sort,' he murmured tightly, desperately trying to swallow the bile which suddenly filled his mouth. 'Arranged exhibitions. I really don't know an awful lot about her, except that she's American and has lived here for several years.'

'Bit remote for a city type, isn't it?' Dr Morrow said in her matter-of-fact way. 'Now then, Evangeline Walter,' she murmured half to herself. 'What exactly killed you, I wonder?' She lifted the gown away

62

from the legs. After a few minutes she replaced it and lightly tied its belt. Then she stood up and addressed herself to Recaldo. 'You've the local knowledge, Mr Recaldo. Do we know her GP? I'd really like to have a look at her medical records.'

'She's not with Dr McCarthy, anyway – he told me so while he was here this morning. His practice is in Duncreagh but also covers Trianach – where we are now. He said he'd ask discreetly around the other groups, see if he could find out.'

'That would be useful.'

'Could she have died of exposure?' Recaldo asked suddenly, ignoring Coffey's glare of disapproval.

'Exposure? I've no idea yet.' She looked at him in surprise. 'Is there some reason you ask?'

He shrugged. 'She isn't exactly dressed for the climate, or the location, is she? That gown is very flimsy.'

'Warm though, it's cashmere. It seems unlikely as a primary cause.' She continued uncertainly, 'She's got a bit of a gash on the back of her head and she's haemorrhaged, copiously.'

'From the operation?' McBride asked.

'Could be,' she said cagily. 'Could be several things.'

'Rape?' he persisted.

'Can't say for sure, yet. Looks as if there's been some sexual activity certainly. Do we know when she was last seen alive?'

'I saw her here, in the garden, early yesterday afternoon. The old guy who discovered the body said he saw her standing over there, last night, at around eight.' Recaldo pointed to a gnarled oak tree by the riverbank. 'He generally goes out about then to bait his lobster pots. She was there when he came in, he says.'

'Eight?' She pursed her lips. 'Too early, I think. At a guess, and that's all it is at this point, I reckon she died well after that, say between nine or ten and em,' she rubbed her hand over her mouth, 'the early hours – one o'clock? I couldn't be sure at this stage.' Her voice fell away to a murmur again; she seemed to have a habit of talking to herself. 'The conditions are too bad to be more accurate. Her clothes are soaked for one thing, which would affect the body temperature. She's certainly been in the open for some hours, probably all night, and may have been in the water for a time. We'll have to see what turns up during the post-mortem.' She fell silent. McBride went off to the water's edge and lit a cigarette and stood gazing out over the estuary.

'The fingerprints done, Mr Coffey? Yes? Well then, that more or less wraps it up,' Dr Morrow said presently and began to pack her bag. She stepped closer to Coffey and lowered her voice until Recaldo had to strain to overhear her. 'I'll phone you tonight, and bring you up to date. We'll have the prints and pics. You'll be in Cork?'

'This evening anyway. After nine probably. Try me at home. If not . . .' He gave her his mobile number.

'I'd like to think over one or two aspects of this,' she waved her arm around vaguely. 'Consult one or two people. We could have a chat when you get back. Meantime, I'd keep an open mind.'

'Is something bothering you, Joanna?'

'Yeah. Something is. It may be nothing. But for the time being I wouldn't put it down as a definite murder. The recent operation confuses things. I may be wrong, however. I'll talk to you tonight.' She gave herself a little shake and raised her voice. 'This is a gorgeous spot, isn't it? Pity about the . . . well. Pity about the poor woman.'

'The van should be here shortly.' McBride strolled up from the water's edge, breaking an uncomfortable silence. 'We can sort out what's to be done once her nibs is off to the mortuary.'

Recaldo flinched. McBride's breezy reference to the corpse offended him. He drew a black plastic body bag over the woman's yellow-white wrinkled feet. When he looked up Joanna Morrow was standing beside him. She smiled. 'Is this how she was found?' she asked in her practical way.

'It's how she was when I got here,' he replied carefully and continued with his task. 'This part of the garden was flooded earlier, maybe she drowned.' He spoke half to himself.

After a pause, Dr Morrow touched his arm. 'Mr Recaldo, did you hear me? Was she found lying like this?'

He cleared his throat. 'No. I'm afraid the old man moved her. He said she was standing against that tree there but he took her down when he realized she was dead . . .'

'Standing up?' Her nose wrinkled in distaste. 'Do you believe him?' Dr Morrow asked softly, after a moment. Coffey and McBride listened to this exchange in obvious disbelief and he knew he'd lost them; they had begun to harbour suspicions about his involvement.

'I've no reason not to . . .'

They exchanged glances. Coffey spoke first. 'The old man moved the body? Have I got that right?' His face suffused with anger.

Recaldo cleared his throat. 'Yes, sir.'

'Why? Did he deign to mention why?'

'No, sir.'

'No? And you didn't think to pass this on?'

'What held her up?' Dr Morrow interrupted. 'Was she tied or something? To something?'

'He described her as standing against that tree, but I wonder if he might have been hallucinating.' His voice grew heated. 'You see, she was in the habit of standing against that tree, watching the sun go down. Smoking. Whatever. He saw her like that most evenings. There was no sign of a rope. I searched,' he said, with finality. Out of the corner of his eye he saw Spain's boat headed towards them down the estuary. 'Why don't you ask him yourself, Dr Morrow? There's John Spain now, he's coming this way.' He pointed to the boat. 'He's the one who found the body on his way out fishing at around half past five this morning.'

'Half five? He goes fishing at that hour?' She huffed out her cheeks. 'God, he must be mad. How old is the guy?'

'Seventy-three or -four,' he shrugged. 'Could be more of course, or less.'

'Compos?' She looked at him shrewdly.

'What?'

'What's wrong with you, man? Is he alert, reliable?' Coffey interjected impatiently.

'Yes, very alert and generally reliable, I should say.'

Coffey touched Recaldo's arm. 'What are you waiting for, call him, man.' There was no need, though; Spain was coming towards them.

They watched him tie up and walk along the shore. 'That what he did this morning?' Coffey asked.

'It is, except the tide was in so he had to wade most of the way.'

'Which is how he got so wet he had to go home?' Coffey raised his eyebrows archly. 'He should have been kept here.'

'I'm aware of that,' Recaldo retorted, losing patience. 'I should have stopped him, run after him, but I told you that would have meant leaving the body with O'Dowd, whom I trust a good deal less than John Spain.' He squinted up at the superintendent. 'I chose the lesser of two evils. If I'd chased after the old man, I'd have had to leave O'Dowd alone at the scene. Nothing he'd have liked better than to be in the thick of it all. The man's into everything, he's a meddler. Our own local Mr Fix-it. I had no intention of allowing him to hang around.'

'Who rattled your cage, then?' McBride asked provocatively. 'What the feck's O'Dowd done to you?'

Recaldo zipped up the body bag and straightened. 'Nothing.'

'Don't you think you're going a bit over the top? You certainly seem to have strong opinions about him, I must say.'

'I don't altogether trust O'Dowd. We shouldn't delay calling on him.'

'*We?*' Territorial lines were drawn up.

'We. You. Or I.' He shrugged wearily. 'Whichever you wish, gentlemen,' he said, as Spain joined them.

'Ah, Mr Spain,' Coffey greeted him. 'We'd just like to ask you a few questions.' He turned to Recaldo and unsettled him with sudden kindliness. 'Look, why don't you go on home for a break, Frank, you must be on your knees. By the looks of things we're going to be hanging around here for most of the day, so we'll have to spell each other. We'll see O'Dowd. Off with you now, have a kip and something to eat and come back in a couple of hours. We should be ready for a conference by then.'

'Thank you, sir.' Recaldo glanced at his watch. 'I'll be back at twelve thirty.' And having given Coffey the spare padlock key, F. X. Recaldo, erstwhile Detective Inspector, late of the Phoenix Park Garda Headquarters, made a dignified exit.

Chapter Nine

IT WAS TEN FIFTY-FIVE WHEN RECALDO PULLED AWAY FROM THE Old Corn Store and eased his battered Jeep slowly along the tortuous drive. He was deep in thought and swore irritably as he pulled on the handbrake and jumped out to wrestle open the rusty gates. It occurred to him that Dr Morrow wouldn't be far behind, and to save her the same trouble he tucked the Jeep under the hedge on the grass verge to one side of the gate to wait for her to come through.

The comb and Cressida preoccupied him. He tried to phone her again but she was still not answering. Spain's evasions also troubled him, and O'Dowd's. Who were they trying to protect? Themselves or someone else? Somehow, deep down, he knew the boat party was at the heart of what had happened to Evangeline Walter. And that Spain, O'Dowd and Cressida and perhaps her husband were all part of it.

After about ten minutes Dr Morrow came bumping along the drive. He unfurled himself from the Jeep and strode swiftly up to the entrance, just in time to guide her through the narrow opening. 'That was kind of you,' she called. 'Thanks for your help.' And with a cheery wave she went skittering down the lane at alarming speed. Recaldo watched her admiringly. She was evidently a woman who took life in both hands. He wondered what strange chance had led her to her macabre profession.

He closed the gates and climbed into the Jeep and, envying Joanna Morrow's elan, eased cautiously forward, his mind still on the previous afternoon and the good ship *Halcyon*. He couldn't see the girl's face clearly as she leaned against the rail beside Mrs Walter, their arms linked. *Linked arms?* – Evangeline and Cressida? It was preposterous.

Had Spain seen the little pantomime as well? Throughout all the questioning Spain never mentioned the boating party. And the voice in Recaldo's head mocked – *nor did you.*

He drove over the causeway but instead of turning right for Passage South, turned left on the main road and made for the old stone bridge over the main spur of the Glár a few miles further upstream. He crossed over to the road on the far bank and, three miles along, forked off towards the Sweeney property. The gate was open but the house was not. He banged at the door, rang the bell and walked around to the back but there was nobody about. No sign either of Finnegan, the red setter. On the slim chance that Mrs Sweeney and son had taken the said Finnegan out for his daily romp, he jumped back in the car and headed for Passage South at high speed.

On the way through the village something else occurred to him. Marilyn Donovan lived next door to Hussey's pub. She was well known to be the best cleaner around, a domestic treasure. He had once approached her to 'do' for him but she claimed she was already overcommitted. He had a faint memory of someone telling him Marilyn only ever worked for the foreigners, because they paid better. She was, it seemed, particularly fond of Yanks. There were several 'Yanks' in the vicinity besides Mrs Walter. But it was at least worth a quick try. He hammered on the door four or five times before it was opened by an undersized girl of about ten or twelve who looked pinch-faced and desperate. He could hear an infant bawling inconsolably in the background.

'Is your mother in?'

'No, she's not.' The girl sniffed and wiped her nose on her sleeve. The background howls turned to piercing screams.

'Aisling, isn't it?'

'How do you know that?' Terror filled her light blue eyes. An axe-murderer couldn't have looked guiltier. He hunkered down to her eye level.

'Are *you* looking after that baby all on your own?' he asked gently.

'Amn't I always?' she blurted.

'Where's Mammy?' He could hardly hear his own voice over the din.

'She's in the hospital. In Cork.' Her eyes filled with tears. He

68

suspected it was more helpless frustration than sorrow which filled her soul.

'What's wrong with the child?' he asked, suddenly impatient with her, life and the furious realization that if he wasn't very careful he was going to be roped in to help her out of her plight.

'I don't know,' she wailed. 'He was awake all night long. He's had two bottles already this morning and I changed him three times as well. I don't know what else to do, my daddy won't be back for hours.'

Oh God, here we go. At least he was wearing uniform. 'Let's have a look at him while you tell me about your poor mammy.' He stepped into the hall and followed Aisling into the back kitchen where a pungent odour left no doubt as to why baby Liam was purple in the face.

Recaldo sniffed and wrinkled his nose. 'I think he probably needs a clean nappy.'

'He does but they're all run out.' She looked up at him tearfully.

Christ. 'Where do you buy them?' he asked tersely and fished a fiver from his pocket. 'Run quick and get some. D'you know the right size?'

'I do, a course, what d'you take me for?' she said but didn't move. The infant sounded as if he was about to burst a blood vessel.

'Go on, go on, for heaven's sake, what's keeping you?'

'It isn't enough.'

'What isn't enough?'

'The fiver. Aren't they nearly six pounds.'

No wonder poor Marilyn had to work. He handed Aisling an additional pound coin. 'Quick, quick, quick,' he said. Aisling still didn't move.

'Now what?'

'Mammy says I'm not to leave him on his own,' she said primly, but made no effort to pick the stinking infant up. 'Or let strangers in the house.'

Recaldo sighed loudly. 'God, give me patience. Amn't I the guard? You know me don't you?' She nodded. 'Right then, go. Off with you?'

'Thanks Mr Recaldo,' she said. 'I'll be back in a minute.' She pulled a roll of toilet paper from the dresser drawer.

His jaw dropped. 'What do you expect me to do with that?'

'Clean him up, I've done it three times already.' Her face broke into a cheeky grin. 'Anyways you asked, didn't you?' She turned tail and darted out the door.

He had been a strictly hands-off father. So much for the hard professional man, he thought resignedly. He picked up the foetid child and held him at arm's length. Liam abruptly stopped screaming and regarded him solemnly, with much interest. Recaldo stood firm and glared back. Fortunately Aisling returned before the racket started up again. He handed the infant over with gratitude and humility.

'Tell me about your mammy? What's wrong with her?'

'Something awful bad.' She looked up at him over the baby's head. 'She fell down the stairs. It was desperate. She was pumping blood – it was all over the place and my dad was away out on a job, so I rang Mrs Sweeney. She took Mammy to the hospital.'

At the mention of Cressida's name, Recaldo spoke more softly to the girl. 'When was this, Aisling?'

'Monday, around tea time.'

'Why did you ring Mrs Sweeney?'

'Cos Mam works for her, I suppose. I tried Mrs Walter first but she said her car was broke down. So I rang Mrs Sweeney and she came straight over and took me mam to Duncreagh. She rang Daddy from the hospital there to say that they told her to go to the Bons . . . the Bons something . . . in Cork City.' The child fought back tears.

'The Bon Secours, was it?' He hunkered down beside her.

She nodded. 'Mrs Sweeney said she'd come back and help us out but she never came.'

'When did Mrs Sweeney say that?'

'On Monday when she collected Mam.'

'And she didn't come back? Not at all?' he asked. Aisling shook her head. 'Was Gil with her?'

'Who?'

'Her little boy?'

A strange look came over her face. Revulsion? 'He's backward.'

'Who says?'

'Me mam. She says he's a dummy.'

God Almighty. 'There's nothing wrong with Gil, Aisling. He's a bit deaf, that's all. But he's learning to talk.'

She paid little heed. 'That's why he doesn't go to school. Me mam says Mrs Sweeney's a saint with him. The noises he makes would drive you mad.' She mimicked an adult voice.

Recaldo's sympathy for Marilyn evaporated. 'Did Mrs Sweeney ring again?'

'She did, but 'twas my dad she talked to . . .'

'Monday night?' he encouraged.

Again she nodded but as an afterthought added, 'He went up to Cork last night after tea and didn't get back till the middle of the night. We've been on our own since morning.'

'But you saw him before he went out to work?'

'I did. He said Mammy was OK, but there'd be no new baby and I have to mind Liam till he comes home.' She stopped and put her hand to her mouth. 'I forgot. He axed me did Mrs Sweeney come to help us last night . . .'

'Say that again.'

'Mrs Sweeney was supposed to come and get our tea last night.' She hunched her shoulders.

'But she didn't?'

Aisling shook her head violently. 'I made banana sandwiches. Mrs Hussey came in after, with cold ham and bread. She washed the baby for me. I put him to bed. Mrs Hussey said for to call her if I was afraid.' She shrugged again. 'But I just fell asleep.'

'Thanks, Aisling, you're a great girl.' He fished in his pocket and gave her another fiver; it was proving an expensive visit. 'Get yourself something to eat down in Molly's café and buy some more milk for that howler.' They laughed and by dint of a little further prodding, Recaldo learned that Marilyn worked for Mrs Walter, mornings, Mrs Sweeney, three evenings a week (by which Aisling meant afternoons), Mr Clancy (another American), two evenings and Saturday morning. Busy Marilyn.

The girl finished up by saying, 'If you want to talk to my daddy, he'll be home around six o'clock. I'm to look after the baby all the time Mammy's in hospital, that's why I'm not in school.'

'So I'm not to arrest you, is that it?' Recaldo reassured her as best he could, then left her to her chores. He picked up some provisions for himself in the grocery shop, somehow managing to stave off Mrs Quinn by freezing her curiosity with over-elaborate politeness and impenetrable reserve. But her unvoiced questions told him, if he needed telling, that the news was out. He could almost hear a faint background buzz as he went back to his car. So far no sign of the press, but Passage South was a long way from the city and it was early in the day yet.

Preoccupied with these thoughts, Recaldo drove home and drank two cups of strong black coffee, brewed from a mixture of freshly ground mocha and Colombian beans. After he'd eaten four slices of toast, he showered, shaved and changed into dark grey cords and a black polo-neck sweater. Then he settled Barker in the back of his car and set off for the cliffs. He didn't hold much hope now of catching up with Cressida, since he'd wasted so much time at the Donovans'. But he still thought it worth a try.

When he found no sign of them, Recaldo decided to cut his losses, dump Barker home and get back to Trianach before Coffey sent out a search party for him. He now wished he'd done what the good superintendent suggested – had a kip – instead of running around like an ineffectual blue-arsed fly. His eyes felt like sandpits and the back of his head was pounding for lack of sleep. Nevertheless, on his way home, as he was passing the grounds of the Atlantis Hotel, a sideways glance triggered a half-buried impression of something vaguely familiar.

He braked sharply, backed up to the entrance and pulled on his handbrake then strode rapidly through the hotel garden, all the time noting the similarity of the landscaping with Evangeline Walter's acres. Eventually he found the gardener working in a semicircular shrubbery. He was a tiny man, almost hidden by the lush foliage of his plants.

'Finbarr? How are things?'

Finbarr Spillane straightened up to his full five feet, pushed his cap back on his head, looked up and gave Recaldo a rather winning gap-toothed grin. It was hard to tell the gardener's age but he had the quiet dignity about him of one who is certain of his calling. In his own environment he looked perfectly at home; it was long tall Recaldo who seemed out of place. Finbarr wasn't at all fazed by the garda towering over him.

'Not bad, then. And yourself?' He wiped his forehead with the back of his hand, leaving streaks of rich black dirt over it. 'That's a grand day we're having.'

'I wondered . . .' Recaldo hesitated. Now that he came to think about it, he couldn't ever remember having actually seen Finbarr working anywhere but in the hotel garden. He realized with a start that he wasn't even sure where he lived. He'd never encountered him in Passage South nor even walking the roads. Perhaps he just squatted down, like a leprechaun, and slept under a bush at night? 'I wondered, Finbarr, if you do other gardens besides this one?' he asked, coming to the point at once.

'I do, then. A bit here and there, from time to time,' he replied guardedly.

'Mrs Walter has a beautiful garden,' Recaldo said vaguely.

'She does. I do work there for her.' He stared up into Recaldo's eyes and took off his cap. 'God rest her poor soul.'

Recaldo recoiled slightly but before he could express his alarm Finbarr piped up, 'I saw you going there this morning when I was just out of bed. I thought there must be something up. Anyways 'tis all around the town by now. She was a grand woman. And very knowledgeable with the plants. Knew all the Latin names.'

'You rise early then?'

'I do. As soon as it gets light. And sometimes before, if I wakes up.'

'Where is it you live, Finbarr?'

'I'd have thought you'd know that by now.' Finbarr looked at him impishly. 'Way out the Duncreagh Road by the Trianach turn. The white house on the right. I live there with my aunt Mona.' He pronounced it ant.

'She in a wheelchair?'

'She is,' he replied. 'But it doesn't stop her doing anything she wants. She's a great woman altogether.' He giggled. 'She keeps *me* on me toes, anyway.'

'When were you last in Mrs Walter's place?'

'Monday, same as always. I do one morning a week there. But I didn't stay long that time. She let me off early, said everything was too wet. With all the rain.' His voice suddenly lacked certainty. He threw his eyes upwards. 'But sure isn't it always raining? It never bothered her before, nor me nayther.'

'It was unusual for her to send you home, then?'

Finbarr nodded. 'A bit. Maybe it was because she had the visitor? That was unusual for her, she was more often alone.'

'A visitor?'

'A gir-rl. Long blondy hair. Bit like young Mrs Sweeney to look at.'

Recaldo gave a little jerk of surprise. 'It was Mrs Sweeney?'

'No, it was not then. Only the long hair put me in mind of her.'

'Who was she? Did you talk to her?' Recaldo asked.

'No-a. I just saw her standing looking out the window at me, while I was pruning back a shrub. I don't know who she was. Never saw her before.' He chewed his lower lip. 'But I saw her again, the very next evening.'

Evening could mean anything from noon. Afternoon and evening were entirely interchangeable in local parlance. 'What time?' Recaldo asked sharply.

'I dunno exactly. After dinner anyway. We usually finish round about two.'

Recaldo froze. 'Where was that?'

'Where was what?'

'Where did you see the girl?'

'Out on the bay, she was, on a yacht. With the grand day that it was, the aunt fancied a bit of an outing. A neighbour took us out by Trabuí for a spin after dinner and 'twas there we saw the big yacht go by with them on it.' Trabuí, at the end of the peninsula, had a superb view over the bay. Spectators often went there when there was a race or regatta.

'Mr Sweeney's yacht, you mean?'

Finbarr gave him an odd little sideways look. 'Maybe you saw them yourself? Weren't you out there as well?'

Recaldo ignored this. 'Could you see who else was on it?'

'I could of course. I have great eyesight, thank God. Jer O'Dowd, Mrs Walter, the gir-rl and some other fella. They were quite plain to see because the sails weren't up. They were using the engine only,' he added, which checked precisely with what Recaldo had himself seen.

'Who was steering it?'

For the first time Spillane's confidence faltered. 'I dunno, I couldn't be sure of that at all – whoever it was had a cap pulled down over his eyes. It looked like Mr Sweeney only I'd heard he was off in London this past week.' He rallied. 'But it was probably him all right. Who else would it be?'

Who else indeed? 'And you're sure the girl wasn't Mrs Sweeney?'

Finbarr gave him a pitying look. 'It was not, then. Sure Mrs Sweeney doesn't care for the sailing at all. That's well known.'

Wasn't everything? 'Anyways, she never stirs out of the house without the boy, God help us.'

Recaldo's face blanked. He was so engrossed in his own thoughts that he almost missed Spillane's next remark. '. . . off in her car.'

'WHAT?'

'I said anyways, Mrs Sweeney was away off in Cork. Didn't she bring Marilyn Donovan to the hospital.'

'Wasn't that Monday?'

'Yesterday as well. She dropped off the child . . .' He looked disapproving. 'With old Spain, I suppose,' he added, watching Recaldo. 'The aunt saw her coming over the causeway around ten in the morning.'

It wasn't exactly confirmation but at least it seemed less likely that it was Cressie on the yacht. Yet somehow the unidentified girl troubled him. The one thing he was clear about was that she held some sort of key. All right, it was a hunch but over the years he'd learned to respect his hunches and the accompanying tingling feeling at the back of his neck. He remained impassive – with no very lively hope that Finbarr would be fooled for an instant. Dammit, the sprite seemed to be able to divine information from the very earth.

'Are you permanently parked at your window?' the garda asked in exasperation.

'I'm not then,' Spillane laughed cheekily, 'but the aunt is. Keeps her entertained.'

'And yourself informed, is that it?'

Finbarr looked delighted. 'That's true for you,' he tittered.

'Where was she headed?'

'Back to Cork I suppose. Marilyn's still in the hospital. Some sort of woman's trouble she has so I suppose it's to the Bons she went. But it wouldn't be hard to find out. You know where she lives, don't you?'

'I do.' Recaldo turned away. Something in Spillane's tone made him suspect that the gardener already knew about his visit to the Donovans. Or maybe he was getting paranoid. 'Thanks, Finbarr. I'll be back to talk to you again later. Would you mind keeping all that to yourself ?' he added, more in hope than expectation.

'I will, of course. My mouth is sealed.' Finbarr drew his finger across his lips then tried to exact his quid pro quo. 'Poor Mrs Walter, what happened to her at all?' he asked slyly. He pulled his cap nervously through his hands.

75

Recaldo gave up. 'She died suddenly,' he said blandly. 'But that's between you and me, mind.'

'She said she might be going away.'

'What?'

'For the heat. She said the winters here do get her down sometimes.'

'When did she say that?'

'A few weeks back. I didn't pay much attention, because she nearly always goes off during the winter, but . . .' He touched his nose and lowered his voice to a conspiratorial whisper. 'I thought when she said it that maybe this time she was off for good. Mind you, I could be wrong, she didn't give me notice or anything.'

Recaldo wondered what notice would be due to someone working one half-day a week? Probably none at all, but Finbarr wouldn't have any difficulty replacing the hours, since there was probably a queue a mile long for his services. He weighed up whether or not he should warn the gardener not to discuss their conversation but decided he would only be wasting his breath. What spin Finbarr would put on it was something else again. Still, unless he was very much mistaken, he would be careful of the interests of his employers; Finbarr was his own man.

Recaldo left him to his plants and delivered the dog home. He stopped just long enough to splash water on his face before heading back to Trianach. He drove sedately through Passage South and out along the Duncreagh Road until he reached the causeway. He slowed down by the white house where a swift glance confirmed the old woman, Finbarr's aunt, peeping through a downstairs window. She was hard to see behind the lace curtain, but not if you looked closely. He worried that he'd never noticed her before.

He crossed the causeway and travelled down the narrow lane to the Old Corn Store at snail's pace, sorting his thoughts. The 'gir-rl' bothered him. If not Cressida, who was she? Had Finbarr got things wrong? Unlikely. In the past he had always found him the most reliable of all his informants. Accurate. Though up to now, he was ashamed to admit that he'd rather loftily supposed Spillane didn't always understand the importance of the information he passed on. Now he humbly and comprehensively revised that opinion and carefully matched what the old gardener had described with his own memory of the previous afternoon. By the time he reached the gateway Cressida Sweeney was uppermost in his mind. The question was, if indeed she went to Cork City on Tuesday, what time did she get back? It didn't make him feel any better to realize that he'd been afraid to ask. *Where was she?* If she was not on the boat, who was? Another of Sweeney's conquests? Or O'Dowd's? His fingers caressed the little comb in his pocket.

'Shit,' he muttered. He had to find Cressida. *Had to.*

He drove past the entrance and tucked the Jeep into the hedge a little further on. He rubbed his tired eyes and wearily switched off his engine. The wind had come up and the sky had begun to cloud over. Recaldo walked up the driveway, still deep in thought. He was missing something. Everything was out of focus.

Chapter Ten

COFFEY WAS OFF HAVING LUNCH AND McBRIDE WAS MAKING A detailed search of Evangeline Walter's garden. 'Had a good kip, then?' His greeting was loaded. 'You certainly took your time about it.'

'Sorry, I went out like a light,' Recaldo murmured.

'Is that a fact? You still look a bit peaky, I'd say.' McBride surveyed him. 'Well, as long as you're here, you can give us a hand.' He stood and looked up at the house with his hands supporting the small of his back. 'This is some place, isn't it? She must have been loaded. A bit gaunt for my taste, but the site couldn't be bettered, could it?'

'Looks best from the water – much less overwhelming.'

Even though the house covered a large ground area, it merged into the land almost organically. Being built of the local stone helped of course, and the way the beautiful, lush vegetation contrasted with the stark architecture. Every detail, as well as its totality, had obviously been carefully planned: a couple of acres tumbling down to the river with enough natural features to provide incident and excitement to an already spectacular outlook. There was the same obvious attention to detail in the way the landscape had been exploited; the gardens had been developed to include and make the most of what nature had bountifully provided.

On the side of the house facing the estuary, there were huge double French windows giving onto a natural granite pavement which had been cleverly extended with stone slabs to form an extensive terrace. A wide strip of turf ran from the terrace to the riverbank in a gentle slope but though it was cut and rolled assiduously it still remained defiantly what it had always been: coarse meadow grass. An army might have marched over it without causing much damage. Whoever had walked on it the night before had left no trace. There was no story marking its surface, no sign of a mighty struggle. True, first thing that morning, it was possible to see where small sections of the dewy grass had been flattened. But that was easily explained by the frantic dash of the old man to the house to make his emergency phone call. Now there were no discernible footprints, no uprooted sods, and no blood-stains, though the overnight rain might have accounted for any or all of these.

'There must have been something of a downpour, last night,' McBride said flatly. He had an uncanny knack of mind-reading.

'Around three this morning,' Recaldo corrected mildly. 'I left my bedroom window open and it woke me up.'

'Did it indeed? You didn't mention that to Dr Morrow when she was trying to time the death. Why was that?'

'That the rain woke me up? Why would I?'

'Ah.' McBride didn't pursue the matter. They went over the ground inch by inch. Every tiny item they picked up was bagged and labelled for the evidence – or what they hoped might be evidence – to be taken to the forensic laboratory in Cork that evening. It was a meagre enough trawl: some fragments of coarse black wool from the branches of a small whitethorn in the shrubbery closest the house, a spring which looked as if it might have come from a small torch, a number of filter-tipped cigarette butts, the top of a Vat 69 bottle, a damaged earring which McBride spotted in a crevice of the terrace paving. Its shaft was broken; it might have been there for years.

McBride was friendly enough, though all the time he covertly watched Recaldo, who was unsure whether or not he was meant to notice this, but soon decided that McBride was playing some sort of game. One-upmanship? Or was he trying to unsettle him?

'Have ye done the interviews with Spain and O'Dowd?' Recaldo asked, and was surprised to discover just how little had been achieved in his absence. Either that or McBride wasn't being quite straight. No more than himself, he thought.

'We've had the pair of them fingerprinted but we've only inter-viewed the old geezer. We put off O'Dowd until one, when the Super gets back. We thought you should be here for that, since you think he's such a slippery customer.'

'How did things go with Spain?'

'We got him to go over what happened a couple of times then made him re-enact his movements. I'll tell you one thing, FX, that auld fella's like a broken record, he stuck solid to his guns. Isn't that a very strange thing? His account tallied exactly with your report. Verbatim.'

'What's strange about it?' Recaldo asked gruffly, determined to keep his cool. 'I wrote down exactly what he said.'

'Aye. That's what troubled us. Don't you see, man? The particulars are too precise. It's unnatural. It's not the way the human brain works. People are not automatons, their speech patterns vary; they add and subtract tiny details. They dig holes for themselves, they stumble, they imagine things, they speculate. Right? But your pal Spain does none of those things. So tell me, Recaldo, just who is this guy? What's his background? I don't see him as your average fisherman, do you?'

'No, he's an educated man.'

'Now you tell me. So what the feck is he doing, masquerading as an old salt then?'

Recaldo sighed. 'He's a retired priest,' he admitted reluctantly. 'Used to be an academic.'

McBride gave him a tight-lipped, wide, mirthless grin. 'Bingo,' he shouted. 'I knew that old fella was trying to pull the wool over my eyes. Retired is it? Is that one of your euphemisms, FX? You're not telling me he was thrown out, by any chance?'

'Yes,' Recaldo said reluctantly. 'I'm afraid he was.'

'Oh Christ. Not one of those child molesters, is he?' McBride's lip curled in disgust.

'No, absolutely not.'

'Absolutely, is it? How come you're so sure?'

'I made it my business to find out,' Recaldo said dourly. 'You can take my word.'

But this, he reflected, didn't mean the people round about didn't continue to speculate as to where Spain came from or from what heights he had tumbled. He'd the particular misfortune of taking up residence when, for the first time in living memory, ecclesiastical scandals were being exposed up and down the country. The age of innocence was over. Henceforth, every cleric, no matter how good or saintly, was looked upon askance. Ex-clerics even more so. And some-how, in the way it does in remote places, the fact that Spain was a disgraced priest became common knowledge by a kind of creeping osmosis.

'So if it wasn't kids, what was it?' McBride wasn't about to be put off.

'Some scandal over a married woman. A diplomat's wife. It was over twenty years ago when that meant more than it does today.' He was protesting too much. They both knew it.

'Well, well, well. What d'ye know? The bishop rides again, eh? Where did all this happen?'

'Rome.' Recaldo's mouth twitched in a ghost of a smile.

But McBride gave a loud guffaw. 'Good location, that.'

'Hmm. Maybe not, if you're a professor at the Gregorian University and some sort of advisor to the Vatican.'

'I see your point, man. Jaysus. We better not let the press have that little nugget, they'd go delirious. Just tell me one thing: was he having it off with your one?'

'Mrs Walter?' Recaldo sounded surprised.

'Well, someone was giving it to her.'

'Surely not Spain? He keeps himself to himself. Anyway he's an old man.'

'Never too old. If I've learned anything in this job, it's that. You're not havin' me on, FX? Are you?'

'Are you what?' Coffey asked as he came into the garden.

McBride gave him a lazy grin and astonished Recaldo by saying, 'Oh, we were just swapping stories, this guy has a fund of great Kerryman jokes.'

'I'm glad you found something to amuse you. Because if you're finished out here we have to start on the house; we're way behind schedule. And bad news I'm afraid, the press has been alerted, my phone hasn't stopped for the past hour. The place will be crawling by tomorrow.'

'If they can bloody well find it,' McBride said sotto voce. He sniffed. 'Maybe we should twist a few more signposts around? Give them a run for their money.'

'Either of you like to guess who told them?'

Recaldo momentarily closed his eyes. 'O'Dowd, for certain,' he opined.

'Well, maybe we can ask him,' Coffey replied. 'He should be here any minute.'

And right on cue, in an unsettling repetition of his earlier visit, Smiler O'Dowd came sauntering around the side of the house.

The first thing Coffey said was, 'I'll have those keys off you.'

'What keys?' O'Dowd asked innocently.

'The ones that let you in through a locked door.'

O'Dowd laughed. 'I don't need keys for that, the lock's faulty. All you have to do is hit it in the right place. Come on, I'll show you.'

'Better get that mended, straight off,' Coffey told Recaldo when they saw how easily O'Dowd punched open the door. 'Or better still, get a new lock. Maybe you have one in your car,' he added archly.

'No, but I have a screwdriver, it's the hinge that's loose. I'll see what I can do.'

The hinge screws were rusted through and had to be replaced. In all the task took him ten or fifteen minutes and when he got back to the others, O'Dowd was being interviewed on the terrace, in an increasingly chilly wind, which didn't please him in the least. He was not permitted into Evangeline's house. He insinuated she was his lover, a claim they regarded with scepticism. When pressed, he admitted jauntily that 'she was as good as'.

'Lonely place for a single woman to settle,' McBride observed innocently.

'Would you say so?' Smiler considered this seriously, as if the idea had never before occurred to him. 'But there are many like her on the estuary. Houses no sooner on the market but they're snapped up.'

'True enough, but usually for holiday cottages, second homes. It seems she lived here the year round. Any idea what brought her here?' McBride asked casually, 'to this godforsaken spot?'

O'Dowd spread his arms as if to encompass the landscape. 'Isn't it obvious? It's a beautiful spot,' he replied as if this would be reason enough for anyone to want to settle there. Somehow, it didn't ring true.

'Maybe, but you can't eat scenery, can you?' McBride said softly. 'You'll have to do better than that. How long was she living here?'

'Must be seven or eight years now.' O'Dowd sounded slightly amazed.

'That long? So tell us, what was her job? What was she doing here?'

'She was an art expert. She advised Mr Bleiberg when he was building the hotel – the Atlantis in Passage – she bought all the art works for him.'

'Mr Bleiberg built this place, didn't he?' Recaldo interjected. 'He lived here.'

'He did the conversion all right but he didn't live here for long. The hotel closed up after a few years.'

'Hold on there.' Coffey held up his hand. 'The hotel's still functioning, isn't it?'

'Otto Bleiberg's son, Joachim, reopened it five years ago. Mrs Walter helped him as well.'

'Two for the price of one, eh?' McBride remarked lewdly. 'Kept it in the family?'

O'Dowd flushed angrily. 'Have some respect,' he said. 'Joachim is a married man with a family.'

'Oh? So just the daddy, then?' McBride goaded.

'She only became close to him after his wife died,' O'Dowd said prissily.

'And who else was she close to, besides yourself? And let me make this clear, Mr O'Dowd, we're not talking friendship, we're talking sex.'

'How would I know?'

'Well, according to yourself, you were very close,' said Coffey. 'So come on, don't be shy.'

This time O'Dowd spoke out. 'No-one, as far as I know. But if you're asking me who was after her then I'd say V. J. Sweeney for one, and Spain for another. That old goat was always "passing by" leaving her presents of fish.' He gave a hollow laugh and his eyes watered. 'She never ate the stuff,' he snorted. 'She was a vegetarian.'

'She was recently in hospital, wasn't she?' Coffey cut in. 'Know where? Why?'

'Dublin. The Blackrock Clinic. She had a stomach operation. She didn't say what it was for exactly and I didn't like to ask. She'd have told me in her own good time.' He looked at them bleakly. 'But she was very sick. I was going to take her away to Florida for a holiday in a fortnight's time. She thought the heat might do her good.'

There was an embarrassed pause before Coffey said brusquely, 'Well now, Mr O'Dowd, let's get down to the incidentals. We want your movements from six o'clock yesterday. In detail.' Recaldo held his breath waiting to see how O'Dowd would handle the boat party, but he skilfully avoided all mention of it, which unnerved Recaldo as much as it intrigued him. All the while Cressie's comb burned a hole in his pocket.

'I already told Frank. I was on the road,' O'Dowd said and repeated his earlier claim to have run out of petrol on the main Dublin–Cork road, about fourteen miles north of Cashel at about eight thirty.

'Which direction were you headed?'

'For Dublin. Ye can check with your colleagues in Tipp,' he said triumphantly, handing Coffey a slip of paper with a phone number on it. 'I was picked up by one of your very own Garda Siochana.'

'Were you, now? Isn't that convenient for you. Maybe you could tell us how that came about?' Coffey asked politely.

The answer came pat. 'The car ran out of juice close to the junction of the N8 and N75. I pushed it up on the grass verge and headed for Twomileborris looking for a petrol station when the squad car picked me up. They gave me a lift to the nearest garage and waited while I collected a can of petrol, then dropped me back to my car.'

He reckoned the whole procedure took a good forty-five minutes. At a signal from Coffey, Recaldo stepped out of earshot to phone the Tipperary constabulary and check the incident. The garda he spoke to duly confirmed O'Dowd's claim.

'. . . after he left I drove back to the petrol station to fill up.' O'Dowd was still talking when he rejoined the group. 'I suppose that took another half-hour. It must have been around half ten by that time and I decided I'd be better off postponing the trip, so I came back.'

When asked for his reason for going to Dublin, O'Dowd asserted loftily that he often spent time in the capital, for social as well as personal reasons. When pressed, he said he was going up to visit his late father's youngest sister who was in an old people's home near Dalkey, on the southern outskirts of the city. He jotted down the phone number and dropped it in McBride's outstretched palm. 'Check it if you like. They'll tell you I get up to see her at least once a month.'

'How far is Twomileborris, when it's at home?' McBride asked after a pause.

'About a hundred and thirty miles from here, I'd say,' Recaldo cut in. 'What time was it when you got back?'

'Just before one.'

Late as it was, O'Dowd said he tried to phone Mrs Walter, but when he got no answer he assumed she was asleep and didn't leave a message. 'I went straight to bed.' His smirk confirmed that he knew he had a watertight alibi. Assuming he should ever need one.

'Wasn't that a bit late to be ringing?'

'We often had a chat late at night, specially in the last few weeks when she had trouble sleeping.'

'You ring her earlier, by any chance?' McBride asked.

'Yes I did, from the petrol station. But the phone was engaged,' O'Dowd replied carelessly.

'So, what time would you say that was?'

'First time? Around half nine, I suppose,' he said. 'I redialled a couple of minutes later, but it was still engaged. I'd have tried again but your fellas told me to get a move on or I could walk back to the car myself.' He looked at McBride's expressionless face. 'What?'

'Don't you have a mobile?' Recaldo asked in some surprise.

'I do, but I didn't have it with me, it's on the blink.'

'Just a minute, let me get this straight,' Coffey interjected heavily. 'You rang at half nine, and a couple of minutes later it was still engaged? But when you rang at one in the morning, the machine was on? That right?'

'Oh, I forgot. I tried again when I drove back to the garage to fill the car up, but 'twas the same thing, still busy.'

'That would have been about a quarter past ten? Forty-five minutes or so? That's a very long call . . .' Coffey said quietly.

'Not for Van— Mrs Walter. She was always yakking, transatlantic and everything. 'Twas all the same to her, she never paid any heed to the cost.'

'Hang on, not so fast,' McBride cried indignantly. 'At one in the morning the machine was back on? Right?'

O'Dowd reflected for a moment. 'Wrong. There was no reply.'

'Was that unusual?' McBride asked. O'Dowd stared at him blankly.

'Come on, man, you just said you often spoke to her on the phone late at night – was that the last time you tried?'

'More or less,' O'Dowd admitted cautiously. 'You see, she always put the machine on when she went to bed so I thought I might have misdialled so I tried again a few minutes later. I only let it ring a couple of times; the machine usually cuts in immediately.' His mouth dropped open as light dawned. 'She was already dead, wasn't she?' He looked to each of the three men in turn but they didn't answer.

'That wiped the smile off his face, all right,' McBride said with some satisfaction as they watched O'Dowd leave, rather less self-assured than he'd been when he arrived.

'Are we assuming it was her on the phone between nine and ten?' Recaldo asked.

'I think so,' Coffey said. 'Unless you have a better idea. Joanna Morrow's window of time was very wide – nine to one. I'd say this narrows it down a bit.'

'In a manner of speaking,' Recaldo murmured.

'In me bollocks,' McBride said loudly. 'He didn't seem too bothered about her death did he?' he added. 'Lover, how are ya.'

'Maybe he expected it,' Recaldo suggested. 'He obviously knows more about her illness than he's saying.'

'That so? So why didn't you press him?' McBride goaded.

'Why didn't I? Why didn't you?' Recaldo cried.

'Shut up, you two,' Coffey said sharply and glanced at Recaldo, who gave an involuntary twitch as if he'd been slapped. It was the first time he had been in contact with his erstwhile peers since coming south and he felt uneasy, unsure exactly how he should act. He was one of them, but not quite.

'I'd prefer to keep that guy guessing. The less he knows the way we're thinking the better. We'll have another go at him once we know what we're up against, and have a few more facts,' Coffey said as the trio traipsed inside the Old Corn Store to commence a detailed search.

Chapter Eleven

WHAT MOST STRUCK THE THREE OFFICERS ON ENTERING EVANGELINE Walter's house was its extreme tidiness. Her upstairs study, in particular, was in extraordinarily good order. They went from room to room, upstairs and down, doing a preliminary check, not touching anything, just taking careful stock. The living rooms and bedrooms and study were all facing the estuary, and had stupendous views. Bathrooms, cloaks, larders and storage were all at the front, facing inland. One of the two guest rooms had a huge double bed beneath an oriel window paned with amethyst glass, which gave onto a great bluff of rock shielding the side of the house. The room was painted white with a pale beech floor and one or two items of austere grey-painted, New England furniture. On one of the bedside tables lay a pair of binoculars and nestling among the embroidered linen pillows was a lavender bag. A small card beside it had *Welcome* scrawled on it.

'This room is made up for guests,' Recaldo said, 'and the en suite bathroom has fresh towels. She must have been expecting someone.'

McBride took a long look around and examined the card. 'Not much help, is it?' he observed laconically. 'A general rather than a specific welcome. She probably always kept it prepared. House-proud, wasn't she?' he added as they went back downstairs.

'How many staff did she have?' Coffey asked Recaldo.

'Two as far as I know: a woman, Marilyn Donovan, who came every weekday morning to clean the house and a gardener who came once

87

a week. He works up at the Atlantis Hotel. Spillane's his name. Finbarr Spillane.'

'Better get on to them.' Coffey motioned to McBride. Recaldo coughed.

'Marilyn Donovan was taken to hospital on Monday night. I gather she had a miscarriage.'

'And when did you gather that?' asked Coffey irritably.

'Mrs Ryan at the post office mentioned it when I picked up the morning paper,' Recaldo said smoothly. 'So I dropped by the Donovans' on my way back here. Her daughter – she's about ten or eleven – told me her mammy was in the Bon Secours Hospital in Cork.' He cleared his throat. 'I wonder, sir, if I might have a word?'

Superintendent Coffey leaned against the side of the desk. 'Go ahead.'

'Look, I know all these people. Maybe not very well, but in a place like this everyone talks and it may get awkward. I want to continue working here. It's taken two years to build up any kind of trust and I don't want to blow it.'

'So you prefer not to be involved in this investigation?' McBride said. 'Or not to be seen to be involved?'

'Yes, something like that.'

Coffey stroked his chin thoughtfully. 'Tell you what, let's talk about this at the end of the day, after we hear from the pathologist and when we have more idea what's involved in the case. I appreciate what you're saying but I may not be able to stay on this one too long myself, in which case Phil here will need a hand. And you would be very useful for background stuff – at the very least.'

'I have a feeling there's going to be an awful lot of legwork,' McBride sighed. 'And not just around here. There's the clinic in Dublin for starters and God knows what else.'

'Right then, we'll talk about it later. Now, Phil, how did Louisa get on with the prints?'

McBride seemed reluctant to spell it out. 'She'll be working on them in the lab even as we speak. Her report will be all written up by the time we get back to headquarters but she reckoned O'Dowd's match several we lifted from various surfaces downstairs. There's certainly a thumbprint of Spain's on the glass top of the phone table downstairs. He has a tiny scar just below the central whorl. Very distinctive.'

'The phone itself?' Recaldo asked.

'Spain again, clear as day.' McBride raised his eyebrows.

'Just Spain's?' Coffey's voice rose. 'The handpiece was wiped?'

'That's what it looked like.' He shrugged. 'The blessed Louisa will tell all later.'

McBride made no attempt to hide the fact that he was obfuscating and Recaldo barely stopped himself challenging him and would have except that the thumbprint, at least, went some way to confirm Spain's story.

'I'd say it only confirms he used the phone, but certainly not when,' McBride opined more ominously. Neither ventured an opinion on O'Dowd. On this and other matters, Recaldo stepped neatly to the sidelines.

'See any sign of a handbag on your travels?' Coffey asked. 'Or a briefcase?'

McBride shook his head and though they searched assiduously again, they found neither bag nor briefcase.

'Perhaps it's in her car?' McBride suggested. 'Presuming there is a car.'

'The garage is locked,' Recaldo said. 'I noticed earlier. There's a padlock on it.'

Coffey took the bunch of keys from McBride and went off to look at the car while the others played and replayed the tape on Evangeline's answerphone. There were six separate messages, plus three or four blanks when nothing but background noise was recorded. Two from one male voice, one each from two others. Oddly, none of these identified themselves by name, so there was no way of knowing who the cheery American was: '*Hi, Evangeline, it's me. Hope you got my message. I'm really sorry about all this. Grace is on her way. I'll try again tonight.*'

By contrast, both female callers were less coy. The first, Rose O'Faolain, confirmed an appointment for Friday at twelve forty-five but infuriatingly didn't say where. The second woman left the last and the longest message on the tape. She had a low, rather beautiful voice, hard to place geographically. '*Sixteenth, eleven twenty. It's Grace. I'm afraid Murray's still stuck in Minneapolis. He'll ring you to explain. I'll come ahead on my own but a day late, I'm afraid. There's a sale in Limerick I just heard about which sounds too good to miss. I'll be in touch as soon as I've some idea what time I'll arrive. See you.'*

'Yesterday was the sixteenth, right?' Coffey said, from the door. He was empty-handed. 'Play the tape through again, Phil. Right, pause there. The message before Grace, the male American – could be the Murray she mentions? Pity she doesn't say what day she's due.'

Maybe she came already, Recaldo thought to himself, remembering the girl in white.

'She may have answered in person next time one of them called?' McBride suggested. 'Presumably she picked up the phone and cut out the machine whenever she was home? It's what I do, anyway.'

'Well, we'll be here if they show up. For a day or so anyway,' Coffey added. He turned to Recaldo. 'Recognize any of the voices?'

'Yes, the message before Grace.' He replayed the tape and listened. 'That sounds like O'Dowd. *It's me, see you later.* That must have been yesterday morning as well.'

'So it's just the recordings for one day? We'll check with his nibs later. Bag up the tape, will you, Phil? Switch off the machine, we'll answer ourselves from now on or get Eircom to intercept,' Coffey said firmly.

'Hold it a second,' McBride said, 'while I work something out. Grace's was recorded yesterday morning before midday. O'Dowd said he couldn't get through all evening and then claimed she didn't answer around one a.m. when Dr Morrow thinks she was already dead.' He looked up. 'It was on when we came in, so my question is, when was it switched back on?'

'And why?' Recaldo murmured.

'Not *why*, FX, *who*,' McBride finished.

'For God's sake, d'you mind?' Recaldo said irritably. He hated being called FX. 'Who? Why? What? When? How? Surely that's what we're here to find out? Maybe Spain inadvertently touched the button when he rang me.'

'Leave it,' roared Coffey. 'We'll tackle the old fellow about it later.

90

Wasn't he in the house, alone? God only knows what else he was up to.' He plonked Walter's keys on the desk. 'The car is as tidy as the house. It's a year-old BMW, 7-series. Some car. She does – did – herself proud.'

'They don't come cheap, that's for sure,' McBride cut in. 'No sign of a bag?'

'No, clean as a whistle. Apart from the logbook and a purse of change there's nothing in the glove compartment either.'

They searched for a diary or address book but found neither. McBride suggested that 'she was probably the kind that'd have an electronic organizer,' and, half-abashed, pulled a Psion from his pocket – 'like this.' But if Evangeline had one they didn't find that either. Everything else of use was also missing: handbag, briefcase, diary, mobile phone – if she had one, and it seemed unreasonable to believe she had not.

Otherwise, the study yielded plenty of information but mainly about Evangeline Walter's job. She was, it seemed, an authority on modern painting and sculpture. Two of the desk drawers were stacked with cuttings from a bewildering range of newspapers, from several continents, all of them over her byline and a tiny youthful photograph. In the neatly annotated catalogues which filled one of her shelves, Walter had written most of the introductions and the captions accompanying the illustrations. The police speculated on the sort of income she'd derive from her work but could find neither accounts nor chequebook stubs. However, there was correspondence from a gallery in Daingean – a largish town to the north-west. Putting two and two together, they were able to identify one of the females on the answerphone, as well as the substance of the message she'd left.

'Mrs Walter is, was, quite a well-known art critic and journalist,' a horrified Rose O'Faolain told Recaldo when he told her why they were calling. 'You'll find her articles in almost every important art magazine, and indeed in some of the serious broadsheets, in the UK and the States. She was due here on Friday to interview an important collector. I'd better cancel that, hadn't I? No, I'm not at liberty to say with whom, unless, of course, you demand I do so. But if I can help in any other way? I've known Mrs Walter for some years.' The precisely modulated voice grated on Recaldo's ears and easily carried to Coffey, who was listening avidly at his side. He signalled acceptance. 'Someone'll be along to talk to you,' Recaldo said smoothly.

'You can do that tomorrow,' Coffey said in a preoccupied voice. He stood for a moment lost in thought. 'Notice, there's been no post,' he said. 'What time is it normally delivered?'

'The postman starts his rounds in Passage at eight. He does the out-lying areas after that and finishes around twelve. I saw the van outside the post office as I came through,' said Recaldo. 'Maybe she didn't have any mail today.'

'Somehow, I think that's unlikely. There's always circulars.' McBride rifled through a neat pile of letters in an in-tray, looking for local postmarks, and found one from Cork, dated the fifteenth. 'These must have arrived on Tuesday. I checked out that old mailbox by the garage earlier but I don't think it's been opened for years, the lid thing seems to be rusted solid,' he said. 'What do people do around here, Recaldo?'

'Usually the mail is delivered, but some people arrange to have it held at the post office either in Passage or Duncreagh. Maybe she did as well?'

'Sound thinking,' Coffey remarked with a rare hint of warmth. 'Nip in to Passage and ask, will you? And if that's no good, try the town.'

'Mind if I try Duncreagh first? If I ask Mrs Ryan it'll be all over the place. Anyway I don't think I ever saw Mrs Walter in the local post office. I've a hunch she'd probably have preferred the anonymity of the bigger place. Such as it is.'

'Whatever you think best. Don't delay, I want you back here, pronto.'

'Yes, sir,' Recaldo said humbly. McBride's loud guffaw as he left put him off making any detours and he returned within the hour with the mail he had collected from Duncreagh post office, amongst which was a letter from a consultant gynaecologist in Cork attached to a huge bill from the Dublin clinic. Coffey read it first then handed it to McBride.

'She obviously failed to show up for an appointment ten days ago. The doctor seems to have got the hump,' Recaldo said.

'So what do you think was wrong with her?' McBride asked.

'I don't know, cancer at a guess.'

'That's very precise,' McBride said. 'For a guess.'

'Hardly, something about the way O'Dowd said the operation was on her stomach made me wonder.'

'Give that doctor a ring, Phil, and get the low-down' Coffey said.

McBride picked up the letter and consulted the heading before dialling the number. After an increasingly terse exchange he asked if the consultant would kindly give him a call. 'When? What do you mean when? As soon as possible, it's urgent,' he roared and left his mobile number. He looked over the room thoughtfully. 'I wonder when that charlady was last here? I don't think I've ever seen a tidier place.'

'I could track down her husband Steve Donovan and ask,' Recaldo suggested, helpfully. 'Except he's probably at work. He's a plumber.'

'No, I wouldn't do that just yet.' Coffey pursed his lips. 'Though it would certainly be interesting to find out when she was last here.'

'Ring the hospital in Cork and ask her,' Recaldo said but neither officer took him up on this.

'Does Mrs Donovan char for anyone else?' McBride asked.

'Yes, several people I believe.' He paused. 'Ted Clancy, another American, who runs a small IT firm outside Passage, and the Sweeneys.'

'That name seems to keep cropping up, d'you notice? So at least two or three people knew she was out of action. When did she get sick?'

'Mrs Sweeney might know. I could see if she . . .' Recaldo's voice died away.

'See if she what?' Coffey interrupted. 'I think we might also leave that for the moment, don't you? No point spreading the word until we decide how the land lies,' he added, as his phone rang. 'Doctor,' he mouthed and left the room. He came back after a few minutes, looking thoughtful, but didn't divulge whether it was the consultant or Dr Morrow who'd telephoned.

'The woman was a real chancer.' McBride filled an awkward silence.

'What woman?' Recaldo bristled.

'The deceased, of course. Who d'you think?' McBride asked. He was absorbed in the collection of framed certificates on the study walls which appeared to be equally divided between awards and degrees, all related to either art (modern) or art history. Three others were in different European languages and one in what looked like Chinese characters.

'And why do you say that?' Coffey asked.

McBride didn't answer for a moment. He pulled over a chair, stood on it and ostentatiously continued his perusal. There were a dozen certificates, of fairly uniform size, arranged in a double column on either side of a large abstract painting.

'Rothko,' McBride identified it carelessly. 'One of my friends has a poster like this. The old bag must have been loaded.'

'If it's an original,' Recaldo remarked dryly.

'Well now, I'd say it is.'

'How would *you* know?' Coffey jeered.

'That it's an original, or she was loaded?'

Coffey didn't reply and McBride didn't press it, but he was chuckling as he climbed off the chair. 'Which is more than I could say about those certs. I bet most of them are fake. Or some of them anyway. Like I said, she was a right bullshitter. Those top two on either side are copies of the pairs at the bottom. Make ya laugh, wouldn't it?'

'Maybe she liked symmetry,' Recaldo said mildly. 'They fit precisely around that picture.'

'Humph.'

'I hope you've as many,' Coffey said irritably. 'She seems to have been a well-qualified woman.'

'She was indeed,' McBride agreed breezily. '*Summa cum laudes* are not to be sneezed at, whoever gives them.'

'What's that supposed to mean?'

'Well, look at this one, it's from some obscure American college for a month's course on Jackson Pollock. I'd say he's worth a bit more than that.'

'Oh you would, would you?' Coffey grunted.

'I wonder what the Chinese one is for?'

'Japanese, FX,' McBride said cockily and touched the side of his nose with his finger. He was clearly enjoying himself and didn't care who knew it.

'You speak Japanese?' Recaldo couldn't keep the doubt out of his voice.

'Ah now, I wouldn't go that far.' He let out a yelp of laughter. 'I don't think me accent helps. But I can read it all right. This is for attending a conference in Kyoto. For a whole week, would you believe,' he mocked. 'Well, I am amazed.'

'So am I.' This time Recaldo was genuinely admiring. He had been battling with Spanish for years and though he could read it quite well, he was reluctant to admit he couldn't master the pronunciation. 'How come?'

McBride shrugged. 'A friend, different one, was doing a course at the Chester Beatty. I went along out of interest.' He winked like a mischievous schoolboy.

Recaldo smiled. 'Well, that's certainly put me in my box.'

'That was the idea, amigo,' McBride laughed.

'Right then,' Coffey called them to order. 'Let's have a look at that computer and see if we've any better luck.' He switched it on and sat down while he waited for it to boot up. It took several minutes for him to grasp that he was denied access as soon as he tried to enter Evangeline Walter's files. 'She must have password-protected it,' he said. 'That figures,' McBride replied. Recaldo said nothing. There was no need, the whole room was witness to a pre-occupation with control. Her diligence was awesome. Somewhere among the neatly stacked papers in her desk and one small filing cabinet or among the tidy shelves of the bookcase, there might be a clue to that password. But Recaldo was realistic enough to assume that someone more familiar than he with Evangeline Walter's lifestyle or history, or, better still, the way her mind worked, would be needed to unlock that particular secret. He glanced at McBride and saw that he was watching him with a knowing half-smile as if he had been going through the same thought process.

'Either of you any good with these things?' Coffey stared glumly at the blank screen. 'Well?' He rubbed his hand over his chin.

'I'm afraid not.' Recaldo shook his head. 'I wouldn't know where to begin.'

'I'll have a go,' McBride volunteered confidently. 'I have one at home. Same as this as a matter of fact.'

After a few minutes he whistled. 'It's not just protected, it seems to have been wiped,' he said in surprise. He looked round at Coffey and stretched out his hands, palms up. 'There's nothing on it.'

'There must be something.'

'I'm telling you, there's nothing except the operating system. No application software, no data. Someone's wiped the hard disk.' He sat back and thought for a moment, then stood up. 'Here, FX, help us pull out the desk till I see what's what.'

They eased the desk away from the wall. It was custom-built for a computer, with cable ducting. McBride followed the Ethernet cable from the machine to a small hub, about the size of a cigarette packet, and noticed there was a second cable plugged into it. This, in turn, he traced to the other side of the desk. 'She had a laptop,' he said and snorted as he fumbled through the jumble of cables. 'And guess what I think?'

'What?' Coffey seemed remarkably indulgent with his sidekick.

'I bet any money some clever Dick has copied everything onto the laptop and then wiped the mainframe.'

'How long would that take?'

McBride considered. 'Let's consult the oracle.' He pulled out his phone and went outside for a better signal. 'Wow,' he said when he returned. 'Jock Barry says six or seven hundred megabytes can be wiped in a matter of minutes across a network connection. If a serial connection cable was used then as many hours.'

'He's sure?' asked Coffey dourly.

'Yeah, pretty sure. Isn't that the bugger. Mind you, I suppose she could have some reason for transferring the files herself.' He sounded dubious.

'Like what, for instance?'

'Well, I suppose if she was getting a new computer, or moving, or . . .'

'But surely if she was getting a new computer she'd just transfer by disk?' Recaldo said.

Coffey brushed him aside. 'McBride, can we do anything to recover what's been wiped? See if there's anything left on it?'

'Yeah. We can drag the whole caboodle back to Cork with us and let Jock's nerds loose on it. They've got gear, stuff. Disk-readers or whatever they call them. Remember that case Kelly was on? He had a problem a bit like this and Barry's lot got stuck in. They'll be able to tell us if there's anything left. If there is, they should be able to recover most of it. But it'll take time.'

'How long?' Recaldo asked.

'Anything up to a few days.' McBride shrugged and made a face. 'Weeks? I remember Kelly saying it took for ever, but that was two years ago and things have moved on a bit.'

'What happens if she protected the files with a password?' Coffey asked.

'Oh, I don't imagine that would worry Jock.'

Coffey rubbed his mouth while he considered what to do. After a moment or two he said, 'I think we'll just leave it for the time being. I'll have a word with Jock tonight and see what he thinks.'

'Well, at least we have discovered *something*,' Recaldo said.

McBride looked at him blankly, then slowly nodded agreement. 'Yeah, I see what you mean. If someone wiped the files then there was something there they didn't want known, right?'

'No. I was thinking more that it would have to be someone who knew a bit more than the average about personal computers. I can't imagine old Spain would fit the bill.'

'Nice one, FX. That why you let him skip off? Jesus, I really like the way your mind works, old son.' McBride put a slight emphasis on *old*, then laughed at the look of disgust on Recaldo's face. His voice softened. 'Only jokin'. You seem to like the old guy.'

'He's all right.'

'Know him well, do you?' he asked casually, but his eyes narrowed.

Recaldo shrugged. 'Pretty well. I see him around. Going up and down in his boat.'

'Develop flippers, if he's not careful.' McBride grinned. Then some signal must have passed between the two detectives because McBride pulled himself up to his full height and puffed out his cheeks.

'Now, amigo,' he said amiably. 'What about you going in search of Mr and Mrs Sweeney, eh?'

Recaldo could hardly stop himself tearing out the door but he acted as though he had something else on his mind. 'What about the press? They'll want a statement.'

'They can wait,' replied Coffey. 'I'll do it when we get back to Cork.'

'Didn't you say some of them were already down in Passage? We'll be besieged.' This was unlikely. Michael Hussey could be relied upon to tip him the wink.

'Stay out of uniform and away from the station and don't bother your head about that lot. Let them cool their heels, it'll only be the junior ones they send in the first instance. They'll save the big guns for when they figure how the land lies.'

'I wouldn't say that . . .'

'I wouldn't say anything,' Coffey said in exasperation. 'Just do what I say, will you? Have nothing to do with that mob. Is that clear? Go on off and take the Sweeneys' statements and we'll see you here first thing tomorrow morning.'

'I wish I was coming with you,' McBride said. 'I hear Mrs Sweeney's a bit of all right.'

Chapter Twelve

RECALDO KEPT QUITE COOL UNTIL HE WAS OUT OF SIGHT OF THE OLD Corn Store but thereafter he shot along the country lanes like a scalded cat. At last he could legitimately look for Cressie without drawing undue attention to himself.

Though the Sweeneys' house was almost opposite the Old Corn Store, the estuary was too wide at that point for anything but a hazy outline of either to be seen from the opposing banks. Coribeen was a handsome and rather grand house which had originally been built for one of Cressida's remote Anglo-Irish ancestors. The early generations of the family had been, for the most part, absentee and the more recent had gradually sold off the land until the house was left marooned in the middle of a field with only a narrow path giving access to the Daingean Road. It had been derelict for years when Cressida inherited it. Valentine Jason Sweeney had had it done up as a wedding present for his young bride, and at the same time bought the surrounding twenty-five acres.

He had been rich then, and indulgent. Newly re-wed at forty-five to a twenty-four-year-old. He looked younger though, with his fading blond hair and his unlined skin, boyish, until closer inspection revealed the fine, faintly etched lines. He had the sort of looks which move effortlessly, but late, from youth to old age. This process was barely discernible when he first came to the estuary, but it had certainly begun. His wife Cressida could have been beautiful had she not been so shy and awkward. She was tall, pale and slender with a gentle manner.

The house apart, there were several reasons why V. J. Sweeney chose to settle on the Glár. He was a world-class mariner who had competed in the Fastnet race several times and knew the whole Cork coast which had excellent sailing and, compared to English ports, cheap mooring. Better still, in this case, free, since the land lay along the beautiful estuary. With the bay less than a quarter-mile away, he could indulge his passion. Within weeks of taking possession of the ruin he and a couple of friends sailed his ketch, *Azurra*, over from Plymouth and moored it within sight of his living room.

In a sense, the acquisition of Coribeen determined the pattern of the Sweeneys' married life. They had originally intended to use the house only in the summer but, from the first, Cressida showed a surprising determination to make it her permanent home. She adored it. By the time Gil was born, two years later, VJ was a regular weekly commuter to his office in London, while she stayed on the estuary. Sometimes weekly stretched to monthly. As their relationship crumbled, it was an arrangement that increasingly suited them both.

When Recaldo rolled up at precisely four forty on Wednesday afternoon, the place was deserted except for a workman repairing pot-holes in the gravel drive who greeted him confidently. 'Fine day, sir. If you're looking for themselves, you're out of luck.'

'Am I indeed?' Recaldo replied, as if the Sweeneys' absence was of little consequence. 'Mick, isn't it?'

'That's right, sir, Mick Moynihan. The boss is in London. Or some-place. The missis took him to Cork airport after dinner Friday.'

'Well, I'm sorry I missed them, but no matter, I'll catch up with them later. That's a fine job you're doing there,' he said casually. 'Have you been at it all week?'

'I have, so. They let it get in a terrible state altogether, it's full of potholes.'

'Not now, it isn't,' Recaldo said jovially. 'Mrs Sweeney must be a real slave-driver.'

'Indeed and she's not. She's a very nice woman,' Moynihan replied robustly. 'She lets me get on with my work, sure I haven't seen her since Monday.'

'What time Monday?' Recaldo asked with a fixed smile.

'She was here all day, till I knocked off at about three.'

'Three? Isn't that very early for knocking off?'

'I had to see to another job. Mrs Sweeney didn't mind.'

'Were you here on Tuesday?'

'No, the way I said, I was on another job.' He looked Recaldo up and down and wiped his hand across his mouth. 'I hear there's been trouble over yonder.' He jerked his head towards the river. Recaldo just grunted and got back into his car.

He started the engine and made a three-point turn, closely watched by the labourer who was leaning on his spade, immobile but alert. Recaldo badly wanted to look around properly but decided he'd prefer not to have an audience. He drove slowly down the driveway and out on to the Daingean Road. He was on the bridge over the estuary when, without warning, his breathing began to tighten and a familiar sour taste filled his mouth. 'Oh hell,' he murmured. He hadn't had an angina attack for months. He gave himself a couple of puffs of nitroglycerine and headed for Whelan's boatyard tucked in under the bridge on the other side, and barely a minute away. He pulled up out of sight of the road, beside the Portakabin which served as an office and lay back in his seat waiting for the symptoms to pass. A dull heavy pain in his chest radiated out to his back until he could hardly bear it. He closed his eyes, willing himself not to panic.

After a few minutes it began to subside and the headache started. He knocked on the office door and went inside.

'Any chance of a cup of tea?' he asked Terry Whelan, who was sitting staring at a brand new PC in the cramped office.

'Of course,' Terry said as he swivelled around. 'God, Frank, but you look rough.' He went to a cluttered table and switched on the kettle. 'What happened to you? Is the heart playing up?'

'Just a small turn, it's passing. I'll be fine.'

Terry looked at him dubiously. 'Right so. I'll put two spoonfuls in, it'll pep you up. Sit down there now for a while.' He indicated his chair. 'D'you want a couple of aspirin?'

'If you've got some.' Frank sat down gratefully. He took his time over the tea and a little colour had returned to his face, when, after fifteen minutes or so, he stretched and stood up. 'That's much better, thanks, Terry. I really dropped in to see if I could borrow the inflatable?'

'You can, but I'll have to fill the tank first. When d'you want it?'

'A couple of hours' time? Could you bring it up to, em,' he hesitated, trying to think of somewhere not immediately on public view, 'where I keep my boat? It's on Trianach.'

'I know where it is, Frank. A small way past Bleiberg's old place?' He swivelled around and raised his eyebrows. 'That's a terrible thing altogether. 'Tis no wonder you're looking exhausted. I heard she was bludgeoned to death.'

Recaldo was usually tickled by the oblique way information was garnered; this time less so. It was quite a skill to parry successfully. 'News gets round fast.'

'Never a truer word. I had a reporter in here earlier, nosing around. A young scut of a lad. Don't worry, I sent him off with a flea in his ear.'

'What paper was he from?'

'*Sunday Tribune.*' Whelan named one of the Sunday nationals.

'Feck it,' Recaldo exploded. 'There'll be a horde of them by tomorrow.' He hoped Coffey would get on with the press statement quick or they'd never be able to stifle the rumours.

''Tis no more than you'd expect.'

'You didn't say anything about, er, bludgeoning, did you Terry?'

'I did not, then. D'you think I'm an eejit or what? I played dumb. But I'd say there'll be shivers going down a few spines around here when that crowd move in. They write what they like. They'll destroy us entirely if we don't protect ourselves. And each other. Have you warned people to be on their guard, Frank?'

'And what good would that do?'

'True for you. There's an awful lot of gullible ones that think they might make a few bob, spreading gossip and getting their pictures in the newspaper.'

'Anyone in mind?'

'Well, there's one or two . . . I wouldn't like to be naming names.'

'You know as well as I do that if people want to talk, they'll talk. We'll just have to keep our fingers crossed. Terry?'

'What?'

'She was not bludgeoned.'

'I see.' Whelan had a hard job resisting the temptation to ask what exactly had happened but somehow he managed. 'By the way, how long will you want the inflatable for?'

'You could pick it up in the morning.'

'OK so. Take the spare key. I'll drop it off myself on the way home.

It'll be there for you by seven, would that do? And I'll have it away by half seven in the morning.'

'That would be grand. Thanks.'

'D'you know anything about these things?' Whelan indicated the PC.

'A bit. What's wrong?'

'Feckin' thing keeps crashin',' Terry moaned.

Recaldo sat down beside him and took over the keyboard and mouse. After a few minutes he said, 'Bit overloaded, isn't it? Have you been transferring files from your old machine? Or moving between folders?' Terry nodded. 'Well then, the disk is probably fragmented or the system registry may have corrupted. I can set up Norton Utilities for you, but it'll take a little time. Best defrag it before you knock off and leave it on overnight. Check it out in the morning and if it doesn't work, give me a call. Or call the supplier. That might be a better bet. I'll be tied up until the weekend at least. OK?' He paused. 'Oh, and Terry? I'd scotch those rumours if you're asked again. It's far from the truth. I'll be seeing you.'

Much refreshed, he left the office and sauntered over to his car. Since he was halfway between Coribeen and Trianach, he decided to try to find Cressie again.

Her troubled face floated through his mind. Where, oh where, was she? How brutally fast things changed. How could he ever have imagined she loved him? A touch of angina was enough to bring it all back. The way his wife couldn't bear to look at him, much less touch him, after the operation. His sons sensed the tension and caught her fear. The memory seared him still. The thin scrawny man who returned to them from hospital bore no resemblance to the distant, cool figure they'd been used to. He'd lost the children carelessly, simply because it hadn't dawned on him that their love and loyalty was not a given, but an option. The surprise was how keenly he felt the withdrawal of their trust. He wondered if this had in some way inspired his growing attachment to Cressie's delightful little boy. He could not bear another parting. From either of them. Cressie, oh Cressie.

Was it from fear or self-absorption that he had been so little moved by Evangeline Walter's dramatic death? He had looked at her lifeless body and felt nothing but revulsion for her emaciated frame. Was that what Sheila had felt, looking at him? Or, more simply, had Evangeline's corpse reminded him of his own mortality?

The Sweeneys were still from home. There was nobody about. Not even Moynihan the workforce, who had knocked off leaving his jacket draped over his shovel which was stuck into the mound of gravel on the forecourt. Must have been in a hurry, then, Recaldo concluded. He knocked, then rang the doorbell without any expectation of being answered. This time he scribbled a formal note addressed to Mr and Mrs Sweeney and put it through the letter box. Cressie would be able to read between the lines. He was turning to leave when a slight movement caught his eye. He backed away from the house and allowed his gaze to range over the large sash windows one by one. Nothing stirred. He hammered at the door again. Frustrated, he walked all the way around the house, his eyes searching each window. All was quiet. But his expression was thoughtful as he drove back to Trianach.

Chapter Thirteen

THOSE INSIDE CORIBEEN HELD THEIR COLLECTIVE BREATH. CRESSIDA knelt by the attic window with her hand clamped to her mouth to stop her crying out. Somewhere below a floorboard creaked. The stairs; he was coming upstairs. Oh God, please let him not come up here, she prayed. She strained her ears but no further sounds reached her until she heard the creak again, more faintly this time. He was going down. Oh thank God, thank God. A few seconds' silence, then the distinctive clunk of the study door on the ground floor. She slowly expelled her breath. Had she imagined it?

She raised her head a fraction above the sill and watched Recaldo drive off. Her dark angel. Hovering around, ready to swoop to her rescue. She was repelled by her craven need of his curiously diffident manner, his tender smile. His silence. His intensity. She never saw him without wanting to hurl herself into his enfolding arms; smell his desire, succumb to his need to cherish her, and her son. He and John Spain had that in common. Gil trusted them, perhaps because they both treated him like a normal – no, like an abnormally clever little boy. 'He's a delight,' Recaldo said one day, surprising her. 'So quick.' And Gil had laughed as if he'd heard.

Everything was changed. Frank couldn't help her now, couldn't help her keep Gil. They would lock her up and put him in some awful place where he would grow silent and frightened again, the way he had been before she and John Spain had worked out how to help him. She'd been warned about Spain but hadn't listened and she'd never had cause to doubt him. She had known him for eight years and he had never laid a finger on her or made the slightest advance. He was more like a father than her own had ever been and was gentle, gentle with Gil. She had not listened to those poisonous stories. Her head was confused with the terrible images of the night before when that appalling woman had shown her a side of John Spain she hadn't allowed herself to believe. And now Val was in the house. Had he found the car? Seen her return? Cressida rocked back and forth, back and forth in anguish. Spain had walked into the trap that Evangeline had sprung for him but it was Val who was somehow at the back of the whole thing. Destroying John Spain so that he could destroy her and get his hands on Coribeen. Gil was just the means. Gil could be sacrificed. They both could. But where did Evangeline Walter come into it? The girl in O'Dowd's car? She couldn't figure any of it out no matter how often she went over it.

After Val had gone off in the launch, she'd bundled Gil into the car and gone to warn Spain. To ask for his help. She had no memory of the drive but when she got to his cottage he wasn't there. She went out to look for him. Next thing she was in the garden . . . oh dear God . . . there was something else . . . Someone else? She squeezed her eyes shut trying to focus on the shadows . . . Val? . . . Laughter. She heard laughter. Then they were back in John Spain's cottage. She couldn't look at him, even while he bathed her eye. He'd examined Gil's arm and made a temporary splint. He didn't speak. Not a word. She had to tell him about Val's threats, accusations. He listened in silence and only at the end said, 'You have to get some sleep.' He made them lie down on his bed and then wandered out into the night but when she awoke, around four o'clock in the morning, she found him sitting at the kitchen table with his head in his hands. 'She's dead,' he said and put his hand over her mouth to stop her screams.

'It wasn't you who killed her,' he told her fiercely. 'Just remember, Cressida, you were not there. No matter who asks, *you were never in that garden*. You couldn't have been. You'd never leave Gil alone at night, everyone knows that.'

Her teeth began to chatter. 'But I killed her . . .'

'You did not. She was laughing, don't you remember?'

She shook her head. 'Frank?' she whispered.

'Not yet. I'll call Frank in a while.'

'You're going to take the blame, aren't you?'

He looked at her strangely. 'No, I will not, then.'

'Val was there, he must have been . . .' Her voice rose. 'She told him you were . . . He'll take Gil away from me.'

'He was in the garden?' His face was like a rock, expressionless, but he let out a deep, deep sigh. 'Cressie, you have got to get Gil away from here. Get him to a doctor. He's hurt. Are you listening to me? Your eye needs stitching.' He ground his teeth. 'You can't go back to that house. You can't.'

'The police?'

'I'll deal with that.'

He took them over the fields to where he'd hidden the Range Rover. He carried Gil and she followed, stealthily, sticking close to the overgrown hedges. They laid Gil in the back of the car, covered him with the duvet and he dropped off to sleep almost immediately. He still hadn't spoken.

'Go back to hospital as if to see Mrs Donovan and stay there till I tell you it's safe to come back. Have you friends in Cork?' When she shook her head he jotted the name of a women's hostel on a scrap of paper. 'They know how to keep quiet,' he said. 'Write down your mobile number. One ring then I'll cut off and a minute after I'll ring again so you'll know it's me.'

'What'll I do about Frank? He'll be looking for me.'

'Leave it. He'll probably not be on the case – the Gardai will send reinforcements – but I'll talk to him. He'll help.' She knew he meant that Frank would lie his head off for her. The last thing he said was, 'Just remember, you were not there. You were not in that garden last night.'

'Oh God,' she wept. She put her arms around him and held her face to his. She could feel him trembling before he pulled away from her. 'Oh, John Spain,' she cried. 'What'll we do?'

'Take care, dear girl. And take care of Gil.' His eyes filled with tears. 'Keep talking to him. He'll come around.'

She took all his advice except for the shelter. She drove straight to the general hospital on the outskirts of the city, carried Gil into casualty and told them he'd fallen downstairs, sleepwalking. Fortunately the young, bleary-eyed doctor on duty was obviously much too tired to press her. Maybe Gil's obvious attachment to her saved them, or the sweet smile he managed when his arm was tied in a sling. Her own bruises she hid by making a curtain of hair and keeping her head pressed to Gil's. And she kept talking, talking. Soothing the terrified little boy with her fluttering lips against his flushed cheek.

Afterwards they sat outside the shelter, huddled behind the wheel, but she couldn't persuade Gil out of the car. At eight o'clock, just as the morning rush hour started, she drove to the Bons and found an empty television room on Marilyn's floor where they dozed until they were thrown out – ironically enough by a cleaning lady. The next few hours passed in a blur but she vaguely remembered spending some time with Marilyn Donovan. She was in a busy ward and the nurses weren't keen on having a small child under their feet. All the time, Gil clung to her, whimpering inconsolably. The ward sister lost her patience at around noon. Since Cressida had no money, neither of them had anything to eat.

She didn't make a clear decision to go home, she just caved in with exhaustion. As she got close to Duncreagh she dithered but by then she was beyond rational thought. She left the car hidden in a wood about half a mile from Coribeen then carried Gil across the fields and laid him under a hedgerow while she checked that the house was safe. She was almost caught out by the workman, Mick Moynihan, whom she'd forgotten, but he was down at the end of the drive and didn't see her. Both garages were empty.

She let herself into the house by the back door and only after she'd checked every room did she go back for Gil. Since then, they'd been holed up while Gil slept, face down, fast asleep beside a jumbled pile of Brio track. Cressida crept towards him and touched his tousled, damp hair with her open hand. Her heart melted with love for him. She crouched beside him, stroking his forehead until she thought she heard the back door bang shut. She tiptoed down to one of the back bedrooms which had an unimpeded view of the estuary and looked out. John Spain was out on the water, in his yellow oilskins. Even as she looked he raised his hand and her phone rang, just once and cut off. Still safe then. For another while at least. Val was either on the yacht or more likely gone off somewhere. How? His car was missing.

As she dialled the number Spain had given she wondered vaguely where and when Spain had acquired a mobile phone. From Evangeline Walter's house? Surely not? She refused to think about it.

He would come to them shortly, when he deemed it safe, probably with something for their supper. Not that she wanted anything to eat. She needed to gather her thoughts. Decide what to do. Alone.

Herself. She touched the throbbing bruise over her eye, tracing its angry rim with the tips of her fingers, then eased her aching leg into a kneeling position and squatted down beside the window. She looked out over the estuary with her burning cheek against the cold glass.

The wind whistled against the frame. *Cressida Sweeney*, it seemed to say. *Cressssida Sssssweeeneee.* She let the sounds roll on her tongue, hiss softly through her teeth. She loved her improbable name, loved its sibilance. She idly watched a light squall race over the surface of the water. Cressssie Sssssweeney. Madame Assonance.

At the beginning, she liked to make believe she had married Val for his name, though she knew it wasn't true. She had married V. J. Sweeney for several reasons but delight in his name wasn't one of them. She had lacked the imagination to recognize it at the time; now it was the only remaining thing about their union that pleased her, or made any sense. Gil didn't come into the equation. Gil was hers. Val had long since relinquished him. From the time the boy's disability was recognized, when Gil was two years old, Val regarded it as a personal affront. People like him didn't have deaf children; it must have come from her side of the family. Her genes. Her heart ran cold at the thought of his threat to take him from her. How could she ever have allowed him to get so much power over her?

Whenever Val said, 'Do you know my wife, Cressida?' she thought, *how could they, when I hardly know myself?* If he varied it to, 'Have you met my wife?' she mentally added, *the tentative Mrs Sweeney.* She only really thought of herself as Gil's mother, determined that his childhood would be full and happy and loving. As far as possible from her own.

Who am I? *Cressssieeee Sssssweeeneee,* Cressida Hollingsworth, that was. The only child of elderly parents, unexpected issue of her mother's menopause, and very, very unwelcome. She was born early and ailing when her mother was almost forty-eight. Her father was fifty-five and already under pressure to retire – for the second time. The army had eased him out when he reached forty-three. After that he'd been administrator of a language school in Corfu, though this was not something to which he readily admitted. Colonel Piers Roland Hollingsworth, proud of his Anglo-Irish ancestry, with the emphasis on the Anglo. He had never set foot in Ireland. An empire man, at heart. Once a soldier, always a soldier, was his motto.

The cost of living in Corfu was relatively low, but the pay was poor. In the circumstances, a sickly baby was an encumbrance for the colonel and his lady, who rapidly gave the infant over to the care of underpaid, undereducated nannies. Mrs Hollingsworth never allowed herself to quite recover from the birth. 'Such a terrible shock, my dear. It isn't even as if she was pretty. Or a boy. Piers would have liked a boy.' Her mother spun the yarn for all it was worth. Cressida must have overheard it a thousand times before she understood the meaning of the words, and the underlying fury, which prompted them. *Baby*, as they always referred to her, had scuppered her parents' retirement plans and ruined her mother's looks. Worse, she was a drain on their slim resources and would continue so into the distant future.

This was something the Hollingsworths hadn't envisaged in their carefree, childless days, when they could afford, just, to live in style – BC – before Cressida. Had there been a convenient maiden aunt the child would have been despatched into her care at the earliest possible age. Unfortunately for Baby, there wasn't.

When Cressida was five, her parents retired to a small village in the Cotswolds. She was sent away to her first boarding school at the age of seven and thereafter was moved down through increasingly poorer, cheaper establishments approximately every couple of years. When she was sixteen, her mother died – though that seemed too strong a word to describe her passing. Mrs Hollingsworth had simply and elegantly allowed herself to fade away. Reduced circumstances didn't suit her. Never had. Cressida left school to housekeep for a father who was practically a stranger. She didn't protest; education had almost completely eluded her, she had no friends.

She proved to be a good housekeeper. Being grief-stricken, the colonel required little else. He lamented – mercifully silently – that the girl had nothing like the pretty looks of her late mother, and despaired for her future. He suspected she was slightly dim-witted and was kind to her. Distant, of course, but kind. Her adolescence was late. She remained gawky and awkward long after her contemporaries. The allowance her father gave her was pitiful, and because he disapproved of jeans she habitually wore long, mimsy Laura Ashley milkmaid dresses, of which the local Oxfam shop seemed to have an endless supply. Thus Cressida turned from duckling to swan, under yards of pastel printed with rosebuds, willows and dancing cupids. No wonder she remained unsure of herself. She lacked social confidence because she so seldom mixed with her contemporaries. Her selfish parents had not equipped her for the twentieth century.

It was not until she was twenty-one, when a small art and craft gallery was opened in the village, that Cressida began to develop an interest in painting first and then art history. It was as if she'd awoken from a long confused sleep. As her interest and confidence grew she began to nurse a secret, timid hope of someday working in the gallery, though she had no idea how this might be achieved.

While Cressie was engrossed in her dreams, Papa was chatting up the gallery owner. Suddenly the spring in his step was restored and the glint in his old eye became purposeful. Immediately, the ubiquitous presence of his daughter became burdensome. Out of the blue, Cressida was invited for interview and swiftly offered a part-time job in the gallery – on condition she smarten up her act somewhat.

'You'll have to get some suitable clothes, my dear. Lose those awful dresses.' Mrs Wallace looked her up and down. 'Let's go shopping,' she said. 'Your father will have to cough up.'

The romance took six months to blossom. The colonel – Cressida never thought of him as anything else – announced he was remarrying and returning to Corfu. The Cotswold house was sold to finance his new arrangements. Mrs Hollingsworth the second kindly recommended Cressida – oh wildest dream come true – to a small Mayfair sculpture gallery and asked a friend to put the girl up until she found a flat. Her father contributed eight thousand pounds by way of inheritance. Poor Cressie thought it was a fortune. But not for long.

'I'm sorry it's not more, but my expenses . . .' He spread his hands in a mock-despairing gesture and left her to discover for herself how many thousands a year it took to eke out a living in London.

The gallery, used to employing well-bred and wealthy gels, paid atrociously but Cressida hadn't the confidence to look for another job. She constantly lived in fear of her ignorance being rumbled. Her social life was practically nil. She spent the following few years moving from one shared accommodation to another, with ever-changing flatmates. One after another these passing ships peeled off to get married, leaving her to start over in another gruesome flat, with another set of strangers. It felt like school all over again, except that now she was slipping inexorably further and further into debt. And then, just as she was reaching rock bottom, she met V. J. Sweeney at a gallery party.

She was immediately dazzled. The fact that there was over twenty years' disparity in age didn't matter. She had always been more comfortable with older people. Her life experience was so peculiarly out of time, worse, out of the spirit of the time, that she often felt like an alien. This suited Val fine. In some ways he was just another, younger version of her father, who expected little of her except her total, unwavering admiration. This she was perfectly willing to trade for security.

Once Val proposed, she convinced herself she was in love. It might even have been true for a time. Val was certainly more realistic than the colonel and more generous, but Cressida Sweeney was of an anxious disposition and quickly grew defensive about her position as the girl-wife of a successful older man. She really and truly wanted her marriage to work but she feared, almost from the beginning, that it was a futile hope. Val liked change, novelty, and a fast-moving lifestyle, which only made Cressie withdraw further into her shell. He didn't bother to hide his boredom nor did he require her to have any ideas. Those were his department.

About the time Gil was born, Val's business went through a sticky patch which somehow became stickier and turned into something more permanent. It was some time before Cressida had any real idea of how considerable these difficulties were. Val was so offhand that she was unable to form an overall picture of their position. By anyone's standards he was still well off, but nothing like as wealthy as he had once been. Then his partner shafted him and the business went pear-shaped. He announced that he was selling the London flat and moving to Ireland to give himself time to recover.

It didn't work out. Whereas he had previously flitted in and out for short periods, often spending more time on the boat than with her, once in permanent residence he quickly became restive. It was a relief that Coribeen was comfortable and roomy enough for them to be able to skirt around each other. He didn't, of course, regard it as his wife's house. Not really.

Cressie herself had no doubt. From the very start she fitted into the house and the land as if born there, so strong was her empathy. Miserable in the overcrowded vastness of London, she never experienced a trace of loneliness on the remote and sparsely populated estuary. She gave herself to her surroundings as to a lover, learned the contours of the land, the feel of the soil. Accustomed to living without constant companionship, she never asked more of her neighbours than was freely given. Being there was all she desired. It was not so for Val. After he sold up in London, Cressida found herself thinking how much better Coribeen suited her when he wasn't around. As a visitor he had been indulgent to his newborn son; as a resident, the constant crying grated on his nerves. Sometimes she wondered whether she had ever actually *liked* him. Failure changed his personality; boredom made him an uncomfortable companion. And when the trouble at the Atlantis Hotel started he became overbearing and dismissive. Gil's deafness was seen as a personal insult.

He who had once the Midas touch could now do nothing right, every project failed. The hotel was the last straw. He'd seen it as a toy, a way of re-establishing his business reputation, even if he regarded Ireland as a poor second to London. It was merely a jumping-off point, he told her, loftily, at the time. His investment, which had seemed chicken-feed when he bought in, eventually turned out to be an important part of his residual resources. He tried to gain control of the board and to his chagrin failed utterly. He had some sort of scheme for shutting down the failing hotel and developing the site more lucratively. This much she had gleaned from overheard phone calls, but he was blocked at every turn. First he blamed the place and pretty soon he linked his family to his ill luck and began to throw the blame for his failures on her and the child.

The boat lay idle on the water. For weeks he'd ignore it and then suddenly would disappear for days on end. Eventually he announced he'd decided to sell up and go. Her heart sank. 'Where?' she asked.

'Anywhere,' he shouted. 'Anywhere, anywhere, away from this bloody climate, the eternal rain.'

Then, a few weeks back, when he sold the *Azurra*, she grew afraid of his filthy temper, his terrible sulks, his fury. She didn't know about the sale until the boat disappeared one day. When it came back it had been repainted and the name changed to *Halcyon*. He moped around for days, staring at it. The change of name seemed to upset him even more than the sale. 'And all because you wouldn't sell the bloody house,' he fumed at her. And then, and then . . .

She wouldn't think about Evangeline. Later, not now. Darkness was falling. She heard a long low whistle. Spain, she thought, and let out her pent-up breath. At the same time she heard Gil stir, then cry out 'Aah.'

He was standing in the middle of his bedroom floor looking like a war victim. His face, like hers, was livid with bruises and he held one arm awkwardly across his chest. She ran to him and enfolded him in her arms. 'I'm here, my darling. You're safe.' She held him out in front of her, her hands on his shoulders, and exaggerated each word with her lips. His face lit up. 'Mmmmm aaaa,' he said. 'Ma-ma.' And then he pointed to the floor. 'Tar?' It was his pet name for John Spain. The old tar. Relief flooded through her.

'Good boy, good boy,' she said. 'Tar is here. We're safe.' She crossed her fingers and thought, we are for the moment. For the moment. She held Gil's hand and led him downstairs.

Chapter Fourteen

WHEN RECALDO GOT BACK TO TRIANACH IT WAS AFTER SIX. HE HAD just turned into the causeway when Jer O'Dowd's Mercedes hurtled past from the opposite direction and turned left for Duncreagh. By the time he got to the Old Corn Store Superintendent Coffey and DI McBride were on the point of leaving. He parked the Jeep outside the gate and walked up the drive to find them in conversation outside the front door.

'You've taken your time,' Coffey growled.

'It's a good fourteen miles by road,' Recaldo protested mildly. 'I hung around for a while hoping they'd get back.'

'Him or her?' McBride smirked. Recaldo ignored him.

'Maybe you should have gone by boat, then, if it's so far by road. O'Dowd tells us you keep your boat up the way,' Coffey said. 'I suppose you saw him on your way in? That man's a bit of a tightrope walker. We'll have him back tomorrow. I'd like to get to the bottom of that relationship, there's something he's not telling us.'

'A lot of things he's not telling us,' McBride offered.

'Any word from the pathologist?' Recaldo asked and was disturbed by the flicker of eye movement between the two detectives. It was Coffey who answered. 'Just the preliminaries, the post-mortem is tomorrow morning. It's murder all right. Violent sex. A blow to the stomach. A haemorrhage. Though not necessarily in that order. I'll know the details tomorrow. Meantime keep that under your hat. No talking to the press, right,' he added, though he'd said nothing that Recaldo hadn't already guessed.

'What do you think I am?' he replied. Coffey looked at him

115

balefully. McBride lifted an eyebrow as if to say – wouldn't you like to know? Recaldo wondered just how much they were holding back and knew if he challenged them they'd say it was only what he'd asked for: to be kept on the sidelines.

'Will you want me here tomorrow?' he asked stiffly.

'Certainly we will,' Coffey replied politely. 'Apart from anything else, you must interview that gallery owner. Keep checking for that Sweeney pair, as well.'

'Right, FX. We're off now. Be seeing you,' McBride said impatiently.

'Conference here at half eight tomorrow morning,' Coffey said. 'Traffic permitting.' His voice softened. 'You've had a very long day, why don't you get off home and have something to eat. If you don't mind me saying so, you look done in.'

'Who's attending the PM?'

'I will. Dr Morrow's scheduled it for early morning.'

'If anyone asks, there'll be a press statement in the morning,' McBride said. 'We'll fudge up something when we meet. Had any trouble yourself?'

'Not so far.' He looked up at the clear sky. 'I might go out for a bit of a sail,' Recaldo said innocently as they got into their car. 'Give me an appetite.'

McBride grinned. 'You might give us a bit of a scorch in your yacht sometime,' he said, tipping the wink that O'Dowd had informed them about his puny little dinghy. Recaldo laughed. 'I'm not sure we'd both fit,' he said. 'I'll lock the gate.' He raised his hand in farewell and walked down the drive after the car, then padlocked the gate when they were through. He wondered uncomfortably what Smiler O'Dowd had told them, besides disclosing the location of his dinghy. That would, almost certainly, have led to him telling them that Spain had taught him to sail. What else? Cressida. He had little doubt that Smiler would have the low-down on most aspects of his life and travails. Feck O'Dowd, he thought savagely.

Recaldo watched the tail lights disappear then strolled down to the shore, though not to his boat. He set off in the opposite direction along the riverbank edging the garden of the Old Corn Store, towards the spit of land which sheltered the house from its neighbours. The ground underfoot was marshy and he disturbed several wading birds as he passed. He wondered who owned the spit, which, as far as he could make out, had no boundary wall. But then there was hardly need for one, he reflected, as his shoes sank deeper into the soft mire.

Having crossed the meadow next to Walter's garden, he turned inland and walked through into the next field until, a short distance off to his left, he came in sight of a faintly smoking chimney. He headed towards it but had some difficulty getting close until he broke through a dense fuchsia hedge bordering a field of sad-looking cabbages. He stood, lost in the hedge, looking at Smiler O'Dowd's bungalow which, hitherto, he had only ever approached from the main road.

It was a tidy enough spread for a bachelor, though the garden was neglected with five or six cattle grazing close to the house. Recaldo shooed them away and hammered on the front door. There was no reply but then he didn't expect one. He walked around the house and would have peered in, except all the curtains were drawn. At the rear again, he looked up at a small dormer window, angled out towards the bay. The pitch of the roof seemed too low for a room, unless of course the ground floor at the back went right up into the eaves. It seemed unlikely somehow. His bet was that the bungalow was as dull inside as out. But he wasn't there to comment on the architecture or decor. He looked around quickly and spotting an old wooden garden bench he dragged it over, turned it on its side and wedged it against the drainpipe. Then he hoisted himself onto it gingerly and from this precarious foothold was able to pull himself up onto the roof. From there, having long arms, he was within reach of the sill and was able to get enough purchase to clamber upwards on the tiles until he was level with the window.

There were neither curtains nor blinds, nor when he could focus could he see any furniture in the miniature room. It appeared to be no more than five or six foot square and was evidently used as a storeroom. His heart began to pound. Scattered on the bare boards there were seven or eight cartons. But he was much more interested in the binoculars lying inside on the window ledge. He pressed the side of his head against the glass and when he eased himself around, he found he was looking straight onto Evangeline Walter's terrace. *Voyeur.* 'Oh Christ almighty,' he swore and drew in a deep, deep breath. He released his grip and allowed himself to slither slowly downwards, regained a foothold on the upturned bench and dropped silently to the ground.

How stupid and blind he'd been. No wonder O'Dowd looked so shifty. Did he make a practice of spying on his neighbour? Or on her visitors? Gossip-mongering or blackmail? Certainly those two had something going, but what precisely? Word was that Evangeline Walter had many admirers and a few affairs too many. With married men. Local married men, some with children. Always the well-heeled, Michael Hussey amongst them. O'Dowd was comfortable too, but being a bachelor, excited no condemnation. He was generally held to be something of a ladies' man. A cute hoor no lady had ever succeeded in pinning down. So safe for Walter to be seen with, particularly if she was having an affair with someone else she wanted to protect. Or to protect herself.

Spain? No, that didn't feel right; he wasn't rich, he was a broken old man. Sweeney? *Sweeney?* Sweeney was no longer wealthy, no longer a success. Who would care if Walter was having an affair with Sweeney? No-one, Recaldo told himself wryly, except his wife and her lover; they would be delighted. He held on to that thought. Sweeney and Walter had been out in the boat. All three of them, counting O'Dowd, were together the previous afternoon. Gil was out of the way with Spain. He was out of the way at Trabuí. A set-up? Where oh where was Cressie at the time? Where was she now? At some stage she was in that blasted garden – but when? Her image lingered until he forced his troubled thoughts back to O'Dowd.

Another thing: according to himself, O'Dowd went off to Dublin – or at least he drove off somewhere, leaving the others together. Where? In the garden? Had Cressie joined them there? Recaldo was almost certain she had because of the comb. But when? He began to tease out the picture in his mind and all his fears came bubbling to the surface.

Suppose Spain also saw her there. Now Recaldo placed Spain, Sweeney, Cressie with Evangeline Walter in the garden together. O'Dowd watching from his eyrie. Oh Jesus wept, he thought and put his head in his hands. One of them had killed her. Spain had woven a very plausible story. Spain was trying to protect someone. Let it not be . . . *Not Cressie? Not my love.* She always said Spain was like a father to her, kind, good, protective. He sat bolt upright as Coffey's words came back to him. Sex, haemorrhage. Where did Cressie fit in with that? He almost laughed with relief. So why was Cressie hiding? Had she witnessed Evangeline being killed by one of the others? Someone she in turn was trying to protect? Her husband? Spain?

John Spain. Recaldo suddenly recalled the danger and power Spain had exuded when he turned on O'Dowd that morning. Over Evangeline Walter's body. Shit. The convolutions of that triangle were beyond him but he guessed that sex was a small part of it and love didn't figure at all. He had to talk to Cressida. If she needed protecting he was the one to do it.

He walked back through the uncut grass to the riverbank and from there back across Evangeline's garden to his car. His head was pounding, he felt utterly drained. Rest was what he needed. Fourteen straight hours on his feet was no joke. A huge drink and oblivion seemed an attractive option. All that sparring with Phil McBride needed a clear head and a good deal more humour than he'd been able to muster; he hadn't acquitted himself well. Maybe he'd simply lost the ability to switch off? It had been a horrible day from start to finish. He was sick with worry.

He went back to his car and drove wearily homewards. He eased to a stop outside the station and stepped inside to check it out and make a few phone calls. He tried Cressida last but she was still not answering. He went down to the village grocery on foot to pick up enough provisions for a couple of days. One of the many advantages of his height was that he could easily avoid the shop assistant's enquiring eye, and another was that he could see over the window screens of Hussey's pub as he passed. Despite what Coffey had indicated, the bar was quiet. Recaldo slipped round the back and found Michael having his tea in the back kitchen. 'Sit down,' he said, with his mouth full. He indicated the heaped plate of bacon and cabbage. 'There's plenty more where that came from. Will you have some?'

'I will.' Recaldo fetched a plate from a nearby press and a knife and fork. Michael piled his plate high and called his brother to get them another couple of beers.

'What d'you think?' asked Michael.

'It's great. That cabbage is just the way I like it, crisp and buttery.'

'I'll tell the wife when she gets back. She's in with the Donovans next door. Marilyn's back tomorrow and the place is a holy show.'

'Any reporters in?'

'A few. Keep an eye out. They were prowling about at your place earlier, but they've mostly gone off to Duncreagh now. They think this place is too quiet altogether.' He tittered and it turned into a great guffaw.

Recaldo found himself joining in the laughter; he wasn't sure why, but it was a marvellous release of nervous energy. He finished his meal and stood up. 'That was mighty,' he said and put his hand on his friend's shoulder.

'You're all right, Frank. We'll keep them guessing. I already told a few of them you weren't on the case; sent them after the McBride fella. It was a bit of sport anyway.'

'You'll have a job keeping Mrs Ryan quiet.'

'That's true for you, but she'll be looking out for your interests. Doesn't she only think you're gorgeous.' He roared with laughter again. 'You've a great way with the auld ones, Frank. By the way, that customs guy was looking for you earlier.'

It seemed light years since the morning before when he and the Customs and Excise officer were tracking a fishing vessel suspected of carrying contraband.

'Damn. I forgot all about him.'

'He said not to worry, he's heard about the— about er . . .' Michael's face twitched with embarrassment. 'Anyway, he said they had it sorted, and that you'd know what he meant. That guy talks in riddles the whole time.' He sniffed. 'Gets a bit above himself.'

Recaldo was just out the door when Michael said softly, 'Is John Spain all right? I'd be worried about him. That feckin' boat is going to kill him, d'you know that? I hear 'twas him that found her.'

'Yes, poor man. He's very shocked.' He rubbed his chin and sighed. 'Tell Aoife thanks for the dinner.'

'Hang on a second, Frank. There's something maybe you should know. All that gossip about Spain's been doing the rounds again.'

Recaldo sat down hard. 'I heard. Any idea when and where it started? It's not true you know.'

'Arra of course I know, but the stuff that's in the papers these days, who's going to believe him? Specially now. I think you better get on up to Lia's and talk to her. It's on your way home.'

Lia Ryan – daughter of the post office – owned and ran an excellent little restaurant on the upper road, which ran between the station and Recaldo's house. He went in the kitchen door and nabbed one of the waitresses who got Lia. They went outside to the yard.

'I don't know if it actually started here but there was a very unpleasant little incident – it must be, oh a couple of months ago. July?

No, June. It was during that hot spell and we were run off our feet. Mrs Walter was in with – I think it was an Englishman, a visitor anyway. It was the only time I ever saw her in here and it's the only time John Spain ever came in as well, poor chap. He was with an elderly woman, also a stranger. Quiet spoken. I have a kind of feeling she might be a nun and related. They looked a bit alike. They passed Mrs Walter's table and unfortunately Mr Spain jiggled it as he passed and knocked over an empty water bottle. I mean it was nothing, but the fuss she made was . . . well it was disgraceful. I could see he wanted to tear out the door. I got it sorted, but you know the kind of quiet that follows an incident like that? Everybody whispering for a few minutes. Mrs Walter called for her bill and when she made sure everyone was paying full attention she said – I swear to God I nearly dropped dead with embarrassment – ". . . one of those child abusers we keep hearing about". That's all she said but it was plain to everyone there who she meant. Mr Spain didn't react at all, nor did his companion, but their evening was spoiled all right, and so was mine.'

'Were there any passengers about?'

'Passengers? Oh locals, you mean? That's a good one. I might take that up.' Her face sobered. 'Well of course there were, not to mention the staff. I had a word with them but . . . It's not true is it?'

'No, it is not,' he said robustly but he could see just how easily doubt could creep in. 'It's a nasty, libellous accusation, but of course the way she said it, it could have been about anyone.'

'That's what I thought. Why would she say a terrible thing like that?'

'That is a very good question,' he said and thanked her.

After leaving Lia's place he went straight home, ran a bath and lay soaking in the scalding water until he dozed off and only woke when the brandy glass he'd been holding dropped out of his hand. He cleared up the broken glass then wrapped a towel around himself and stretched out on his bed. Forty-five minutes later he awoke refreshed. He dressed in an old pair of black cords and polo-neck sweater and padded barefoot to the kitchen where a neglected Barker was asleep beside the boiler. One eye opened as Recaldo came in and another when he filled a jumbo dish of grub and a bowl of water. He brewed himself a pot of strong tea and sat for a few minutes' quiet contemplation, planning his next foray, while Barker had a run in the yard.

He packed a small knapsack with a couple of large torches, some tools, a hip flask of brandy, a bar of chocolate and a pair of deck shoes, then he switched on several lights, closed the blinds and turned on the radio. Last, he put on a couple of pairs of woollen socks and his wellingtons, a black knitted hat and a navy waterproof jacket with a black sleeveless fleece underneath.

At nine thirty F. X. Recaldo slipped out the back door and skirted the village through the back lanes on foot. It took him a good twenty-five minutes to reach the spot where the dark grey dinghy was waiting. The sky had darkened and the wind was up. With the thick cloud cover, the only light was a vague shimmer on the surface of the inky water when John Spain slowly put-putted past, on his way home. Recaldo drew back. No wonder Michael was worried. The old man was out unusually late. But then he seemed to be in his damned boat all day long, as if he couldn't rest on shore. Recaldo searched the surface for a directional wake and spotted a slight disturbance stretching across the river. Spain might have come from the opposite side or on the other hand might as easily have turned for home from midstream, the way he usually did. Had Recaldo been a betting man, he'd have plumped for the first option. He'd always felt curiously protective of Spain. Lia's tale had chilled him to the marrow. It just added a whole new layer to the story, but, as yet, an unfathomable one.

The old man and the estuary. His endurance was awesome. It was possible to think of him as he always had, with admiration. His was a strange, spartan existence. Alone when he came, alone ever since. Rolled up in a battered Cortina towing his blessed boat and pitched a small tent inside the tumbledown walls of the abandoned Trianach schoolhouse, then set about salvaging it with his own hands. This must have been a purely economic decision, since he was extremely cack-handed. The slow and laborious restoration was watched with interest by his neighbours who were too shy or too polite to push forward with help he might not want. They allowed him time to get his bearings, make his own decisions as to what he did or did not want to do to the old place. But gradually, as they came to admire his stoical persistence and to despair of his ham-fisted lack of skill, first a carpenter, then a roofer and finally a plumber casually volunteered some desperately needed help.

John Spain, aloof, proud and unhappy, gratefully accepted and suggested payment in the only way he could: by offering to tutor any children who needed scholastic help. Since this offer was politely but invariably declined, he insisted on providing his benefactors with freshly caught fish.

When the need for immediate help was over his saviours melted away, leaving him to his fishing and his books. He was neither harried nor bothered but was treated with distant reserve. There seemed to be an unwritten rule not to share their knowledge – or speculation – with the other strangers in the area. He was protected in this way because, deep down, the people retained respect for what he was, or had been, and as knowledge of his distinguished scholarship slowly spread, that too was a protection of sorts. While the locals remained aloof, the incomers didn't particularly notice him. Or if they did, they dismissed him as a recluse. Everyone except Cressida Sweeney, who came in for much unsought-for advice and some condemnation when Gil began to be seen, frequently, in company with the old man.

Recaldo thought hard about all these things as he followed Spain's progress until the boat disappeared around the spit of land a couple of hundred yards beyond the boundary of Evangeline Walter's garden. He was either going home or further upriver. He knew from experience that the old man was one of the few who was willing and competent to navigate the river in the dark, when the lack of markers made it especially treacherous. All his skill would be needed tonight, he thought, looking up at the threatening sky. He wondered how many people had witnessed the old man's attempts to teach him his lore. That was one of the strange mysteries of Passage South and its inhabitants. Even when you didn't notice them, or were out of sight of the land, every man jack of them seemed to know exactly what you were doing and with whom.

He felt uneasy that he'd missed his colleagues' interview with Spain. The old fellow could be both curmudgeonly and imperious, sometimes both at the same time, and McBride particularly, with his provocative ways, would have brought out the worst in him. But then, Recaldo chided himself, Spain had to endure worse than McBride could throw at him when he first settled on Trianach. Even after twelve or more years' residence he was still talked about, still regarded as a blow-in. *Same as yourself*, Recaldo always thought, when he heard that careless description. Now he thought of it again and it sent a chill down his spine. They were all incomers; all except O'Dowd. Walter, the Sweeneys, himself, Spain.

Blow-ins could be blown away.

He waited in the shadows a good fifteen minutes before he quietly slid into the inflatable, untied it and pushed away from the shore. It was cumbersome but its powerful outboard motor made it extremely fast. He usually hired it when he wanted to go some distance, more often than not with his Customs and Excise pal. Its dark colour made it almost impossible to spot in the gloom, which was why he'd chosen it instead of his own dinghy, which, in any case, had no motor.

Balancing the oars on the chunky, rounded sides was awkward, but he made steady, if slow, progress and reached Evangeline Walter's boat, *Cynara*, within fifteen minutes. Rowing across the current later would be a different matter, but he hoped by then he might be confident enough to risk the outboard motor. He slunk in under the starboard side and got to his feet gingerly. His hands easily reached the gunnel. He felt along the inside until he found a cleat then slipped the line from the dinghy through, pulled it taut and secured it. Now for the tricky bit. A side wind was whipping across the surface of the water and it was difficult to keep the dinghy steady enough to scramble up, but by dint of hanging on tight with both hands to the rail he eventually managed to get one knee on *Cynara*'s deck. He thanked his stars for his long legs as he rolled awkwardly into the cockpit.

He didn't need the tools; the hatch was unlocked with no sign of a padlock or any securing device. This made him pause for a moment before he switched on his torch and, pointing it downwards, descended into the cabin. It was too low for him to stand upright, nevertheless he allowed himself a brief moment of envy. Of all the boats on the river this was the one he'd most like to own. It was in beautiful condition and, like the house, it was as neat as ninepence, shipshape, though there was a vague musty smell. Little patches of black mould were sprouting on the bulkhead and in the porthole rims. Not enough to spell real neglect. He drew his hand over the ceiling and sniffed his fingers and reckoned the boat must have been thoroughly scrubbed down within the past few weeks. Even more interestingly, it had quite obviously been cleared of all personal effects. He wondered when Evangeline Walter had last stepped on her boat.

Had she been thinking of selling it? He knew *Cynara* hadn't left her moorings all summer. Mrs Walter was a skilful and much-admired single-handed sailor, a keen and regular participant in the coastal regattas and her absence this season had given rise to much speculation, and some ribaldry, about her state of health. But if she'd put the boat on the market, wouldn't Terry Whelan have mentioned it? Probably, unless he hadn't the selling of it.

A thorough inspection yielded nothing but an ancient snapshot on the floor under the chart table. He smelt something else as he bent down. He sniffed. Whiskey. He ran his hands, in the dark, along the base of the bulkhead and pricked his finger on a piece of broken glass. He covered his hand with his handkerchief and picked it up. It had a strong, lingering scent. He wrapped it in the hankie then examined the snapshot in the dim glow of the torch. It showed three figures, hard to make out because the photograph had obviously been folded or crumpled at some time or other and the colour had faded where it hadn't actually peeled away. It showed a young couple with a child sitting on a table between them. Both adults were smoking. There was a scribbled date on the back which was impossible to decipher in the half-light. Recaldo slipped it in his pocket, switched off the torch and climbed back on deck with his booty.

The inflatable was barely visible in the dark and getting into it was even more difficult than getting out. He landed painfully and winded, spreadeagled on the side while the wretched thing bounced up and down like the proverbial rubber ball. He needed a strong gulp of brandy to recover. He untied the ropes, brought the bow around, and pushed off into mid-channel. After some hesitation he turned over the engine. The din rent the air like a burst of thunder. He held his breath as he cut it well back to almost idling speed and headed downstream towards Val Sweeney's floating palace.

Thursday

Chapter Fifteen

FRANK RECALDO SLEPT LIKE THE DEAD. TWO LARGE BRANDIES WHEN he got back from the estuary and he was out like a light. He didn't come to until seven thirty on Thursday morning. He lay dazed for a moment then shot out of bed, showered and dressed in record time. He checked his answering machine when he got downstairs. There was a total of fifteen messages, including seven from importunate reporters demanding 'a word'. He was tempted to wipe the lot but something made him keep playing through the tape. The second last was Cressida. 'Frank? Don't worry, we're safe. I'm sorry.' He leaned against the wall, almost sick with misery. Had she got his message? He dialled her home and mobile; both went unanswered. This is going to drive me mad, he thought. Why couldn't she trust him? Or was she trying to protect him from himself? The answer came in a flash: no, not him. The person Cressie would be most anxious to protect was Gil. It was a kind of relief. But it didn't explain why she was hiding nor what she'd been doing in Evangeline Walter's garden. By her own admission, she disliked Evangeline intensely. It was going to be another terrible day.

The *Cork Examiner* had been shoved through his letter box by hands unknown. He glanced through it while he grabbed a cup of coffee, then paused just long enough to shove a bowl of food under Barker's accusing eye. He had the mother and father of a hangover.

The village was staggering to its collective feet as he hurtled through but no-one paid him much heed; 8.05 was clearly too early for even the most eager newshound, the Irish variety at least. It took barely seven minutes to check that the inflatable had been collected and another five to reach Evangeline Walter's house. As before, he parked the Jeep on the verge beside the gate and made his way up to the house on foot.

To his surprise, O'Dowd was standing at the front door, peering through the sidelights. He was not in the least fazed when Recaldo asked him what he was doing. He turned and stood with his feet apart and folded his arms. He held a bunch of keys loosely in one hand, which he made no attempt to hide. He wore his usual fixed smile. 'Just checking,' he answered genially, as if it was the most natural thing in the world.

'Are those the keys of the house?' Recaldo asked suspiciously.

'Hmm.'

'Is that yes or no, O'Dowd?'

Smiler shrugged his shoulders. 'Whatever.'

'What the hell does that mean?' Recaldo's blood began to boil. O'Dowd could get under his skin like nobody else. A little fighting cock. Almost everything he said seemed to be a challenge. Of what? Manhood?

'You haven't been inside, have you?' Christ, he thought, this is all getting away from me.

'Why would I do that?'

'Stop farting about, O'Dowd. Have you or haven't you?'

'No, Frank, I have not. These are my own keys, you omadhán.'

'So what are you doing then?'

'For God's sake, I was just checking the place was secure. Same as I always do when Evangeline is away.' He winced. 'Was away.' He sucked in his breath.

'And what business is that of yours?'

O'Dowd looked at him for a slow moment, relishing some secret information. The smile had faded; he wore a look of total self-satisfaction. Triumph, even. 'Every business,' he said softly. 'She was my neighbour, as well as my friend.' His flinty eyes fixed on Recaldo's confusion as he added, 'It's my house after all. I had it set to Mrs Walter.'

Recaldo was so surprised he fell back a step. 'Come again?' he said.

'You heard me. I own the place. She was my tenant.' The happy smile was back.

Recaldo didn't bother to hide his astonishment. 'But I thought Bleiberg owned it?'

'He did the conversion all right, but he never had more than a lease on the place.'

'You have proof of that, I suppose?'

'All the proof I need.'

'Why didn't you say?'

'What you mean is, why didn't *you know*. You didn't ask. Thought ye were too feckin' superior.'

'You tell the others?'

'No. They didn't ask either.'

I am stumbling around in the dark, Recaldo thought, disgusted with himself and suddenly nervous at how seriously he had underestimated O'Dowd.

'You seem to enjoy keeping me guessing,' he said lamely.

'Yeah, you could say that.' Jer O'Dowd rocked back and forth on the balls of his feet. For a wild moment Recaldo thought he might start dancing a hornpipe. 'Yourself and that other pair.' He was hugging himself with glee. 'You're eejits, the whole lot of you. And *you* don't know your feckin' arse from your elbow, do ye?'

'And what's that supposed to mean?'

'You said that before,' O'Dowd answered insolently.

'And I'll say it again,' he shouted, completely losing his temper. They eyeballed each other furiously but it was Recaldo who cooled down and looked away first. His brain felt scrambled. Was O'Dowd taunting him for a particular reason? He had somehow managed not to mention exactly when he'd set out on that journey to Dublin, by pulling his garda witness out of the hat like a conjuror. Economical with the truth.

He would not discuss Cressida with Smiler O'Dowd. Recaldo toyed with the notion of confronting him with the boating party but decided to hold that piece of drama in reserve for the time being. He needed some leverage but he was still mystified about the significance of the expedition; deep down he sensed it was important. He glossed over his own reaction to the incident. The thought of exposing his emotions made him shudder.

'You stand to gain by her death.'

'Is that a question or an accusation?'

'You obviously know more about the woman than you're saying, or have said so far.'

'About her death or her life?' He looked up at Recaldo, not at all

131

disadvantaged by being at least eight inches shorter. The smile was in place as he suddenly half raised his hand in farewell and walked away. As he pulled open the car door, he called over his shoulder, 'There were a couple of reporters nosing around here last night. I chased them off. That's why I came over this morning.' He grinned. 'Just in case anyone's enquiring.'

'You haven't been shooting your mouth off at them have you, O'Dowd?'

O'Dowd gave him a withering look. 'I didn't get where I am today by blabbing. You'd do well to remember that. I'm as careful of what I say as you are, Frank Recaldo. So you might try to stop looking down your nose sometime; you never know what you might see.' He came back and stood quivering with rage in front of the garda. 'I didn't kill Evangeline, and I don't know who did. But I'm bloody well going to find out. You seem to be forgetting – she was my friend. If you want my help, let me know. But try asking for it, you might get a bit further that way. You're a stuck-up bastard, you know, for a fellow that's fallen so low. And as for that other pair of jokers,' he snorted, 'what the hell would they know about what goes on around here?' He returned to his car and started the engine.

'We'll need to talk to you.'

'I talked till I was blue in the face yesterday. I won't be around today. I've a few calls to make and I don't give a feck whether they like it or not.'

'Mind telling me where you're going?'

'I do mind. I'm not under arrest, am I?'

'You can't just . . .'

'Just watch me. I'll be at home early tomorrow morning, if you want to talk. Just you, mind. You'll be needing to hold your own with your superiors, I've no doubt.' With that final shaft, O'Dowd smiled sweetly as he drove past.

There being, as yet, no sign of Coffey and McBride, Recaldo went through to the garden. Locking the side gate behind him, he walked down to the water's edge and began to skim pebbles over the water, something he often did when things got on top of him.

'Ah, there you are, FX.' He turned around to find McBride standing on the terrace outside the house, beckoning him. 'Better get a move on,' he said. 'I have to get back to Cork by two. We have appointments with the consultant and the computer man, as well as a solicitor and the bank,' he counted them off on his fingers.

'Superintendent Coffey not here?'

'He's covering the PM and he has a few things to attend to – he'll try to get along later. By the way, that woman in the gallery – O'Faolain, was it? He wants you to see her today. I don't suppose you've had any luck with the Sweeneys overnight?'

'No. Has the time of death been established?' Recaldo asked, as they went into the house.

'She's narrowed it to between ten and one. We'll get the details in an hour or so. You can add hypothermia to the list you got yesterday. So there's plenty to confuse us. But the old geezer was right. She died on her feet.' He eyed Recaldo. 'You seem to know what you're talking about,' he said slowly. 'About some things anyway. So would you mind tellin' me why you asked Doc Morrow if the woman drowned?'

'I asked if she died of exposure.'

'So you did, but you also asked if she drowned, didn't you?'

'I may have.' This was followed by silence until Recaldo eventually muttered, 'Her feet were very wrinkled. Washerwoman's feet, they call it. I've seen it a couple of times around here. We have several accidental drownings each year, fishermen usually,' he added by way of explanation.

'But then she was *standing* in the water, wasn't she? Or so the auld fellow says. *Propped*, was it?' McBride sounded extremely sceptical. Worse, he looked at Recaldo as if he, somehow, was responsible. For what? Recaldo asked himself grimly. For pulling the wool over their eyes? Maybe. They could hardly be accusing him of the deed, could they?

McBride's phone rang. He listened for a moment and then sat down on one of the sofas and began to take notes. Recaldo went into the kitchen and made some coffee while he was waiting. Why not? He felt a bit like a tea boy.

'Dr Morrow thinks she was in the water for some time.' McBride came in and sat down at the kitchen table. He accepted coffee and nursed the hot cup in his hands.

'After she died?'

'That's not clear yet but, it seems, she didn't drown.' His voice was tetchy. 'You haven't really said what made you mention exposure, have you?' he persisted. His nose was almost visibly twitching. It was obvious that he couldn't quite put his finger on what was bothering him, but he made it patently clear that his initial mistrust of Recaldo was hardening.

'I can't remember. Does it matter?'

'You tell me. You were right about exposure and almost right about drowning. Have you second sight or what?'

Recaldo snorted impatiently. 'No. I don't have second sight.'

'So something made you say it.' McBride was like a terrier.

'Look, it was a stupid thing to say,' Recaldo started, then fell silent. Better to be thought thick than that he was trying to shield someone. 'She was soaked through, her clothes, everything. I just wondered, that's all. What about the blow to her head?'

'The blow to her head is neither here nor there. The blow to her stomach is something else. The woman had had an operation. Concentrate on the haemorrhage.'

'Could it have been caused by the sex?'

'It could indeed. And so what we need to know is whether the sex or the blow to the stomach was responsible for her death. And we definitely need to know who the hell was she entertaining. Nice guy whoever he was.' *Guy*. Recaldo forced a cough to cover his little cry of relief.

McBride said softly, 'How does a gang bang grab you? I'd say there was more than one in at the death. We need to know a lot more than we do about this woman. She's an interesting case, I'll say that for her. I wonder why she was propped against the tree?'

'If she'd been left lying down, nobody would have seen her, she might have been there for hours, days . . .' Recaldo said slowly then stopped. 'Oh . . .'

'Right,' McBride said laconically. 'She hardly propped herself against the feckin' tree, did she? I think we can take it, it wasn't the missionary position.' He laughed. 'Think that leaves your priest friend out, then?' he asked provocatively.

Recaldo rose to his full lean height, tall enough to look down into McBride's sleepy eyes. 'Watch your lip, McBride,' he said through gritted teeth.

'Now FX, ya want to watch that temper,' McBride retorted, 'what with your heart and everything.'

'Spain would hardly claim she was standing up, if he was responsible, would he?'

'That's a point. But he's a clever man, that one, he may have worked all that out. No?'

'Oh, come on. I'm perfectly certain he didn't make it up, it was too graphic . . . No, I don't think so.' Recaldo shook his head. 'I really think that was genuine. Even if it's just a gut feeling.'

'I've nothing against gut feelings – I get them myself. Like now. Where exactly was she when you arrived yesterday morning?'

'Exactly where she was when you got here. Lying face down on the grassy bank. Maybe she banged her head against the root of the tree?'

'Joanna Morrow is adamant that the blow to her head was super-ficial. It might have shocked or surprised her, at most it would only have stunned her; it seems it wasn't powerful enough to kill her. On its own. But that and the blow to her stomach . . .' He pursed his lips and looked at Recaldo before dropping his small ballistic.

'There was *one* other thing. Joanna also says there are traces of some sort of restraint marks under her arms.' The words doused Recaldo like a cold shower.

'Now, I didn't hear mention of anything like a rope for instance, Recaldo, did you? How many times did we go over that story with your man Spain? Four, five times? *Propped* against the tree, he said, as I recall. And so did you. You read his account from your own note-book, as I recall.' This time he didn't trouble to mask his hostility. 'Maybe the auld fella pulled her out of the water? Or pushed her in, then pulled her out?' He stabbed the air with his finger. 'But he's an old man. Would he have the strength, d'you think?'

'He wouldn't need all that much strength,' Recaldo said heavily. 'There's a small winch on his boat. He uses it for lifting lobster pots.'

'I noticed that, all right,' McBride said. 'So where does that leave us? She wasn't attached to the boat at any time, was she?'

'As far as we know,' Recaldo said, half to himself.

'And how far is that? We need to know an awful lot more about that old man, so spill the beans, Recaldo, you must know a whole lot more than you're saying. An estuary is a great place for red herrings, but they seem to be scattered a bit too liberally around here for my liking. Something's amiss somewhere, I can feel it in me water.' He looked about him and then pounced. 'And so can you, Recaldo.

We're being led up the creek, if you'll forgive the pun. Someone has made damn sure that we can't time her death precisely. And that stinks of alibi to me.'

'Hmmm.' Recaldo sighed heavily. 'What was the operation for?' he asked. 'Did Dr Morrow say what was wrong with her?'

'Cancer. Looks like you were right again, FX. Most of the organs are affected but it seems she originally presented with a banjaxed womb. The poor bitch was riddled with it. An open and shut case as my mother would say. Someone could have saved themselves a hell of a lot of trouble. She hadn't long to live – weeks at most. The boss had a long chinwag with the consultant last night.'

'Maybe she would have preferred to go out with a bang?' Recaldo remarked, then put his hand to his head when he realized what he'd said. 'Oh Lord,' he started but McBride just laughed. 'That'd be one way of putting it, old son.' Somehow, after that, the tension eased a little.

McBride rinsed his empty cup in the sink and put it away. 'Where are all her friends?' he asked. 'That's what I'd like to know. Nobody has come to the house. I'll just go check with Eircom and see if there's been any calls. I'll use the upstairs extension.'

'One,' he said when he came back. 'Someone rang last night, about nine thirty, but didn't leave a message. All I got was "number withheld".'

'That's a fat lot of use. It hasn't been in the papers yet, has it? I mean apart from that small mention in the *Examiner* this morning?' Recaldo said blandly.

'Ah yes, the editor was on to Coffey last night. He said he warned him not to release the name.'

'He didn't. The article just said a woman's body had been found in mysterious circumstances.'

'One of the blessings of a remote place, at least,' McBride said heartily.

Recaldo snorted. 'You wouldn't say that if you lived around here. I hope your press release will do something to stop the speculation. There was a bloke from the *Sunday Tribune* nosing around here last evening. It'll be splashed all over the papers by tonight.'

'They'll only stay interested if they start dredging up salacious details,' McBride said. His eyes narrowed. 'Are there any? About her and,' he paused significantly, 'old Spain?'

Recaldo shook his head. McBride watched him quizzically from the window. 'If there are, the hacks will have them in jig time,' said McBride. 'And then there's her self-styled lover, O'Dowd. But somehow, I'd say that claim might just be a smokescreen. By the way, did Walter own a yacht?' he asked over his shoulder.

Recaldo joined him at the window and pointed. 'That one moored nearest to the shore, *Cynara*. Up to this year, she used to race it almost every week, single-handed mostly; she was a fine sailor.' He saw that McBride was watching John Spain row past, dressed in his yellow oilskins with the hood up against the rain.

'Who owns that big one, way over the other side?'

'Sweeney.'

'Ah, I wondered when that name would crop up again,' McBride murmured, his eyes still glued on the water. 'Strange how we've still had no word from them. Why is that, I wonder?'

'They're not answering the phone and there was no-one there all yesterday. There was a labourer working on the drive who said he thought Mr Sweeney was away since last Friday. Mrs Sweeney brought Marilyn Donovan to the hospital on Monday and I assume she must still be there, because no-one has seen her since.'

'Phew,' said McBride. 'Aren't you the informative one, all of a sudden?' He looked at Recaldo thoughtfully. 'O'Dowd tells me Mrs Sweeney was supposed to be a friend of the deceased. Odd she hasn't rung, isn't it? Women are usually good at keeping in touch.'

'Depends on how friendly they were,' Recaldo said tightly. 'Anyway, she probably doesn't know Mrs Walter's dead.'

'Everybody else seems to,' McBride cut in. There was a slight emphasis on 'everybody'. 'Wherever she is, I bet the phone lines around here are red hot. You know her well?' he asked Recaldo.

'I sometimes see her when I'm walking my dog on the cliffs.'

'What about the husband?'

'To pass the time of day, no more. He's seldom enough around. He comes and goes. There are rumours of financial difficulties. He has or had a PR firm in London, raises sponsorship for major sporting events or something like that. But as far as I know, it went bust some time ago.'

'Not by the look of that gin-palace parked over there,' McBride

137

interrupted. 'You better check that, old son. A tub that size doesn't suggest bankruptcy to me.'

'He's not exactly on skid row. I believe he has some sort of financial interest in the Atlantis Hotel. I've occasionally seen him and his wife together there, having a meal, a drink. Apart from that, he spends most of his time on the boat. But he hasn't been around for several weeks, as far as I know. At least I haven't run into him.'

'That lets them out of the picture, do you think?' It was a loaded question which Recaldo avoided answering.

'Not on your nelly,' drawled McBride and gave a derisive little snort. 'I'd say we're getting nowhere, real fast. Let's have another go at that bloody study.'

They went upstairs. 'Look at this place,' McBride said. 'It's like an unoccupied feckin' hotel room.' It was true. Evangeline Walter's life and lifestyle was still mostly a blank. It was almost as if someone had erased her. Cancelled her out, vacuumed her up. It seemed unlikely that, in the few hours between her death and the discovery of the body, the whole house could have been stripped so efficiently. For one thing, there was no sense of disturbance, none of the hallmarks of panic. It wasn't just the study which was so unnaturally neat; the whole house was pristine. When, on a hunch, Recaldo picked up a small maquette of a bull from a side table, sure enough there was a tiny star marking its exact position. And the same proved true of the other few sculptures in the living room. That was another odd thing, there were many valuable items in the house, some small enough to shift easily, but nothing had been disturbed. The markers had proved doubly useful. In all senses, everything was in its place. Except for her personal effects.

'Should I go and collect the post?' Recaldo broke an awkward silence.

'No, that's OK. I picked it up on the way through Duncreagh this morning. There was nothing of interest.' McBride was rifling through a box file, one of ten or more relating to art topics on the shelf above her desk. 'Bingo!' he shouted and held out a clutch of utility bills. They appeared to be for the previous six months, all neatly in order and marked paid, including some very large phone bills. Yet there were no itemized printouts of calls, such as generally accompany the quarterly accounts. Frustrating because these, of course, would be potentially the most useful for tracking friends and business contacts.

McBride immediately made a long and intensely irritable call to the Eircom accounts office which finally, after a huge outburst, got him in direct contact with the head mucky-muck who promised to fax the printouts to headquarters. 'I'll get onto it straight away,' he said – this was close to eleven o'clock. 'I'll get them to you by the morning.'

'No, today,' McBride barked. 'I will be along, in person, to collect them around four. Make sure they're ready.'

'These all run from April,' Recaldo said. 'I bet there's a tax file somewhere. Is there an attic, I wonder?'

There wasn't. But somewhere, somehow, Evangeline Walter had stashed all her personal papers.

'It's like going through treacle. Do you think she might have cleared everything herself? Surely she must have known she was dying?'

McBride paused for thought. 'We don't know that for sure – until Coffey passes on the consultant's verdict. Anyway very few people act like that. In my experience most people continue to hope to the bitter end.'

'Didn't O'Dowd mention that she was thinking of a holiday in the sun? Florida? I'd guess she may have been looking for alternative treatment?'

'Not bad. But would she have moved to the States permanently?' McBride said. 'I wish I could see a pattern in all this. Apart from frustration. You know, I think someone has been very, very clever. But who? That's the question.'

After that they fell silent and, having divided the dozen or more box files between them, they went through the contents page by page. It was tedious and worryingly unproductive; nothing relevant turned up. McBride finally called a halt at twelve.

'I'll have a word with the boss and then I'm off down to Hussey's to talk to the hacks. This might be the moment to see if you can dig up anything useful from Ms O'Faolain. We need to know more about her lifestyle. Link her with other people. Where did her money come from? That kind of thing.'

'Are you coming back here?'

McBride scratched his head. 'I'm not sure. There's a few things to sort out in Cork and I want to talk to Dr Morrow. I'll let you know my movements. After you finish in Daingean come back here in case that Grace woman turns up. You're to get in touch immediately if she shows up tonight, with or without the man. Keep hold of her till we get a chance to talk to her tomorrow. Oh and find out exactly where that Donovan woman is, phone us with the ward number and we'll pop in and talk to her. Is that everything?'

'Marilyn is getting out of hospital sometime today. If you don't nab her, I'll call in and see her later. What about DNA testing?'

'What about it? You can't test if there's no-one to test, can you? Apart from O'Dowd and Spain, of course. No, don't look shocked. Coffey thinks we should wait for a day or two.' He rolled his eyes. 'Not a man I like to argue with.'

'But surely . . .'

'I'm relieved you're so anxious, FX. Are you volunteering yourself, by any chance?'

'If you wish,' said Recaldo stiffly, realizing he had neatly boxed himself into a corner. 'After I see Ms O'Faolain, I'll see if I can track down the Sweeneys, and keep an eye on O'Dowd as well. OK?'

'Jaysus, FX, you won't have time to bless yourself with all that,' McBride joked. 'Are you sure you're up to it?'

'In what way?' Recaldo asked blandly.

'Any way you care to take it. Adios, FX. See ya tomorrow.'

Chapter Sixteen

AS THE TWO MEN LEFT THE HOUSE MCBRIDE OBSERVED, 'I WAS thinking, FX, you must be falling a bit behind with your routine stuff. D'you think it might be a good idea to put it about that you're no longer on the case?' He made it sound as though the idea had just come to him. 'Otherwise you're going to be mobbed every time you show your face down in the village,' he added. He raised his eyebrows and gave Recaldo one of his more duplicitous grins. 'Don't look so suspicious, I'm only thinking of you − it might be a way of shifting the interest, don't you know.'

'Where to? Cork? Or are we not talking geography?' Recaldo asked smoothly.

McBride laughed. 'Well now, I wouldn't say that.' He got into his car and rolled down the window. 'See ya,' he said breezily and shot away.

Recaldo followed him down the drive and, though he knew it was a pointless exercise, laboriously secured the gate. The Jeep was reluctant to start. 'Don't let me down now,' he pleaded. The engine coughed and spluttered four or five times before it fired, then wheezed and groaned along the lane, protesting vigorously every time he hit a pothole. He took the twenty-five miles to Daingean at a leisurely pace but by the time he arrived it was running smoothly enough.

The entrance to the O'Faolain gallery was through a sombrely painted, unobtrusive, traditional shopfront, which opened into a vast white space about the size and shape of a modest warehouse. Subdued natural lighting came from milk-glass panels in the roof, with directional artificial light from tiny spots on a system of steel tracking high on the walls. There were seven hugely colourful canvases on display and in the centre of the room an open grand piano. He went over to it and let his fingers hover silently above the notes.

Ms O'Faolain was talking on the phone in a small office at the back of the room. He recognized her voice before he caught sight of her in the open doorway. She waved a hand. 'Won't be long,' she mouthed, and pointed to the receiver. Recaldo wandered around the exhibition until she came bustling out to meet him. He was relieved to discover that her phone voice was in no way indicative of the way she normally spoke. Posh Cork certainly, Montenotte at a guess, but in the flesh she was not nearly so affected. She was affability personified.

'I'm Rose O'Faolain.' She was an attractive, florid, handsome woman with unruly pepper-and-salt hair and a terrific smile. She looked comfortable with herself and her looks. A big woman in all senses: weight, size and personality. She was wearing a long, loose, deep red garment – dress was too mean a word for it – with a finely knitted dark maroon jacket. A pair of bright red spectacles was dangling from a chain around her neck. Rose. Her name suited her. He almost burst out laughing when he noticed that her large feet were encased in fuchsia-coloured satin track shoes.

'Mr Recaldo, is it?' She crushed his hand in both of hers. There were rings on every finger. 'What a name you have,' she gushed. 'A vice-admiral of the Spanish Armada was called Recalde, did you know that?' She threw up her hands and laughed. 'But of course you did, what am I thinking of, at all?'

Recaldo smiled. 'I see we've been reading the same book,' he said, but he was so tickled that she knew his putative ancestor's rank, he became unusually animated. 'Don Juan Martinez de Recalde. He ran his ship through the Blasket Island Sound in a storm. An amazing feat, if you know that part of the world. The ships pursuing him were smashed to bits. Or at least that's the story in our place. My family's always lived around Dingle. We claim his ancestry but there's no real way of verifying it – not that I haven't tried.'

'You certainly have the looks.' She held back her head and surveyed him sideways. 'Velasquez? Goya?' He noted, with relief, that she didn't suggest that specialist in canvas cadavers, El Greco.

'He wasn't Spanish, by the way, he was Basque,' Recaldo said, getting well into it.

'Oh? That's interesting,' she smiled. 'So you're from Dingle, eh? My mother-in-law's family was from Kerry, not far from the Blaskets as a matter of fact – Ventry. *De Recalde.*' She rolled the name around her tongue, emphasizing the final e with satisfaction. 'Splendid name. When did the o get tacked on?'

'There are those who say we'd have done better to put it first,' he said laconically.

'O'Recalde?' She wrinkled her nose. 'Ah come on, that'd be a bit contrived – but then so is O'Faolain I suppose. The family was plain Whelan until my father-in-law started using the Irish form. He felt it sounded better.' She laughed. 'And I must say I agree with him.' She snorted. 'But I don't suppose you came here to swap family histories, Mr Recaldo? Or names for that matter. Though I wouldn't mind doing that some other time.'

'Neither would I, Mrs O'Faolain,' he said, mildly surprised by the warmth of his response.

'Oh for heaven's sake, call me Rose,' she said impatiently and glanced at her watch. 'I usually go to the pub next door about now, for a bite to eat. Would you like to join me? My assistant should be back from lunch any minute.'

When Recaldo demurred, she said briskly, 'Look, I don't know about you, but I'm ravenous. A bowl of chowder and a sandwich is what I always have, and that's what I'm offering you. You can eat or not, as you wish, but if you want to talk the pub's usually quiet at this hour and the phone won't interrupt us. Ah, here's Martin now.'

'Didn't Cressida Sweeney once work for you?' Recaldo asked as they left the gallery.

Rose O'Faolain looked at him with interest. 'She used to, but that was a while ago, before Gil was born, though she still comes in from time to time, to help out when I'm stuck.' She cocked her head to one side and smiled archly. 'You look disappointed, Mr Recaldo.'

'Not at all,' he protested.

'Cressie's much too busy these days with Gil. She teaches him herself, the poor child couldn't manage school at all. He's deaf, did you know?'

'Yes,' he said. 'But I believe he's coming on well.'

'That new hearing device they fitted him up with is great altogether. It's some sort of radio-controlled thing, I must say it's made a huge difference. She dropped in with him early last week. His speech is also improving in leaps and bounds. Mind you, he's a very bright little boy, he was reading and writing before he could say a word. I really admire young Cressie. She's a great girl, never complains.'

All this was music to Recaldo's ears and he encouraged Rose to continue her paean as they strolled the few yards to the pub. They were shown to 'your usual, Rose?' table tucked away in an old-fashioned snug at the back of the bar. It was already set for one, complete with a starched white linen cloth. A young woman quickly added a second place setting. Rose ordered a half-bottle of Volnay and a jug of tap water. 'I hate that bottled muck,' she explained. She and the waitress had an elliptical discussion – more a series of grunts – on what to eat.

'Prawn chowder and smoked *wild* salmon sandwiches,' Rose announced firmly. They made small talk until two large bowls of pale pink soup and a heaped plate of sandwiches were brought to the table.

She watched him taste the soup. 'Well?' she asked.

'Terrific.'

'Don't sound so surprised,' she countered robustly. 'You look half-starved. When was the last time you ate properly?' It was like getting caught up in a maelstrom, but, oddly, this most private of men found her friendliness infectious. She was easy to like, relax with, and he found himself wishing they could socialize the afternoon away. He'd had more than enough male company over the past couple of days. Weeks. Years.

'Do you play the piano?' she asked, catching him off guard as he was about to start quizzing her. 'I noticed you admiring it while I was on the phone,' she added hurriedly.

'I'm a bit out of practice – my cottage is too small for a piano.' He gave her a self-deprecating smile and shrugged. 'I sometimes play at my local hotel in the evenings. Wallpaper stuff mostly but I throw in a bit of Bach when they're not looking.'

'Aha. I thought your fingers were itching.'

He let out a great guffaw of laughter. 'You're an observant woman, Mrs O'Faolain – Rose. Tell me, what's a Steinway doing in the gallery?'

'It lives there,' she laughed, then held up her hand. 'Not all the time, but we have a recital on Sunday night – you should come, a young chap called Matthew Rosen will be playing some Field nocturnes and Chopin.'

'I'd like to, if I can. Actually, I heard him playing in Dublin a few months back. I enjoyed it.'

'Well I'll save you a ticket so, and put you on my mailing list, will I?'

'Do.' He cleared his throat. 'Now, if you don't mind, I'd like to ask you a few questions about Mrs Walter,' he said.

'Poor Evangeline. What can I tell you?' she asked.

'Everything. For a start, what was she doing here? What sort of woman was she? How long have you known her? Who were her friends? Anything at all would help.' He had already gleaned from her casual manner that Mrs Walter had not been a close friend, since she didn't seem especially distressed about her death.

'Whoa,' she laughed, 'I get the picture. Let's see . . .' She massaged her chin thoughtfully. 'I suppose I first met her about, oh it must be almost twenty years ago. We were both doing some course or other in London – at the Courtauld. I recognized her name because I'd begun to see articles by her in various art publications – I've been in the business nearly thirty years, by the way. We kind of fell in together and afterwards kept in vague touch. I suppose it was inevitable that I'd one day ask her to do some catalogue notes for me. It was really a pretext for sounding her out about something else.'

'Oh?' He pricked up his ears. 'What was that?'

'Well, the Atlantis Hotel in Passage South was just about to open – first time around – that's where you play presumably? Yes? Well, the owner, Otto Bleiberg, was an old customer of mine and asked if I'd be prepared to buy some "art works" for the public rooms. I knew Evangeline did a bit of that sort of thing from time to time, so I ran the scheme past her. She came over and met Otto. They got on like a house on fire. He was very much more impressed by her than me.' She smiled ruefully. 'Still, I managed to hang on in there.' She leaned towards him confidentially. 'We evolved a sort of casual arrangement and put together a few – not many – collections for other hotels over the years, including the new Atlantis. Nice work when you can get it,' she cackled. 'Pays well.'

145

'Did you have a contract between you?'

'What?' she asked, puzzled.

'A formal contract – did you use a solicitor?'

'Oh, of course, I see. We did, but only on an ad hoc basis, whenever we took on a commission together. We used a chap called Gough – his office is on the South Mall in Cork.' She tore a page out of a pocket notebook and jotted the address and phone number on it. 'There, in case you want to get in touch. He's not my family solicitor, by the way, nor hers either. I'm fairly certain she had her own – in Dublin.'

'Any idea who?'

'Well now, I believe she mentioned a name once, let's see what was it?' She sucked in her lower lip. 'It was a series of names . . . Boland was one. Boland and . . . Boland Callaway and something hyphenated. Very Dickensian.'

'That's marvellous, thank you. I should be able to track them down. Can you tell me when she settled in Trianach?'

Rose seemed surprised at the question. 'It was some considerable time after that first Atlantis job. The funny thing is, I hadn't actually realized she was living in the vicinity until she dropped in to see me one day. Let's see, it must have been about six or seven years ago. She just turned up, "to show her face", she said, and offered to do some more catalogue notes for me. I was quite surprised when she casually announced she'd recently moved into the area. I only found out by accident exactly where – she was careful not to mention it herself *or* that she'd been in residence in Otto Bleiberg's old place for nearly a year. I was surprised, to say the least.' She made a sour face. 'Mind you, it took me even longer to figure out she'd been living with him since his wife died. Maybe even before,' she added half to herself. She looked at him thoughtfully. 'Evangeline Walter certainly didn't let the grass grow under her feet. She was some operator. Other than that, what do I know about her? Let's see.' She began to count the items on her fingers. 'American, of course. Midwestern. Minnesota – St Paul, I think, would that be right? But she's lived all over the place: Kyoto, Rome, Munich, Vienna, London, France – Pont Aven, among other places – that's where she became interested in Roderick O'Conor and other Irish painters who worked there at the turn of the century. From that she got hooked into the modern scene here.'

She smiled across the table. 'I seem to know more than I thought, don't I?' she chuckled. 'But of course I'm cheating, extrapolating from what I remember of the various collections she's written up. And the list is even longer. Her age? I can only speculate on that, my guess would be about mid to late forties, though she looks younger. She's a walking advertisement for the old nips and tucks. Was. Sorry. She could always pull the men. Her favourite phrase was *he's wild about me*. Indiscriminately and universally applied,' she added cattily. 'It would appear that all the men were mad about Evangeline.'

'Did you socialize much? Were you often at her house?'

'Not often, she was a surprisingly poor host. Well, perhaps not all that surprising, she hadn't a very . . .' she shrugged, '*giving* personality. I went a few times to drinks parties. Gruesome affairs they were too – Evangeline was strictly anti-food, she never served anything to eat and she always scrimped on the wine. Oddly enough, she was rather awkward socially; never quite got it right. At parties she only drank mineral water, so while the rest of us got paralytic, she remained cool and collected. Ah well, some of us never learn.' She made a face. 'I seldom went there, more often than not we discussed business at the gallery.' She paused for reflection. 'Oh, hang on, one time she loaned a couple of paintings for an exhibition and I went to view them beforehand.' She laughed. 'Extraordinary. It's a fantastic house but the way she kept it . . .' She threw up her hands. 'Like an operating theatre. Unreal. Unbelievably tidy. The sort of place that makes you sure you're dragging in dog shit on your shoes. I was so uncomfortable, I could hardly sit down. That how you found it?' she asked cosily. 'And of course, not a bite to eat. She was always on some flaky diet or other. To tell you the truth she was a bit punitive about food. God knows, I was lucky to get a drink out of her.' She gasped, as if suddenly recollecting the old adage of not speaking ill of the dead, or perhaps she had simply remembered the purpose of his visit; in any case she clapped her hand over her mouth. 'Can you tell me how it happened?' Her face was sombre.

'I'm sorry, Rose, all I can tell you is that her body was found in the garden early yesterday morning. She probably died late on Tuesday night.'

'I hope she didn't suffer and I hope there wasn't a mess, she couldn't have borne that.'

He shook his head. 'I'm afraid death is messy, even natural death.' He paused. '*The harvest fields are dunged with rotten death,*' he misquoted, half to himself.

'That's a line from Thompson, isn't it?'

Recaldo looked mystified. 'I've no idea. It's just something that's been running around my head the last day or so.'

'Francis Thompson. "The Hound of Heaven". Though I'm not sure you've got it quite right.'

'I'm surprised I got it at all,' he laughed. 'We had that wretched poem drilled into us at school though I never managed to learn the whole thing.' He paused. 'You might like to know that the person who found her described her as beautiful,' he said.

'She'd have expected that. Evangeline was very vain.'

'Yes, so I gathered. Odd there are so few photographs of her in the house.'

'Come again?'

'We could find only a couple of photographs, old ones, and very few personal effects.' Coffey would have his guts for garters if he heard him. 'Apart from her clothes, that is.'

Rose O'Faolain screwed up her eyes as if she was looking back into the past. 'There were certainly three or four rather beautiful black and white studies framed in the living room.' She laughed. 'Of herself of course, who else?' She thought for a minute. 'But there was something . . . The day I went to collect the paintings, I arrived a bit earlier than she expected. It was the sort of thing that irritated her – though you'd have thought she'd be used to it, living here, where no-one pays any heed to punctuality. Anyway, while she went to the kitchen to open a bottle of wine, I walked down the steps into that wonderful living room. I remember the blinds were half-drawn and the lights were on, everything in its precise place except the Rothko, which had been taken down and was standing on the floor, leaning against a small table. It's a nineteenth-century mahogany card table,' she added precisely, 'with one of those tops which swivels around to reveal the storage space beneath. I don't suppose I'd have particularly noticed it except that it was standing open. I was just about to snoop when she came back, casually twisted it closed and set the drinks tray on top. I'm almost sure it was full of cuttings, photographs.' She thought for another minute. 'Yes, there was one of a beautiful young girl on top. It might have been her, though I didn't get a good enough look.'

'Do you know anything about her background? She was a divorcee, wasn't she? What about her husband?'

'Next of kin, you mean?'

'Well, yes, that would be of great assistance.'

'She was divorced when I met her, or at least that's how she described herself, though she never actually referred to a husband by name. Mind you, someone once told me there was more than one. But I can't help you there, I'm afraid. Maybe the Dublin solicitor might be able to?'

'Had she a family?'

'Children?' Rose gave a snort of derision. 'I see you didn't know her, did you? She was one of the few women I've ever met who seemed to have a complete antipathy to children. Ask Cressie Sweeney, she'll tell you.'

He pricked up his ears. 'How's that?'

'She used to be very nice to Cressie while she worked here.' She paused. 'Now that I think about it, Evangeline made the running with Cress, kind of wooed her, in a strange sort of way. There was quite a disparity in age, of course – Evangeline was almost old enough to be her mother,' she laughed, 'though she wouldn't thank me for saying so. Nonetheless a friendship of sorts developed between them. But then, blow me down if Evangeline didn't casually drop her. It was while Cressie was pregnant with Gil and she was hurt and upset. God knows she has little enough companionship.'

'What about Mr Sweeney? Was she friendly with both of them?'

Rose sighed. 'Alas and alack,' she said dramatically.

'How so?'

Rose raised her eyebrows at him. 'She met VJ here. The whole thing was very unfortunate. It was at an opening. Usually he didn't show up but that time he did. Gil was with them, bedded down and fast asleep in my office, and Cress was helping with the drinks. I was talking to VJ when Evangeline suddenly appeared at my elbow. I thought she would have already met him through Cress – after all they are more or less neighbours – so I was surprised when she asked to be introduced. I left them talking and spent some time circulating. The place was crowded. I suppose it was about half an hour later that I noticed

149

them in a huddle in the corner. By then VJ was well oiled. Evangeline was all over him – shining eyes, dazzling smile, the whole bit.'

'When was this?'

Rose thought for a moment. 'It was shortly after Gil was diagnosed and Cressie was still in a state about it. Blaming herself for not spotting the hearing problem earlier. It hadn't been picked up in the early baby tests and it was only when he turned two that she became really worried that he hadn't made any attempt to talk, specially since he was such an alert child otherwise. He'd just had his birthday, so it would be around five years ago.'

'Did they see much of each other?'

'Evangeline and VJ? Don't ask me.' She shook her head sadly. 'She knew I was very fond of Cressie so she'd hardly discuss that particular conquest with me, now would she?'

'I don't suppose so. If it was a conquest?'

'I'm not sure Evangeline was into any other sort of relationship,' Rose said shortly.

'Do you know Mr Sweeney well?' Recaldo asked neutrally.

Rose wasn't quite so cautious. She wagged her head sadly from side to side. 'Not a very nice man. Charming – certainly when I first met him shortly after he and Cressie were married. Extremely goodlooking, tall and blond, athletic, youthful, though he was in his mid-forties then, I believe. His looks began to go, of course, once he started in on the booze after his business in London collapsed.'

'Do you know why it failed?'

'Too many eggs in too few baskets, it seems. One of those Eighties bubbles which went' – she made a cutting gesture with her hand – 'just like that, right down the tubes. He arranged sports sponsorships but only took on really big accounts with high-profile sports: Grand Prix cars, round-the-world yacht races, eventing, that sort of thing, matching them with sponsors in the tobacco and drinks industries. They were pretty well scuppered with the UK legislation banning tobacco advertising, but it seems they would have survived if one of his partners hadn't done a runner taking two-thirds of their remaining client list with him.'

'And this all happened after they came to live here?'

'Oh yes – several years after, though I'm not entirely sure when. It was certainly sometime after all the renovation work on the house was done and Cressie was living here permanently. She'd pretty well stopped going to London once she became pregnant. So it must have happened some months after Gil was born because Cressie was back here part-time.'

'How did she come to be working for you?'

'She had a job in a friend's gallery in London where I'd met her a few times. This was before VJ appeared on the scene. When they moved here my friend recommended her to me. It worked out very well. She was very keen and I loved having her around.' Rose cupped her chin in her hand. 'Ireland has been good for Cressie – given her confidence in herself.'

Recaldo smiled faintly. 'Maybe you had something to do with that?'

'Well, maybe.' Rose sounded doubtful. 'But she's very good with customers. They feel comfortable with her low-key approach.' She laughed. 'It's a pretty effective sales ploy – people seem to feel they have to impress her. She can have a full-time job here any time she likes.'

'How long did she work for you?' The unaccustomed pleasure of talking openly about his beloved knocked him momentarily off-track but Rose gave no indication that she noticed.

'On a regular basis for three or four years before and after Gil was born. The child was always with her but he's a good little fellow so I never minded that.'

'Why did she continue?' he asked curiously. 'She didn't have to, did she?'

'You mean they're wealthy?' Her eyebrows shot up under her fringe. 'Dear me, Mr Recaldo, you're not very PC, are you?' She lowered her voice conspiratorially. 'But as it happens you have a point. Dear VJ was not a generous man.'

'How do you know?'

'Little things. For instance, how much the pittance she earned meant to her. VJ was a great one for the big gestures, at least until the crash. He spent a fortune doing up the house – and I'll tell you an interesting thing about that, though perhaps I shouldn't. Cressie came to see me a couple of weeks ago, in an awful state. She'd only just found out what a precarious situation she was in.' Rose absently polished her glasses before continuing. 'It seems that the house – Coribeen – came with only a small parcel of land which just about covered access to the road and an apron of garden around the house. But when she inherited it, VJ cannily bought the surrounding land including about five acres of river front, making twenty or thirty in all. Now I don't quite know how he managed this, but apparently *he* is registered as owner of *all* the land, even the original access which isn't used any more since the driveway was laid down. What it seems to mean is that Cressida only owns the bricks and mortar. Which could make for certain difficulties, wouldn't you say?'

This was news to Recaldo and he was appalled Cressie hadn't told him. He sat back in his chair and rubbed his chin with his hand, over and over. 'But that can't be, can it?' he asked eventually.

'You wouldn't think so, would you? But somehow it is, however it was done. When she tackled him it seems he tried to convince her that she'd knowingly *and* willingly surrendered the land against the cost of doing up the house. What she thought was a gift was nothing of the sort.' Rose looked outraged. 'Can you believe it? What it amounts to is that his nibs can sell the land, but she can't sell the house. What do you think of that?'

'Not much. You?'

'Ditto. I sent her off to Cormac Gough for proper legal advice, as a matter of fact. It's outrageous. The girl has no money of her own and a disabled child to bring up, otherwise, I believe, she'd have left him long ago. Frankly, if he did that to me, I'd kill the bastard.'

'How was Sweeney with the boy?' Recaldo asked, as if he didn't know.

'Oh, he was delighted with his splendid son until he realized the unfortunate child was deaf. After that, a total jerk,' Rose said acidly and, once started, let forth a furious diatribe. 'He blamed everyone: doctors, hospitals, and most of all his poor wife. Well, I mean macho man himself would hardly have brought forth an oddity, would he, now? Given his disdain for the Irish health service you'd have thought he'd have whisked the child off to Harley Street, wouldn't you? But not a bit of it. He just ignored the boy, wouldn't have anything further to do with him. And not all that much to do with Cressie either,' she added half under her breath.

'She confides in you.' There was relief in his voice.

Rose shrugged regretfully. 'She used to but sadly, not so much recently. She's become very, very isolated, poor girl. Obsessed with the house. She won't leave it. But then why should she? It's practically all she's got. And no matter what VJ thinks, Gil is getting excellent treatment here and is coming on splendidly. She has some old chap tutoring him, which is marvellous. She's hoping he'll be able to cope with school soon.'

Recaldo was silent for a moment. 'Was Sweeney's affair with Evangeline still ongoing?' he murmured presently.

'Ah, I wondered when you'd get back to her. Look, Mr Recaldo, I'm not even sure if there was an affair. I really shouldn't have shot my mouth off about the Sweeneys. Cressie would be very upset.'

'It's all right, Rose, I'll be discreet.' He paused. 'Now, can you tell me anything more about Mrs Walter? Her friends, for instance?'

Rose pushed her plate away and leaned across the table. 'She used people, including me. Until now I never admitted that, even to myself. So while I'm being honest . . . I wasn't really a friend of hers. She did a lot of work for me but that's different, I couldn't fault her there. But she never once, in all the years I knew her, passed on a single useful contact. Or introduced buyers to my gallery. What Evangeline had, she kept. She was very businesslike, very, very sharp about money. Sometimes unpleasantly so. In the end, I was just someone who provided her with work, that's all. She was reliable, hard-working and meticulous. If she promised copy for my catalogues, it would be on time with all the facts checked. She even copy-edited her own work. Always. She was a rather pedestrian writer, but accurate. However, her nose for an up-and-coming artist was absolutely spot on. Another thing, she could charm even the most reluctant collector into sharing his thoughts with her. Provided they were male, of course.' She paused while the waitress cleared the table and poured coffee for them from a large cafetière.

'What brought her to Ireland?'

'Well, you know, I've often wondered that myself. I mean you and I might think of it as the centre of the earth and all that, but I do think it strange to cut yourself off so entirely from your roots. But then she was odd, a one-off. She seems to have led a very nomadic existence.' She looked at him slyly.

'Have I caught you on a raw spot, by any chance?' she asked, seeing his expression. When he didn't reply she grew serious. 'Actually, this is not a bad place for her kind of work. She syndicated all over the world so I guess she did quite well, financially. And I suppose it was rather perspicacious of her to get stuck in here so early on, what with the Celtic tiger and all that. There's a great deal of new money in Ireland these days, some very exciting young artists and, most important from her point of view, a number of international collectors have settled, or have second homes here. For the last few years she's made a speciality of writing profiles of collectors and their collections.'

'But why here, specifically? Does the same hold true?'

She shrugged. 'Well, there are certainly some very well-heeled people about and of course Otto Bleiberg knew most of them. He was an expansive host, with a real gift for friendship.'

'And she hadn't this gift?' Recaldo asked diffidently.

Rose was silent for a moment. 'I'd be very interested to know if you manage to find *anyone*, any single person, who knows – knew – Evangeline Walter well,' she said softly. 'She compartmentalized her life more than anyone I've ever encountered. She kept her friends separate and her business to herself.'

'Was that particularly odd?' Recaldo asked innocently. It seemed broadly similar to his own modus operandi, which he considered perfectly normal.

Rose raised an eyebrow and looked at him knowingly. 'Well, *I* think so. But what really bothered me was the way she magpied *my* friends and never let on. I was hurt because a lot of them were also professional colleagues. The art world in Ireland isn't that extensive. There's quite a lot of gossip and rivalry. And friendships. These were all valuable contacts for a woman like Evangeline Walter.' She sat back in her chair and watched him unblinkingly.

'I'm puzzled about her settling on Trianach. It seems very isolated for someone with her' – he hunched his shoulders – 'rather urban interests.'

'Aah. Now that, as they say, is a point verging on the moot. She certainly never volunteered any specific reason. Otto Bleiberg's house – and his contacts – would be my bet. I assume it was hers for the asking. I suppose you know it was originally a grain store? There's quite a few of them, built along the remoter estuaries of the county, just far enough in not to be too noticeable, but with easy access for shipping. Vast quantities of grain were being exported even during the famine times. Something that sticks in my throat, I'm afraid.'

Listening to her, Recaldo decided she must have been a teacher in a previous, less flamboyant incarnation. He was intrigued that she thought the hotel man owned the house but made no attempt to enlighten her. His real interest was that the house connected Bleiberg to Walter to O'Dowd – and thus to the hotel? Busy with these thoughts he let Rose ramble on, listening with only half an ear for stray bits of useful information.

'The place was derelict when Otto did the conversion. He and his wife lived there until they retired to Madeira, to the very hotel which inspired the Atlantis in the first place – Reid's Palace. It's a fabulous old place, wildly expensive. Built into the living cliffs, overhanging the sea, as the Atlantis is.' She hooted with laughter. 'We spent a short winter break there, a couple of years ago. The clientele was so old, I told my husband I felt like a young chick. Very good for the morale, it was. For both of us.'

'Did Mrs Walter live with Otto Bleiberg in Madeira?'

'She never said but I wouldn't have thought so. I believe he left Madeira after his wife died and went back to Switzerland – Zurich. That's probably a more likely location. Much more Evangeline's scene.'

The list ran single file through Recaldo's head: Bleiberg, Walter, O'Dowd, Sweeney. The Atlantis seemed also to have shimmied into the picture. Sweeney had some involvement in the hotel. He felt a familiar tingle of excitement at the back of his skull.

'I believe the Trianach house was idle for a long time before she moved in.' He paused, trying to frame his next question and at the same time feeling ashamed that he was being so devious with her. 'Was it ever for sale?'

Rose shrugged. 'It was certainly never on the open market. The gossip is that old Bleiberg left it to her. I've no idea if that's true or not. You could ask his son Joachim I suppose, though he's rarely around these days.'

'I'll do that,' he promised.

'I'd be circumspect, if I were you. I'm not sure how well Joachim knows – knew – Evangeline. To be honest, I've only just realized how little I knew her myself. Speculation or even facts don't make a person and that's the truth.'

'Did you like her?' he asked bluntly.

Rose refilled her cup and slowly sweetened it with sugar, grain by grain. 'Evangeline Walter puzzled me,' she said at last. 'To be honest, I never knew which way the wind was blowing with her. She had a strange trick of beaming specific pictures of herself. One for you, a different one for me. In multiple variables. Odd woman. Utterly, utterly self-absorbed. The un-ageing appearance was part of it. The obsession with her figure. For Evangeline, artifice was all.'

She huddled closer to the table and shuddered slightly. 'I had respect for her scholarship, but no, I'm afraid I didn't like her. But then, she was never a woman's woman. Men were her natural prey.'

'Mrs O'Faolain? You mentioned on the phone that she was to meet someone on Friday, can you tell me who? I know you'd prefer not to, but it may be important.'

She sighed. 'Oh dear, I don't know why I was so uptight about that. The phone does that to me sometimes. Sorry. I was going to ask you what I should do. I haven't liked to ring and cancel, since you seemed not to want it known she was murdered. I take it she *was* murdered? There was a small mention of it in this morning's *Cork Examiner.*'

It seemed pointless to prevaricate. 'Yes, so there's not much we can do about the papers, I'm afraid. This morning's little effort was just the start. We're expecting the stampede any minute now.'

She frowned. 'Ghouls,' she pronounced succinctly. 'So what'll I say to my Canadian?'

'Your Canadian?'

'The man she was to meet on Friday.'

'Well, if you prefer, I could speak to him.'

'Yes, that might be best. His number is ex-directory but I'm sure he won't mind if I give it to you. His name is Alex Mure-Robertson, usually known as Mure. He has a horrendous Victorian castle on the Suir near Thurles which he seldom uses, but I happen to know he's there at the moment. He collects sculpture and stained glass – Harry Clarke, Evie Hone – wonderful stuff. When he rang to say he'd be coming over to see the exhibition tomorrow, I tipped Evangeline the wink. I knew she'd been wanting to meet him for ages.' Rose looked as though she deeply regretted this indiscretion and he wondered if this was the basis of her earlier reluctance to divulge the man's name.

'This may seem an odd question, but has Mr Mure-Robertson any business interests locally?'

Rose ran her fingers through her hair. 'I don't really know. However, he was a friend of Otto's so he may have shares in the hotel. At least in the original company – but other than that I don't know.'

Recaldo pushed his chair back and stood up. 'You've been a great help, Rose. Thank you very much for lunch. You were right, it was excellent. By the way, was Mrs Walter meeting Mure-Robertson in your gallery?'

Rose gave a hoot of laughter though she didn't look much amused. 'Oh Lord no, not Evangeline. You'd have to ask him where they arranged to meet.' She sighed and waggled her head in disbelief. 'I can't imagine why I kept doing her favours. Sometimes I think I need my head examined.'

'Natural generosity?' he said, with a faint smile. 'One last thing, did you ever see her with a fellow by the name of O'Dowd?'

She shook her head. 'I don't think so. The name's not familiar.'

'On the short side. Late forties, grey hair, fresh complexion. Smiles a lot.'

Rose looked at him thoughtfully. 'Does he drive a dark blue Mercedes?' Recaldo nodded. 'In that case, yes. He collected her from the gallery a few times. He never came in, just waited in the car.' She got up from the table and walked him to the pub door. 'Will there be a funeral?' she asked before he took his leave. 'Do you know where? Or when?'

'That'll depend on the relatives and when the body is released. But I'll let you know when I find out.'

'I'd be grateful.' Her expression as well as her voice was serious. 'And thanks for not warning me to keep quiet about all this. But I will, anyway.'

He treated her to another of his rare smiles and held out his hand.

'I wonder what sort of woman she really was?' Rose said. 'What she felt about anything?' She gave a little shiver. 'I'll never know now, will I?'

'I don't suppose you will.'

She looked past him, lost in thought. 'I wish I'd really liked her. I feel sad that I didn't make a bit more effort to get to know her properly. It seems a little pious to regret that now, but it occurs to me that she must have been very, very lonely.'

'Surely she lived the way she wanted?'

'I wonder. Think about it for a moment. We're all capable of putting on a brave face now and then, but all the time?'

'Why brave? What makes you think she was brave?'

'Because making your way alone – living alone – *is* brave.' She shuddered. 'I couldn't stand it five minutes.'

'But did she live alone?' he asked. 'You said yourself she had many male friends. Lovers.'

'Ah. I said that's what she *claimed*. Companionship, someone who really cared for her is something else again. I wonder who really knew her? I wonder whom she loved or who loved her? Who she turned to when she was down?'

He looked at her steadily. 'If we knew that, we'd probably know who killed her.'

Rose took his hand in both of hers. 'You'll come back and see me, when you've laid all this to rest? Resume our historical deliberations?'

'I'd enjoy that.' He was halfway across the road when she called him back.

'What about you, Mr Recaldo? Did *you* not know her?'

He slowly shook his head. 'Not really, I've lived in Passage South less than two years.'

'Surely you must have seen her around?'

'True enough, but not all that often. Why d'you ask?'

Rose looked him up and down. She was only a few inches shorter than him and her large brown eyes bored into his. She grinned mischievously. 'I would have thought you were exactly her type, Mr Recaldo. A bit of a mystery man. Tall, dark, handsome – or you would be if you took better care of yourself. Yes, you'd have interested Evangeline, all right. I'm surprised she never made a play for you.' She stuck her head to one side. 'Or perhaps she did?' she added archly.

He gave a little snort. 'You seriously think she'd have any truck with a country guard?'

'No, I'd guess she liked her lovers well heeled. But then you don't much look like a country anything, do you? Or act like one either. Pianos and poems, Mr Recaldo? So tell me, what is your story?'

Chapter Seventeen

IT WAS JUST BEFORE THREE WHEN RECALDO LEFT DAINGEAN. A FEW miles down the road he pulled into a lay-by and checked out Twomileborris on his road atlas. He dithered between phoning Coffey or McBride with his report, decided to play it by the book, and contacted Coffey with an edited but succinct report on his meeting with Rose. The superintendent listened without comment.

'Check the downstairs windows on the front have been boarded up, would you? I asked Phil to see to it,' Coffey said. This was news to Recaldo but when he drove to Evangeline Walter's house he found that McBride had indeed had the windows boarded, giving the house a neglected sad look. There was no sign of either journalists or what Coffey was pleased to call 'the American couple' who had left messages on the answerphone.

Recaldo blocked the padlocked gate with his car and walked rapidly down the lane to the shore to wait, as instructed, for the couple to show up. He sat on the low bank, held his face up to the dying sun and closed his eyes. While he soaked up the rays he mulled over his conversation with Rose O'Faolain. For the first time since the case started he felt properly in control.

It was a beautiful evening, with snowy white clouds tumbling and racing over the mountaintop, playing hide and seek with the radio masts on the summit. It had rained in fits and starts during the early part of the day, and shortly it would come rolling in again, as it had done, at regular intervals, since the previous morning. A stiff sea breeze ruffled the surface of the deep, deep aquamarine water. Out in the bay, a flotilla of tiny red and white sails whizzed about like a swarm of demented flies.

John Spain hove into view, instantly recognizable by his yellow overalls. His boat moved gently up and down with the swell. He sat hunched in the stern, one hand on the tiller, guiding it through the troughs and risers, up and down, down and up. Spain had a line out which he occasionally touched, then reeled in and recast. There were several other little fishing boats gathered where the river met the bay, near a perilous cluster of partially submerged rocks where a small flock of cormorants sat motionless, drying their outstretched wings. Overhead the seagulls dodged and wheeled, their strange raucous keening filling the air. A gannet or two flew nonchalantly past, surveying the scene.

Tiny wavelets danced along the surface, becoming more animated as the river narrowed. Further up, where tide met current, the water boiled in great swirling vortices as it scurried in and out of the little coves and inlets. Seagulls swooped and skidded along the surface and at the river's edge stilted wading birds bent and ducked. As the wind and water became more agitated the mast stays jingled and clanged like distant bells on mountain cattle. The *Halcyon* turned and twisted on her mooring rope as if inviting the smaller and drabber *Cynara* to join the dance. A partial rainbow appeared fleetingly in the spray, perhaps caused by the sun behind the boat, sparkling off the steel uprights of the deck stays.

On the opposite bank, at the very edge of the water, perky little dunlins dipped their heads in time to their rickety gait. A flock of late swallows swooped low over the rim of dead seaweed deposited by the tide. It was coloured pink and green, vibrant against the endless muted variation of the grey-brown stones. The fickle sun shone on the rolling hills, picking out the autumnal colours: gold, purple tinged the brown. In the distance a speck of red – a tractor – moved over and over the landscape. The fields were edged with low drystone walls. Not neat and ordered, but scrambled together as if in a despairing attempt at clearing the land of their irksome presence.

A maze of walls zigzagged down the hill to the bank on the opposite side to a small walled famine graveyard by the ruined church at the water's edge. There were fifty or more children buried beneath one simple cross there. Unnamed, unknown victims of the 1840s famines.

Country people carved their history into the land, he thought. Incomers were ephemeral. Tossed about until they washed up on some shore or other, temporary, fleeting, surprised that they were neither much welcomed when they arrived, nor missed when they drifted off to some other dreamland. Coming and going with the seasons, rushing about, clashing with the even rhythms of local life; causing turbulence with their restlessness, deluded by the natural beauty into thinking their transient lives could be transformed and enhanced by change. Invariably they remained essentially untouched. They brought their hang-ups and discontents with them and took them away when they left, intact and unresolved. Ill prepared by city life for humdrum permanency, they plucked and plundered what caught their eye and disrupted the frail economic stability until the inhabitants could no longer afford to live in the dwellings their forefathers built, nor till their ancestral soil.

The sun glinted on the blank windows of Coribeen. Recaldo focused his glasses, eagerly looking for some sign of life. His heart ached for a sight of Cressida. But the place was still deserted.

He set the binoculars down and pulled out his mobile, then dialled the Donovans' number on the off chance. The phone was answered by Marilyn's husband Steve who confirmed, through loud bellowing from baby Liam, that his wife had indeed had a miscarriage on Monday evening but was recovering.

'She's in Ward 10. They'd have let her out today but I can't manage to get up there till dinnertime tomorrow.'

'What time did she go in Monday?' Recaldo asked.

'Sometime around five, I think. No, it might have been nearer six. I wasn't here at the time. Mrs Hussey next door took the kids while Mrs Sweeney drove Marilyn to the hospital.' He had no idea when Mrs Sweeney got back, or even if. 'I'd say she's likely still in Cork,' he said.

'Why would you think that?'

'Well I would be, in her shoes. Things aren't so hot for her,' he added, 'from what Marilyn says.'

'Was Gil with her?'

'The dog? No.'

'Gil is her son,' Recaldo said tersely. 'The dog's called Finnegan.'

'Sorry,' Donovan said and told him that as far as he knew the child

162

hadn't been with her and he wasn't sure, but he thought the dog was in Mrs Reilly's kennels, near Kishaun.

Recaldo allowed himself a few minutes' reflection before ringing Coffey again to report his conversation with Donovan.

'Right, I'll try and have a word with Mrs Donovan, while she's here. Wait, hang on a second.' There was a murmur of voices in the background. Recaldo thought he recognized McBride's Dublin accent. 'Recaldo? Could you give me Donovan's home phone number? I better have a word with him before I see the missis. What about the Yanks?' he asked in a surly tone.

'No sign. I've blocked the gate with my car and I'm here waiting for them.'

'Hang on for another hour or so, will you? I'll give you a ring later, at home.'

If I'm there, Recaldo murmured and slipped his phone back in his pocket.

He thought about Rose O'Faolain again. She was right, getting a fix on Evangeline Walter was difficult. Trying to assess the local reaction to her death was more tricky, and at the same time, more disconcerting; as if, by getting killed in their midst – *getting herself killed* – the entire population was somehow implicated. The shame of it hung over the place like a miasma. A shiver ran down Recaldo's spine.

A plethora of information was whizzing around but leading nowhere. Like players in a demented game of poker, they were all offering theories rather than the truth: Spain, O'Dowd, and the Sweeneys, whose continued absence looked more damning with every passing hour. And himself, of course, for shielding Cressie.

In the light of his conversation with Rose O'Faolain, Recaldo reconsidered Smiler, and could not rid himself of the thought that O'Dowd would yield a great deal of information if he only knew which buttons to press. He worked carefully through O'Dowd's alibi, not just to the incident at Twomileborris but right back to the early afternoon on Tuesday. By implying that his destination was Dublin, Smiler had neatly avoided all mention of that afternoon's outing, thus signalling – to Recaldo at least – that it had some special significance he didn't want known.

Smiler had neatly implied that he was travelling to Dublin. 'I was on the Dublin–Cork road,' he'd said with a sly emphasis on Dublin.

Producing the corroborative garda from his hat was a masterstroke.

Might his destination have been much nearer? Like Twomileborris. Or Thurles?

Rose had offered a neat explanation which had rung a bell at the time and which he now examined again. The collector Evangeline was supposed to meet lived within spitting distance of where Smiler claimed to have broken down. This was confirmed by checking the exchange of Mure-Robertson's telephone number and his earlier consultation with the road atlas of Co. Tipperary. Had Evangeline sent O'Dowd there? And if so, why? Or had his journey – Recaldo turned this next thought over gingerly, since it was the wildest supposition – something to do with the girl Finbarr claimed was not Cressida? *Or was this yet another connection to the hotel?*

This brought him neatly to the woman herself. Somewhere in the back of his mind was the germ of an idea that Evangeline Walter had orchestrated the whole tragedy. Not her death – that would be too far-fetched – but the circumstances which led to it. The conditions for making it happen. Furthermore, he had the strong impression that there was one moment when each facet had been revealed to him, if he could but interpret what he'd heard or seen. Perhaps he would have done, he told himself disgustedly, had not his whole intelligence and ability been distorted by his confusion over Cressida. His concern for her and, to a lesser extent, John Spain irretrievably compromised his professional integrity. But even having accepted these uncomfortable truths he knew that he could not walk away. Would not. How else could he protect her?

He hesitated by the shore a while longer, watching the dying light play upon the water. Spain was still there, sitting forlornly in his boat with the hood of his jacket up, almost as if he was unable to leave the river. *Watching me, watching you.* And suddenly his heart was in his mouth. The answers were all there, spread out before him; the meaning was right there on the estuary.

He trained his binoculars onto the far bank and slowly ran his eyes along the surface of the water, looking for he knew not what. Something was changed but he couldn't see quite what it was. He ranged around an ever-decreasing circle until his eyes came back to rest on Spain's little clinker boat. As if aware of his scrutiny, the old man turned and seemed to look directly at him. He raised his hand to the hood of his jacket, as if in salutation, then pulled away, closer to the opposite bank. With a sickening jolt it occurred to Recaldo that he might not be looking at John Spain at all. The hunched figure in the boat, habitually wearing that bright yellow oilskin, might be anyone. Anyone at all. Man or woman. Cressida.

Oh bloody hell, he cried. He sprinted along the shore and into Walter's garden and around to the front of the deserted house. It had clouded over and the light was fading fast. Nearly seven. It seemed unlikely that Coffey's Yanks would show up. Either way, Recaldo no longer cared. He had things to do.

He drove at full pelt to Coribeen and then, more cautiously, up the drive. The mound of gravel had mysteriously disappeared. The Range Rover was parked outside the house.

Chapter Eighteen

HE PULLED UP HIS JACKET COLLAR AGAINST THE SEA MIST AS HE walked around to the front of the Jeep, where he leaned back against the bonnet, calmly watching Cressida through her filthy windscreen, giving her, and himself, time. He had no idea whether or not her husband was around. She had the engine idling. He waited until she turned it off and reluctantly opened the door. A sleepy blond head appeared behind her shoulder. She half turned and Gil crashed down on the back seat again. Cressida stepped out of her car.

'Mrs Sweeney.' Recaldo unfurled himself but remained half propped on the Jeep bonnet. She registered his formality with a nervous flick of the eye. 'Mr Recaldo,' she said awkwardly. After a moment she took a few steps in his direction, then stopped. She held her head unnaturally to one side, her eyes slewed off to his right. Her face was without make-up and very, very pale. She wore a mouldy old green Barbour jacket, buttoned up to the neck, with grimy gold-coloured cords stuffed into green wellingtons. Her hands were thrust deep into her pockets. Her long tawny hair, tucked behind her ears, was greasy and unkempt, as if she hadn't washed it for several days. She looked wretched. The mist formed a dim aureole around her. She reminded him of a drooping sunflower. All he could think of was how much he longed to hold her, protect her.

'Mrs Sweeney,' he said quietly, looking down, 'I've been looking for yourself and your husband.'

'I'm sorry, Val's away.' Her light sweet voice floated through the confusion of his thoughts. It was like hearing it for the first time and

166

he felt a rush of desire. He desperately wanted to lick the dew from her hair, run his tongue over her skin. He could almost taste the salt. I'd die for her, he thought. Die. Idiotically, he wondered if she could sing. Madrigals, he thought, or forlorn French ballads of courtly love. He cleared his throat. 'Where?'

'Where?' Her voice rose. 'I'm not sure. London, I suppose,' she said evasively, then immediately overdid it. 'I haven't spoken to him for a few days. Why do you want to know?' Her eyes darted this way and that. They were the same tawny colour as her hair. All he knew was that he was utterly and hopelessly in love with her and the present circumstances didn't change that one iota. On the contrary, his feelings were intensified.

'When does he get back?' He phrased the question carefully. The little boy stirred on the back seat of the Range Rover, then settled again. He was wrapped in a red and black chequered rug. Recaldo watched the movement as though through the wrong end of a telescope. The mist was soaking his hair and running in tiny rivulets down his face but she made no attempt to invite him into the house.

'Why do you want Val?' She kept her distance halfway between the cars as if poised for flight. Her cellphone rang once, then stopped.

'Have you not heard?' he started, then abruptly changed tack. He didn't want her to think he was trying to trip her up when he, most emphatically and against all his investigative training, was not.

'About Mrs Walter?' she asked hoarsely. She cleared her throat. 'Yes, I heard about it from Georgie O'Shea. I dropped in on her on my way through Duncreagh.'

'Who?' he asked, trying to curb his rampaging thoughts. A chill fear ran through his long spare frame like an icy stream.

'She runs the restaurant, Georgiana O,' she replied.

'Of course.' For a moment time stood still. Georgiana O was where he first laid eyes on Cressida Sweeney, only three or four months after he arrived. It was a bitterly cold Saturday in December and he'd gone into the bistro for lunch only to find it crowded. She had been sitting alone at a table for two just inside the door, wearing the same old Barbour jacket. When he asked if he could share, she'd sighed and put down her book. 'As long as you don't mind me reading,' she said, but at the same time pulled her shopping off the vacant seat. And smiled.

He packaged up that smile and took it away with him to remember during sleepless nights.

Her phone rang again. She smiled nervously. 'You better come in, Frank,' she said abruptly. She fumbled for her keys. 'I'll just carry Gil up to bed.'

He walked over to her car where Gil was struggling to sit up, still half-asleep. 'I'll do that,' he said quickly. As he leaned in to pick up the child, Gil sat up and rubbed his eyes. 'Tank.' He giggled sleepily. '. . . all Tank.' Tall Tank. Recaldo picked him up tenderly and to his utter joy the boy snuggled comfortably into his neck. 'Tank,' he whispered. 'Tank, Tank.'

As they went through the front door Recaldo glanced down. The note he'd dropped in the previous day wasn't there. He followed Cressida up the stairs to the second floor. He had never been inside the house. Gil's room overlooked the driveway. Their feet clattered over the bare boards. It was a large brightly painted room, full of toys and books and his own double bass leaning against the wall by the bed. He almost trod on the bow on the floor beside it as he laid the child gently on the bed. Only then did he notice that Gil's arm was bandaged and that a cut above his eye had been recently stitched. He didn't remark on it, nor on the fact that Cressida had dark bruising down one side of her face.

'Your phone keeps ringing,' he said. 'Why don't you answer it? I'll make a cup of tea.'

'Oh? Are you sure?' He couldn't tell if she was questioning his competence or if her uncertainty was due to some other, unspoken fear. *Of being surprised by Val?* 'I'll be down in a few minutes,' she said at last.

He padded quietly down the carpeted stairs to the hall. A large bowl on the hall table was chock-full of unopened mail. He rifled through it swiftly but didn't find the note. He noticed that the telephone jack was out of its socket.

The kitchen had a huge curtainless picture window behind the sink which faced south-west to the bay rather than straight onto the estuary. Recaldo kept the light off while he checked the view. Because he was tall enough he could lean over the sink and, twisting himself at an awkward angle, could catch, through the gloom, a glimpse of the handful of boats moored just below and to the left of Coribeen's dock. There was no sign of the yellow-clad Spain.

He looked around the kitchen. It was a large untidy room, strewn with bits of unglazed pottery and piles of books, with a vast old-fashioned oak dresser along one wall, crammed full of crockery with an old brass telescope on the lower shelf. A carton by the back door contained five empty wine bottles and four Vat 69. Pope's telephone number, he thought inconsequentially. The counter surrounding the sink was piled with dirty dishes, the floor was covered in muddy tracks. He compared the state of the room with Evangeline Walter's house. The women shared the same cleaner but it was clear that Evangeline, rather than Marilyn Donovan, was responsible for the unnatural tidiness of the American woman's house. He wondered when Marilyn had last cleaned for Cressie.

He filled the electric kettle, switched it on and checked that the tap water was hot before systematically attacking the dirty dishes, washing and stacking them neatly on the draining board. A couple of rather dubious looking tea towels draped in front of the cold Aga were examined and rejected. He'd almost finished when he heard a footfall and the sound of the front door opening.

He strode out to the hall. 'I put your double bass in your car,' Cressie said.

'Why?'

'Don't you have a gig in Duncreagh on Thursdays?'

'Someone else is standing in. You can hang onto it.' A few weeks back, he'd suggested that Gil might be able to 'hear' the sound through his bare feet. Cressie had learnt to play a few simple little tunes – nursery rhymes – on the instrument, to Gil's utter delight. He held out his wet hands. 'Is there a towel?'

'There's one in the hall cloakroom. I'll make the tea. Or would you prefer a drink?'

'Tea will be fine. I won't be a second.'

She was standing with her back to the window when he returned. She sensed him putting his hand out to switch on the light and swung around. 'Don't,' she said. She'd cleared a space at the end of the table for the teapot which had two china mugs beside it. She seemed more together, less nervous. She'd washed her face, tied her hair back and changed into a pair of khaki jeans and a long russet sweater. She looked more like a sunflower than ever.

'Frank.' She gave him a slow sweet smile. He went to her and swept her up in his arms. 'Oh Cressie, love, I've been so worried about you.' He held her close and traced the outline of her lips with the tip of his tongue, teasing her gently until she began to respond. They swayed together like dazed dancers. 'I love you,' he said. 'I've been out of my mind with love for you,' he whispered and kissed her.

She pulled away and gazed at him as if she was trying to memorize his face. She had dark rings under her eyes. 'You look tired,' she said, pre-empting any comment on her bruised face. She sat down at the head of the table with her back to the window. He took a chair to one side, where he could keep both door and window in his sights.

'What time did she die?' she blurted.

'Late on Tuesday night.'

'What does late mean?' she whispered.

'Somewhere between ten and one. It's not established yet. May never be.' *Another rule broken*. She took this in. He watched her struggling with some demon. 'Was your husband having an affair with her?'

She swallowed. 'I don't know. It's what I thought,' she murmured and put her hand unconsciously to her cheek. The tension between them returned. They sat quite still, as though separated by an invisible barrier.

'What happened to your face, Cressie?'

'Nothing. An accident. I bashed into a . . .'

'Door?'

'Yes. A door.'

'Gil too?' he asked, but she wouldn't answer.

She picked up the teapot and slowly filled the two mugs, pushed one towards him and held the other cupped in her hands. 'Georgie said she was murdered.'

'I wonder where she got hold of that? The papers?'

'She says it's all round the town that she was blu . . . bludgeoned.' The same source as Terry Whelan, then, Recaldo concluded grimly. 'On the head.'

'No. She was not,' he said tiredly.

She stared at him, her eyes like saucers. 'What then?'

'Cressie, love, you know I can't tell you that.' He was confused by her proximity and the unfocused questions. His future with her was hanging in the balance and he desperately did not want to lose her. He wanted to help her, tell her what to say and how to act. But suppose she wasn't there that night, suppose she wasn't involved? What then? Wouldn't she, ever after, blame him for suspecting her? By the same token, he could not lead her into incriminating anyone else, especially if that someone turned out to be her husband. Or John Spain: the man she regarded as a surrogate father. A man who would be hung drawn and quartered for the slightest involvement. Lia's report of Walter practically accusing Spain of child molestation in a crowded restaurant swam to the surface. Walter must have seen Spain in the boat with the child on Tuesday.

'Has Gil seen a doctor?' he asked. She nodded mutely. 'When, Cressie?'

Her phone sounded again. Twice. Her face flushed. 'I've been away, you know,' she said absently.

'Yes, Cressie, I know that. I was told you took Marilyn Donovan to the hospital in Cork.'

'She was so scared. She wouldn't let me go,' she babbled nervously. 'So terrified, I couldn't leave her. Look, I'm sorry but d'you mind coming back later, Frank? Or tomorrow? I'm really tired . . .' Her voice trailed away and her shoulders slumped.

'Where's Finnegan?'

'Huh? He's with . . . I took him to the Kishaun kennels before I picked up Marilyn on Monday. I didn't know how long I'd be.' Her fingers drummed on the table. He noticed three tiny, perfectly round scabs on the back of the hand he'd seen bandaged the previous week. They looked like cigarette burns. The bastard. She pulled her hand away when she saw him staring.

'Your husband's car is missing,' he persisted grimly.

'What?' She kept turning her head to the window. 'Val's away.'

'When did you last see the car?'

'Friday, Saturday?' she said vaguely after a moment's thought. 'I can't remember.'

'Was it here on Tuesday?'

'I was in the hospital with Marilyn. Why do I have to keep telling you?'

'It's a silver Lexus, isn't it? What's the registration?'

She sighed. 'Oh Frank, for heaven's sake . . . it's an English regis-tration. L 812 FLR,' she said. She bit her lip. 'I think.' Recaldo jotted it down on the back of his hand.

171

'The motor launch is gone from the dock.' He spoke firmly, grabbing for her attention. She frowned but her mind was elsewhere.

'What does that matter?'

'Oh shit, Cressida. We're investigating a woman's death. Don't you understand? It matters. Everything matters. This is *serious*. You've got to get a grip. Concentrate.'

'Yes, of course,' she said vaguely. Cressie was gone, Mrs Sweeney was back. She glanced off to the side again, wall-eyed, almost as if she had a cast. She looked as though she hadn't slept for a week. 'Kevin Corkery must have collected it and taken it to the boatyard. Or Terry Whelan. One of them anyway. I think it was to be overhauled and varnished.' Her hands constantly moved to her face, then pulled at her sweater. Everything about her screamed guilt.

He stretched out his hands to take hers but she pulled away. He eased himself towards the question he most wanted to ask. 'Where were you on Tuesday? I was waiting for you at Trabuí.' He spoke loudly and firmly.

'Oh Frank, I'm so sorry,' she cried. 'Oh I wish . . .' Her eyes began to swim.

'Cressie? Listen to me. Were you out sailing on Tuesday?'

She gave him a startled look. 'I never go out sailing . . . Anyway, Val's away. Didn't I say that?'

'Yes, you did.' He could barely stop himself from shouting: no, he is not. He tried a different line. 'Was Gil with you in Cork?'

'Gil is always with me.' She was close to tears. 'Don't you know anything?'

'Not on Tuesday, Cressie. I saw him out with John Spain.' Echoes of what Lia said resounded in his head. Oh my God, he thought. *They must have seen the boy with Spain.* Did Walter repeat then what she'd said in the restaurant?

She sat quite still. 'John helps with his lessons sometimes.'

'I know. But on his fishing boat?' She didn't answer. 'Are you sure you weren't on the yacht on Tuesday?'

'Why do you keep asking me that? No, no, no, no, no.' Her face was flushed and angry.

Who was that girl? And, more important, why did he keep harking back to her? Because the whole set-up struck him, even at the time, as odd. Now it occurred to him that the important question might well be, *where did she disappear to?*

'Val was out sailing on Tuesday. He wasn't away, I saw him myself.'

'You did?' She looked distraught. 'I was in Cork,' she said. 'I swear to God I wasn't in that boat.'

'But you know who was?' he said softly. Her face turned to parchment. She stared at him, and though she opened her mouth to speak the words didn't come. He waited.

'No,' she whispered. 'No, I don't know. I was with Marilyn.'

'There's something else I have to ask you. Why did he change the name?'

'The name?'

'Your husband's sailing boat,' he said patiently. 'The name's been changed. Why was that?'

She didn't answer for a while and when she did her voice was cold and distant. Abstracted. 'He sold it.'

He leaned towards her. 'What, the name?'

'No, the boat. He said it was too big, he couldn't afford it. He said he'd keep the name *Azurra*, for his next boat. For luck. I can't think why. But he's not always very communicative. Specially when he's not well.'

'If he sold the boat, why is it still on your moorings?'

'He had some arrangement. That he'd teach whoever bought it to sail, I think. Or that he'd crew and generally look after it. Said it was a brilliant scheme. He got the cash and still had use of the boat.'

'And does he?'

'Does he what?' She brushed the air impatiently with her hand, as if trying to get rid of a troublesome gnat. 'Frank, I'm really tired . . .'

'Have the use of it?'

Her head sank to her chest. 'Val doesn't discuss business with me.' She looked so bleak he could hardly bear to continue, but it didn't stop his brain going into overdrive.

'Know who bought it?' he asked casually. 'It wouldn't be Jer O'Dowd, by any chance?'

That startled her. Her jaw dropped. 'Him?' She shook her head violently. 'I . . . He . . . he gives me the creeps.'

'He was out with Val on Tuesday.'

Her head turned slowly, her eyes wide. 'Who was out where?' She avoided looking at him.

'O'Dowd. Out on the *Halcyon*. Four people including your

173

husband. Mrs Walter, O'Dowd and someone I thought at the time was you. My darling, I saw them.'

Her jaw dropped. The phone sounded again. Cressida sat up in her chair. 'Me? How could you have seen me? I wasn't there. I was with Marilyn Donovan.'

'You drove her to the hospital between five and six on Monday, not Tuesday,' he said grimly. 'Stop lying to me, Cressida. Trust me.'

'I came back late on Monday and went straight to bed. I went up again early on Tuesday morning,' she retorted without hesitation. 'It's the truth. I tried to ring you to put off Trabuí but my phone wouldn't work in the hospital. I had a terrible time persuading Marilyn not to discharge herself. She's a stubborn bloody woman. I don't know where Val was, he wasn't here on Monday.' She bit her lower lip. 'Maybe if I'd stayed in Cork . . .'

'Maybe what? Cress?' But she wouldn't answer. He sighed. 'Was Gil with you the whole time?'

She took a little time before she said, 'I left him with Georgie on the way through Duncreagh on Monday. John Spain took care of him on Tuesday. As you know, since you saw them.'

'But you came back, didn't you? You wouldn't stay away from the child for two days, would you? Answer me, Cressida. What time did you get here on Tuesday?'

She put her head down on the table. 'I collected Gil from John's house about six,' she mumbled. 'I promised Marilyn I'd get back to see her. We stayed with a friend in Cork.'

'Where is your husband?'

She looked up. 'I don't know,' she wailed in desperation. 'I don't know what's happening.'

She hadn't given a single straight answer. Not one. She hadn't said Val was still in London. Didn't say she drove straight back to Cork on Tuesday – she implied it. The boat was sold – but she wasn't sure to whom. Didn't deny it when he suggested Val and Evangeline were having an affair. The one thing he at last believed was that she was not sailing that afternoon. *That bloody girl just wouldn't go away.* The boat party crowded in on him again. A small chink of light was suddenly cast on the passengers and immediately he became terrified of asking her exactly what she was doing on Tuesday night besides getting beaten up.

'Frank,' she cried suddenly. A sweat had broken out on her forehead.

'Are you all right, Cressie? Can you hear me?' He moved swiftly around the table and grabbed her arm. She felt brittle as a bag of bones. 'I need . . .' Her body seemed to collapse. 'Hold me,' she whispered. 'Hold me, Frank.' He gently eased her head to her knees and stood over her with his hand resting on her shoulder. When she began to recover he went to the sink and filled a glass of water. He had to get her away, out of here, where she and Gil would be safe. Only then could he begin to think straight, get on with the investigation without continuing to compromise himself.

'Drink this,' he said. She sat up and took the glass from his hand. He gave silent thanks that McBride wasn't present, pulled over a chair and sat beside her with his arm around her shoulders and his head close to hers. 'You didn't go to see Marilyn Donovan on Tuesday night, did you? You brought Gil to the hospital. But something happened when you got back here the first time, didn't it?' he asked urgently. His voice was low. 'Something that made you run away. Cressie, tell me? I can't help you if you won't trust me.'

'I can't,' she whispered. 'Oh darling Frank, please go. Please, please go, Frank.'

The long-case clock in the corner struck the hour. Eight o'clock. At that moment there was a tap at the back door and Spain came into the kitchen, in his stocking feet. He was carrying a couple of crabs, which he threw in the sink. 'I'll prepare them for you, if you like,' he said gruffly and took a large saucepan from under the counter. It was an extraordinary performance. He seemed entirely at ease. He took off his jacket and slung it over a chair.

'Would you mind telling me what you think you're doing here?' Recaldo asked.

Spain blinked rapidly. 'What does it look like?'

'Don't come the innocent with me, John Spain. Don't you realize that you're under surveillance?'

'I'm only trying to look after her. She shouldn't be here.'

'Shut up,' Cressida suddenly exploded. She jumped to her feet. 'Both of you. Shut up. Stop talking about me as if I wasn't here. I'm not dim-witted, I can look after myself.'

Exasperation seized Recaldo; the lover rather than the policeman. 'Really? Then why do you let that lout of a husband beat you up?' he said angrily.

175

'What business is it of yours?' she blazed.

He looked at her for what seemed for ever. 'I care about you,' he said quietly. 'And I care about what happens to you and Gil. I would give my life to keep you both safe.'

Cressida burst into tears. 'He only did it once before,' she sobbed. 'Twice. And he never hit Gil until, until . . . Honestly . . . it was my fault . . . I shouldn't have . . .'

'Oh Cressie love, for God's sake,' he said wearily, 'will you stop taking the blame? He's been at it for weeks.'

Cressida sat down and put her head in her hands. 'I wish you'd both go,' she said.

Recaldo drew himself up. 'That's it. Enough pussyfooting. You're leaving here right now. Tonight. You and Gil. This is not about murder, this is about Sweeney beating you up. I'm not asking where he is, because wherever he is, we all know he's going to come back – like every other wife-batterer I've ever met, he's going to have another go. And that's what you're afraid of, isn't it? Afraid for Gil, if not for yourself. This has got to be sorted out, Cressie. Please.'

'It was my fault,' she whispered. Recaldo looked at her sadly. Why did they always say that? But then it struck him. She's telling the truth. For once, she must have provoked him. Tuesday night, Tuesday night. His brain crashed; he could no longer think straight.

John Spain was about to say something when Recaldo held up his hand. 'Tell me what happened, Cressie, or I'll kill that bastard myself.'

She put her hand to her bruised eye, and spoke in a low mumble. She didn't look at either of them. 'I wouldn't sign over the house. He said I was a bad mother, that he'd have Gil put into care unless I signed. He said I had to be back tonight to sign otherwise he'd . . . he'd . . .' She faltered. You could have heard a pin drop.

'Cressie? You're the best mother I know. There's no way he can do that.'

'Yes there is,' John Spain said hoarsely. 'He accused her of letting a paedophile teach her child. He accused me of sexually molesting Gil.' He swallowed. 'You know as well as I do that an accusation like that is enough, with the kind of gossip that's already been spread,' he said despairingly. 'The damage is already done. I cannot defend myself.' He looked pleadingly at Cressida. 'But I swear to you, Cressida, and to you, Frank, I have never, never in my life . . . oh dear God. I could never ... I cannot even say it. Gil has always been safe.' His eyes wavered from one to the other.

Cressida said quietly, 'I know that, John. I've never doubted it.'

'Jesus.' Recaldo's breathing became shallow and rapid. 'Jesus.' He went over to Cressida and held her. He looked at Spain. 'Evangeline Walter put that into his head, didn't she?' Spain nodded.

'What was that fucking woman up to?' The three of them stood in stunned silence as the horror of the accusation, put into words, was made real and urgent. Who would defend Spain? He, Recaldo? The local copper who was shagging the boy's mother? Some chance. God, but she was clever. But why? What was it all about? He put his hand out to the old man. 'Over my dead body,' he said. He hardly knew what he meant.

'We need to get you and Gil out of here for a few days, Cressie,' Recaldo said decisively. 'I have some friends who might be able to help. They live about twenty miles away, in the hills on the other side of Duncreagh. Jim and Mary Dillon, they're called. They have three children so there'll be company for Gil. Will you go to them? Just for three or four days?'

'What about John?'

'John knows how to make himself scarce.'

'You're out of your mind, Frank,' Spain growled. 'If you don't watch out, you're going to lose your job.'

'Let me worry about that. Don't argue, John,' he warned as Spain opened his mouth to say something more. 'Cressie, let's get you packed. Now. We'll hole up somewhere till it's good and dark then I'll drive your car and John can follow in mine. Go on, Cress, what are you waiting for?'

When Cressie went upstairs Spain said, 'Frank, my car's outside, I came to take her away. We can go in that.'

'No, I'll drive her in the Range Rover, I don't want her marooned. You can follow in mine and we'll come back together.' There was a moment's silence.

'I killed Evangeline Walter,' Spain said.

Recaldo looked at him. 'Did you now? How did you do that?'

'Sex,' he mumbled and looked up shamefaced. 'She was only just out of hospital and I had sex with her.' Recaldo's face went blank. Not now, he wanted to scream, not now.

'Ever had sex with her before?'

'A few times, when she first got here.'

177

'But not since? Are you saying you raped her?'

'No, I don't think you could call it that.'

'What then? Did you strike her?'

'No, she fell. I wouldn't strike a woman, you know that, no matter what.'

'She came on to you?' Recaldo asked.

Spain nodded his head slowly. 'But who would believe me?'

Recaldo took his arm. 'I believe you. I always have, John Spain, but sometime, in the next few hours, you are going to have to tell me exactly what went on in that damn woman's garden on Tuesday night.' He looked at the old man fiercely. 'And, more to the point, what Cressie was doing there.'

'What?'

'Do I look stupid, John Spain? I *know* she was there at some point. And no, she didn't tell me. Now, that may or may not have something to do with trying to protect you, but I've been running around in circles long enough. And I'll tell you this, though I shouldn't, somebody thumped Walter, not only on the head, but smack in her stomach as well. Somehow, no matter what the provocation, that doesn't seem to be your style. So, three guesses who I think did that? The trouble is, I can't work out why. Nor, more specifically, why *then*? I simply can't get to grips with what incident, or series of incidents, triggered the attack. Not yet anyway.'

Cressie came into the kitchen. 'I'm ready,' she said. 'Apart from Gil. He's fast asleep, I'll need a bit of help carrying him down.'

'I'll bring him down,' Recaldo said. 'You go on ahead, John, and drop your car home. We'll drive separately and meet you at the edge of the woods near your place in about twenty minutes.' He waited for a moment until Cressida had gone back upstairs and out of earshot and Spain was halfway through the front door. 'You dined at Lia's restaurant one night last June,' he said. 'D'you mind telling me who was the lady you were with?'

Spain's leonine head swivelled slowly, his expression appalled. 'You heard about that?'

'Only recently.'

'It was my sister,' he replied. 'She was visiting for the day.' He pulled the door closed, leaving Frank Recaldo not much wiser. Or so he thought at the time.

Chapter Nineteen

INSPECTOR MCBRIDE HAD JUST ARRIVED BACK AT HEADQUARTERS and was sitting in conference with Coffey, when Recaldo rang to report his conversation with Steve Donovan, Marilyn's husband. Five minutes later, Coffey rang Steve. 'Superintendent Coffey here. I believe the hospital will allow your wife home this evening, but that you're having trouble getting someone to collect her, is that right?' he said smoothly. 'Well now, we could give her a lift home, if that would be of any help? We'll be driving that way in about an hour or so, and since we'd like a word with her, we can kill two birds with one stone. Would that suit? It would? So, will you give her a ring and tell her we're on our way?'

Half an hour later McBride arrived at the hospital and was directed to the small day room where Marilyn Donovan was sitting in a wheel-chair, in full warpaint, with a small overnight bag at her feet. His first reaction was that she took her name seriously, unless it was a co-incidence that she had the full voluptuous figure and the gorgeous pouting lips of her famous namesake. Her cropped hair was bleached, though her eyebrows were dark. She looked to be in her late thirties. Marilyn Donovan was an improbable charlady.

'Mrs Donovan?' McBride showed her his card. She looked him over.

'Marilyn,' she lilted and smiled, showing a set of perfect teeth. 'Steve said it would be a Superintendent Coffey.'

'He was tied up. He sent his apologies. I'm afraid you'll have to make do with me.' He looked pointedly at a plate of curled sand-wiches on the table beside her. 'That your supper?' he asked. Marilyn glanced at it with disgust and stubbed out the cigarette she'd been surreptitiously smoking on the plate.

'I couldn't stomach it. The food here is desperate.'

'Seems to be the same in every hospital,' McBride said, then looked at her as if an idea had just occurred to him. 'If you're feeling up to it, we could stop for something on the way? I haven't eaten myself since morning and, well, to be honest my stomach thinks my throat is cut.'

Marilyn was at eye level with his beer gut. 'I can see you're fading away,' she laughed. 'I'd give my back teeth for something lovely to eat.' She made to get out of the wheelchair.

'Stay where you are. I'll push you. Is that bag all you've got?'

'Yeah,' she said laconically. 'I was in a bit of a hurry.'

McBride picked up the bag. 'All set then, madam?' On the way down in the lift he said: 'Italian? French? Chinese? Hamburger? Indian? Thai? What'll it be? Take your pick.'

'Something simple would do nicely.'

His car was parked right outside the hospital entrance with an irate porter standing beside it. McBride flashed his card. 'I'm just taking her to the clink,' he joked as they settled Marilyn in the front seat.

'How much of a hurry are you in?' he asked as they set off.

Marilyn considered this for a moment. She looked a little less frisky after her marathon in the wheelchair. 'Well, to tell you the truth I'd prefer not to get back until the baby is settled for the night. He's a bit of a handful and I haven't my usual energy.'

'Would the Arbutus Lodge suit you?' Inspector McBride fastened his seat belt and rolled away from the entrance.

'You're having me on? That's very smart and look at the cut of me – straight out of hospital. Ah no.'

He glanced down at her. 'Ah yes. Anyway, you look lovely – if you don't consider that a bit cheeky.' His voice sobered. 'Look, I need to ask you a few things and I need somewhere quiet to do it. You'd be doing me a favour, Mrs Donovan – Marilyn.'

He was greeted like a good and valued customer and they were soon settled at a small table at the back of the restaurant, overlooking the city. Marilyn sat back, delighted. 'I love this,' she said simply. 'I love the style.'

'So do I.' He grinned at her. 'Of course Superintendent Coffey may not see it in quite the same way when he gets the bill. So eat up, for tomorrow I may die.' Despite his brave words they had a half bottle of wine and ordered from the set menu: he opted for rack of lamb, Marilyn for a fricassee of chicken. They made small talk until the waiter had served them.

'Were you called after who I think?'

She laughed. 'Yeah. I was born two days after my mother saw her in *The Prince and the Showgirl* – not her best, but Mam thought she was the greatest. She said Marilyn made Laurence Olivier look like someone from the Duncreagh amateur dramatic group.'

'Duncreagh? Is that where you come from?'

'No, I'm Passage South, born and bred. I've lived there all my life.'

'Why do you work as a charwoman?' he asked bluntly.

'Am I not what you expected, then?' Marilyn gurgled. 'Think I should have a scarf around me head and a mop in me hand? You're a bit old-fashioned, aren't you?' She looked at him shrewdly. 'My job is the reason you have me sitting in this gorgeous place, feeding me this delicious food. Am I right?'

McBride held up his hands, palms outwards. 'You're right. I meant nothing by it. Sorry, my tongue runs away with me sometimes.'

Marilyn Donovan was not short of confidence, nor, as McBride soon discovered, intelligence. She was quick-witted and extremely direct.

'Look, Mr McBride, I have nothing to be ashamed of. I do what I want to do. I'm the best charwoman for miles around, maybe the best ever. I can hire a baby-minder when I need one and still earn more than Steve and he's a skilled plumber. I like what I do. And no, I don't call myself a home help or a housekeeper though some of my employers do. I hire myself out by the hour. My rates are as high as Dublin or London, because, when all is said and done, the work is the same wherever you are, and I'm worth it. I'm efficient, discreet, and, given respect, I return it. I enjoy my job.'

She took a gulp of water and sat back. McBride poured them each a glass of wine, then spoke to her directly without any of the hail-fellow-well-met attitude he'd previously employed. She liked him better for it.

'Mrs Donovan – Marilyn, I'll be honest with you. I'm shooting in the dark here. We're investigating a killing and I don't know the lie of the land. I'll have some specific questions for you later on, but really

181

what I need most is someone to fill me in on the ins and outs of the place.'

She mulled this over. 'What about Frank Recaldo?'

'In cases like this the local garda doesn't run the investigation – for one thing he wouldn't have the resources and for another he needs to keep on with his day-to-day activities. That's why an investigation team is sent from headquarters.'

'Dublin?'

'No, I just happen to be from Dublin but I've been stationed in Cork for the past year or so. Superintendent Coffey is running the case. There's nothing sinister in that, it's just the usual practice. Frank is part of the team.'

'So what do you want me to tell you?'

'Everything and anything you can think of. How did you come to be working for Mrs Walter?'

'That's easy, I only work for the foreigners. Apart from the better pay, I'm appreciated as their first real contact with the locals. A position of trust and an education in itself. Something I missed – an education, I mean.'

'How come?'

'I'm from a big family: four boys and three girls.' She sniffed. 'I was the eldest. Mam died giving birth to her last child when I was fourteen so that was it school-wise, but I saw to it that the rest of them got a good education. They all have great careers. And I include myself among them. I'm quite bright, you know. I read all the time.' She dimpled. 'I often thought of getting myself qualified, but then what? Of all my family I'm the only one left at home, which is great. I've never wanted to move away. It's where I belong, the place I know. Once I decided to go out to work, it didn't take a genius to realize that I should do what I was good at. I like housework, always have, I don't know why. I suppose I like putting things in order. I set myself up when my own daughter, Aisling, started school. Being a plumber, Steve was able to point me to the households that would pay what I'm worth. We're a good team.

'After raising our own crowd, I never really wanted more than one child, but Liam made a surprise appearance when Aisling was nearly nine. He's a holy terror. I don't think we've had a night's sleep since he was born. To tell you the truth I was a bit upset when I found out

I was pregnant again. I didn't really know how I was going to manage three.' She sniffed again. 'Funny the way things go.'

'You went into hospital on Monday? Is that right?'

'Yeah, I missed all the excitement.' She leaned towards him earnestly. 'Isn't it weird how one thing follows another like that? I'm not saying my miscarriage had anything to do with Mrs Walter being killed but I can't help feeling that it could have been myself that found her body, couldn't it? Wednesday was one of the days I worked for her. Except that I usually don't start work until about nine and she was discovered earlier, wasn't she?'

'How do you know that?' he asked.

Marilyn looked at him pityingly. 'Steve told me.'

'When?'

'Yesterday evening when he came in to see me,' she said matter-of-factly and then stunned him.

'He'd heard she was standing up against a tree even though she was dead.'

'He what? Where did he get a story like that?'

Marilyn shrugged. 'Of course I didn't believe a word of it. He got it from old Mona Spillane when he went to change the washers on her kitchen taps yesterday. She lives beside the Trianach causeway. The news bulletin, we call her. She was full of it, he could hardly drag her from the window to show him what she wanted him to do.'

No wonder FX is so buttoned up, McBride thought.

'How did you get on with Mrs Walter?'

'OK,' Marilyn shrugged carelessly. 'I was with her for about six years – with time out for Liam. She had her ways,' she added enigmatically, though she didn't remain enigmatic for long. 'It's not that I didn't like her, because I did in a kind of a way, though she could be very changeable and say wounding things, right off the top of her head. I think she was the most discontented woman I ever met. It showed on her face too, otherwise she would have been really attractive. She was forever lamenting the passing of time. If she'd asked me I'd have told her to have a bit more faith in herself, stop thinking people were always out to get her. There are many would find that a surprising conclusion to come to, because Mrs Walter had a great air about her; she could be very aggressive, always anxious to be the best, but at the same time worried about everything. Did she look good? Were her clothes right? Had anyone changed a word in one of her old bits of writing? Who was trying to get one over on her?

'But then again, she wanted to be friends. "I wish you'd call me Vangie," she'd say. I told her that if I was called Evangeline I would never, ever, shorten it to something ugly like Vangie. "Evangeline's too old-fashioned," she said. "It's an old woman's name. My silly mother got it from a stoopid poem."' Marilyn added mimicry to her charms. 'I thought it was a beautiful name, whenever I heard it I thought of her twirling around in one of her lovely long dresses, like a girl waltzing. When I said that, she turned on me and told me I was being fresh. Maybe she thought I was getting at her by mentioning the long dresses? She only wore them to hide her thick, beef-to-the-heels ankles. But I swear it never crossed my mind. I loved the name but I stuck to Mrs Walter. It was better that way.'

'You didn't like her much, did you?'

'Not a lot. She was very vain and spoilt; an old man's darling. She didn't know how to have real fun, or let herself go,' Marilyn summed up succinctly. 'She was with old Otto Bleiberg for years and got the house when he died. It's a big old place that was derelict when I was a little girl. We used to be chased away by Smiler O'Dowd's auld fella – the Pouncer he was called. He used to graze store cattle there from time to time.'

'Was she married?'

'Divorced. I think maybe she was married several times. It's just a hunch, she was very close with that kind of information. I never saw a husband. Since Mr Bleiberg died the Smiler has been very attentive. I wouldn't fancy him myself but she seemed to like him well enough. Otherwise she didn't exactly stint herself, always had a string of admirers. To my certain knowledge Dr McCarthy had a fling with her and Mick Hussey until Aoife found out about it and nearly gave him his walking papers. There was also an American that came a few times and an old guy from Tipperary someplace. I used to see him in the house from time to time. And of course poor old John Spain was putty in her hands. She once told me she liked elderly men because they were not so demanding.' Marilyn snorted. 'And if I believed that I'd believe anything. She liked them because they were rich, though Father Spain was hardly in that category. But V. J. Sweeney was, though she was very careful never to be seen in public with him. God love us, she thought her interest wasn't noticed. But how could I help it? Don't I also work for Mrs Sweeney? Or at least I used to until a few weeks ago.'

'You left?'

'Yeah, I didn't see what else I could do.'

'What happened?'

'Nothing and everything. I could see she was finding it harder and harder to pay me – I only take cash. I didn't cop on at first that he was keeping her short. Of course *she* didn't say that; just some old rigmarole about not being able to justify me any more because she wasn't earning. Poor thing was mortified.'

McBride had opened his mouth to say something when Marilyn answered his unspoken question.

'I like Cressida Sweeney, she's one of the nicest women around. The genuine article. Her little boy is deaf, you know. I really admire the way she looks after him, specially when she gets not a bit of support from that man of hers. The Lord only knows how she puts up with him. I suppose you've heard about him? No?' She wriggled more comfortably in her seat. 'Well, a couple of years ago his business went – ouf.' She pulled her finger across her throat. 'Then he took to the bottle. And mean with it. When they came here first they were the best-looking couple for miles – with money to burn. They were from London, though with a name like Sweeney I suppose he must have come from Ireland originally. She had some Irish ancestors for certain, because she inherited the old Hollingsworth place on the far side of the estuary. It was falling to bits but they made a lovely job of doing it up. Once it was finished he brought that huge yacht over from Portsmouth.'

'How long have they been here?'

'They first came about ten years ago, but only for the summers. Once little Gil was born *she* settled here permanently. Not VJ though, he commuted back and forth until – oh, about two years ago when the London business went. It's not what I'd call a marriage, he's always treated her as if she was thick, which she isn't. She's paralysed with shyness, that's all, and can't stand up to him. I wouldn't let any man treat me like that. Full of himself for pulling a lovely young girl, I'd say. He never showed any respect for her but it's got really bad in the past few months and lately he started thumping her. That or disappearing for weeks on end. God only knows what he's up to. At first I believed her when she said she fell, or banged into a door or something; it took me a while to cop on. Steve would never do anything like that so I suppose it wasn't something that would naturally occur to me,' she sniffed.

'How come she drove you to the hospital?'

'Steve was out on a job. I called Mrs Walter first, which was stupid, because she was only just out of hospital herself and wasn't feeling well enough. Cressida was over like a shot. She took me to Duncreagh first but they sent us on to the Bons. I felt terrible dragging her all that way but she said she was glad to get away. She didn't say why but then I wouldn't expect her to, she never complains. I'll tell you something, I wouldn't sleep alone in that old place for all the tea in China, it's awful isolated and most of the time she's there on her own with little Gil. He never leaves her side. But I suppose better alone than with Sweeney rampaging around drunk.'

'Was the boy with her?' he asked and Marilyn flowed seamlessly to his next target.

'No, I suppose she got John Spain to look after him. They're great friends. The old man teaches Gil for an hour or so every day – to help Cressida out. Between the pair of them, the child is nearly talking. He used to make terrible noises altogether. He's still hard to understand but he's getting there, and these days he has a lovely sunny nature. Mind you, there are plenty around here think she's mad to trust the old man with the child, but I don't, because I can see he loves the pair of them like the children he never had, God help him.'

'Why do people say that?'

'Because they've nothing better to do,' Marilyn said robustly. 'And they don't know what they're talking about. In my humble opinion Spain's problem isn't children. It's women.'

'How do you know that?' he asked.

Marilyn ran her hand sensuously down the front of her blouse. 'Well, to tell you the truth, Mr McBride, I consider myself something of an expert on the subject.'

He frowned. 'Are you . . . Did he?'

'No I am not, and no he did no such thing. You've a filthy mind, d'you know that?' she said indignantly.

'I didn't say anything.'

'You didn't have to.'

'So how come you're so het up about Spain? How do you know what he's like?'

'I just know, that's all. I pass the time of day with him every day when he comes down to drop off his catch at Lia's restaurant. She's a great pal of mine and she thinks the same as me. All those terrible rumours about him had long since died down until this summer when they started up again. I'm telling you, someone has it in for that old man.' Marilyn's indignation boiled over. 'It's disgusting. He's been here nearly twenty years and not a whiff of scandal apart from the original one about the Spanish woman. And believe me, if there was anything to come out of the woodwork, we'd have heard about it by now. Lia Ryan told me that Mrs Walter was responsible this time. That there was some incident this summer when I was visiting my sister in England. And Aoife Hussey was full of it as well. I told her to stop making mischief. I mean, she's not exactly a fan of Mrs Walter's since Michael went off the straight and narrow. Anyway I worked for the woman so I couldn't be seen to be gossiping, now could I?'

'Who is Mrs Sweeney friends with?'

'I don't know about friends, but Frank Recaldo's been paying her a lot of attention.'

'Has he now?'

'Yeah and I'd say they're well suited. The pair of them are mad about each other, sure they can hardly keep their hands off of each other. Or their eyes. Transfixed, I'd say.' She sighed. 'And we all know what that's like. I often felt like saying to her – why don't you just go for it? But they're very discreet. Just as well. VJ'd have their guts for garters if he found out. He may not want her himself but he's the sort that regards a wife as his personal property and God knows he has little enough of that left to him. I had to laugh when Frank got the pup. Putting it about that he needed the exercise when the whole of Passage knew well 'twas only so he could go up on the cliffs where Cressida and Gil walk their red setter. There are some who think he shouldn't be seen out with a married woman, but I don't blame him one bit. Nor Cressida either. Frank's a dish. The sort who could throw on a few things from Dunne's Stores and look as if he was straight out of Armani. Not exactly a bundle of laughs but a decent man all the same.' She fell silent.

'He's not in very good health, is he?' McBride prompted.

'He's much better now. It's a real shame about the heart attack, isn't it? He told my Steve it came on after a game of squash. Imagine something as simple as that? And him only thirty-eight at the time. There must have been a weakness there all the same. He looked desperate when he first came. I never saw anyone so thin and pale, but he's getting stronger all the time. It always surprised me that Evangeline Walter didn't snap him up. She was interested, because she was always asking me questions about him. He certainly had the looks but I suppose, in the end, a country guard wasn't quite her scene. I'm not sure she realized he has a few more strings to his bow. Literally. He plays the double bass in a jazz quartet with Steve, who's handy enough with the fiddle.'

'Recaldo plays the double bass? You're kidding me.'

She made a face. 'No I'm not.' She laughed at his surprise. 'He's even better on the piano. Classical stuff. Plays up at the hotel the odd night. Liberace isn't in it.'

'Busy man.'

'I don't suppose he earns much and he has a family to keep,' she said pointedly and drained her glass. 'So tell me something, Mr McBride, how come *you* can afford this place?'

McBride threw back his head and laughed. 'Do you think we could sting Coffey for coffee?'

She giggled. 'Not for me. The chicken was beautiful but if you don't mind, I feel a bit worn out.'

He got the bill while she went to the cloakroom. She looked very shaky when she rejoined him in the hall. He took her arm and led her to the car. 'Are you up to the drive?' he asked.

'Thanks, I'll manage.' He drove at about half his normal speed. She lay back in the seat and dozed for the first half-hour and then sat up, apparently refreshed. 'D'you hate people smoking in your car?'

'No, as long as you open the window.'

Marilyn lit up, inhaled deeply and lay back again. 'Do you know who killed Mrs Walter?' she asked quietly.

'No, not yet, but at least we're beginning to assemble a list of possibles,' he said.

'A sort of cast list?' she asked and after another silence began to reminisce. 'One of my sisters lives in Stratford upon Avon,' she said. 'The very first Shakespeare play I ever saw was *Hamlet*. You wouldn't believe how exciting it was. I must have been the only person in the whole audience that didn't know how it was going to end. All those bodies.' She sighed. 'I wasn't there when Mrs Walter died. I worked for her last on Monday morning. Sad isn't it? I didn't know what happened until Steve rang yesterday dinner time. Cressida Sweeney and Gil were just about to go home. She never said anything about it. I was a bit anxious about her to tell you the truth. She turned up with a terrible bruise on her face and Gil's arm was in a sling. She wouldn't tell me what had happened to her. But every time I asked her if she was expected at home, she said no, her husband was away. She started crying when I told her that Mona Spillane told Steve that Finbarr, who does Mrs Walter's garden, was warbling on about a crowd, including Mr Sweeney and Mrs Walter, out on his yacht on Tuesday.'

McBride slowed down and turned to her. 'I understood Sweeney to be in London.'

'Yeah, that's what Cressida said. D'you know, I don't think she went home at all. She looked that rough I wondered whether she was sleeping in the car. So there's something odd there. Finbarr and his aunt Mona don't often get things wrong. Not information anyway, though they sometimes get the details a bit twisted in the telling. For instance, they don't seem to know that the yacht doesn't belong to VJ any more. But you know, something tells me to lay my money on Finbarr. He is very upset about Mrs Walter and hasn't he every right? Finbarr thought the sun shone out of her.' She giggled. 'Though I doubt he was one of her elderly gentlemen. By the way, Mr McBride,' Marilyn said as they finally pulled up at her door at half past eleven, 'didn't you have some questions you wanted to ask?'

McBride helped her from the car. Steve was standing in the doorway with a large screeching baby in his arms. 'Home sweet home,' Marilyn groaned.

'There isn't a thing you haven't already answered,' McBride said. 'Oh, just one little query. Where did Mrs Walter keep her working papers, household bills, that kind of thing?'

'Mostly in her study, the rest in a wooden chest in the lounge. It's easily recognized, it's got scenery painted on it and gold decoration. She said it was from Italy. Sometimes she puts cushions on top so you might think it's a seat. You can't miss it.'

189

Friday

Chapter Twenty

SOMETHING WOKE HIM. FEAR? HE WAS SWEATING PROFUSELY. IF HE wasn't protecting Cressida, who was he protecting? He lay slooming half-asleep, half-awake, thinking about Tuesday afternoon. In his mind's eye he could see the two women sitting in the cockpit of the yacht. The wind lifted the girl's hair as she looked out to sea to Spain's fishing boat with the child in the prow, the white-blond curls glinting in the sunshine. And suddenly the two heads, boy and girl-woman, began to twirl around and around in his mind, merging and separating like the shapes in a kaleidoscope. He let the images fix in his mind, then slowly opened his eyes and held his watch up to the bedside light. Friday morning, five past six. Five hours' sleep felt like five seconds. He lay quite still, filled with anxiety about the coming day and what it might bring.

His concern for Cressida had intensified and with it his confusion. Had he protected her or endangered her by spiriting her away? Would his action have the opposite effect to what he intended and bring her more closely to McBride's attention? Fear that he had let her down almost overwhelmed him.

He hauled himself out of bed into the shower and was shaved and dressed by twenty-five to seven. Only stopping for a single cup of coffee, he set out to call on Smiler O'Dowd. He wanted to talk to him alone, and he wasn't sure what time Coffey and McBride would show up.

O'Dowd was up and dressed and greeted him without surprise. Yet as usual he somehow managed to imply an underlying, if slightly unhealthy collusion between himself and Frank, as he insisted on calling him. The whole inside of his house had recently been done up. The smell of fresh paint and new carpet hit him as soon as the front door was opened. There were open cardboard cartons lying in the hall, similar to those he'd spied through the attic window. They appeared to be full of books and videotapes. Through the open door of the front room he noticed a brand new dark blue sofa still encased in clear plastic wrapping and a large empty newly painted bookcase. He wondered why on earth anyone with a river aspect would have the orientation of his sitting room directly away from it onto the scruffy meadow in front.

'I hadn't realized your house was so close to the estuary,' Recaldo remarked pleasantly as he followed his host to a smart modern kitchen. Even here the windows were placed too high to afford a view from the table where Smiler seated him. 'Pity you haven't the view.'

O'Dowd looked to see if he was being wound up, but evidently decided not. 'When I want to look at the view, I go outside,' he said. He wedged the back door – no window, no view – slightly open, letting in the soothing sound of water lapping the riverbank. He busied himself frying a panful of rashers, eggs and sausages, then left the pan sizzling while he set the table for two and made a pot of tea, which he covered with a grubby pink knitted cosy. He was neat in his movements, rather fussily so, and even put out a coloured paper napkin on either side plate.

'Could I have the keys of next door?' Recaldo launched in without preamble. O'Dowd gave him a backward glance but didn't reply. 'You've got spare keys, I take it? Would you mind letting me have them?' Recaldo repeated casually. 'Just until the investigation is over?'

'I already handed them over. Didn't your Cork pals tell you?'

Shit. Recaldo glimpsed contempt in Smiler's eyes. 'That story you told me was true, then? How you came to acquire the Old Corn Store?'

O'Dowd shrugged carelessly. 'It was an arrangement I made with Mr Bleiberg, years back when he first had the notion of converting it. It had been lying idle for ages, since my father bought it from the Land Commission.' O'Dowd brought two overfull plates to the table and set one in front of his visitor, who almost got sick at the sight.

'Tell me about Otto Bleiberg?' Recaldo asked.

'I'm sure you know it was him built the original Atlantis Hotel. In the early Seventies, that was. He was from a famous hotelier family in Switzerland. They had luxury hotels in other parts of the world, though not in Ireland. Otto wasn't actually in the business himself – he was an industrialist. But when he retired early he got the notion of building the Atlantis. He'd been looking for a site for some time when my father sold him the few acres on the cliff. They became friends. I've known Otto since I was a young lad.'

'An unusual place for a hotel, isn't it? Particularly an expensive one like that.'

'You mean no passing trade?' His eyes crinkled. 'It's not run like that – people who can afford the Atlantis don't go on package tours.'

'No, I was thinking more of the weather. Most people like a warm climate, sunshine and entertainment – all in fairly short supply around here.'

O'Dowd laughed. 'What? With the triple glazing, you'd think you were in Florida. You never have to step outside. You can be all cosy looking out over one of the best views in Ireland. It's a great place altogether. Very popular with the sailing crowd, and they don't stint themselves,' Smiler said with a faraway look in his eye, and went into nostalgic mode. 'You should have seen the place when it first opened. The Fastnet race was on and the Taoiseach arrived in his helicopter, with Hollywood stars and all sorts. It really set the place up. The weather was fantastic and the guests had a fabulous view of the yachts racing across the bay. The party went on for the weekend, and by the time they left many of the guests, the Taoiseach included, had booked themselves in for future stays. Otto knew what he was doing, all right. God be good to him.'

'You were friends,' Recaldo murmured when he could get a word in edgeways.

'We were, then. The best of friends. I did a lot of work for him when he lived here; managed things for him, saw to the house, hired workmen, all that kind of thing.'

'I suppose that's why he left you the house?'

Smiler drew himself up. 'He didn't leave it to me. It was part of an agreement we made when he took on the renovation; the building was on our land to begin with. We gave him a lifetime lease on it.'

Cute hoor, Recaldo thought, not for the first time. 'That was a great arrangement altogether. He paid to have it renovated, then

195

it reverted to you on his death? Is that what you're telling me?'

'Yes, that's what I'm telling you. But it was his till he died. He had it loaned out to Vangie.' He paused reflectively. 'I honoured his request that she could live in it as long as she wished.'

'And how long was that?'

'That was up to her. Until she wanted to move on. Or died,' he added bleakly.

'What about Bleiberg's family?'

'What about them? His wife and son had an option for an extension of the lease. Also cheap. But Inge died long ago and Joachim didn't want to take it up. He has a much bigger house of his own down near Glandore, which he hardly uses. He wasn't interested in this place.'

'I have to wonder about that.'

'Do you?' Smiler held his glance, then slowly put down his knife and fork. 'You're all the same, you blow-ins,' he said witheringly.

'I'm from Kerry, not from Timbuktu,' Recaldo protested mildly.

'You might as well be,' Smiler replied. 'You just don't get it, do you?'

'What don't I get?'

'It isn't the foreigners who have the money, you omadhán, it's the natives. The money *and* the land. Outsiders may have it for a while, sometimes a long while, but it's really only a kind of loan. You know the old saying?' he grinned. 'Everything comes to them that wait?'

'You going to tell me how that works?'

'I have to laugh at you sometimes, Frank. And I'm not the only one either. You don't go to mass, do you? You should, it'd save you a whole lot of shoe leather as well as the bother of asking questions – at least it would have in the old days. It was the quickest way of getting to know what was going on around here. All you had to do is keep your head down and your ears open. Much better than Hussey's bar.' His eyes crinkled up and the amused smile played around his lips. 'I bet you remember it all from when you were a child? The old fellas at the back of the church slipping out for a fag and a deal? Remember the priest asking for prayers for the sick or the dying? Well now, weren't them boys at the back the ones that realized just when the farm would be on the market and when to go talk to the widow, or whatever. People are often glad of a private sale when times are hard; no percentage for an agent. My old fella was in a class

196

of his own at such times. Did you know what they called him?' he said, with pride. 'The Pouncer.'

'Is there some point to all this, O'Dowd? I'm very interested and all that but . . .'

Smiler held up his hand. 'But that's what I'm trying to tell you, man, you're not. Not really.' He shook his head in mock disbelief and for a few minutes devoted himself to his breakfast. He was adroit at hiding his thoughts when he wanted to. Then a rather curious thing happened. As Recaldo grudgingly began to respect him, he grew ever more uneasy. Smiler had skilfully pointed out not just that he knew all about him, but that he could also make a decent stab at following his thought processes. Which left Recaldo with the empty feeling of having spent the previous couple of years floating above, rather than being any real part of Passage South. He had deluded himself; he'd never really fitted in at all.

'I could point you out fellas around here who look like paupers and are millionaires,' Smiler continued unperturbed. 'My own father spent his whole life in one feckin' suit, but could have bought and sold any blow-in without even noticing. Wasn't he the smart one? I know, because I watched him and I learned from him. But it took a while. I came back with my economics degree from the National University and sat around waiting for someone to offer me a job. I thought I was way above the place and everyone in it.

'The house was a pigsty, the roof was leaking and the auld fella travelled the county in a broken-down Ford Prefect. He let me get to desperation point, waited till I announced I was emigrating before striking. I can see him now tapping me on the shoulder and saying, "Before you go, there's something I've been meaning to show you." He took me out on his rounds, as he called them, and that's when my education really began. I realized I was a rich man's son, and it was all for my benefit. Wasn't I the only one he had? And he'd made every penny piece himself, the tight-fisted old bastard,' he said admiringly.

'Listen to me, Recaldo, Bleiberg was in the ha'penny place next to my da. The Pouncer knew the secret of places like this. It isn't what you *do* with the land that makes it valuable, not what it yields; it's the land itself, no matter how poor and stony it is. If you can hold onto it long enough. And hold onto it he did.' He paused for effect. 'He died owning eight hundred and forty acres, most of it along the banks of the Glár. When he started buying, in the 'forties, times were hard and nobody wanted land that was under water half the year. He was before his time and regarded by some I could name as a fool – hardly anyone except the Pouncer saw the potential of the estuary for leisure activities. He had no interest whatsoever in farming.'

He sat back, waiting for Recaldo to react, challenging him to ask the right question. There was a raffish devil-may-care look about him, which illuminated for the first time just where his attraction lay. He really didn't give a damn what anyone thought of him, least of all a demoted policeman. He was in control. Recaldo sighed and obliged.

'And you added to that? I suppose you're going to tell me how the pair of you managed to finance all this? And managed also to fight off the opposition? Assuming there was any?'

Smiler gave a self-satisfied chuckle. 'I won't then, 'tis too long a story. I wouldn't want to be filling you up with extraneous inform-ation, now would I. Some other time, maybe.'

'Suits me. What about Mrs Walter? Where did she come into this . . . deal . . . this arrangement you had with Otto Bleiberg?'

Smiler took his time answering. He poured a cup of tea and pushed it across the table. 'She was his . . . em . . .' He seemed shy of actually saying the word mistress.

'Mistress. Lover,' Recaldo said firmly. O'Dowd slapped a huge lump of butter on a thick slice of brown soda cake. Recaldo was surprised at his modesty but envied his appetite. The cholesterol-laden fry remained largely untouched on his own plate, though the tea was welcome and excellent. It ran down his parched throat like a warm river. Without waiting to be asked, he picked up the pot and poured himself a second cup.

'I don't know whether she was or not.' O'Dowd was unusually sober, as if he had been troubled by this point himself. ''Twasn't some-thing she was likely to tell me, or anyone else for that matter.'

'And what exactly was your own relationship with her?'

'Exactly, is it? I'd say now, *exactly* is not something I'd discuss with you. Over breakfast. Or indeed at any other time. Why don't you leave it that we were just good friends.' There was an archness to his mood.

'You implied you were lovers, that . . .' Recaldo began, but O'Dowd quickly cut him short.

'I liked her well,' he said with surprising simplicity. 'There was an excitement about her, terrific life altogether. You couldn't ever be bored of her, she was as unpredictable as the weather. And a very, very intelligent woman. A fit companion for any man.' He spoke admiringly. 'She had style,' he added, as if this was worth more than diamonds. 'I'll miss her sorely.' He drained his cup.

'What time did you get back on Tuesday night?'

'We've been through all that.'

'You weren't in Dublin, were you? You went to Thurles.'

To his surprise O'Dowd gave a shout of laughter. 'And what in hell would I be doing there?' he asked defiantly.

'Seeing Mr Mure-Robertson.' Recaldo put as much conviction as he could into this supposition. He was fairly sure that this was indeed the case, though he had no idea, as yet, why.

And O'Dowd obviously had no intention of telling him. 'I see you've been talking to Rose O'Faolain.'

Recaldo immediately changed tack. 'Mrs Walter was ill, wasn't she? Seriously ill?'

'I already told the others that she was more than ill, she was dying. She hadn't got long at all, the creature.'

'Did she have many friends?' he asked.

'Around here? Few enough then. She saw a bit of the Sweeney woman.' He glanced up slyly under his dark lashes, with a knowing look. 'For a while, anyway. But of course you probably know that.'

Recaldo kept his face blank while he grasped at certain key words, speculative clues he sensed O'Dowd was dropping in amongst all the verbiage. *Land, money, relationships*. Christ, he thought, what else is there? He could see that O'Dowd wasn't sure where he stood; trusted him, yet didn't trust him. There was something he clearly wanted to convey. Or find out. Ah yes, that was more like it. Recaldo pondered the wisdom of asking about the tiny attic or the boat party, but decided to hold back for a bit. The chink of his cup against the saucer seemed unnaturally loud. O'Dowd continued to eat, complacently. He poured them each another cup, then took his empty, and his guest's still full, plates to the sink. 'Haven't much appetite, have you, Frank? I thought your old trouble was cured.'

'It is,' Recaldo replied gruffly.

'Doesn't much look like it. You talk to her yet?'

'Talk to who?'

'Mrs Sweeney.'

'No, not yet. She took Mrs Donovan to hospital in Cork.'

'That was Monday, wasn't it? Not seen her since, then?' he asked casually. Which told Recaldo that O'Dowd had either seen her himself, or at the very least knew where she was. Now was the moment. 'I noticed you out sailing with Sweeney on Tuesday,' he said.

Smiler stepped lightly off at a tangent. 'It's *him* you should be looking for,' he said. The boating party was a no-go area, then?

'V. J. Sweeney?' Recaldo held his head half turned, his expression masked. 'Are you going to tell me why, Jer?' he asked evenly.

But Smiler didn't get a chance to, because at that very instant McBride strolled airily through the back door and looked from one to the other with a broad grin. O'Dowd looked put out, but Recaldo remained impassive.

'Jaysus, FX, you're a difficult sod to keep up with. I must have lost a stone chasing after you.'

'So much? In so little time?' Recaldo said calmly and raised his eyebrows.

'Do you usually barge into people's homes, unasked?' demanded O'Dowd.

'Only when I'm investigating murder,' McBride declared sweetly. 'Are you going to offer us a cup of tea, or what?'

O'Dowd stepped over to the sink and refilled the electric kettle. 'I'll be back in a minute,' he said and left the room. After a minute or so the other two heard the sound of not-so-distant plumbing which didn't quite block the ping of the telephone.

McBride leaned towards Recaldo. 'So, where were we?' he asked in a low voice. 'Got anything out of yer man?'

'Well, that depends on what you've already got out of him yourself, doesn't it?'

'Ah now FX, don't be hostile,' he murmured as O'Dowd came back into the kitchen. He made a fresh pot of tea, plonked it down in front of McBride and fetched him a clean cup and saucer.

'You can be mother,' he said contemptuously and sat down. 'What are ye doing about Spain?' he asked abruptly.

'Is there something we should be doing?' McBride asked smoothly.

'He was always hanging around, watching her. Evangeline couldn't stand the sight of him. No child is safe from him,' he added savagely.

'Did she say that?' McBride asked softly. 'Those are dangerous rumours about anyone. But an ex-priest? Was there something between them?'

'Don't make me laugh, she had no time for the old goat.'

'You don't sound as if you've much time for him yourself,' McBride observed drily.

'Vangie knew all about him. Couldn't believe he'd have the cheek to show his face.'

'Share all this *knowledge* with you, did she?' Recaldo asked, tight-lipped.

'Didn't have to, I can work most things out for myself.'

'With embellishments, no doubt,' Recaldo said sourly. He couldn't fathom why Smiler was repeating the old gossip. It didn't seem his style somehow. He turned to McBride. 'Mind telling me where all this is leading? Besides traducing an innocent man?'

'Innocent? Oh, stop messing, FX.' McBride had no qualms about calling a spade a spade. He turned his attention to O'Dowd. 'Were you Mrs Walter's lover?' he asked, and to their utter amazement Smiler actually blushed.

'No,' he muttered reluctantly. 'No. It was a kind of game she . . . we . . . played.' The smile was replaced by a more humble expression, which might also have been shaded with anger.

McBride examined him intently. 'Like that, is it?' he said softly. 'Just pals, then?' He smiled to himself. Smiler swallowed painfully and slowly nodded his head. Lord, Recaldo thought, how bloody slow I am. Who would have guessed? All that garbage about ladykillers hadn't fooled McBride for an instant.

O'Dowd leaned across the table and hissed viciously, 'If you ever mention this conversation, or the conclusions you may have come to, I'll feckin' destroy the pair of you. And don't think I can't.'

'So how come you and she . . .' McBride left the question hanging in the air.

'First of all we were very close, and having me around stopped other fellas pestering her. They thought she was already *doing a line* with me.' He made a face and fell silent. Recaldo was struck by the old-fashioned expression. There was something innocent in it, virginal almost. Smiler might nod and wink and touch the side of his nose but he rarely used or abused sexual expressions, except the ubiquitous 'feckin'', but that hardly counted. The man had been knocked completely off balance. Had he not been so implacable about Spain, Recaldo would have been touched, even saddened by this casually merciless exposure. Evangeline Walter must have been party to the ageing bachelor's secret also, since she had so neatly pinned him by his Achilles heel. Recaldo, ashamed to have been part of Smiler's humiliation, began to truly loathe her.

McBride, too, obviously found himself unable to pursue the subject. But within a few moments the Smiler had recovered his equilibrium enough to question the gardaí about how much they'd discovered about the dead woman. In particular he was interested in whether they had found a will.

'That's absolutely none of your business,' McBride rebutted robustly, but then O'Dowd further flummoxed them by giving them the name of Evangeline's Dublin solicitor and her bank in Cork. McBride impassively noted the name and number in his notebook though he seemed to be having trouble keeping a straight face.

'Did you notice any activity around the house when you got back from, er, Dublin that night?' Recaldo asked.

'I told you, I went straight to bed, once I couldn't raise her by phone. It was too late to go calling.'

'You didn't look to see if there were lights on or anything?'

'You mean go over to the house?'

'No,' Recaldo said, 'I was thinking more about your attic window. You might have looked out.'

There was a minute hesitation before O'Dowd replied. 'It's a store-room,' he said, looking shifty.

'But you phoned her?' McBride butted in. 'What made you so anxious to talk to her, so late at night?'

'That wasn't unusual, we often had a bit of a gossip during the night when she couldn't sleep. But that time I rang her because she wasn't well. I was concerned for her.'

'Why did you go around so early next morning?' he asked. 'Weren't you afraid of disturbing her then?'

'She was an early riser like myself. Anyway I wanted to talk something over with her.'

'Mind telling us?'

Smiler shrugged. 'It doesn't matter now, it wasn't anything important.'

'You don't know what's important,' McBride chided, but the devastation on O'Dowd's face stopped him and he allowed himself to be sidetracked.

'I knew her better than most,' he said with curious dignity. 'I'll do anything to help you get the blackguard that killed her. But what I had to say to her was of a personal nature and it doesn't concern either of you. You'd be much better off getting out there and asking John Spain a few questions.' He sounded less sure of himself now, as if his heart was no longer in it. As if he would like to have done some questioning himself. He stood up.

'What is it with you and the old man?' McBride asked. 'Just what is it?'

'Nothing. If you want to know about him, ask Cressida Sweeney,' he said venomously. 'I've seen her talking to Spain on many occasions. In and out of his house, day and night. She leaves that young boy with him as well.' He implied that only a fool or another pervert would be seen doing such a thing. But it wasn't a convincing performance. For one thing, he didn't make any obvious connection to the Walter killing. Was O'Dowd just digging? Diverting interest from himself to Recaldo by trying to provoke him into defending Cressida Sweeney, or at least admitting his interest? Recaldo shuddered and on glancing around found McBride's beady eye fixed on him. He had a very knowing expression on his face. McBride pushed back his chair. 'Could I use the bog?' he asked and went through to the hall without waiting for directions.

'Uncouth lout,' O'Dowd bristled.

Recaldo got up from the table. 'Thanks for the breakfast, Mr O'Dowd, even if I didn't do it justice,' he said as McBride returned, looking from one to the other with a provocative grin on his face.

'Be seeing you, Jeremiah,' he said breezily. 'I really dig the names around here, they're an education in themselves. Me own's so ordinary I'm beginning to feel a bit deprived.'

He left the kitchen, and when Recaldo caught up with him he was standing in the cabbage patch looking up at the attic window, turning sideways, this way and that, trying to line himself up with the window and the gable end of the Walter house which was visible over the tall laurel hedge planted close to it. He didn't appear bothered that

O'Dowd was at the kitchen door watching. 'That the window you mentioned? I wonder what it looks onto?'

'The edge of the terrace away from the house and the lower part of Walter's garden,' Recaldo replied.

'That's very precise, FX.'

'I climbed up on the roof yesterday and looked for myself.'

'I wouldn't have thought you were that athletic,' McBride said mildly. 'O'Dowd's more my height though, he mightn't have such a good view.'

'Not necessarily. I couldn't manage to stand upright on the sloping roof – he could if he was inside.' He coughed. 'There's a pair of binoculars on the window sill.'

'That figures. He'd call it looking out for her but I'd have a different name for it. Prurience,' McBride said with disgust. 'What a good friend he was. I think I'd prefer an enemy. At least you'd know where you stood. Here, he's looking out the window at us. That's all I wanted – to unnerve the old bugger. I'm not going to let that guy out of my sight this day. Let's go.'

They started across the field towards the Old Corn Store. McBride contacted Coffey with the solicitor's number on the way. He fell behind Recaldo as he talked.

'I checked Walter's answering service before I came calling on friend O'Dowd,' he said when he caught up. 'Coffey's Yank, who isn't a Yank at all but a well-spoken Englishwoman by the name of Grace Hartfield, will be turning up sometime today or tomorrow. It wasn't clear whether or not the husband will be with her. Can you check them out? I'll see you anon, as they say. I've a few things to do. One or two people to see,' he said breezily. 'A bit of checking up here and there.'

'Coffey not coming today?'

'No, he has a couple of appointments. Then he's off to Dublin to see the solicitor.'

'Did Dr Morrow happen to mention,' Recaldo began, then carefully rephrased his question. 'Is it known whether Walter ever had a child? They can usually tell if there have been any pregnancies, can't they?'

McBride stared at him. 'Yes, as it happens,' he said slowly, as if releasing the information was painful. 'A long time ago and maybe more than one. Any reason you ask? Any *particular* reason?'

'No, I just wanted to fill in the picture, that's all. I find it hard to figure out where she was coming from.'

'Well, we sure as hell know where she's gone to . . . Here, hold on a tick.' McBride touched Recaldo's arm and looked back at O'Dowd's house. 'He's disappeared. He must be on the move. I want to keep tracks on him so could you sprint back and stall him long enough for me to get to my car? I left it in the lane outside the Walter place.' He winked and raised his voice. 'So long, FX, see you.' He walked rapidly through a gap in the hedge. As Recaldo watched him disappear he looked at his watch and wondered what time McBride had set out from Cork that morning. It was still only twenty-five minutes past eight.

He strolled back up the field and when he saw O'Dowd still glued to the window he appeared to change his mind and turned around and took a tangential path down to the shore. He walked slowly along the grassy bank into the next plot of land and from there to Mrs Walter's garden. McBride's car was gone. Recaldo sat in the Jeep and looked out over the estuary. He could only see halfway; the opposite bank was shrouded in a heavy mist. His mind was on Sweeney. There were two ways of getting from one bank to the other: by water or by road. Recaldo started the engine and drove away. He was still lost in thought when he knocked on the Spillanes' front door.

'It's open,' a woman's voice sang out. 'It's on the latch. I'm in the front room.'

Chapter Twenty-one

'WELL, MR RECALDO, I'VE BEEN EXPECTING YOU SO I HAVE,' MISS Mona Spillane greeted him as he entered the room. She was from the same mould as her nephew Finbarr though she looked younger than him, a small neat woman, sitting, or rather perched, in a wheelchair by the window of a large bright room which ran from the front to the back of the house. It was nicely but sparsely furnished, to make access and movement of the wheelchair easy, with shelving on either side of the chimney breast, on one side books; on the other a sophisticated electronic system with three rows of CDs. There was no television but Lyric FM was playing softly in the background. Miss Spillane watched him glance over a group of five framed black and white photographs of a young ballet dancer before saying, 'Now you know all about me.' She had a light melodious voice and merry eyes. 'Won't you sit down?'

'You were a dancer?'

'Yes, before this.' She banged the armrests of the chair and smiled up at him. 'In the corps de ballet, I was never a star.' She laughed. 'My principal work was teaching at the Royal Ballet School in London,' she said proudly. 'With Dame Ninette.' She looked pleased at his surprise, satisfied that she'd established her credentials.

He sat down in an upright cane chair, conveniently placed beside her at the window. 'When did you retire?' he asked politely.

'Eighteen years ago,' she replied, 'but I don't think you're here to talk about my brilliant career.'

He glanced out the window and was amazed at how good the view was. Not only was the house directly opposite the causeway to Trianach but because it was slightly elevated from the road, the view was panoramic. She was perfectly placed to clock all the causeway's comings and goings. He turned to Miss Spillane – somehow it never occurred to him to address her in the familiar – who was examining him with interest. 'You took your time,' she said complacently.

'Have you something to tell me?'

'Depends on what you want to know,' she said, clearly expecting to have the information wooed out of her. She was enjoying herself hugely.

'Do you spend much time here?'

She gave an elegant little shrug. 'All the time there is. Day and night. I sleep on that sofa bed there – if you'd call it sleep – but rarely more than two or three hours,' she said in a slightly martyred tone, 'at a time.'

His mouth twitched. 'That's terrible, Miss Spillane. I hope you manage a nap during the day?'

'Sometimes,' she conceded graciously, then gave a little titter.

'And what time do you retire at night?'

'About eleven, or twelve.' She whipped some field glasses from under the blanket covering her knees. 'But I have a great view from the bed,' she laughed. 'I suppose you want to know about Tuesday night?'

If he was surprised at her perspicacity he didn't show it. 'Yes. Did you see many cars coming or going to Trianach? Say from seven o'clock onwards?'

'I don't suppose you want me to list the normal routine of residents going and coming?' She raised an eyebrow. 'Just unusual traffic then, is that right?'

'That's exactly right.'

'Let me see. Hannah Foley brought us out to Trabuí for a spin after lunch and from there we went over to Daingean, so we didn't get back until a bit after six. Mrs Sweeney's Range Rover went in shortly after and about a quarter of an hour after that Smiler's hearse of a thing came out with a young one in the front with him.'

The girl, the girl, the girl moved in and out of his sights like a will-o'-the-wisp. 'Do you know who she was?' In spite of a little leap of excitement, he kept his tone light.

'I don't, but Finbarr thought it might be the girl that was staying with Mrs Walter.' She sounded slightly impatient at the interruption. 'They turned right towards Duncreagh. Mrs Sweeney followed a few minutes later, with her little boy sitting up beside her. She also went off down the Duncreagh Road – though Smiler was well gone by then. About half an hour later, at around seven, John Spain drove out in his ancient Cortina and headed off in the same direction. You came out of Passage soon after and went over to the island but you didn't stay long, did you? Was it to see Mr Spain you went?' she asked slyly but didn't wait for an answer.

'After that we had our tea and Finbarr helped me get settled for a small nap. I was feeling a bit tired after the outing – all that strong sea air as my mother would put it.' She laughed.

'So I suppose you didn't see much after that?'

'Well now, there you'd be wrong. Mrs Sweeney came back over – it must have been about half nine or ten – it was quite dark – she was driving that fast she nearly skidded on the turn. I didn't notice if the child was with her. I was surprised to see her. It isn't often she's over this way so late. I half wondered if old Spain was sick or something.'

Recaldo's heart leapt to his mouth and as he beat back the panic she suddenly burst out, 'Isn't she the foolish girl, consorting with that old fellow? She should think of the child if not of herself. The things I've heard . . . And as you well know there's no smoke without a fire, is there?'

'I don't know about that,' he started but she wasn't listening. 'I must have missed her coming back,' she said archly. 'I had an early night – much good did it do me.'

'So you saw no more comings and goings?'

'I didn't say that,' she said and gave him a little slap on the hand. 'Have you no patience at all? Something woke me around midnight – the screech of tyres, I think. I looked out and saw Mr Sweeney's car going across the causeway. Maybe he went looking for his wife? It was beginning to rain so I couldn't make out whether he was alone but I'm almost certain he was.'

'How do you know it was Mr Sweeney?' he asked, hardly able to control his voice.

'Sure don't I know all the cars?' she mocked. 'A good car is the one thing I really miss – and can't afford. So I pick and choose the one I'd get if I won the lotto. Mr Sweeney has a gorgeous silver Lexus. Next to Mrs Walter's BMW, that's my favourite.' She grinned at his surprise. 'It isn't only men that like fast cars, you know. There's life in the old woman yet.

I lost the use of my legs when a lorry saw off my Triumph Herald.' She sniffed. 'I was a bit of a goer in those days. Ah well. Roll on the lotto.'

'I think I might apply to be your chauffeur, Miss Spillane.'

'Join the queue, Mr Recaldo,' she laughed with delight. 'I'm beating them off with me cap.'

'How long was Mr Sweeney beyond?' he asked as casually as he could.

'That I don't know, but till sometime in the small hours. Usually when he goes over late at night he stays till morning, though he hasn't done that for a very long time. That's why I was surprised to see him.'

'And that was it?'

'No. I was just dropping off when the lights on the ceiling woke me and there was Mr Sweeney's car coming back over the causeway again. I didn't notice the time, I was half asleep. You woke me again going past at six. Your old banger isn't much better than John Spain's, d'you know that?'

'It was a bit later than that,' he said lightly.

'Not much,' she said firmly. 'Finbarr's alarm goes off at quarter to six. He sleeps in the room above, I could hear him moving about. He brings me a cup of tea at quarter past six every morning. He's very punctual.'

'You haven't seen the Lexus since?'

'No. I haven't been out since Tuesday and it hasn't been around here. But I'll keep an eye out – if you like, Mr Recaldo?'

'Frank will do. That would be a great help.' He stood up. 'Has anyone else been to see you?'

'You mean the other detectives?' she asked shrewdly. He nodded. 'No,' she said. She hesitated. 'Sit down for another second, Frank. Finbarr and I have a lot in common besides our age. We've always been close. Although he's my nephew he's actually a couple of years older than me. I am the youngest of thirteen, his father was my eldest brother. But that's by the by. That window is like live theatre for me. I make up little stories about the strangers, Finbarr fills in the rest for me. Yes, I know everyone thinks he can't keep his mouth shut, but they're wrong. He always says you have great respect for him. So I suppose you realize Finbarr always knows a bit more than he lets on – except to me.' She smiled. 'And I'm pretty careful about what I pass on. And who I talk to. It was concern for Mrs Sweeney that made me say what I did about Mr Spain. People are talking about her, you know.' She paused. 'What time was it you went in?' If she'd touched the

209

side of her nose in conspiracy mode, he wouldn't have been surprised.

'I'm not sure it matters, Miss Spillane. She'd been dead for some hours in any case.'

A rather shaken Recaldo dropped in at the station on his way home from the Spillanes'. Not only had she linked Smiler and the girl, Mona had also confirmed his own persistent hunch. She had given him the first hint of evidence of Sweeney's presence on the Trianach side of the estuary on Tuesday night. Moreover, her sightings were more or less at the material time. Had he also gone there earlier? By the river launch? Was it he who'd cleared her personal effects? Against that she'd definitely placed Cressie on Trianach without clocking her out. Damn. But first things first.

He rang the duty officer in both Duncreagh and Daingean garda stations and asked them to keep an urgent lookout for V. J. Sweeney's car, giving the registration. 'Hang on a second, Frank.' He could hear paper being shuffled in the background. 'We're already looking for that vehicle.'

Recaldo closed his eyes in frustration. *One step behind McBride again*.

'Just checking,' he said casually. 'You know how it is when there are three people on the . . .'

'Not sure who's the chief and who's the Indian? That it? I know how you feel. Don't worry, it's all in hand. It was a general call. Ports and airports.'

'Great,' said Recaldo, though he didn't mean it. He had just begun writing an edited report of his encounters with O'Dowd and Mona when there was a knock on the door. He opened it a cautious inch or two. A young woman lounged against the jamb. He pressed himself against the door, blocking the view into the office.

'Yes?'

'Sergeant Recaldo, I presume? I've been looking for you,' she said with a wide and conspiratorial grin.

'Have you?' he said coldly.

'I have.' Her hand shot out. 'Fiona Moore. *Sunday Independent*. I was in Daingean for a few days' holiday when the story broke.'

'How convenient.'

He knew her column. She specialized in chatty celebrity interviews, taking the sting out of what she wrote by injecting witty, self-deprecating little comments on her own life and general sluttishness.

She was gifted and occasionally lethal. He had always wondered how she got her victims to unbutton but now he understood. She looked harmless. Pushing forty and a little bit too plump, she was nevertheless a very attractive woman, with good skin, clear and innocent baby-blue eyes, and a wide friendly smile. She wore improbably tight silver leather trousers and a pale grey fluffy jumper, the combination of which screamed cuddleable danger. He knew perfectly well she was quite capable of constructing a profile without a word from her victim.

'So, how are things going, Frank?' she asked with easy familiarity and a lazy smile. Her accent was more mid-Atlantic than Dublin.

'Was there something specific you wanted?'

'Oh, just a few words about the job.'

'My job?' He raised his eyebrows.

'No, Mr Recaldo, *the murder*. You're the most elusive bloody policeman I've ever encountered.'

'Not all that elusive, since you've tracked me down. Anyway what are you doing here? You're a columnist, aren't you?'

She made a face. 'Oh, very funny.' She turned off the charm. 'Why hasn't there been a press statement today? Is there going to be an arrest?'

'To tell you the truth,' he said sweetly, 'I've no idea.' He shrugged. 'I'm only the local mule. This is not my case. You'll have to ask Inspector McBride or Superintendent Coffey – if you can find them.' He gave the ghost of a smile. 'I'm afraid I can't stop, you'll have to excuse me, I'm snowed under with paperwork.' He could have kicked himself later for being so bloody naïve. For thinking anything he said could possibly affect her. She saw him coming a mile off. He had almost got the door closed when she blocked it with her foot.

'Ouch,' she said. 'That hurt.'

'Then get your foot away,' he said tersely. 'I've nothing further to say.' She threw back her head and stared up at him, but after a moment's stand-off moved her foot. He banged the door shut and shot the bolt. It didn't make the slightest difference.

'I think I'll do a piece about you in next Sunday's paper,' she shouted in her husky voice, 'since I've nothing else to keep me busy. You'd make great copy, Frank Recaldo. I've a terrific pic of you from the old days.' She stopped and for a moment he thought she might have gone away, then she started again. 'It'll be interesting to see what the headline writer comes up with. I can make a few suggestions. *Sex* seems the most obvious, with your smouldering looks. Like to tell me what the hell a guy like you is doing in this effing backwater?' She waited, and when he didn't reply shouted, 'See you later, Frankie. I'll make you a star.'

He tried to deal with mail and phone messages but he couldn't concentrate. After checking the coast was clear, he picked up the pile of papers and shot out to his car, only just managing to get away before a phalanx of press boys and girls came round the corner and advanced on the station. They reminded him of a crowd of marauding football supporters except they were almost uniformly dressed in urban black leather. He blew his horn and drove straight through the middle of them, then hared home, fully expecting another mob on the doorstep. There wasn't, but maybe the dog had seen them off; he was barking his head off and the back door was scarred with fresh claw marks. Recaldo looked at him sadly. 'Poor old fellow, I don't treat you very well, do I?' he said gently, stroking the soft floppy ears. 'I can't take you for a walk this morning.' Or any time for the foreseeable future. He made a sudden decision which seemed so obvious that he was disgusted with himself for not thinking of it sooner. With his free hand he dialled directory enquiries, asked the number of the Kishaun kennels and arranged to lodge Barker with Mrs Reilly for long enough for her to teach him better manners. 'When will you bring him over?' she asked. 'Today,' he promised.

He was gasping for a coffee. Following Mona's little bag of surprises, his encounter with the journalist had disturbed him, but even so, he hadn't dealt with it well. He should have sent her packing at once. Not said a word. *Shit.* He filled his cup and sat down at the kitchen table with Barker's happy head on his feet. He desperately wanted to go up on the cliffs for a long and vigorous walk. Anything to get away for long enough to sort out his emotions and, even more importantly, decide what to do to ensure Cressie and Gil's continued safety. He had to get to grips with solving the murder, since everything hinged on it: Cressie, their future, his job. His integrity. Acting out of character had only added to the mess. When McBride found out about him spiriting Cressida away, as he inevitably would – probably had already – there would be hell to pay. There was the danger that the Dubliner would storm over and haul Cressie back screaming. The Dillons didn't deserve that. They were his closest friends, one of the reasons he'd chosen to settle in the area, and he valued them too much to impose on their generosity too long. With Cressie safely with the Dillons, Coffey in Dublin or Cork and McBride shadowing O'Dowd, he had at least a few hours in hand. From now on it was think first; act second.

It wasn't only that the murder had fundamentally altered his life and position vis-à-vis Cressie, the timing was particularly poignant. It had happened just at the point when he might have been able to take the first tentative steps towards a new life with her: first the book deal, immediately followed by the offer from his ex-wife of financial freedom. Her letter had been burning a hole in his pocket since Tuesday. Now his dreams were up in smoke. He opened the letter and read it sadly.

Dear Frank, I'm writing because I have some news that I wanted to tell you myself before you heard it from the boys. I've tried ringing you several times but never manage to make contact.

I'm getting married again. I've told the boys and they seem to be all right about it – though it's hard to say since they do more grunting than talking these days. I asked them not to say anything until I had a chance to tell you myself. His name is Martin Doyle and we've known each other for years. He emigrated to the States directly after college and lived there about fifteen years but came home after his wife died six years ago, and set up his own business in Dublin.

This is the hard bit. We got together soon after he got back. I could say I didn't mean to fall in love, or that it just happened, but you know yourself we weren't getting on, that things were going from bad to worse between us. I'd made up my mind to leave just before you got sick and then I thought the least I could do was stay and look after you. It was not a good decision, was it? I can see that now. I was too frightened and unhappy and maybe too resentful. At the time, I know you thought the illness was what caused the break-up but it wasn't, we were already washed up. I should have gone earlier.

So I feel I owe you. Martin is doing well, his IT business is flourishing. He has a house in Blackrock where we intend to live. Andy and Feargal are (for them) reasonably enthusiastic, so I don't need this place. With your agreement, I propose to sell it and divide the profit between you and the boys, one half to you, the other half invested for their college fees. House prices are astronomical in Dublin at the moment, so it's a good time. It's been valued at over two hundred thousand and the auctioneer thinks that with enough competition we might get more. You may think I'm being short-sighted but I've thought this through and I'm sure of what I'm doing. Martin and I are very happy together.

It's not blood money. You were more generous than you could afford when we broke up and I know you've had a difficult time, so maybe this will help you get on your feet. The boys say you're coming up to Dublin again in a couple of weeks' time – maybe we could arrange a meeting then and get the process started? I hope you're keeping well. Sheila.

Somehow the letter made him realize that his mind was already made up; about the job, at least. He let Barker out into the back yard and went upstairs to his desk and replied to his ex-wife, then wrote a letter of resignation pleading ill health and giving three months' notice, but asking to be replaced sooner, if possible. With that out of the way he felt he could pursue his own line of enquiry unencumbered with worries about protocol.

There was no good reason, no absolute clincher, linking V. J. Sweeney with the murder. None but Recaldo's strong and growing belief. Could it be he was just blinded by love? Some things he knew or almost knew: Spain and Cressie were on Trianach that evening. This wasn't proof that they were in the Old Corn Store garden: that was where the hunch – and the comb – came in. But then again, the comb was just proof of her presence there *at some stage*. Providing it belonged to her and not to either of the other females, both of whom had long hair.

Sweeney was also on Trianach; Mona had marked his card. Sweeney, Spain, Cressida, Evangeline. What bound those four? What was the catalyst to the violence? What had caused one or more of them to punch that malicious bitch to death? What was the motive? Gossip (Spain)? Jealousy (Cressida)? Rejection (Sweeney)? Viewed that way none seemed strong enough. So why did the mysterious girl again come tripping into his thoughts? Gil? O'Dowd? Even as he linked the names he knew he had the whole cast list in front of him. That being the case, what, specifically, ignited the violence?

He needed a clear run at it for a few hours. He hoped it would be long enough to get Cressie and Spain out of the frame before McBride started homing in on them – and him.

As for the future? He had absolutely no idea whether his proposed travel book would earn more than its advance but even if it failed, there were other things he could try, surely? He reread his wife's letter before replacing it in its envelope, then he sat back in his chair, slowly and methodically working out a plan of campaign for the rest of the day. He was determined to concentrate on the case and absolutely nothing else. He put all thoughts of the future out of his head.

He rang the hospital in Cork and asked to speak to Marilyn Donovan. Fifteen wasted minutes later he was told she'd been discharged the night before. He rang her home number and a rather hesitant voice answered.

'It's Frank, Marilyn.'

'Oh thank God. One of those bloomin' reporters got hold of our number and he's been pestering the life out of me. I feel like ripping the blasted phone off the wall. No, no I didn't talk to him. Told him my daughter Marilyn was in hospital.' She tittered.

'Good. Keep it like that. Could you answer a few questions for me?'

'God, Frank, I talked myself silly last night with yer man McBride. Didn't he only drive me back from the hospital. Gave me dinner in the Arbutus Lodge, if you please.' Blast and damn. Why was he not surprised? No wonder McBride had been so bright and breezy that morning.

'It won't take a minute, Marilyn, d'you mind?'

'For you, Frank, anything,' she said flirtatiously. 'But make it snappy for to tell you the God's honest truth I feel like I've been steamrollered. The drive back took it out of me and of course Liam was up half the night.'

'When did you last work for Mrs Walter?'

'Monday as usual, though I didn't actually do much. I made up the guest room and changed the sheets on the sofa bed in the lounge. She's mostly been sleeping downstairs for the past few weeks.'

'Did she say who she was expecting?'

'Some American relatives is all she said.'

'Did she work on the computer on Monday?'

'Lord, Frank, she hasn't worked on that for months. Once she got the laptop she hardly used it. It was that much handier for the bed.'

'What bed?'

'Stop eejiting, Frank, the sofa bed in the lounge of course – didn't I tell you she's been sleeping downstairs? She stored the laptop and all her personal papers in that painted Italian chest beside the sofa nearest

215

the window. Bills and things. She couldn't bear bits and pieces lying around the place. It all had to be neat and tidy with Mrs Walter.'

'The chest was there on Monday?'

'Of course it was. Actually she had it open, she was putting new batteries in her little dictating machine. Is it not—'

'How big is the chest?'

Marilyn thought for a moment before answering. 'I suppose about the size of an old-fashioned cabin trunk with a flat top. You may not have noticed it. There's usually a couple of embroidered cushions on top of it or a blanket.'

He cut across her. 'Thanks a million, Marilyn, you must be tired answering the same old questions.'

'Ah Frank, would you give over. You were great with Aisling, I owe you. Look, Mrs W was a good employer. Poor woman, it was a terrible thing to happen to her altogether. I didn't really take it in when your man was talking to me last night. He must have thought I was a heartless cow. But now, since I'm home . . . Look, d'you mind if I ring off? Aoife has Liam for the next hour and if I don't get some sleep I'll die.'

'Leave the phone off the hook, I'm surprised more of them haven't sussed out you worked for her.'

Marilyn gave a little giggle. 'Didn't Michael Hussey put it about that she had a butler. He's supposed to be living over Daingean way, I believe.'

Recaldo replaced the receiver. A chest the size of a cabin trunk would fit easily into the boot of a car. As well as a laptop, for that matter. The question was – was there some specific reason for taking it away? Other than to cause delay? On reflection, it seemed to him that there could be two reasons for such a tactic: one to keep the investigating team tied up, and two to give some interested party information as well as time . . . But for what?

Recaldo was worming his way along this labyrinthine path when Cressida rang. She sounded less tense and said that Gil and the nine-year-old Dillon twins were getting on like a house on fire.

'They don't talk much, do they?' he snorted. 'Mary says they have their own secret language.'

'But that's the point,' she said. 'They seem to understand Gil really well. They're on the same wavelength. The three of them were up at seven – nattering away as if they've known each other all their lives.'

She seemed less stressed. They spoke for a few minutes, but neither mentioned her husband or the murder. She promised to stay put until he contacted her again.

He put down the phone and tried to work out how he could get out of the house without being mobbed. After a few minutes' thought, he rang Lia Ryan who agreed to loan him her car for an hour or so. 'I'll leave it parked by the church with the keys on top of the front wheel,' she said. He switched the house phone to the station where it would be answered automatically and put a message on his mobile to say he was unavailable.

On his way out he left a bowl of water in the back yard for the dog. 'You're to savage any intruders,' he instructed. 'And bark your head off if anyone comes within a mile of the house. I won't be long, old son,' he said and vaulted over the fence into his neighbour's garden. From there he made his way, garden by garden, up to the church and picked up Lia's venerable but carefully maintained Audi. Ten minutes later, Recaldo was walking up the lane to Spain's house.

He knocked on the front door and when he got no answer, pushed it open and stepped directly into a large room which constituted the main room of the small cottage. He stood, blinking uncertainly in the gloom. After a moment he made out the figure of John Spain sitting at one end of his kitchen table with a bottle of whiskey in front of him. The curtains on the small windows were still drawn. Dim light was provided by a small oil-lamp in front of him which left the rest of the long table and the surrounding room in deep shadow. There seemed to be a pile of junk on the other end but it was hard to see anything save only the lined face of the old man who pushed the empty glass across the scrubbed board. 'Have a jorum,' he said shakily.

It was the last thing Recaldo wanted; nevertheless he sat down, poured a tot and took a tiny sip. It felt bloody marvellous. He took another. 'Well?'

'They had me in last night. Picked me up an hour or so after you dropped me off.'

'McBride?'

'No, the other one, the superintendent, hauled me off to Duncreagh station and kept me till the small hours.'

'McBride wasn't there?'

'No, just the other fellow and a doctor – a stranger, I'd never seen him before – took some samples.' His face twisted in distaste. 'I'm expecting them back any minute to arrest me.'

Spain toyed with the glass, running the amber liquid, mesmerically, around and around. 'You in trouble yourself for spiriting her away?' he asked.

'Probably, but I'm throwing in the sponge anyway. I'm resigning.'

'I'm sorry about that, Frank. I'm afraid I've put you in a desperate situation.'

'No, you haven't,' Recaldo said gruffly. 'It was already on my mind to resign. I'll be well pleased to be out of it.'

There was an uncomfortable hiatus before Spain cleared his throat. 'Last night you asked who was with me in Lia's restaurant back in June?' Recaldo nodded. 'It was my twin sister. I didn't think it was relevant until you mentioned it.' Recaldo waited, suddenly alert. 'I talked to her early this morning.' He looked up. 'You were quite right.'

'Right about what?'

'I think it was her presence which must have upset Mrs Walter.'

'How do you work that out?'

'It's a roundabout story. My sister is a nun. She was a missionary in Africa for many years but about six months ago she retired to a convent in the Galtee mountains. There's a home for the disabled there – the mature mentally disabled. The unfortunates who find themselves homeless when aged parents pass on. It used to be a huge place, once upon a time, but these days there are few vocations and it's gradually been dwindling in size and numbers.' He looked up blearily at Recaldo. 'There's a young inmate there, a girl of eighteen or so who turns out to be Mrs Walter's daughter.'

Recaldo could hardly trust himself to speak. 'You knew about this in June?'

'No, that's what I'm telling you, I heard it this morning for the first time. My sister knew nothing about it in June either. The whole incident was very upsetting for us. You see, Mary was in Africa at the time of my disgrace so it was the first time she had to confront it. She didn't know what to think when she heard what Mrs Walter said that night. She knew the reason I left the priesthood of course, I wrote to her at the time. I've always been open and honest with her. I didn't spare myself the truth, which she accepted,' he said harshly. 'But that night she heard something she didn't expect or know what to make of and she began to doubt me. Her own brother. I think that was the worst I ever had to endure. We've hardly spoken since.' His hand was trembling as he poured himself another measure.

'Life is very unforgiving,' Recaldo murmured helplessly.

'Amen to that,' the old man said, and after a moment added, 'the odd thing is that my sister hasn't anything to do with the girl or Mrs Walter. She lives in a small community quite apart from the main house. She only realized the connection recently when she got talking to another sister who'd worked in a similar home in New York for twenty years. When I rang this morning she told me that when the American institution closed down, Mrs Walter arranged to have the girl transferred to Ireland with the nun who'd looked after her since she was a child. The girl travelled in her charge.'

'What's wrong with her?'

'Some sort of brain damage.' He looked up again. 'Mary reckons the mother may have been in contact with measles when she was pregnant because the girl is also deaf. She has little or no speech.'

'You mean because she's deaf or is that part of the condition?'

'Mute and deaf. Mary says the sight can sometimes be affected as well. But fortunately not in this case.'

'How did Mrs Walter know your sister?'

'She would have recognized the outfit. The nuns don't wear the full habit any more but the older ones wear a kind of watered-down version of it. A navy blue coat with a silver cross and chain around the neck. They also wear a kind of kerchief thing on the head. The habit was much more becoming. The main thing is – the older sisters all dress the same. And there aren't many young ones. Ergo . . .' He drew a deep, deep sigh.

Recaldo put down his glass. 'Are you saying Mrs Walter traduced *you* because she couldn't bear anyone to know she had a disabled daughter? That doesn't make sense, John.'

'I'm not trying to make sense,' Spain said irritably. 'You asked who was with me that night. You seemed to imply that it might be important.'

They looked at each other. 'And I still think it might be,' Recaldo said, 'if I could just work it out. Who was with Mrs Walter that night?'

'She was with O'Dowd, and another man I didn't recognize. About my age.'

'No idea who he was? No? Who else was in the restaurant? Can you remember?'

Spain thought for a moment. 'V. J. Sweeney was there with three or four men who'd been crewing for him earlier. I saw them going out that afternoon. I can't remember anyone else specifically.'

'Do you know anything else about the girl? What does she look like?'

'I didn't think to ask that. My sister just said she was a "sweet poor little thing".'

'Do they know who the father is?'

'That I did ask. Unknown.'

'Is the convent near Thurles?'

Spain took this with some surprise. 'Yes, how did you know? Very close. On the Suir near a small place called Twomileborris.'

'Ooooh.' A long moan erupted from the depths of Recaldo's very soul. 'Did the mother visit her?' he asked softly.

'Seldom.'

'Does *she* visit the mother?'

Spain shrugged and shook his head. 'I didn't ask.'

Recaldo said, 'I'm almost certain she was here on Tuesday.'

'Was she?' Spain sounded surprised and from the look on his face was completely flummoxed. 'When on Tuesday?'

'Same time as you had Gil out on your boat. You remember? You warned me there was a tree down. Mrs Walter and O'Dowd were on the *Halcyon* – Sweeney's boat. There was a girl with them.'

'Oh.' Spain looked up. 'That's what the girl is called.'

'What did you say?'

'My sister referred to her as Halcyon Walter. Though I may not have heard right. I'd forgotten the name of the boat was changed. *Halcyon*?' He stared into the far distance and Recaldo knew him well enough to realize that he would say no more while he figured it out. *Halcyon*. A tingle of excitement – or was it fear? – ran through him.

He handed John Spain his mobile phone. 'Could you please ring your sister again, now, and ask if Halcyon was with her mother on Tuesday afternoon?'

'You do it,' Spain said and jotted down the number from memory. 'Ask to speak to Sister Agnes – she looks after the girl.'

Sister Agnes said yes, and without any prompting added, 'I don't think it was a great success. Mr O'Dowd brought her back. He was very flustered and Halcyon was up to high doh. She hasn't settled yet. Oh dear, I'm sorry sir, I have to go . . .' The connection was abruptly cut.

Recaldo sat quite still, rigid, his mind racing. Spain was off in another world by himself.

So that was it. O'Dowd sent up a flyer by mentioning Twomileborris. The sleeveen was trying to establish if the existence of the girl – Halcyon as he must now call her – was known. He had brought the girl back in his car. Was she *his* daughter? Was this what bound him to Evangeline? It fitted, but somehow Recaldo couldn't quite believe it.

Because of course there was another link with Twomileborris: the outsider Mure-Robertson who also lived in that area. His connection to the dead woman had been established by Rose O'Faolain as art. Was there some other connection? It was coming together all right, but the pieces still didn't fit. He stood up abruptly. 'I must get back. Lay off the whiskey, John, and get some rest. Did you go out this morning?'

Spain shrugged dispiritedly and knocked back another slug of liquor. 'I don't have the heart for it any more.' His speech had become slurred.

Recaldo leaned over the table. 'Don't, for God's sake, go to pieces, John Spain. We're both out on a limb. Drink enough of that stuff and they'll have you saying whatever they want.' He didn't specify who 'they' were. 'Keep up your routine. And keep your eyes peeled for V. J. Sweeney. We need to find him. Urgently. You haven't seen his car by any chance? No? Well then.' He drew himself upright. 'I'll be back later. You are going to have to tell me *exactly* what happened on Tuesday evening, everything, from the time I saw you on the estuary with Gil. Are you listening to me? You'll have to trust me to figure out just why that unfortunate woman was plastered to that tree. Who put her there? And, more to the point, why? Think about it. Sober up. I'll be back around seven.'

He left the old man rocking back and forth, and saw himself out. Time to stop chasing his tail. At last he had a good idea how the mysterious girl fitted into the puzzle. The trouble was that Spain and Cressida were still in the shit. Maybe even more so.

He didn't drive directly to Passage South. When he crossed the causeway he turned left. He took a circuitous route over the hills and approached the Atlantis Hotel from the cliff track, with Lia's poor old Audi protesting the whole way.

Chapter Twenty-two

THE NOON-DAY ANGELUS WAS RINGING WHEN F. X. RECALDO PULLED into the hotel car park. Five minutes after that he was sitting in the manager's office, having a beer and making small talk with Flor Cassidy.

'Escaping the crowd down below in the village?' was Flor's greeting. 'They were in here till all hours last night. So how are things with you, Frank? Bearing up?'

'With difficulty,' Recaldo smiled. 'Nice to get a break for a few minutes. And yourself? Things going well, then?'

Cassidy hesitated. 'It's been a bit sluggish all summer.' He shrugged. 'It's an uphill battle to tell you the truth.'

'So you'll have no trouble holding a room? We have a couple coming in and I'd guess they'll be wanting a place to stay. Relatives of the dead woman. I'm not sure when they're going to show up.'

'Don't worry, we've plenty free. I'll do a discount seeing as who's in it. You won't want them dropping dead with fright at the cost,' Flor said, then closed his eyes in embarrassment. 'Oh Lord above, Frank, what am I saying? I didn't mean anything.'

Frank smiled. 'I know that. We're all feeling nervous, don't worry about it.'

'I take it you won't be able to play tomorrow night?'

'No, I'll pass on that, this week, if you don't mind.' He took a sip of his beer. 'Look, there's something I'd like to talk over with you. In confidence.' He asked, as circumspectly as he could, about V. J. Sweeney's interests in the hotel and was rewarded beyond his wildest hopes.

'I have a list of shareholders and directors, I'll make a copy for you,' Cassidy volunteered with surprising alacrity. Recaldo glanced down the names: ten board members including Sweeney and O'Dowd, and a further fifteen shareholders listed alphabetically with Evangeline Walter at the bottom.

'D'you think we should put a notice up or something? About Mrs Walter's death? She being a shareholder,' Cassidy asked anxiously.

'I don't think so. Let's get the case sorted first,' Recaldo replied. 'Did you know her personally?'

Before he answered, Cassidy made sure the door was properly shut. 'This may not be . . .' He cleared his throat and hitched a leg on the edge of his desk.

'You know anything you say will be perfectly safe with me,' Recaldo observed quietly.

'It's just that there was a bit of a barney at the last annual board meeting,' Flor Cassidy told him. 'In early June. I don't attend, of course, but I heard a couple of the members griping about it afterwards. What they said might not be true – I may have got the wrong end of the stick, or they may just have been describing a clash of personalities. But since you're asking about her, Mrs Walter's name was mentioned. Something about interference from an outsider.' His voice lacked conviction.

'Outsider? But she's a shareholder?'

'Yes, but not on the board.' He looked at Recaldo unhappily and held his joined hands against his lips. 'You have to be so careful in hotels. One rumour can wreak havoc with the staff. A hint of something wrong at the top and they all start fearing for their jobs. So I'd be grateful if you didn't say who told you this.'

'You have my word. Why don't you start by telling me how the board functions.'

Instead of answering directly, Flor asked, 'Do you know how this place came about? Who built it and so on?'

Recaldo groaned inwardly and glanced surreptitiously at his watch, but gave no sign of his impatience to be off. 'Is it relevant?'

'Yes, I think it may be. Let me just fill you in, then you can decide for yourself. Most of what I'm going to tell you I got from Joachim Bleiberg,' Cassidy said. 'The people around here called it Bleiberg's Folly when it was first built. The white elephant to end all white elephants. Still, there was a lot of goodwill for the project, though there's many now claim that they always knew it was doomed. Others, of course, saw it as the opportunity of a lifetime. The likes of Jeremiah O'Dowd, for instance. They say he was in there like greased lightning and before you could blink he was Bleiberg's right-hand man. The guy with his finger on the local pulse, and a dab hand at getting things past the planning authorities.

'In the late Eighties Bleiberg took a tumble with the collapse of Lloyd's and closed the hotel. It remained closed for a couple of years until his son Joachim rallied enough support to reopen. There was a lot of refurbishment to do, so, naturally enough, the first person he consulted was his father's right-hand man, Jer O'Dowd. Joachim formed a new holding company with ten shareholders, including old Otto, each with a seat on the board. Most of them are still with us.' Flor picked up his copy of the list of directors and ran his finger down the names. 'Those two chaps. They were the ones I over-heard. They claimed someone was trying to buy out several of the older shareholders and was hell-bent on ousting the chairman. I got the impression that whoever it was thought he was only a front, that there was someone else behind him.' He paused. 'Mrs Walter's name came up.'

'But you've just said she's not on the board.'

'No, she hasn't enough shares for that, I believe there has to be some sort of minimum. That's what they meant by outside interference.'

'So why would she be involved?'

Cassidy shrugged. 'I've no idea. But she was definitely mentioned in that context.' He sighed. 'I don't have to tell you that things have been on the slide.' Another slight hesitation. 'When the Bleibergs were in control, they used to be in and out the whole time. First the old man, then Joachim. Discreetly, of course, but the staff liked the way they were individually known. It gave them an interest in how things were running and so on. It was definitely a family affair. Now the old man is dead and Joachim's been much less in evidence over the past couple of years. He doesn't always attend board meetings.' He turned his mouth down. 'Which sends out the wrong signals, in my opinion. What those two guys said confirmed my own feelings that things weren't quite right. I mean, to be honest, this place is a wild and wonderful dream. For one thing, our standards are very high and that doesn't come cheap. For another, the upkeep is horrendous – you can imagine – with the wind and weather howling in across the bay.

'The indication was that the board was split over three proposals. One, keep things as they are: a top-class private hotel, no packages, and no tours. Two, develop corporate events, conferences – on a small and exclusive scale, of course. *Or*, and this is the rub, a group headed by Sweeney, who is acting chairman, wants to sell up and turn the place into a conference centre or convert it into apartments.' He hunched his shoulders and rubbed his palm across his forehead.

'And which of these were the plotters alleged to subscribe to?' Recaldo asked, and Cassidy's answer made him suddenly sit up and take notice.

'Ah well, that's the interesting point. Neither. Or rather both. Again, it was only what I overheard, but it would appear their sole interest was in ousting V. J. Sweeney, and either getting Joachim back or else making someone, unnamed, chair in his place.'

'Any idea who?' Recaldo asked innocently. Then, almost as an afterthought, added, 'When exactly did Sweeney become chairman?'

Cassidy shrugged. '*Acting* chairman. A couple of years ago. Joachim was busy setting up another hotel in the Pyrenees and was spending less and less time here. It seemed like a good idea at the time but now . . .' He threw up his eyes. 'It's all too obvious that V. J. Sweeney is up the Swanee. Without a paddle. His company in the UK is all washed up and don't tell me you haven't seen him the worse for drink. He's all the time smashed out of his skull. I don't know how that poor wife of his puts up with it,' he added, and Recaldo allowed himself the fervent hope that she wouldn't have to for much longer.

'OK, but where does Mrs Walter come into all this?' he persisted.

Cassidy threw up his hands. 'God, you tell me. I have no idea. I was really surprised because I thought Sweeney was a friend of hers. At least I used to see them around the hotel together.' He bit his lip thoughtfully. 'Not for quite a while though, and those two guys kept mentioning her name, as if there was some sort of personal vendetta.' His eyes were troubled. 'The word manipulation was used a lot. It will be interesting to see,' he said softly, 'exactly who inherits her shares.'

'Ah,' Recaldo let out his breath. 'Indeed it will.' He took out his list and ran his finger down the names until he got to Mure-Robertson. 'Know anything about this chap?'

'You must be psychic, man. He hardly ever shows his face but believe it or not he's in the hotel, I saw him myself not half an hour ago having coffee in the lounge.'

Recaldo jumped to his feet. 'Is he still here?'

'I'll check.' Cassidy went out of the office but was back instantly. 'He's in the spa, having a swim, but he's booked lunch in the dining room in half an hour. D'you want me to leave a message for him?'

'No, I'll find him on my way out. What does he look like?'

'About your height, heavier, seventy-odd and . . . er . . . eccentrically dressed. You'll spot him a mile off, he's into bright colours. Frank?'

'Yeah?'

'Funny you asking about him just now. I'm pretty sure I heard those two guys mention his name that day though I can't remember in what context.' He winced. 'I may not have heard it properly, because there's also someone called Robert Kelly-Moore on the board, which is a bit confusing. I couldn't exactly stand around with my ears flapping. But whichever of them it was, my chaps seemed to be afraid he was thinking of selling up.'

'To Mrs Walter, you mean?'

'I dunno.' He looked distinctly uncomfortable. 'I assumed O'Dowd, until they implied that they thought she was involved. It really puzzled me because of her not being a director. I suppose that's what made me prick up my ears in the first place. It's all a bit iffy.'

'Any ideas, yourself, what was going on?' Recaldo asked. He could feel the excitement rising in him. 'Come on, Flor, I told you I'll be discreet.'

'Well now, this really is gossip and based on nothing more than a hunch. The two guys were still talking when Jer O'Dowd showed up. They seemed to be expecting him, but the minute he appeared they clammed up. Nothing more about the board was said while I was within earshot. But later, after O'Dowd had gone, they were chatting just outside my office – I had the door slightly open,' he confessed sheepishly. 'By then I was all ears. Sure as hell, one of them said: *O'Dowd is the fly in the ointment. The pair of them are as thick as thieves.* And the other said something about a majority shareholding.'

'Any idea who he meant?'

'Well, yes and no. God, I shouldn't be telling you this, Frank, but old Bleiberg gave Jer O'Dowd's original shares to him or sold them to him, or whatever. He got more when the old man died. Same time as Mrs Walter did, I believe. Everyone knows the pair of them are an item. You must have heard that yourself? I wondered if she was trying to accumulate enough shares to get on the board and he was trying to help her. Or something like that.'

'Is this place more valuable as a going concern or for development?'

'I think you'd have to ask someone better qualified than me and with less of a vested interest to answer that. But I'll tell you this much: one of those scutty little holiday cottages near you recently changed hands for nearly a hundred thousand. Which doesn't make me feel too secure, I can tell you.' Nor me, thought Recaldo, thinking of his wife's letter.

'How much support had Sweeney?'

'I couldn't say but he wasn't universally unpopular, you know. He could be very effective and he generally appeared sober for board meetings.'

Recaldo was miles away. Were the pair manoeuvring Sweeney into a position where he was forced to sell cheap? They could then turn the tables, backing his scheme when he could no longer benefit. Neat. When added to O'Dowd's recent revelations, Flor's story was indeed very illuminating. Strange, how Smiler kept popping up and always in tandem with Evangeline Walter. But stranger still that O'Dowd, a Passenger born and bred, had overlooked how easily speculation was passed around as gospel. Recaldo contemplated this, but only for a moment. Smiler was nobody's fool. Whatever was known about Smiler was because he himself had orchestrated it. But what if – and Recaldo took his next line of argument a little more hesitantly – what if Smiler had recently suspected that he, arch-manipulator that he was, was himself being duped? What then? What a blow to his ego that would be.

He found Alex Mure-Robertson sitting at a window table in the dining room. Cassidy had been right about the clothes – bright green polo shirt and loud check slacks – but the Canadian was courteous and informative.

'I spoke to Mrs O'Faolain on Wednesday when I heard about poor

Mrs Walter's death. It's very sad. I knew she was ill, of course. But to be struck down like that? Such a terrible thing. Dreadful, dreadful. I don't suppose you know . . .' He was very softly spoken with a pronounced Violet-Elizabeth Bott lisp. It took Recaldo several moments to tune in.

'I'm afraid not.' Recaldo took a deep breath. 'May I ask the purpose of the meeting you arranged with Mrs Walter?'

'She arranged it, not me – here as a matter of fact. She wanted to do an interview for *George* magazine in the States. I wasn't very keen, and would have told her so, but I agreed to meet her for lunch anyway because I felt I owed her that courtesy. She kindly introduced me to the work of a very talented young Croatian artist recently.'

'So your meeting had nothing to do with the Atlantis?'

'What makes you ask that? Mr, er, Mr . . . I'm sorry I didn't quite catch your name.'

'Sergeant Recaldo. Just routine, we are going through her effects, and trying to fill some gaps,' he dissembled artfully.

Mure-Robertson chuckled. 'Well, if that isn't a coincidence. Mr O'Dowd dropped in to see me on Tuesday evening, to talk over the last board meeting and to offer to buy out my shares. It seemed Mrs Walter had mentioned that I might be interested in selling, though where she got that idea I cannot say.' He twinkled mischievously. 'Things have changed a little since then, of course.'

'How so?' Recaldo felt a cold blast of air at the back of his neck.

'Well, as I told Inspector McBride this very morning, I've bought out V. J. Sweeney's interest in the Atlantis. We struck a deal last evening.' His face creased with mirth when Recaldo grimaced with irritation. 'Mr McBride asked me to tell you if you happened to get in touch. Don't you guys co-ordinate?'

Blast and damn. 'Mr Mure-Robertson? May I ask if it was a cash deal?'

Mure-Robertson laughed outright. 'Well now, I can see Mr McBride was quite correct when he said you and he thought as one. Yes, indeed, though I wouldn't like you to think this my usual practice, I paid him forty-five thousand pounds sterling in cash.' He beamed.

'How on earth . . . ?'

'Tut, tut, Mr Recaldo. No, no, I'm afraid I must decline to tell you how that particular little deal was arranged.' He chuckled again. 'But I can assure you the bargain was in my favour. Even as things stand, the shares are worth twice that. Look around you, sir, and on your way out take a good look at the site. You got that?'

'I got it.' Recaldo kept his voice firmly controlled. 'Was the transaction completed last night?' His question was answered by a slow enigmatic smile but Mure-Robertson didn't enlighten him further, from which Recaldo deduced the reason for Sweeney staying out of sight. He had been waiting for the deal to go through. Now he could scarper.

'You stole a march on Jer O'Dowd then?'

Mure-Robertson laughed again. 'Good for you, young man. Your colleague didn't make that connection. But yes, O'Dowd did me a favour by muscling in and making Sweeney a much lower offer. All I had to do was discover what it was and up the ante a little.'

There was nothing more to be gained. McBride was probably, even now, sitting hard on O'Dowd. Recaldo fervently hoped he wasn't right on Sweeney's tail. He walked around the outside of the Atlantis before he went home. Only a semi-circular single storey was visible from the lush gardens. The rest was hanging off the cliffs: four or five storeys built down into a natural ravine. It was a spectacular design. The balconied rooms dangled below him like shining crystal with an unparalleled view across the bay and the foaming water breaking on the rock beneath. They would make heavenly apartments.

He met Finbarr Spillane near the gate on the way out and stopped for a second to pass the time of day and tell him how much he enjoyed meeting his aunt. Finbarr beamed and eyed the Audi, clearly expecting to be filled in, but Recaldo murmured something about being in a tearing rush. He delivered Lia's car back to her restaurant and left the keys in the kitchen. Home was only a five minute walk down the hill but to avoid unwanted confrontation, he went back through the gardens again, dodging under clothes lines and over discarded toys.

Once he got home, he found a pad and pencil and wrote a list of names across the top of the first page. First the boat party: EW, O'Dowd, VJS and Halcyon as he now knew she was called. Below it he wrote Gil, Spain, Cressie. Halfway down the page he wrote the names of those who had been mentioned or interviewed over the past couple of days: Rose, Flor, Mure-Robertson, the nun, Finbarr, Mona and Marilyn. As an afterthought he added himself to the equation. In another column he listed Bleiberg, Atlantis shares, yacht, land and, once again, Halcyon.

He tore off the page and laid it in front of him and began a new one. This time he grouped the characters he had seen on the estuary as they had been on the Tuesday afternoon. Was the outing simply a woman, her friend, and her daughter pottering around on a sunny day on a lover's boat? Except it wasn't his boat. Whoever bought it renamed it for the girl. This led to two possibilities: O'Dowd bought it and renamed it to please EW or EW herself bought it. Recaldo thought about this for a long time and it seemed to him unlikely that pleasing her backward daughter would be high on EW's priorities. Specially when the cost of such a boat was considered. It was about ten years old, so, conservatively, it might fetch anything up to two hundred thousand pounds sterling. More if the deal was in Irish punts. Which of them was rich enough? O'Dowd probably. But he was fixated on land. *The land's the thing*, he said that morning.

EW's finances were an unknown quantity. But a woman who worked as hard as she was hardly in the super-rich bracket, or was she? The third and most persuasive option was that it was yet another example of Evangeline and O'Dowd joining forces and buying it together. Aha, now he was getting somewhere. Cressie had mentioned that VJ had sold it to someone on condition he would keep it on his mooring and teach whoever it was to sail. It was a joke. Much more likely the intention was *to resell immediately at a massive profit*. To do that successfully the purchasers would have lined up a buyer. The question was who? Recaldo almost immediately crossed out *who* and substituted *when*. When had Sweeney discovered what they were up to? Tuesday. 'Yes,' he said aloud. 'Yes.' He wondered, briefly, if the wily Mure-Robertson had been offered the yacht as part of the package but then dismissed the idea.

The name change remained a bother. He wrote Halcyon/girl/boat/father? He looked at it for a long time then pencilled O'Dowd/unknown/Sweeney. Motive? Flattery/revenge? Why revenge? He drew a little circle and placed Halcyon and Gil inside it and thought about them. He scribbled revenge and circled Sweeney.

Cressie said Sweeney wanted to leave Ireland, that he had sold or was trying to sell the land. To O'Dowd? Not if he wanted to make a profit, he wouldn't. No, O'Dowd would get the best of the bargain.

But, on the other hand, O'Dowd would be able and willing to deal with the thorny problem of access to the house. Selling the property would take time. Meanwhile it was quite clear that if his theories were correct Sweeney was being systematically stripped of his assets. It seemed improbable that he didn't realize this, yet he was more often drunk than sober, these latter weeks at least. Had the worm turned? To get away he would have to liquefy everything. And if he wanted to get away it was because he was guilty.

This brought Recaldo neatly back to the Old Corn Store garden and the problem of Cressie's comb. That she was in the garden that night there was no doubt in his mind. He was almost certain Spain was, as well. Sweeney too? Cressie had definitely seen something or done something which made her very afraid, not just of her husband but of him. As policeman, or as lover? Was she lying to protect herself and therefore Gil? Or to protect her husband? This was, for Recaldo, the most difficult question and he still couldn't quite cope with it.

DNA testing was the only certain way of identifying Walter's assailants. He wondered if his supposed colleagues had tested O'Dowd as well as Spain. Come to that they'd probably been trying to figure out a context for making him produce a sample as well. Somehow or other he had to shift their interest to Sweeney.

They seemed remarkably relaxed about his absence so far. And the reason for that could be that they thought they had already identified their killer. He wondered how far down the list the name Recaldo appeared. Somehow or other he had to come up with conclusive evidence before they swooped. Viewed that way, time was of the essence.

Having checked the coast was clear he bundled the dog out to the Jeep and headed for Duncreagh post office via Kishaun. It was shortly after three and beginning to rain when he posted his letters. For the first time he felt he was getting somewhere. Running around in circles was no substitute for plodding thought. He walked quickly down the street to the best fish restaurant in the county, the Georgiana O, where, Cressie claimed, she had first heard the news of Evangeline Walter's death.

The restaurant was closed. Shading his eyes, Recaldo peered through the window. Inside he could see Georgie O'Shea setting up the tables for the evening. When he rapped on the glass she let him in. 'Sorry, Frank, we're closed, but if you like I could grill some fresh scallops for you?'

He sat at the bar while he ate with Georgie perched beside him. He buried the question in a series of general remarks about the dreadful happenings at Trianach. Georgie told him she hadn't clapped eyes on Cressida Sweeney since Monday.

Chapter Twenty-three

RECALDO WAS GRIM WHEN HE LEFT GEORGIANA O, AS WELL AS worried, upset, anxious, tense, stressed. Georgie's simple little remark had set him off and for the first time he allowed himself the luxury of being utterly furious with his beloved. Much too angry to go and confront her. Instead he dropped into Terry Whelan's yard and borrowed a small motor boat. He spent the next couple of hours in search of Sweeney, though he had no intention of tackling him without the burly McBride as back-up. Locating his whereabouts was his intention, and, if possible, cutting off his means of escape. In the end it was wasted time. There was no sign of life on either the *Halcyon* or *Cynara* – though he didn't actually go aboard either – and Coribeen was forlornly deserted.

Recaldo returned to Whelan's, collected the Jeep and drove out to the Dillons' where he found Cressie making bread in the kitchen. She looked up and gave him a nervous little smile. He stood just inside the door, calmer now, watching her. 'Where's everyone?'

'Mary's taken them all swimming.'

'Bit cold for the sea, isn't it?'

'Not the sea. Apparently there is a good pool in a hotel about five miles away.'

He nodded at the dough she was kneading. 'Will you be long at that?'

'No, I'm just going to leave it to prove. Why?'

'We need to talk. Come into the garden when you're finished,' he said abruptly and turned on his heel. She had to come to him of her own volition. She had to stop putting all men into the same box as her violent husband. She bloody well had to trust him.

234

He found it almost impossible to be near her and not touch her, crush her in his arms. He sat down on a secluded bench under an apple tree within sight of the house. Cressida joined him about five minutes later. This is the woman I love, he thought as she approached. The delight of my muddled heart. This business is going to kill me.

The shock of seeing her poor battered face in the sharp daylight was so intense he almost cried out in anguish. His anger evaporated. There were bright spots of colour on her cheeks below the yellowing bruising round her eye. She looked fragile and anxious and yet even so he thought her the most lovely woman he had ever seen. He longed to take her hand, run off into the shadows and make deep and gentle love to her, kiss away her fears. Cherish her. But there were more days to endure, more mountains to climb. She came hesitantly and sat down beside him without speaking.

He put a tentative arm around her shoulder. To his utter joy, she leaned into him for a moment before edging away again. He framed and reframed what he wanted to say but couldn't get the words out. They sat in awkward silence.

'Do you suppose you could recognize someone after twenty odd years?' she said presently.

He considered her question. A word wrong now and he'd lose her again. 'Depends, I suppose,' he said slowly, 'what age we're talking about. Child to adult would be difficult. Otherwise, less so. Some people change a lot, others little,' he added warily.

'That's what I thought.' She looked over her shoulder. 'I didn't believe it,' she said, as if he knew or could guess what she meant. 'But then I'm not very bright.' Her voice was higher-pitched than normal.

'You can trust me, Cressida.'

She gave a little snort. 'Isn't that what every copper says?' she retorted wryly.

'Not every copper fancies you,' he said lightly, almost as if he didn't really mean it. The implied vulgarity oppressed him. 'Not fancy, *love*. I love you, Cressida.' Her beautiful name whispered gently through his head.

She looked a million miles away. Lost. He stretched out his hand and covered hers. She was all tensed up.

'Frank? I'm sorry.'

'How well do you know John Spain?' It was his turn to face what he most feared.

'As well as I know anyone around here.'

'How well is that?'

She gave him a startled look but took her time about answering. Her speech was hesitant, as if she was marshalling her thoughts. 'Apart from you, John Spain is the only man who ever took me seriously, as if I had a functioning mind. I've always been treated like a nitwit. Yes, I know his history. But not Evangeline Walter's lurid version. You realize who spread all the gossip about him, don't you? No-one need ever have known.'

'How so?'

'She must have been in Rome when the scandal broke. Of course it was all over the papers. *Priest seduces diplomat's wife.* God. So bloody pathetic. All she had to do was pass on the details to her sidekick. O'Dowd did the rest. A whisper here, a whisper there. Drip, drip, drip. John fell in love, that's all. He made a mistake.'

'I think, in fairness, a lot of people around here already know all that.'

'Way back, maybe, when he first arrived. It had all died away when she stirred it up again and started those other, much nastier rumours.' Cressida swallowed hard and looked away. A deep blush slowly spread up her neck. Observing the transparency of her feelings about the dead woman, something he hadn't thought of before occurred to Recaldo: Evangeline Walter had been adept at diverting attention from her own past. Had she done so by focusing on her neighbours' foibles? Was she afraid of John Spain? Not disgusted, afraid? Afraid of his intelligence? *Afraid of what he knew about her?*

'Why did she dislike him so much?' he asked, in an abstracted voice.

Cressie shrugged. 'I don't think Evangeline Walter liked anyone. Not really.'

'I heard she liked you. That you were friends at one time.'

She glared at him. 'Especially not me. She thought I was pathetic. Stupid. I know, because I heard her say so. She only cultivated me because she fancied Val and like a bloody fool I introduced them.'

'So, this isn't just about John Spain, is it? It's about you, Cressida.' He used her name with tenderness and allowed the tips of his fingers to rest on her shoulder. Her hand reached up and clasped his and a thrill of pure joy seized him. He sat quite still, for fear she would pull away.

'She said he was having it off with me,' she burst out, and turned around violently. 'They said that's why I was always running after him. Called him a dirty old man. Said he's a . . . he's a danger to Gil. I can't tell you all that's being said, but now I feel people are avoiding me when I go into Passage. They look away or else straight through me as if I was dirt. The worst thing is that nobody says anything. They don't need to; I know what they think. But it isn't true. He's a good man.' She looked up at last. Her eyes were shimmering with unspilled tears.

'He's never laid a finger on me,' she said fiercely. 'And as sure as hell he would never, never touch Gil in that way. He is the most gifted teacher in the world.' She turned to him earnestly. 'He couldn't achieve results like that unless he had Gil's absolute trust. And he does. Gil's a fluent reader and writer now,' she said proudly, 'and he's even learning Latin. John Spain is kind and good. I love him, but not in the way people say. What Evangeline Walter said disgusted me. He's the only real friend we've got around here.'

'Not quite, Cressie.'

'Oh darling Frank, I didn't mean you, but you shouldn't have come. It's wrong. You're the bloody policeman aren't you? John said you'd lose your job. That those guys from Cork would have your guts for garters.'

'Never mind that. You have to tell me what happened Tuesday night,' he ordered sharply. 'I want to help you. To do that I have to work out exactly what went on.'

'You should have stopped her.'

'Stopped her doing what? For God's sake, what do you think she was trying to do?'

She didn't answer. 'Cressie? Please?' But she stayed mute. He retreated wearily, remembering how he felt when he first picked up the rumours that she was forever in and out of Spain's house and he hers. That they were an item. The old man and the girl. He had been heart-sick when the whispers had floated past. He tightened his grip on her hand. 'Cressie? What happened Tuesday night wasn't really about John, was it?' he said slowly. He could feel the gallop of his heart in his voice. 'It's not what she said, is it? It's who she told?' Failure. As she went off on another tack, he saw that once again he hadn't got it right.

'She told Val. She told him I was unfaithful. She convinced him. I was such a little fool. I thought they were having it off. I couldn't understand why she wanted him so badly, he's drunk practically the whole time these days.' She closed her eyes and rested her head on the back of the chair. 'She kept inviting him over. He was always sneaking away. I saw him. He denied it, told me it was a business matter, said I was a fool. But I saw him, out in the boat with her. O'Dowd too.'

'Just the three of them?' He kept his voice neutral. 'When was this exactly?'

'A couple of times. By chance. Gil had a bad cold a few weeks ago. He was fed up being indoors so we tidied the attic. There's a good view.'

'On Tuesday as well? I saw them on the boat that afternoon. O'Dowd was with them.'

'I didn't see them then,' she said evasively. 'I was at the hospital, remember.'

'What time did you return?' he asked softly. Keep it cool, he told himself, let her come to it in her own way.

She shrugged. 'Late, late,' she mumbled distractedly then suddenly burst out, 'That two-faced O'Dowd, sweet as pie to your face but always up to something. Val playing the big guy, was he? Giving them a spin in that fucking, fucking boat? That would be just like that bastard.'

'Was O'Dowd bothering you?' he asked, unsure whether he was heading her off or pandering to his own jealousy.

'O'Dowd?' Her face wrinkled in disgust. Then to his surprise she gave a hollow, despairing laugh. 'Oh darling, darling Frank, you really do care about me, don't you?' There was wonder as well as sadness in her voice. 'So you think everyone else fancies me as well?' She sniffed and shook her head slowly from side to side. 'Poor you.'

This time he was not to be diverted. 'What happened when you came back from Cork on Tuesday?' She pulled away from his troubled gaze and began to prowl up and down in front of the bench.

'Cressida? Why did you go to Evangeline Walter's house on Tuesday night?'

She stood still with her back to him. Her shoulders were slumped. 'You haven't answered my question,' he said quietly. *But it's not the question I want to ask. I want to ask you to live with me. I want to close the door on the whole world, overwhelm you with tenderness. Melt you. Make you love yourself. I want to sleep for ever with you clasped in my embrace. I want to . . . I want to take you away from that awful drunk.*

She spun around and he saw from her face that she'd read his thoughts. He watched the ripple of her throat as she swallowed. The tip of her tongue moistened her parched lips.

'How did you know I was there?' she whispered.

He took something from his pocket and as he held it out he shivered with fear that he might have missed other little clues to her presence that night. Her finger snaked out to touch the broken tortoiseshell comb she had worn the night they fell in love. Then she simply caved in.

'I killed her,' she whispered. 'I killed Evangeline Walter.'

'What time was that?' he asked calmly, though his heart began a wild quickstep.

'What time? What's that got to do with anything? Didn't you hear what I said?'

'I heard. What time?'

'Eight, nine? I don't know what time . . . it was coming on for dark. What are you asking me the blasted time for? I told you . . .' Her voice rose dangerously. She tried to pull her hand away but he wouldn't let go. 'I killed her,' she shouted.

'Where was John Spain at the time?'

'I knew it, I knew it,' she shouted. 'You think John Spain killed her, but he didn't. I did.' Her voice was defiant, her face closed. 'I was there, in the garden, I saw them.'

'Who did you see?' His voice sounded hollow even to himself. 'What did you see?' He sounded stilted, walking on eggs. What happened on Tuesday would have happened without her. Why, oh why, had she not stayed in Cork with Marilyn? Safe.

'Cressie? Tell me from the very beginning. I want to help you. Was Val there?'

She went off at another tangent. 'He never told me. I don't suppose I ever really asked. Can you imagine that?' She was talking more to herself than to him. Then she looked at him squarely. 'I killed her, but not for that,' she whispered. 'I killed her for shaming him. I couldn't bear him to be so humiliated.'

'Val?'

She shook her head slowly and closed her eyes. 'No, of course not. John Spain.'

'How? Cressie, how did you kill her?'

'I attacked her, pushed her over. She hit her head on the paving.'

'Where was this exactly? Where in the garden?' He rapped out the questions, not giving her time to think. 'Answer me, it's important. How near the house was she?' As he forced himself to stay neutral, he closed his fist on the comb.

'On the terrace . . . near the window. I ran away. My comb must have fallen out when she grabbed my hair. She was laughing when I killed her,' she whispered. She looked up at him fearfully. 'What's going to happen to Gil?' He grabbed her shoulders and pulled her down to him and held her close.

'Then you went and got John Spain to help you?' he said in her ear.

'No,' she cried. 'No, he was already there. He saw me do it. He dragged me away.' Her shoulders hunched up and she said nothing further. She didn't have to.

'Listen to me,' Recaldo said. The deep voice rumbled in her ear, pressed to his soft sweater. 'You're going to have to tell me exactly what happened. Every single detail and then some. And you have to do it now – we're running out of time. Why did you go to Evangeline Walter's house? Why that particular night? Why, Cressida?'

She sat down on the grass and looked up at him. 'I know about the girl,' she whispered. 'I was so, so stupid.'

He expelled his pent-up breath slowly. 'How did you find out? When?'

'On Tuesday.' She spoke so softly he had to strain to hear what she said. 'It must have been about seven. I'd picked up Gil from John's, but I had to go back into Duncreagh because I'd forgotten to get petrol. The Ross Street garage was closed so I went to the one on the north side of the town. I was really tired and I must have pulled in too quickly, my front bumper glanced off the rear wing of the car parked at the pump in front of me. At first I didn't notice it was Jer O'Dowd's Mercedes. There wasn't any real damage. The paintwork might have been slightly scratched, that's all. But you'd think I'd totalled the blasted thing. I got out to apologize and of course Gil jumped out after me. I thought Jer was going to hit me he was so angry. There was an odd-looking girl sitting in the front of the Mercedes who started to wave and smile at Gil. Gil laughed and waved back at her. Then she got out of the car. She was quite tall, but acted like a child. Long blonde hair, almost exactly the colour of Gil's. Gil was frightened when she began to paw him. He grabbed hold of my leg and the girl did too. They were both shouting "Mama". People were stopping to look. That absolutely infuriated Jer, but then suddenly, he began to laugh.

'"Who's that?" I asked. He didn't answer me, he spoke directly to Gil. "Don't you know Halcyon, Gil?" he asked. My mouth must have dropped open. His voice was so creepy, it was like he had suddenly realized something that had been bothering him. "Isn't that a strange thing, now?" he said. "Your daddy's just had us out on the boat. We had great sport." He kept smiling. "Pity she can't tell you herself." He was looking directly at Gil and I knew what he was insinuating. I felt sick. There were spots in front of my eyes. "Who?" I asked, meaning *who is she?* He said, "Oh VJ and me and Evangeline." By then she was making a fuss and I had to help him get her back in his car. Next thing he was driving off. The girl turned around and kept smiling and waving at Gil. She had the same colour hair. Blonde, just like Val.' She threw her arms around her head. 'I told you I was thick. Thick as a bloody brick.'

'Then what did you do?' He took her trembling hand in his and held tight.

'I drove home. I was trying to calm down. Val was in the hall on the phone when we got in. Doing some deal or other. I brought Gil straight up to the bath and then put him to bed. Val was in the kitchen when I went downstairs. He was looking out the window with a bottle in one hand and a glass in the other but he seemed to be sober. Friendly, even. Trying to be nice. He is only ever like that when he wants something. I didn't mention meeting O'Dowd. I was afraid to. I knew he'd tell me I was imagining things. I made supper – bacon and eggs or something. Everything was OK until he started on about selling the house. Suddenly I looked up and Gil was standing at the door. He had his teddy in his arms. "I saw the lady, Dada," he said, just like that. "I saw the lady, Dada." As clear as clear could be.' There was wonder in Cressida's voice. 'Sometimes he doesn't manage to form the words but that night, poor, poor darling, he spoke really clearly, and I wished – oh how I wished I had never taught him to . . .' She began to sob. 'Val must have thought Gil saw the girl on the boat, because without any warning he lunged across the room and took a side swipe at me. "What was *your* child doing out in that old pervert's boat?" he

241

shouted. It was always your child or that child or that dumb kid. He could never bear it that Gil couldn't hear properly.

'I don't know what possessed me. I said, "What was *your* child and that bitch doing on yours?" That was as far as I got. He went for Gil, thumped him with the bottle and when I tried to pull him off, he started in on me. He kept shouting that he would have Gil taken into care, that John Spain was molesting him. And I knew he could do it. He wouldn't even have to have any proof, would he? Just the accusation would be enough for Gil to be taken away and it would be months before we could prove it was all lies, if we ever could, and Gil would be in some awful home . . .' She broke into wild sobbing. Recaldo held her tight.

'He's mad,' he said. 'Mad and dangerous. What happened then?'

'I think he knocked me out. When I came to, he was gone. I ran to the window and thought I saw the launch out on the river. The lights were on in the yacht. All I could think of was that I better warn John. And then I had to get away. I didn't care about the sodding house any more. I picked Gil up and put him in the car. I was shaking with anger. I don't know what I meant to do. All I remember was thinking, I have to get out of there.

'I can't remember driving to John Spain's cottage but when I got to it he was out. I ran down to the shore to look for his boat. I thought he might be still fishing or else on the way in, but I couldn't see beyond the spit. I don't know what made me drive round to where you keep your dinghy. Maybe I hoped you'd be there? There's a good view out to the bay. I jumped up on the bonnet and looked for John's boat and all the time it was tied up to a boulder right in front of me. Then I saw him walking along the shore towards Evangeline's. I followed him straight over to that bloody, bloody bitch's house and killed her.'

'What was happening in the garden when you got there?' And he realized from her terrified reaction that at last he had asked the critical question. 'Cressie love, what is it? What was so terrible?'

'If John won't tell you, I can't,' she said at last.

He tried another approach. 'Where was Val?'

She looked up at him, dumbstruck. 'I don't know. I don't know where he was. I should have . . . but . . .' As she nervously traced some complicated pattern on her cheek with the tip of her forefinger, he noticed the nail was torn and broken.

242

'Cressida? Where is he now? You're going to have to tell me.' Oh how weary he felt of repeating that stupid phrase. She looked spaced. Her eyes were smudged, her cheeks wet. She nodded miserably.

'Was he at home all this time?'

'Around and about. On the boat.' She spoke so quietly he could barely make out what she said.

'Not just on the boat. I boarded it the other night and I was there this afternoon.' He raised her chin with his finger. 'I noticed a light in the dormer window at the top of your house, the other night.'

'He was in and out. I didn't realize . . .'

'Was he there when I called yesterday?'

'On the yacht.' She looked even more wretched.

'That charade with John Spain was for my benefit, was it?' he asked sharply.

'Yes, I called him while you were downstairs.'

'But he was out on his boat. I saw him myself. How could you phone him?'

'He has a mobile, like everyone else.'

He looked at her in total disbelief. 'I am not a fool, Cressida. John Spain is the last man on God's earth to have a mobile phone. For one thing, he couldn't afford one. And if you're going to tell me it's in case he runs into difficulties at sea, forget it. You know as well as I do that John Spain doesn't give a stuff whether he lives or dies.'

She avoided his eye. 'He had one yesterday, that's all I know. He said he'd come if I needed protection,' Cressida said.

'From me or from your husband?' he demanded.

'Both,' she admitted miserably. 'I thought you were going to arrest me.'

'You? Not John Spain?'

'Why would you arrest him?' she asked, in genuine puzzlement. He knew then that she was unaware Spain had never mentioned her presence in the garden.

The question was, did they kill her together? Or had the old man finished her off himself? And where, oh where, did V. J. Sweeney come into it? Halcyon, of course. Cressie, having seen the girl once, assumed her to be her husband's child. Another abandoned disabled offspring. 'Oh Jesus wept,' he murmured. It was all too flimsy. Somehow he had to get proof of Sweeney's presence in that blasted garden. 'Did John Spain tell you how he found Mrs Walter's body?' he asked.

'How do you mean? She was lying on the ground near the house. That's all I know.'

'Was VJ there? Concentrate, Cress, was your husband in the garden?' She looked at him blankly and shook her head. 'Did you see him there that night?' he asked. 'Think, Cressie, for God's sake, think back. Was Val in that garden?'

'I don't know. I told you what happened . . .'

'No you didn't. You said you killed the woman,' he said urgently. 'But whatever you did, it wasn't that. Your story doesn't make sense. Same as Spain's. The pair of you are stumbling around in the dark.' *Me too*, he added grimly to himself. 'Did you see VJ there, that night?'

'No.' She sounded uncertain.

'Cressie, your husband was abusing you and Gil.' She was about to interrupt him when he put up his hand. 'For heaven's sake, Cressida, don't take me for a fool. Why are you protecting him?'

'Because of killing Evangeline,' she whispered. 'If I'm arrested then there will be no-one to look after Gil,' she sniffed.

'But Cressida,' he said wearily. 'Gil's father beat him up, there's no way you could leave the boy in his care. What were you thinking about?' As he said it, another fear hit him in the solar plexus. 'You're not pregnant, are you, Cressida?' he asked. 'Is that why you're protecting him?'

She blushed. 'That's a very personal question.'

'Yes, I'm sorry, I shouldn't have asked.'

'Those who don't fuck, can't conceive,' she said harshly and gave a high-pitched little laugh. 'I told you that long ago.'

'Cressida, look at me?' He spoke slowly, deliberately forcing her attention. 'You did not kill Evangeline Walter. Don't be afraid, nothing is going to happen to you. I'll see to that.' He sounded surer than he felt. 'Was VJ's car at the house when you got home on Wednesday?' he asked abruptly, surprising her.

'No, of course not. I wouldn't have gone in if it had been,' she answered without hesitation.

'Now Cress, this really is important so think carefully. When did you last see your husband's car?'

She hesitated. 'On Tuesday,' she whispered. 'In the drive. That was the last time. I can't remember seeing it again.'

'Where did you go after you hit Evangeline?'

She pondered this even longer. 'Back to John Spain's house. He dressed Gil's arm and my face and made me drink brandy or whiskey or something, then he made us lie down. We slept for a while or half slept. I think he went out. I woke up around four and found him sitting at the kitchen table. There were bits of engine spread all over it. Gil was fast asleep. I picked him up and we carried him over the fields to where John'd concealed my car. That must have been what he was doing when he went out . . . I can't remember anything about the drive to Cork . . . I brought Gil into the City Hospital in Cork early next morning. The nurse kept asking awkward questions so I told her that he'd fallen down the stairs, sleepwalking. At least I think that's what I said. I don't know what time I got to the Bons. We had no money and nothing to eat. I was scared of coming back home but in the end I didn't know what else to do. I hid Gil until I checked the coast was clear.'

'Why didn't you come to me?'

'Oh Frank,' she cried. 'How could I? I killed her.'

'I keep telling you, you did not.'

But she shied away, her eyes like saucers. 'What'll happen now?' She started weeping again. 'Would you, would you look after Gil if . . . if I'm . . . They'll let you. You're a policeman.'

He took her wrists and held them fiercely. 'My dearest love, have no doubt about it. I'll look after you both, I'll never let you out of my sight again, either one of you. You've got to trust me.'

'But Frank, I killed her,' she sobbed.

He pulled her to him. 'You did not. Just hold onto that one thing. You did not kill Evangeline Walter. She didn't die until much later,' he said with a good deal more conviction than was justified. 'Listen, my love, I have to go now. There's something I have to chase up. Stay here until I come for you, then we'll go together to see John Spain. This time you're both going to tell me exactly what happened. But together, so there'll be no misunderstandings.'

He walked back to the kitchen with her and left her sitting at the table with her head in her hands. Mary Dillon arrived with a carload of children just as he left. He stopped only for a few words but promised to be back next day.

Chapter Twenty-four

IT WAS GROWING DARK WHEN HE GOT BACK TO JOHN SPAIN'S cottage. Spain was waiting at the open door, watching the sunset. He looked terrible: his skin had developed an unhealthy yellowish tinge, as if the blood as well as the life had been leached from his features. There was also a more subtle change in him: he was on the point of breaking. Recaldo stared into the old man's eyes: dark, fathomless, despairing. Whatever happened was too late for him. He was almost visibly shrinking, diminished by the traumas not just of the previous week but of his whole wrecked life. Evangeline Walter had done for him; in death as in life.

'There are lights on upstairs in Mrs Walter's house,' he said. 'I thought you'd like to know.'

'What?' Recaldo looked at him grimly. God, he thought, Coffey's feckin' Yanks. Fine bloody timing. He'd forgotten all about them. But then maybe the ubiquitous McBride had it sorted. 'I'll deal with that later,' he said curtly. 'I need to talk to you.'

'The house is closing in on me – walk with me to the spit,' Spain asked gruffly. The two men walked along the lane to a low hillock which jutted out into the estuary. It was in fact a huge rocky outcrop on which small patches of bright green grass snuggled into an almost uninterrupted smooth sandstone pavement. They sat down and Spain lit his pipe and drew on it deeply.

'I want to tell you what happened on Tuesday night,' he said heavily. 'The whole truth this time.' He looked out over the water and sighed. 'But first I need to go back to that incident in June. Before we went to Lia Ryan's restaurant that night my sister and I came up here

246

and had a glass of wine before going to the restaurant. We sat, just like we are now, looking out over the estuary. It was a beautiful evening. I hadn't seen Mary for many years and it was a happy occasion for me. She had some photographs with her taken on the last day we spent together when she was already a nun and I a novice priest. I remember thinking how incongruous a pair of twenty-two-year-olds looked in those grim clothes with Mary's flaming red hair all shaved off. I asked her if she'd ever regretted her decision, regretted not having children. At first she gave me the usual claptrap about the hundreds of children who'd passed through her life, the ones she'd cared for in Africa, but then after a few minutes she took my hand and said quietly, "Every single day of my life."

'And so it is with me. I perverted my own nature; in that way Evangeline Walter was right. I completely discounted my desire and need of love, marriage, a family. I thought I could vanquish those dragons. I bought celibacy as I would something from Mrs Ryan's shop. I took it down from the shelf, dusted it off and convinced myself it was what I wanted. In the days when Mary and I became religious, sexuality wasn't much discussed or taken into account. *I* didn't take it into account. It was something awkward one learned to pretend didn't matter. But the girls and women I met weren't so easily fooled. I slowly began to realize that how I actually appeared was very different to what I tried to project. Had I been more honest I would have taken a good look at myself and left the order before I took my final vows.

'But I didn't, I ignored my sexuality and embraced the intellectual life. I made quite a job of it, I thought. Until my fortieth birthday when I had a classic midlife crisis. I found myself standing naked in front of a mirror wondering where my youth had gone – probably like every other man in the universe. And as I looked I had a spontaneous erection. I had never seen myself like that: massive, powerful, alive. I was appalled at how primitive I seemed. But while I was admiring myself, my penis just as spontaneously drooped. It was like a warning, showing me up for the sham I was. For the next three years I screwed every woman who made herself available – I choose my words carefully – I made no effort and invested no emotion. I became the sort of worldly cleric I most despise. It was so, so easy. In the circles I moved in I was much sought after as a personable spare man for smart dinner parties – I could talk and flirt in several languages.

247

And I suppose my cloth added a pleasant little frisson of corruption.

'I carried on teaching and continued as a priest but in all that time I did not once search my soul or my heart about what I was doing or how I was living. That is what I mean by perverted.

'And then I met Consuela. I had been given an honorary degree by a Spanish university and the ambassador in Rome gave a reception for me. It was quite a crowded gathering. The ambassador was about my own age, ascetic-looking, impeccably dressed. When I stood beside him I felt like a peasant. I remember turning my head as his wife was announced. It was a kind of premonition. My nemesis. She stood in the doorway trying to locate her husband. It was as if the room had suddenly emptied and she was crossing it, straight into my arms. Her eyes held mine as she joined us. For the rest of the party we spoke only to each other. Next day I wrote to thank them and the day after she wrote back and we began to correspond. I saw her from time to time but only in company, socially.

'My philandering stopped from the day I saw her. I left the order. My superior tried to persuade me to stay. He knew what my life had been like but felt it would pass by the time my dispensation came through – in those days it took several years. I think that, more than anything, made me determined to go. The extraordinary thing was from the time I left the priesthood I imposed celibacy on myself. I found a small apartment in Trastevere and I continued to teach at the university. I didn't see Consuela alone until two and a half years later, when she came to my flat.

'Her husband was being posted to London the following week and she'd called to say goodbye. I can see her now. She was wearing beige trousers and a white shirt with a pale grey cashmere sweater draped around her shoulders. She had little pearl studs in her ears and a large bag on her shoulder. When she came through the doorway I had the same sensation as I had at the embassy that first night, but this time she did walk straight into my arms. She never left me.

'When the scandal broke, my old order came to the rescue and somehow arranged a visiting post at Harvard. For three years we lived in utter bliss. A thousand days of perfect happiness. She was my life, my soulmate. Love enveloped us and protected us. We lived in an isolated bubble that we thought would last for ever.

'Then one day a young Irish girl came to my college room, mistaking it for another professor's, or so she said. Since I was about to give a class in his building, I said I'd show her the way. When we got down to the quad, she hailed her boyfriend who was sitting on the grass. The three of us walked to the faculty building together and before I left them the boy asked if I'd let him take his girlfriend's picture with me, a real Harvard professor. I was charmed by them.

'The photograph was in the *Boston Globe* two days later with a full résumé of the scandal. There were blown-up pictures of Consuela's grown-up children as babies. The press absolutely pilloried her. Every detail of her defection. How she had left her glittering life, her distinguished husband, her three children. The headlines were lurid. I innocently picked up a paper, as usual, on my way to college and ran straight home. Consuela was distraught. We holed up in the apartment for five days without going out, while the reporters besieged us. They interviewed our neighbours and my students, they shouted through the locked door.

'Then we ran out of food. I slipped out to an all-night supermarket at six that morning, leaving Consuela asleep in bed. The girl who had started it all must somehow have seen me drive away. She got into the building and started banging on our door and shouting at Consuela through the keyhole. One of our neighbours came out to berate her and a fight started. Consuela left by the back way and ran up the service stairs to the roof. When I got back she was lying dead on the ground outside with the neighbours around her.' John Spain looked up. 'She was four months pregnant.'

He fell silent. Recaldo picked up a handful of flat pebbles and began to skim them over the water. 'Did you come here straight away?' he asked eventually.

'Not for some time. I had a nervous breakdown. I was in hospital in Boston for eighteen months until a friend of my old superior rescued me and loaned me a small place to live outside Chatham on Cape Cod. It was a whaler's cottage just by the shore. One day I found a clinker rowing boat rotting in the garden. When I asked the owner if I could have it he put me in touch with a retired fisherman who fixed it up for me. He also taught me how to handle the boat and fish. When I left I took it with me. Come,' he said. 'Let me show you something.'

They walked down to the water's edge where the boat was gently moving in the calm water. 'See?' Spain pointed proudly to where *Consuela* was written in neat cursive script on the prow, inside. 'When I'm in the boat I feel she's with me. I talk to her all the time,' he said simply.

'John? Can you tell me now what happened on Tuesday?'

John Spain took a long, deep breath. 'Cressie brought Gil over around noon. Marilyn had been very upset the night before and she was anxious to get back to her. The little boy was exhausted. He slept for a while and then I gave him his lesson but all the time he kept begging me to take him out in the boat. But I didn't want to be seen with him. I was nervous of gossip. I was still thinking of . . . well, you know. Anyway it was such a lovely day I gave in. We went upriver first but unfortunately we were turned back by the fallen tree. Then Gil asked if I'd take him to see the seals. "Mama says they laugh like me," he said.'

'He *said*?' Recaldo asked incredulously.

'Oh, yes, he said. Not very clearly but I don't find it difficult to understand him and if I do, he writes it down. The boy has a very remarkable mother. Cressie taught him to communicate long before I entered the scene. Anyway he kept pestering me so, at last, I gave in. As we rounded the spit I saw Mrs Walter in her garden, smoking, as usual, by the tree. I headed off out into the middle hoping she wouldn't notice us, but of course she did. I heard her laughing. "My, my," she called. "What have we here? Naughty boy. I may have to tell Papa." And then she laughed and laughed.

'I brooded on it all day. Decided she had gone too far and had to be stopped. Not just for me but for Gil and Cressie's sakes. He's getting on so well and I've helped. It is one of the things I am most proud of in my life. Between us, we have given the child the gift of speech. But more than that, he gave me back my self-respect.

'After Cressie picked him up I had to drop off a box of lobsters to Georgiana O in Duncreagh – I couldn't get there earlier because of minding Gil. All the time I kept asking myself why Evangeline was so vindictive to me personally; we used to get on well. When she came here first she seemed to know all about the scandal, but she went out of her way to befriend me and yes, I'm ashamed to say we did have sex once or twice. But for the past few years she's been poisonous and

I couldn't think what the reason was. I stupidly felt the only way was to have it out with her. So when I got back I took my boat out and rowed down to her house.

'I knew it was a mistake the minute I saw her. I think she must have been drugged or something, but she was wild, out of control. I've thought about it a lot over the past few days and I've come to the conclusion she was acting out a part for someone else. I was only incidental.'

'Cressida?'

'No. I'm almost sure there was someone in the garden or in the house before Cressida ever got there. The windows were wide open. Someone she was trying to impress or punish or – she kept talking all the time. "Do it, do it. Show us how a man does it." Those are not the words, she was much cruder than that . . .'

Recaldo wasn't interested in crude, he was interested in 'us'. 'She said, us? What do you think she meant?'

'I don't know but after Cressie hit her I thought I heard laughter. A man laughing. God, but this disgusts me.'

Bit by bit, Spain recounted the whole incident as it happened, without sparing himself, and Recaldo learned precisely why Cressie had shielded the old man, why she had said he'd been humiliated. But even while Spain talked, Recaldo's mind was racing through the reasons why Evangeline Walter had grown to hate the old man and Cressida so specifically and so virulently. Was it because they had given Gil what she could not give her own daughter? He shuddered. They had given Sweeney's second child what had been denied his firstborn.

'Was the laughter you heard Sweeney's?' he asked and willed the old man to confirm his supposition.

'I have no idea who it might have been or if I imagined the whole thing.'

'What happened to Cressie then?'

'I dragged her out of the garden towards the boat but she got away from me. Her car was at the slipway. I pushed her into it and got in after her and drove them to my place. They were both badly bruised, beaten. I was afraid Gil's arm was broken. She was in a woeful state. Incoherent. I could barely take in that she was telling me her husband was having an affair with the Walter woman and that she'd persuaded him he could get Cressie to sign over the house by threat-ening to report that I was corrupting the child. Paedophile.' The lethal word whispered past. Recaldo watched the old man rock back and forth, back and forth, pain and bewilderment etched into the craggy features. He let out a long pent-up breath. 'I couldn't leave my boat there, I had to go back and get it.' He looked up. 'I had to. I didn't know what I was doing. It was where I had left it. I got in and was well out into the river when I looked back at Mrs Walter's place and as I watched she stood up.

'I couldn't believe my eyes. She was alive, leaning on the picnic table with her head thrown back, laughing. A radio or gramophone was playing . . . the wind carried the sound . . . Ella Fitzgerald.'

'Think, for God's sake, John, think. What did she do then?'

Spain sat stock still, bewildered. 'She went in the house and put out the lights.' He stopped. 'No, that's not right. The lights went out and she went into the house.'

'What did you do then?'

'I rowed like hell. I had to tell Cressie. . .'

'Wait a moment. Think back. Look along the bank of the Walter garden. Is there anything there? Think back, John.'

'Oh, oh.' He put his hand to his mouth. 'Sweeney's motor launch. It was tied up to the, to the tree . . . It must have been there all along.'

Recaldo clasped his hands in front of him, trying to batten down his excitement. Had Spain got it right?

'The tide was running so fast and I was being pulled upstream. Before I knew it I was past the spit and I had a hell of a job getting back. I moved Cressie's car to a secluded field in case VJ came look-ing for her. It was as I got back to the cottage that I heard the roar of a boat's engine.

'I ran down to the spit and saw a launch racing across the river. I'm almost sure it was Sweeney's. I don't know what made me go back to Walter's garden – this time on foot, along the shore. The motor launch was gone but I could still hear the engine, faintly, over the other side, but now there was someone by the tree. I crept closer, tak-ing care not to be seen or heard. When I got near I saw it was her. I said her name but she didn't stir. My heart was in my mouth. I put out my hand and it came away all bloody. Her head was bowed on her chest. I whispered her name and held her wrist. She had no pulse.'

252

His eyes met Recaldo's. 'I had absolutely no doubt she was dead. I'm sorry I lied to you.'

'I'm beginning to see why,' Recaldo said wryly.

'I couldn't think straight. My only reaction was to get Cressie and Gil away. I had to go back the long way, the water was too high to wade. There was one other thing . . . I don't know if I imagined it,' he said hesitantly. 'It was lashing down so I went to pull the tarpaulin over the boat. By then I was exhausted and maybe I was hallucinating but I began to wonder if I'd imagined the whole nightmare. I climbed the spit and stood looking back at Walter's garden. For a split second I thought I saw the lights come on and someone come out of the house.'

'Man or woman?'

Spain hunched his shoulders. 'I couldn't see, I was too far away, but someone big.'

'Big as in tall?'

'No, in bulk. A big bulky figure.'

Or a tall slim person carrying something big? Recaldo thought. 'What time was it when you got home, John?'

'I'm not sure – three – half past? I took off my things and washed myself in the river, then I went inside and waited for Cressie to wake up. She got up at about four and I took her and the child to the Range Rover and sent her off to Cork. She was in no fit state but I couldn't think what else to do. I sat up drinking hot milk and whiskey until dawn. Then I got ready to go out again.'

Recaldo and Spain walked slowly back down the lane to the cottage. When they stopped by the Jeep, Spain said, 'I saw a young woman in Passage South yesterday, from one of the newspapers, I think. She's the girl who was in Harvard that time. The girl who had her photograph taken with me. Fiona Moore, she was called.'

Recaldo froze. 'Did you speak to her?'

'No,' he snorted. 'She didn't see me. At least I don't think so.'

'Stay away from the village, John. For God's sake keep out of sight.'

'Frank? I couldn't face all that again. I couldn't.'

Chapter Twenty-five

IT WAS HALF PAST NINE WHEN RECALDO GOT HOME AFTER HIS turbulent interview with John Spain. He'd left the old man broken and exhausted, back at his kitchen table, with his hands clenched around a large glass of whiskey.

As he drove home half of him was tense with the excitement of at last pinning Sweeney to the murder scene, the other half was shaking with such anger that if Evangeline Walter had still been alive, he knew he would have gone and torn her limb from limb. The old man's appalling story had left him feeling dirty and guilty that love or desire could be so easily subverted into something so degenerate. But then, if his theories were correct, Evangeline too was corrupted by love. She had dished out what she had got herself.

It was as well, in his present mood, that he didn't encounter Ms Fiona Moore. He let himself into the dark and empty house and went straight to the shower, where he let the scalding water cascade over him. After he had dried himself, he padded downstairs in his dressing gown and poured a double brandy. God, but he felt tired. There was a diatribe from Coffey when he turned on his answering machine and lest there were others he switched it off again. He put the Verdi Requiem on his CD player. It exactly matched his mood.

He was making himself an omelette when Flor Cassidy rang to say his Americans had checked into the hotel a couple of hours before and were having dinner in the main dining room. 'I didn't say anything about Mrs Walter and they didn't either. I'm going off duty now, Frank. Will I tell them you're coming or what?'

'I'll drop up for a few minutes,' Recaldo said wearily. 'Unless

Inspector McBride's already talked to them?' Flor replied that as far as he knew they'd spoken to no-one and had kept to their room until dinnertime.

Recaldo abandoned his supper and walked slowly up to the hotel, isolating in his mind those questions to which he urgently needed answers. He hoped like hell that Mrs Walter's visitors were not cut from the same cloth as herself.

The dining room was vast and could easily, and on occasion did, double as a ballroom. It had a colonnaded central area with galleries on either side and floor-to-ceiling arched windows facing due south. The ceiling of the central section was ornately decorated, the columns faced with pale green, pink and white marble. Vast Waterford glass chandeliers hung at regular intervals. It was as bright and airy as a Mediterranean palazzo, which was something of an achievement considering the cold northern sea light. An array of orange and lemon trees in huge pots at the windows further enhanced the illusion of sun, and rose-shaded lamps glowed on pink-linen-covered tables.

The couple were sitting in a window alcove perched high above the sea, holding hands and smiling into each other's eyes. Recaldo stood back while the waiter served their main course and discreetly withdrew. The woman was straight-backed and very well groomed. She wore a simple long-sleeved black dress with no jewellery. As he crossed the room, she suddenly threw back her head and laughed at something her husband was telling her. He had a winning, rather goofy grin and looked the very picture of an academic. In another few years he'd be positively shambling. He seemed to have a keen sense of fun – Recaldo observed the laugh lines etched around his eyes as he came nearer. He felt a familiar pang of envy and regret as he watched their easy intimacy. They didn't notice his approach, but the woman glanced up with a start when he put his hand on their table.

'Excuse me,' he said politely.

She had the most astonishing eyes – pale grey with a dark circle around the iris. She looked calm, vaguely amused, and though she was no longer young, he thought her quite beautiful. As she would remain, well into old age, he decided, and was surprised by his own sentimentality.

He addressed himself to the man. 'Mr Murray?' he said.

Murray Magraw looked up and grinned. 'Yeah, that's me. You from Evangeline, by any chance?' He had a soft American drawl.

'In a manner of speaking,' Recaldo replied. 'I must have missed you at the house,' he said vaguely.

'She's back now, is she? So why didn't she come herself?' Murray Magraw asked.

Recaldo didn't answer. 'Is either of you related to Mrs Walter?' he asked.

His wife shot him a sharp look. 'Yes, my husband is her cousin.'

Murray paid no attention. 'You can tell her we're staying put—' he began but Recaldo cut across him. 'I'm afraid I can't do that, Mr Murray.'

'Magraw. My name is Murray Magraw, surely she told you that much? This is my wife, Grace Hartfield,' he said, then stopped short. His voice was slightly slurred from the wine and his reactions were slow. His eyes narrowed, as if he was having difficulty focusing. 'I didn't quite get what you said?'

'I'm sorry, Mr Magraw, I have something to tell you. Look, do you mind if I sit down?'

'Not at all, not at all,' he said and drained his glass. 'Any friend of Evangeline, etc., etc. Care for some wine?' He raised the bottle and when Recaldo refused, poured himself another glass. 'Why can't you give her my message, huh?'

Grace shot a glance at Murray, who was clearly gearing himself for a chat. His habitual friendliness turned to garrulousness when he'd had a few drinks. Now he was barely the right side of blotto.

'Are you going to tell us who you are?' he slurred.

'My name is Frank Recaldo.'

'Ooh, that doesn't sound Irish.' Murray gave his goofy grin, as if he'd just said something remarkably perceptive. He insisted the stranger share a glass of wine. 'Join us, we've had a very tiring day. So where are you from?'

Recaldo sighed and took the proffered wine, turning to Grace, who appeared the more sober until she spoiled it by giving a nervous little giggle. Perhaps it was as well that the waiter appeared at that moment with the sandwiches and mineral water Recaldo had ordered on the way in.

'I'm from Kerry,' he said stiffly, when the waiter had gone. 'But I live locally, here in Passage South.' He poured a glass of water for himself and then one for Murray. 'Drink that, would you please, Mr Magraw?' he instructed, firmly. Grace looked at him questioningly. This time Murray must also have noticed that something was up, because he readily gulped the water down, then poured and drank a second glass. He was sobering up fast and suddenly sat up straight.

'You're a policeman, aren't you?' he said.

'Yes, Mr Magraw, I am. Forgive me, but I'm afraid I have bad news for you.'

'Evangeline?' Murray turned to his wife and grabbed hold of her hand. 'Is she back in the hospital? We knew something was wrong. The house was so cold,' he said inconsequentially.

'You were in the house? You have keys?'

'No, my cousin left a key for us in the old letter box – just in case we missed each other. As indeed we did.' He brushed back a dangling lock of hair impatiently. 'What's happened to her house? The sidelights in front are boarded up. Did she have a burglary?'

'Mrs Walter is not in hospital. I'm afraid she's dead,' Recaldo said quietly. Grace gave an odd little cry, then clamped her hand to her mouth. She half rose to her feet.

'Murray, Murray. Oh darling, I'm so, so sorry,' she cried. Murray rose, took her in his arms and held her tight. He looked at Recaldo over her shoulder.

'We knew she was ill, but this is very sudden. It's very good of you to come and tell us.'

'No. It was not her illness, I'm afraid it was . . .'

'An accident? I wouldn't listen when Grace thought something like that might have happened. We were waiting at the house for hours.'

'It wasn't an accident either, I'm afraid. She was attacked.'

Murray sat down with a bump. He'd got it at last. 'Are you saying she was murdered? When? How did it happen?' The words tumbled out of him. 'Why?'

Recaldo slowly nodded his head. 'She was found dead in her garden early Wednesday morning. Look, I'm sorry, I know this is a terrible shock and you've probably been travelling all day, but I need to talk to you both. It'll only take a few minutes.'

'Tell us what happened,' Murray persisted.

'An old fisherman, John Spain, who's a neighbour of hers found her in the garden early on Wednesday morning.'

'How did you know we were here?' Grace interjected abruptly.

'You both left messages on her telephone-answering machine,' Recaldo said pedantically. 'We've been waiting for you to arrive.'

'No, no,' she said impatiently. Her clear, guileless eyes disturbed him. 'I mean, here, at the hotel?' She stood behind Murray with her arm protectively around her husband's shoulders. She didn't look shocked, Recaldo noted with interest. She was slightly flushed and seemed, if anything, rather angry.

'We were expecting you,' he repeated. 'I didn't think you'd be able to get into the house so I asked the manager here to look out for you, in case I missed you at Trianach,' he added hastily.

'We were in the house for ages,' she said accusingly. 'If you were so concerned to . . .' Her voice fell away as Murray cut across her anxious questions.

'It's all right, Grace.' He turned to Recaldo. 'Tell me what happened, I want to know.'

'But, Mim, if he could wait for several hours, he can wait until morning,' she said irrationally. 'You're tired,' she added. 'You've been up all night.'

'My love, I need to know. Now.' Murray spoke with sudden authority. 'See if you can get some brandy, would you, Grace? And tell them we don't want to be disturbed. I don't want that waiter wandering in and out.' He turned to Recaldo, who was reminded of his primary-school teacher. 'I would be grateful if you would kindly tell me precisely what happened to my cousin.'

Recaldo silently took out his notebook, rifled through it busily, more to order his thoughts than anything else, before he began. Halfway through, Grace came back, carrying a bottle of brandy and fresh glasses. She plonked these on the table, then poured three generous measures before sitting down. Recaldo resumed his story and the couple listened in silence until he was done.

'I'm afraid, simply as a matter of routine, I'd like you both to account for the past few days,' Recaldo said diffidently, wishing he could think of some other way of getting them to talk. 'It's just a formality.' Murray looked as though he was about to protest, but instead told him he'd got in to Shannon that morning from Minneapolis via Chicago. He waved an airline ticket under Recaldo's nose. Grace had met him at the airport, having crossed on the Swansea–Cork ferry on Tuesday night. She gave the address of the friend in Lahinch she had stayed with, one Seamus Crowley. Recaldo also made a note of the auction house in Limerick where she'd attended a book sale the day before. 'We're booksellers,' she offered by way of explanation. 'We have an antiquarian book business in Oxford.'

He felt faintly ridiculous as he laboriously noted the details which he knew would not mollify Coffey, but at least he'd have something to show him.

'So, you've no idea who killed her? Or why?' Murray spoke half to himself.

'No. We're a bit stymied, not least because we could find very little information about her private affairs in the house.'

'So she *has* been burgled?' Murray wasted no time coming to the point.

Recaldo nodded. 'We've no evidence of it, but it would seem so, yes.' He paused. 'How exactly are you related to Mrs Walter?'

'Our mothers were cousins. We've known— knew each other from childhood, but I'm not the next of kin, if that's what you're asking.' Murray looked curiously troubled when he said this, as if he were breaking a confidence. He looked from Grace to Recaldo and back again.

'Any idea who is?' Recaldo asked.

Murray thought for a moment. 'Probably her husband – I can't call him ex because I don't believe she ever divorced him. His name is Edward Cairnley. He used to edit some glossy art magazine or other in London, or did the last time I heard, though he must be pretty ancient now. I can probably dig out his address. As I recall, he lived in Dulwich, near the art gallery.'

'On good terms, were they?'

'I've no reason to doubt it, though the marriage ended a long time ago. But he helped her get her career started and still takes articles from time to time, so she'll certainly have his address in her files. She's always been very meticulous.'

'Did they have children?' Recaldo asked smoothly, and watched them glance at each other.

'No,' Murray said firmly. 'There were no children of the marriage.'

It was rather a pedantic way of saying it. Recaldo felt encouraged to keep digging.

'Who was Mr Walter?'

'What?'

'Who was Mr Walter? I understand she married several times?'

'Not as far as I know. She certainly had several partners, most of them elderly, but no other husbands. Walter was her maiden name,' Murray replied, and then took the floor from under Recaldo with his next question. It was not just what was said, but the way he said it; his timing was startling. 'Who owns the boats moored near her house?'

'Mrs Walter owned the *Cynara*, the boat that's moored at the bottom of her garden.'

'There's a very large yacht moored towards the other side of the estuary, who owns that?'

'The *Halcyon*.' Recaldo pronounced the name clearly, hoping for he knew not what, and saw Grace glance at her husband. 'I understand it's owned by a man called O'Dowd. A neighbour.'

'Her landlord?'

'How do you know that?'

'Why? Is it a secret?' Murray asked testily. 'Of course I knew, I was thinking of renting the house.' He turned to his open-mouthed wife apologetically. 'I'm sorry, hon, it was to be a surprise. Depending on whether you liked it, of course.' He blinked rapidly as he turned for help to Recaldo. 'Vangie was going to the States in a few weeks. She thought we could use it while she was away. See if we liked the area.' Recaldo watched their interaction with interest. Grace got to her feet, involuntarily. She looked as though she couldn't believe her ears.

'No way. *No way*,' she said loudly, with feeling. 'Nil nisi bonum and all that crap, but that woman had an infernal cheek and she seems to have infected you. Are you completely mad, Murray? I'd as soon live in Ballymahon, God help me. And you know how I feel about that.' Her husband stretched his hand to her. He looked stricken. Grace ignored him and turned to Recaldo.

'I don't suppose you need me, do you? I think I'd like to go to bed now.'

Recaldo stood up. 'I'm afraid I do, but it will keep till tomorrow.' He looked down at Murray who was staring after her miserably as she left. She walked the length of the room without looking back, her spine rigidly straight.

'Oh boy. Now I've really blown it.' Murray Magraw hunched his shoulders helplessly. 'Sorry about that. Grace had a difficult time as a child – in East Cork where she was brought up. A very unhappy time. I hoped by coming here she might get over it. Lay the ghosts, finally. But I guess it's too close for comfort?' He held his head. 'This is really going to put the kybosh on my stupid scheme.'

'Is that the only reason you came?' Recaldo asked quietly.

Magraw hesitated, but only for a moment. 'No. Not really. My cousin was very ill. I'm her executor, she wanted to make sure everything was all square before she went away.'

'When was Mrs Walter intending to leave?'

'I'm not real sure. Sometime in the next few weeks; she was going to some alternative clinic in California but I believe her friend Jer O'Dowd had persuaded her to go with him on holiday in Florida beforehand.' He gave a wry little laugh. 'She's been spared that anyway. Florida is the very last place on earth I'd have chosen for Evangeline. Not her scene at all.'

'I wonder what was?'

Grace Hartfield rejoined them at the table. She put her hand on her husband's shoulder. 'I'm sorry, darling, I shouldn't have walked away like that.'

He took her hand and kissed it. 'I didn't mean to upset you,' he said contritely.

'Yes, I know that. It's . . . never mind.' She gave Recaldo a trace of a smile. 'I interrupted you. What were you saying?'

'I was asking your husband why Mrs Walter agreed to go to Florida if she disliked it that much?'

'I guess maybe she knew she wouldn't make it?' Murray spoke sadly.

'You can't mean she knew she was going to be killed?' His words fell like raindrops. 'Mr Magraw?'

'Certainly not. But she hadn't long. A few months at most. I don't believe she'd have gone to the States at all.' He paused. 'She thought I'd like the house. She was right, I did. It reminded me of my boyhood home. Not the sea of course, just the position by the water. I was born in the American Midwest.' His voice trailed off. 'We lived on a lake.'

Grace looked at him suspiciously. 'Murray? You're not levelling with me, are you?' Her eyes opened wide. 'Murray?' she said sharply. 'Oh help, you haven't gone and committed us? You have, haven't you?'

'I guess.' He avoided his wife's dismayed gaze, and brushed his hair out of his eyes. 'Did Evangeline sell the *Halcyon* to Mr O'Dowd?'

Recaldo froze. 'Why do you ask?' he asked softly.

'Oh, no reason.'

'I get the impression the name bothers you, Mr Magraw,' Recaldo persisted.

Magraw fell silent and when he spoke at last it was as if the words were being dragged out of him. 'I just wondered. It's the name of her only child who was very badly brain-damaged in an accident. The association would have upset her.'

'Oh?' Recaldo's face was blank. 'When you say badly damaged, what do you mean?'

'She had a mental age of three or four as far as I know.'

'Had? Is the child dead?'

'No.' He looked vague, evasive. 'She was in a home in New York for a long time. Evangeline rarely talked about her.'

'Until recently.' There was a faint flush on Grace's face. 'What do you think I've been going on about?'

'Yes,' Murray added reluctantly. 'Grace is correct. It was one of the reasons we came. Evangeline wanted us to meet the girl.'

Grace flushed. 'Rubbish. She wanted us to inherit her.' She turned and spoke directly to her husband, completely excluding Recaldo, as if she could no longer contain herself. 'How could you do this, Murray? How the hell could you undertake to act as guardian to a handicapped girl – woman – without consulting me? I really can't believe it.'

'But she's all taken care of, we . . . All Evangeline asked was for me to make sure there was enough income to support Halcyon in the home. You needn't have got involved. You're the one who demanded to see her.'

'I don't believe I'm hearing this. How could you be so naïve? Homes close, Murray. Where have you been living these past few years? Patients are dumped. If not on relatives, on the street.'

'This is different, this is an Irish convent. Evangeline said the nuns are utterly devoted.'

'Oh for God's sake, she would, wouldn't she? How often did she go there, I'd like to know? Did she say how old the nuns are? Did she tell you they are overwhelmed with vocations? That the place is bursting with rosy-cheeked young Irish girls with angelic smiles, tripping about the place with bedpans at the ready? She used you, Murray. She used us both.'

'Stop,' Murray shouted. 'Stop. I can't cope. I just can't cope with this now. You should have told me this when we first discussed it or else shouldn't have come.' He looked a bit like an angry child.

Grace sat still and held her breath, clearly embarrassed to have quarrelled, particularly in front of an audience. 'I'm sorry,' she said. 'I better go.'

Murray Magraw grabbed her hand. 'No, Grace. Please don't go. I'm sorry too. I want you to stay.'

Recaldo felt mortified, not least because it was clear that the couple were not habitual fighters and were obviously deeply distressed by the incident. Grace looked as if she was in a state of shock. He was less sympathetic to Murray who just looked petulant. 'Shock makes us all act out of character,' he said helplessly. 'I should have waited till morning. I apologize. I'll go now. Perhaps we can meet in the morning? I'm really sorry about your cousin's death. We're doing our best . . .' His voice died away. The three of them stood up simultaneously. Recaldo cleared his throat. 'Would you be willing to identify the body, Mr Magraw? I'm sorry to have to ask.'

Murray nodded miserably. Grace asked if it could wait until morning.

'Yes, of course. Forgive me if I gave the impression that I meant now.' They walked down the long, deserted dining room to the foyer. Recaldo was just about to leave them when he tried one last shot, hating himself for it even as he spoke. 'By the way, Mr Magraw, Mrs Walter didn't sell the boat to O'Dowd. A man called Sweeney did. He lives on the other side of the river.'

Murray stiffened. That the name meant something to him was obvious. Recaldo knew then that the secret of Halcyon's parentage was in the head of the gentle-looking man, blinking nervously at him.

'Isn't that Halcyon's . . .?' Grace started.

'Valentine Sweeney?' Murray said incredulously. Recaldo nodded.

'Valentine Jason Sweeney?'

'Yes, do you know him?'

'Of course I know him. If it's the same guy. He's Halcyon's father.'

'You sure about that?' It was so easy after all, so easy. 'Are you absolutely sure?'

'Oh yes, I'm sure all right.' He looked furious as he turned to his wife. 'She never said a word. Not a syllable.'

Recaldo opened his wallet and found the small, black and white snapshot from the *Cynara*. He held it out to Murray who peered at it myopically then brought it to the reception desk and examined it under the light. Recaldo held his breath.

'They sure were a handsome couple, Evangeline and VJ,' Murray said softly. 'Look, Grace, that's Halcyon, such a pretty little thing.'

Recaldo joined them. 'You're certain that's Sweeney with your cousin?'

Murray smiled up at him sadly. 'Sure I'm sure. I took the picture myself. Evangeline never told me he lived here,' he added.

'If the father was on hand, Mim,' Grace said quietly, 'then what the hell did she invite us for?'

'Good question,' he replied.

Chapter Twenty-six

IT WAS WELL PAST MIDNIGHT. RECALDO, REELING WITH EXHAUSTION, was at last preparing for bed when there was a knock on his door. He ignored the banging until it was repeated, getting louder each time. He cursed fluently and continuously as he pulled on the socks he had just taken off, and slipped into an old tracksuit. He banged his bedroom door shut and shouted, 'Stop that infernal racket, I'm coming.' The hall floor tiles felt cold and dank underfoot. He peeped through the spyglass and saw, to his fury, McBride's spud of a face grinning at him.

Now what? he thought, as he yanked open the door.

'Howya, FX?' McBride greeted him brightly. He had the look of a man with a few drinks on him, though he was still well in control. He stepped inside the narrow hallway. 'Mind if I come in?' he asked belatedly in a relaxed and amiable voice.

'Have I any choice?' Recaldo snarled. 'This is outrageous, McBride. D'you know what hour it is?' He was so stupefied with weariness he could have wept. 'What the hell are you doing here, anyway? I thought you were in Cork.'

'Well, now you know I amn't.' McBride sniffed and, unabashed, pulled a half-bottle of whiskey from his pocket. 'Now, me old segotia, which of those questions do you want answered first?'

'None of them. I want to get back to my bed. I'm exhausted.'

'Feckin' dead on your feet, you look, old son. A drink will warm the cockles for you. Get us a coupla glasses,' he said, 'and I'll even make it hot for you.'

'What?' Startled, Recaldo jerked away.

265

'Ha, ha. Wrong-footed you there, FX.' McBride flicked his head to one side and grinned broadly. 'Only jokin'. Have you no sense of humour at all, man?' He brushed past his reluctant host and headed for the kitchen.

Recaldo closed his eyes and rocked back and forth on the balls of his cold feet. But seeing there was no way he could get rid of McBride, he followed him into the cramped kitchen, where he was busy pulling open the overhead cupboards. 'Have you the doings?' he asked.

'The doings? Jesus. What the hell are you talking about?' He walked around after McBride, irritably banging the cupboard doors shut again.

'The doings, FX, the doings. For making hot whiskey. You know? A lemon, brown sugar, boiling water. Oh, and a clove or two while you're at it, FX.'

Recaldo's frustration flared. 'God in heaven, will you stop calling me FX. The name's Frank. I'm sorry to be inhospitable, McBride, but I'm in no mood for company. Go home. Get the hell out. I don't drink whiskey. And I specially don't drink it hot.'

'And there was I, thinking we were getting on like a house on fire. Sit down, FX, I want to talk to you,' McBride said with surprising authority. Whereupon Recaldo, seeing it was no use arguing, sat down meekly and buried his head in his hands. McBride found a couple of glasses and poured two generous measures from his half-bottle. 'Drink that.' He sounded perfectly sober and not in the least perturbed by the lack of welcome. He pushed the whiskey towards Recaldo. 'Sláinte,' he said and raised his glass. 'How's the heart?'

'Fine.'

'Great. That's what a pal of mine in Dublin told me.'

An awkward pause followed before Recaldo snarled, 'You've no business discussing me or my health with anyone.'

'Sorry about that, old son. My enquiries were purely in the line of duty, I meant no harm,' McBride replied sheepishly.

But Recaldo wasn't mollified. By now he'd worked up a fine head of steam, which he intended letting off, preferably right in McBride's self-satisfied fat face. He leaned across the table and hissed, 'Let me tell you something, McBride. I'll say this once, so watch my lips. I resigned my job for many reasons but when I came here, I had a clean bill of health which I don't discuss with anyone. I'm not an invalid. OK?'

'I never said you were,' McBride kept a very steady eye on Recaldo. He was not in the least put out by the other's antagonism. 'I can read more than Japanese, y'know, FX,' he said softly. 'I'd say you have the look of a man who's shitting bricks.' He stabbed the table with his thumb. 'Worrying about something or someone. Or maybe you're not getting enough sleep. Or both. Would I be right?'

Recaldo snorted. 'And you came here in the middle of the night to tell me that? You've a feckin' nerve, McBride. Did Coffey send you?'

'No, this is on my own initiative,' McBride retorted primly. He loosened his collar and rubbed his lips. 'I don't get on all that well with Coffey, to tell you the God's honest truth. He's an awful man for the book. Bloody slow, as well. He browns me off.' He circled the table and settled in the chair opposite his unwilling host, who eyed him warily. McBride poured himself another drink.

'I want to ask you something,' Recaldo said. 'Do you make a habit of rounding up old men in the middle of the night?'

'Not me, old son. Didn't I warn you Coffey was hot on the old DNA?'

'And?'

'And what exactly?'

'Are you going to tell me about it?'

'No, as a matter of fact, I'm not.' An awkward silence held until Recaldo broke it. 'You going back to Cork tonight?' he asked.

'You mean I shouldn't be driving and drinking? Naw, I'm hanging around. A couple of days ago I never heard of the place, now I can't get enough of it. Gorgeous, isn't it?'

Recaldo rubbed his forehead, bewildered at the other's rapid changes of mood. He had to think straight. 'McBride, you've had too much to drink.'

'It's still gorgeous.' McBride smiled lazily. There was something almost reptilian about that confident leer. '*You* seem to have got well stuck in. Wouldn't mind livin' here meself.'

'In a pig's ear. You can't wait to get back to Dublin.'

'That's true enough.' He grinned again. 'The hotel's tremendous, though. The guy gave me a great rate. He didn't mention it, then?' He noted Recaldo's start with some satisfaction. 'I suppose it was because I was so late checking in. Only thing, I have to be out early tomorrow morning. Bit of a waste, but there you go.' His ramble petered out and both men fell silent, though McBride gave no sign of pushing off.

'I wanted to discuss a few things. About the case,' he said at last.

Recaldo got up and opened the window. 'Well, since I don't seem to be able to get rid of you, we better go in the front. There's a bit more space.' He was finicky about his kitchen and hated being in such close quarters with the other man who gave off an overwhelming odour of booze and sweat.

McBride tipped Recaldo's untouched whiskey into his glass and followed his host to an extremely chilly front room. He watched in silence while Recaldo deftly built a small tripod of turf briquettes in the grate, lit it, and blew until the flames licked around the fuel and up the chimney. The small parlour warmed fractionally. It wasn't much more than three metres square, close carpeted in sombre grey and furnished austerely. Whether by design or frugality it achieved a kind of minimalist chic: a glass coffee table, a bookcase, a couple of Jack Yeats prints on the otherwise bare, whitewashed walls.

McBride took a gulp of whiskey. 'You've one thing in common with her nibs, haven't you, FX?' he said thoughtfully. 'The one of you is as neat and tidy as the other.'

Recaldo pursed his lips. 'Oh?' he said tightly.

'Well, you know, something has been bothering me from the beginning. So I got to thinkin' about Ms Walter and that museum piece of a house and why there was just enough stuff left to keep us hangin' around but not enough to answer any of the important questions. D'you get me?'

'Like what?'

'Like, none of the information that might possibly push the case forward. Was it yourself wiped the PC?'

'I told you I know nothing about computers,' Recaldo said shortly.

'That's not what I've heard. All right, you may not have enough knowledge to write a friggin' book on the subject but you certainly know enough to do that. So what exactly were you and old man Spain up to before you deigned to call us in? Mind tellin' me that?'

'I reported the incident as soon as was humanly possible.'

'That so? Somehow I have me doubts about that.' McBride stretched out his hand for the bottle. 'I was a bit slow. Showing off when I should've been keeping my eyes peeled. You're a dangerous man, FX, you make the likes of me want to impress you. You're an

arrogant bastard. You must've been an awful tough guy to work for.'
He sucked his teeth. 'In your day. They say you were.'

'Do they?'

'They do. They say you'd give a man just enough rope to hang himself, but that you always knew how to keep one jump ahead.'

'Your friend talks too much,' Recaldo said mildly. 'I'm not sure what you're trying to get at.'

'It took me a while to put my finger on it. But I've got it now, all right. Ms Walter didn't clear the house herself, and she hasn't an office anywhere else, either. Coffey was right about that, it doesn't make sense. I asked pal Smiler about it and if anyone should know, it's him. He thought – and I quote – that it was a very queer notion. And for once, I believe him. No, it's much simpler than that. I think someone who knew exactly what we would be looking for cleared her stuff. And you, FX, would be just the right guy for the job.'

Recaldo laughed. 'Is that an accusation?'

'No, a question. Did you clear the place?'

'And why would I do that?'

'Not *why*; for *whom*. *When*. Who would you do it for?' He threw back his head and made a great play of examining the ceiling with a look of total innocence on his face. 'You haven't managed to locate the elusive Mrs Sweeney, I suppose? No?' He looked his host straight in the eye. 'Tell me, FX,' he asked softly and paused for effect. 'What exactly are you up to?'

Recaldo's eyes narrowed. 'I did not disturb her belongings nor did I kill Evangeline Walter, if that's what you're implying.'

'No, I *know* you didn't. But I'd lay evens that you know, or *think* you know who did. Would I be right?' he asked slyly. 'I think you bought time. Know what else I think?'

'I'm sure you're going to tell me.'

'We should have examined her boat first thing. That'd be a good place to hide stuff.'

'There's nothing on her boat,' Recaldo said dismissively. 'I had a look.'

'Oh, and when was that?'

'Wednesday night.' He went back to the kitchen and returned presently with a quarter-full bottle of Hennessy and a fresh glass. He raised an eyebrow at McBride who waved the brandy aside and

269

topped up his own glass, then peered suspiciously into his bottle. 'Still one left,' he said. The two men sat down on either side of the fire in a couple of antique leather-covered wing chairs.

'Well then, McBride, are you going to tell me the real reason you're here?' Recaldo, marginally back in control, spoke quietly. The gloves were definitely off; his whole demeanour had suddenly changed. The resigned irritation which followed his first outburst was gone. Now he looked at the younger man with something approaching respect.

'Cut the McBride crap. My name's Phil.' He paused. 'Just to clear one or two things up. I didn't stay in Cork last night, I drove Marilyn Donovan home from hospital. Now there's a looker.' He smirked. 'And bright as a bloody button. It must be the air around here. The women are something else. I didn't go back on Wednesday night, either. I've been holed up in that dreary guest house on the main road. Except for tonight's little treat, of course.'

Recaldo fixed him with his unwavering basilisk stare. 'Some reason you didn't mention that?'

'Oh no, not really. It was Coffey's idea. He wanted me to keep an eye on O'Dowd and Spain. And on things generally,' McBride said. 'Thought you weren't looking too hot. Thought you might need a hand.' It was a neat enough warning.

'You might have told me.'

'I might, but then there's a few things you haven't told us, isn't there?'

'And what's that supposed to mean?'

'I saw Rose O'Faolain. Don't suppose I mentioned that? Now, there's another fine-lookin' woman. A bit of a flirt, for one so long in the tooth, but then that seems to be a general rule around here, from what I gather about our corpse. Anyway, Rose was very impressed; quite fancied you, I'd say.' He leered. 'D'you know, she seemed to think *you* sent *me*. Wherever she got that idea I can't imagine. She was quite put out when she realized *I* was the senior officer. Got all uppity. Anything she had to say about Ms Walter she'd already *shared* with you.' He opened his eyes in mock surprise. '*Shared?* Imagine that. Very cosy. I didn't know what she was talking about, FX, but I suppose you might? You obviously made quite a conquest there. But then, I hear you're good at that.' He clicked his teeth. 'So, how come you didn't *share* with us whatever it was Rose *shared* with you?'

'It was nothing of interest,' Recaldo said smoothly. 'Just the name of the guy Walter was supposed to interview this lunchtime. Mure-Robertson, he's called. A Canadian industralist, apparently. Collects stained glass – Harry Clarke, Evie Hone. And sculpture.'

'Is that a fact, now?' McBride sucked in his cheeks and let them out with a pop. 'Well, y'know, she told me that much herself. Any idea if he's the same fellow that has a house on the river Suir, north of Thurles?'

'Probably. I wouldn't know,' Recaldo said, then looked at McBride as if he'd had a brainwave. 'I see.' He leaned his arm back and reached for an Irish road atlas on the bookshelf.

'No need for the amateur dramatics,' said McBride briskly. 'I expect you already worked that one out for yourself, same way I did.' He paused. 'As luck would have it, as soon as I stepped out of Rose's gallery who comes mooching around the corner but the bold Smiler O'Dowd. So I was able to have a word with him as well. Funny that he happened to be in Daingean at the same time, wasn't it? If I were a suspicious man I'd almost say he was keeping an eye on me.'

'Or vice versa?'

'Well, yes, now you come to mention it.' McBride was not in the least put out at being rumbled. 'Of course, he sticks to his story that it was Dublin he was headed for the night Walter died, but somehow I wouldn't trust that fella as far as I could throw him. What d'you think?'

'Bit of a coincidence, all right.' Undaunted, Recaldo consulted his road atlas. O'Dowd and the girl were invading his thoughts again. He pushed them to one side to concentrate on Mure-Robertson. 'Twomileborris. About twenty miles the other side of the Galtee Mountains. No more than three or four miles from the Suir. The N75 crosses it. Any idea how far up Mure-Robertson's castle is?' He raised his head, desperately trying to control his tired features. 'You think that's where O'Dowd was that night?'

'Coming or going. I could see it written all over him but he wasn't budging an inch on his story, I'll give him that much. By the way, FX,' McBride added slyly, 'how d'you know it's a castle?'

'Mrs O'Faolain mentioned it,' Recaldo replied smoothly.

McBride shook his head slowly from side to side. It wasn't entirely clear what was causing his scepticism. 'I'll have another go at O'Dowd tomorrow,' he remarked mildly. 'He's a cute hoor. I rang that garda who gave him the alibi for Tuesday night. The car was pulled up on the grass verge at the N75 turn, face out with its backside stuck in the ditch. It could have been headed in any direction.' McBride grunted and continued to wag his head. 'Amn't I going to be the busy one? Unless of course you'd care to fill in some of the blanks? I hear you've been buzzing around the countryside like a demented bee.'

This was a game Recaldo wished he could play with a clearer head. Before he pooled information with McBride he wanted to work out the details. Cressie's safety depended on it. He put his head back and closed his eyes, overcome by drowsiness. Undaunted, McBride droned mercilessly on.

'I got the phone printouts from Eircom, by the way,' he said. Recaldo didn't react, not even to protest at not having been told. 'I hauled off to the billing office after I dropped the stuff at forensic. They gave me copies of the itemized bills for the last two quarters. And very interesting they are too. Coffey has them. While I was about it, I asked to have a squint at the list of calls Walter made over the past couple of weeks. They were able to oblige, right up to Tuesday.' Recaldo opened his eyes and sat up as McBride pulled a small notebook from his jacket pocket and flicked it open. 'A call to Oxford was logged in at six fifty-eight, duration one minute six seconds. Plenty enough time to listen to a message and send a short reply, I'd say. The number is registered to Hartfield Magraw Rare Books. Ring a bell? Remember a Grace Hartfield left a message on Monday? So I called the number and got her recorded message. Except it wasn't her, it was a male American voice.' He referred to the pad again and read the message out. ' "Hi. Sorry neither Grace nor Murray can take your call right now. Leave a message, we'll call right back." Exactly the same guy on Walter's machine.' He looked up. 'And what do y'know? Mr and Mrs Magraw booked into the Atlantis Hotel at eight fifteen this evening.' He grinned broadly.

Recaldo bowed his head. 'Yes, I know. I spoke to them.'

McBride's eyes narrowed. 'Would that have been at the house?'

'No, at the hotel. But they got into the house. Did you know that?' he asked, with some satisfaction.

'How come?' McBride seemed to be caught on the hop. 'I had the keys.'

'Yeah, but they knew where there was a set concealed.' As he explained, McBride became less confrontational. 'Something we all missed. Not good, eh? I thought the blasted letter box was rusted through. Just goes to show you.' He puffed out his cheeks. 'I wonder who else knew about them?' They were both quiet while they contemplated this awkward development.

'What time did they get to the house?' McBride had a neat way of wrong-footing him.

'I'm not exactly sure – early evening, I'd guess.'

'Guess? Christ, Coffey will go ballistic. Why weren't you waiting at the house?'

'I was looking for Sweeney, among other things. Same as you, Phil. You happen to find him?'

'I'd dearly like to know just why you keep harping on about Sweeney. It's her I want to interview. I take it you know where she is?'

'Yes. I've asked her and Spain to come and talk to you tomorrow.'

'That'll be nice. Did you interview the Magraws?'

'Yep. We had a bit of a chat. He'll do the business at the mortuary tomorrow. That's what Coffey wanted, isn't it?'

'He wanted you to contact us when they arrived. That's what he wanted,' McBride said belligerently.

'I am not a messenger boy.'

There was a moment's stand-off before McBride conceded, 'No, that's one thing we're both sure of.' He didn't explain whether he was aligning himself with Recaldo or Coffey. 'Are you going to tell me what they had to say?'

'He's her executor. He knew she was dying and rolled up to make sure things were straight.' He smiled sweetly. 'And to make sure her daughter was properly taken care of.' If Recaldo thought this would be a surprise for McBride, he was disappointed.

'Ah, you know about the daughter? We should have pooled resources and saved me the bother of tracking O'Dowd. But then,' he added reflectively, 'I might not have had such an interesting chat with one Mure-Robertson, might I.'

'The shares?'

273

McBride burst out laughing. 'Would you ever do us a favour, FX? Would you ever stop trying to pull the wool over my eyes?'

'Only if you'll do the same,' Recaldo said warily.

'That feckin' woman was into everything.'

'Is it pax then?' Recaldo said.

'Yeah, go on then, pax it is.' McBride grinned. 'So now, tell me, FX, where were you since I left this morning?'

'Or pretended to leave.' Recaldo kept his end up. 'I had some routine stuff to do. I had lunch, talked to the people in the boatyard, the manager of the hotel, Mure-Robertson.'

'Ah you got around to that, did you? You work out why O'Dowd was so anxious to buy the shares?'

'Yes, I think so. Did Mure-Robertson tell you he'd clinched the deal with Sweeney?'

'No, he feckin' well did not.'

'Cash transaction: forty-five K.'

McBride whistled. 'Jay-sus. When?'

'He wouldn't tell me. But I'd guess today sometime.'

'Sweeney again. You think it was him killed her?'

'Yes. Don't you?'

McBride thought about this for a considerable time before replying. 'No,' he said reluctantly. 'I kinda put my money on Spain. With a little help from your girlfriend. Though I can't see how either of them fit into the whole picture. One or two little items of evidence and little snippets of hearsay don't make a motive. Spain's been DNA'd, you know.'

'It'll be positive.' Recaldo swallowed. 'But he didn't kill her.'

'I think you'd better tell me why you're so sure of that.'

Although Recaldo ran rapidly through his case against Sweeney, it took him a good half-hour. 'The trouble is we have absolutely nothing concrete. I'm pinning my hopes on finding something in his car.' His face was serious. 'I didn't clear her house, by the way. I think Sweeney did. There seem to have been all sorts of convoluted financial deals going on between him and Walter and our pal Smiler.'

'You have any theories as to why?'

'It would take all night, so I'll leave it till the morning if you don't mind. But in a word I believe Walter was systematically ruining him and whether knowingly or not, O'Dowd was giving her a helping hand.'

McBride nodded slowly. He took a Kodak envelope from his pocket and held it out. 'I found an undeveloped roll of film in the house. It was under one of the sofas. Tell me what you think?' He watched lazily while Recaldo pulled out the photographs and went through them one by one. There were twenty-four in all, five ruined by overexposure or a shaking hand, eight taken at a party. One of these was a partial shot of V. J. Sweeney leaning against a pillar. He thought he recognized the O'Faolain Gallery. There were two shots of the *Halcyon*, one a close-up of the name. The rest were of various different groupings of the same five people: Cressida and V. J. Sweeney, Gil, Evangeline Walter and her daughter. She looked to be in her late teens or early twenties. In the distance shots she was very pretty but close up, there was something odd about her face. She had a slight cast in one eye and her expression was childlike and unfocused. In one shot she was sitting with her back to the boat rail as the yacht passed John Spain's boat with Gil sitting in the prow. The juxtaposition of the two crafts drew their heads close together. Recaldo turned the photo over and saw that it was date-stamped on the back. September the fifteenth. He looked up.

'They were all there, weren't they, on the good ship *Halcyon*? Mrs Walter, her daughter Halcyon, O'Dowd and their unsmiling host V. J. Sweeney,' McBride said. 'Tuesday afternoon. None of them look very happy, do they? Except the girl, and she doesn't really count, does she? Except she does.' He passed over another photograph which he conjured out of nowhere. 'This one I had blown up. Look at her carefully. And the boy as well. See what I mean? They could be brother and sister. And you know what else? I think I know why you've been keeping the hapless Mrs Sweeney out of my way. The blessed Marilyn filled me in. Cressida Sweeney came home from the hospital each evening. Early each evening. She wouldn't leave that little boy alone, would she? By all accounts she adores him. No-one has a bad word to say about her. They love her nearly as much as you do.' For once he dropped his bantering tone. 'I'm sorry, old friend, she's in it up to her armpits.'

Recaldo sat still as a statue and thanked his stars that he had talked to the Magraws that evening, otherwise he would have lost control. Lost her. Cressie, oh Cressie. He drew out the *Cynara* snapshot for the second time that evening and laid it on the table. McBride picked it up and examined it silently. 'Cressida Sweeney ran into O'Dowd and the girl in Duncreagh on Tuesday evening. I suppose she told you? A bit of bad luck from her point of view. Ran into O'Dowd with the girl on their way back to Halcyon's convent. Mama was taken sick so good friend Smiler obliged, he told me himself. He was getting petrol when Mrs Sweeney rolled into the petrol station and bashed into the back of his flippin' car.'

'But that doesn't mean anything. How would *she* know who the girl was?'

'Oh Frank. Would you look at the feckin' photograph.' He paused. 'I went to the convent – that's where I was today.' He looked at Recaldo intently. 'This will spook you. That unfortunate girl is not just backward, she's deaf and dumb. Always has been, it seems. Born that way.' He put his hand out and took away the photographs.

'Not surprised, are you? We've had parallel agendas haven't we, old son? I'm not Coffey, you know, you should have trusted me. *I* would have told you Dr Morrow is linking the fatal haemorrhage with both the sex and the blow to the stomach and Spain's DNA matches one of the semen samples – that one was quite a goer. Your pal Spain is up the creek without a paddle, unless . . .'

'She had sex with someone else?'

'Doc Morrow thinks she might . . .' McBride smiled like the Cheshire cat.

Recaldo leapt out of his chair and stood threateningly over him. 'Stop winding me up, McBride. Stop playing games. You're going to have to DNA others besides Spain now, aren't you?'

'You?' McBride asked lazily. 'I don't think so. Not with you so hot on the lady Cressida. O'Dowd? Ah no, I don't think we'll bother with him either. But you've just made quite a good case for having a go at Sweeney . . .'

'Why not O'Dowd?' Belligerence rather than conviction made him say it.

'O'Dowd? You think O'Dowd's screwed her?' McBride grinned at him knowingly. 'Then I'm a Dutchman. No, I think we can safely discard that notion.'

'What makes you so sure?'

'*Aithníonn ciaróg, ciaróg eile,*' McBride said quietly. *It takes one to know one.*

'So? He's still capable.'

276

'Perhaps. But I think you might be barking up the wrong tree.'

Recaldo thought about it. 'Yes, probably. Whatever his pre-dilections, Smiler is not a violent man. No, Sweeney did it. I'm sure of it. I'm absolutely sure. We have to find his car.'

'Then how hard can you pray?' McBride drained his glass and pulled himself out of the chair. 'Because we're looking for a feckin' miracle and I don't think Miss Mona Spillane's little article of info will swing it for us.' He looked straight at Recaldo. 'Thank God it's the weekend. That'll keep Coffey off our backs. I've just had word of a nasty double knifing at a disco in the city. Poor guy'll be up to his oxters.' He winked. 'I'll see you about at the hotel early tomorrow. Give me a ring before you set out. Something tells me you're an early riser, and I'm feckin' not. Adios amigo.'

'Wait,' Recaldo said tersely and went into the room on the other side of the tiny hall. When he came out he was holding a clear plastic bag in his hand which he held out to McBride. It was sealed with three or four metal staples and contained two empty Vat 69 bottles.

'What's this?' McBride held it up to the light. The base of one of the bottles was caked with brown mud and the label was torn. 'Where did you find this?'

'In the middle of one of the shrubberies at the front of Sweeney's house. The other I got out of his kitchen. I used a handkerchief, so if there are prints they may be recoverable.'

McBride held his gaze for a moment. 'I wouldn't be at all surprised,' he said softly.

'I posted off my resignation today.'

McBride grinned. 'Very dramatic. I'll see you in the morning.'

Recaldo stood framed in the doorway until McBride had woven his way out of sight. Then he went back inside. He cleared the living room and washed the glasses. It was almost three in the morning by the time he staggered into bed.

Saturday

Chapter Twenty-seven

RECALDO WAS RUDELY ROUSED FROM THE DEPTHS OF HIS BRIEF sleep by a high screeching noise. He surfaced groggily to find it still dark outside, though there was a faint glow appearing just above the horizon. For once it wasn't raining but the wind was howling like a banshee around the draughty house. He got out of bed, eased open the window and got a swift damp blast in the face. Demented bell-like clanging made by loose halyards rattling against the aluminium masts of the boats moored in the cove below travelled up to him on the wind. It was going to be a blustery day. He banged the window shut and trundled down to the kitchen to put on the kettle and, while he waited for it to boil, absent-mindedly filled the dog's water bowl before he remembered Barker was still at his finishing school. He was surprised at how empty the place seemed without him.

He swallowed the scalding coffee, showered, and dressed formally in dark slacks and tweed sports jacket for his meeting with the Magraw couple. Judging seven o'clock too early to wake McBride, he made a couple of short phone calls then set off towards the cliffs to clear his head. The temperature had dropped considerably from the day before; there was a real touch of autumn in the air and a seasonal mist over the bay where only a few fishing boats battled slowly over the choppy surface. He searched for John Spain but could see no sign of him. Nor were there any of the usual Saturday sailors, though with the horizon shrouded by sea fog they would probably be few and far between until it cleared. The weather didn't look promising and yet he found himself wishing he could go out and even if briefly tussle with the elements. The day stretched before him mercilessly; he dreaded what it might bring.

There were few people about even after half an hour's brisk walk, so he was surprised to come upon McBride strolling around the garden as he went through the Atlantis entrance.

'Trying to get my feckin' head clear,' he greeted Recaldo succinctly. 'I have a desperate hangover. I thought a turn around the garden might do the trick. Come on, slow coach.'

They walked around the flower beds in silence. The ceasefire had held overnight, their confrontation replaced by mutual respect, if not yet trust. They were edgy but not unfriendly.

'Coffey woke me up at twenty to seven,' McBride said eventually. 'Can you bloody believe it? Thought it better if *I* told the Magraws about the arrangements. He's a great one for avoiding emotional scenes or passing on unpleasant news. Still, they didn't seem unduly bothered, they went off to Cork ten minutes ago. Coffey will waylay them on the outskirts in a squad car, to lead them to the morgue. I sent your little bottle bank with them by the way, suitably disguised in a padded envelope. Let's hope it keeps the boss occupied for a while.'

'Did you talk to them at any length? Or was it too early?'

'Not for them it wasn't, they were roaming the cliffs when I caught up with them. Having had breakfast,' he said incredulously. 'They must have been up at six.'

'I don't suppose they got much sleep, with what they have to face. How did they strike you?' Recaldo asked curiously.

'I liked her a lot. Bright, straightforward, unreserved. Striking-looking as well. Struck me as the honest type. A bit tense. Him I found more difficult. Maybe it's shock or grief or both but he wasn't very forthcoming.' He bit his lip. 'At a guess I'd say there's a spot of bother between them.'

'I'm not sure husband Murray has been telling her the whole truth and nothing but. She was pretty furious last night. He obviously made some pie-in-the-sky commitment to look after the Walter girl without fully consulting her.'

'Hmm. Then she's in for a bit of a shock. I met the young one when I went to the convent yesterday,' McBride admitted casually, then laughed at Recaldo's incredulous expression. 'Didn't I tell you that? Oops, sorry. Bad habit. Halcyon – god-awful name, isn't it? – seems happy enough but the nun says she's liable to fierce bouts of

282

temper and can be quite a handful – being backward *and* deaf. Or should I say disabled? I trotted delicately around the deafness – i.e. could it be congenital? – but didn't get anywhere. How long can places like that stay open, d'you think?'

'That's precisely what Grace Hartfield wanted to know. Gave her husband a shock, I can tell you. Reality may be beginning to set in with our professor.'

'Was he, er, romantically involved with the victim?'

'I think I might say yes to that, but in what way? Now there's a can of worms. You?'

'Hard to say, I only saw him for five minutes and anyway I'm not at my intellectual best at seven a.m.' He sniffed. 'I gave Coffey a rundown on our,' he cleared his throat, 'our theories. He isn't buying, but he suggests we meet this evening at Walter's house, at four, to hammer things out. The Magraws will be coming back at the same time.' He scratched his head. 'It was the best I could do. I better warn you though, he's all gung-ho about making an arrest.' He coughed. 'Two, in fact. Spain and your lady friend are for the chop, unless we can come up with something pretty spectacular in the next few hours,' he said, declaring his shift of allegiance without fuss.

'We better find the Sweeney car PDQ, then,' Recaldo said grimly. 'I woke that Canadian up this morning and put the squeeze on him.' He pursed his lips. 'He eventually admitted that the money changed hands at ten on Thursday night in a bar in Thurles. His lackey didn't mention what Sweeney was driving but I think we can assume it was the Lexus. Cressie has the other family car so unless he hired one, it must have been.'

'I'm not sure I'm with you on that, old son. My bet is that Sweeney's probably halfway to Europe by now, or at least crossed to the UK. You know yourself finding cars at airports is a long, laborious business. I mean, have you seen the size of the car park at Dublin airport recently? And then there's Cork. Feckin' thing could be anywhere.'

Recaldo considered this dubiously. 'You know, I can't get rid of the feeling the bloody thing is around here somewhere, under our noses. It's the yacht that's his obsession. If he's going to scarper, he'll go in the ketch, I'm sure of it.'

'That thing? Single-handed? You're having me on. Anyway I thought you said it was sold?'

'I did, but he still has the use of it.' He bit his lip. 'Come on. Let's go see O'Dowd and get the low-down. His phone was engaged when I tried him earlier.'

They found O'Dowd at his kitchen table reading the newspaper. He looked up and nodded at them resignedly when they walked in through the open back door. 'I usually prefer a solitary breakfast,' he said plaintively, but nevertheless he poured them a cup of tepid tea apiece. A cooked breakfast didn't seem to be on offer. They asked him about the outing on the *Halcyon*. And the arrangement with Sweeney.

'I think she must have known just how little time she had left,' he replied obliquely. 'I couldn't make out or fully understand what was going on.' He leaned back in his chair and considered for some time before he continued. 'The yacht was contracted for sale to a consortium from Kinsale,' he said, mentioning the port on the east side of the county. 'Four e-commerce princes,' he added dryly. 'It was only before we went out with Sweeney on Tuesday that Evangeline told me they were coming up to complete the sale this weekend.' He paused for effect. 'To complete *and* sail the *Halcyon* to their home port.'

'Are they still?'

'No, I rang them on Wednesday night and put them off.' He shrugged. 'I didn't see what else I could do.'

'Why's that?' McBride asked. 'I thought it was you bought it from Sweeney?'

O'Dowd gave his awful, inappropriate grin. 'No, we bought it together. At the start I thought it was a mad idea but she managed to persuade me. *And* find a buyer the way she said she would – at considerable profit too,' he added admiringly.

'You fronted the purchase, didn't you?' Recaldo said laconically. 'Would you like to explain to Inspector McBride how the deal worked?'

O'Dowd shuffled around in some embarrassment before replying. 'I kept her involvement quiet, that's all. As far as I know – the way Vangie told it – she got the idea when she happened to see an ad in a yachting magazine which described a small consortium looking for a boat in these waters. Vangie spotted that their specification almost exactly matched Sweeney's ketch and from that she hatched up the whole scheme. Sometimes she was a wonder to me with her outlandish plans.' His smile turned to a grimace. 'We both knew he was on his uppers so she got me to approach him with the notion that I wanted to buy a boat *and* learn to sail. At first he laughed and told me to hop off to the sailing school in Passage South but then he got greedy as Vangie guessed he would. I gave him a lot of plámás about how much I admired his boat and how convenient it would be for me to have it on hand with such an expert to teach me. I put it to him that it would be like him still owning it while at the same time having the readies. I knew he wanted to buy more shares in the hotel so I had him . . .'

'By the short and curlies?' McBride obliged.

O'Dowd cleared his throat. 'Well, I wouldn't put it as crudely, but yes. He has a fine opinion of himself as a businessman and doesn't rate us peasants, so it wasn't hard to play him in. I gave him the impression that my wanting to sail was a passing fancy – something to impress Evangeline maybe – and that I would quickly tire of it all, specially when I realized what an expensive toy I'd acquired. I made myself into a right eejit so of course he swallowed it wholesale. As Evangeline predicted. The one thing I didn't realize was that she had more on her mind than making a fast buck. I tried to back out. It seemed too personal. I'm sorry I got involved, it's not my way of doing business.'

'You're getting very particular all of a sudden, aren't you?' McBride said sourly.

But O'Dowd only shrugged. Much of his swagger was gone; he looked diminished. 'The trip was to be our last.' He sighed.

'Why was the girl with you, Jer?' Recaldo asked quietly.

'God only knows. It was a surprise for me, I can tell you,' O'Dowd said heatedly. 'I'd never met her before Monday. I knew about her, but it was only the day before that I saw her for the first time. We drove up to collect her together. *I* thought the purpose of that trip was to see Mr Mure-Robertson but halfway there Vangie sprang it on me. She told me she'd arranged for her cousin to become the girl's legal guardian after she died, but that his wife had insisted on meeting her first and since they were due on the Wednesday she wanted to . . . I don't know what . . . Maybe to give the impression that she was used to dealing with her or that she was easy to manage? Familiar with the house?' He shrugged. 'It didn't matter anyway, I'd have done anything

285

she asked.' There were tears in his eyes. 'You see, she'd never actually mentioned *dying* before, so I was shocked into doing what she wanted. But then,' he added sadly, 'she was good at that.' He scratched his head. 'The young one was a desperate nuisance all the way home, mauling the seat leather, pulling out ashtrays, and anything else she could get her hands on. We had an awful job keeping her in the car. Vangie was fainting with tiredness by the time we got home. And after all that, the very next day she told me the cousins were delayed and wouldn't be here till the end of the week. She thought she'd better keep the girl with her. I told her she was out of her mind, that we should just get her back to the convent as quick as possible.' He shook his head ruefully. 'But she wouldn't listen. Instead she came up with the notion of taking the young one for a jaunt in the boat. I could hardly credit it but as usual I went along.' He gave a parody of a smile. 'Anything for a quiet life.'

He looked at the two gardaí earnestly. 'Listen to me. I had absolutely no notion that Sweeney might be the father. Even on the boat that day, I didn't cop on. And of course *she* didn't say a word about it. She could be very devious when it suited her. I knew they'd had an affair all right, but he broke it off suddenly when his son was born – Evangeline didn't like to be dropped like that. Who would? I'll make that bastard pay, is what she always said.

He took a deep breath. 'It was only when I saw Gil and Halcyon together at the petrol station that it dawned on me. And like a fool I said something to poor Cressida – broke the habit of a lifetime doing it as well. I spoke out of turn. I think I may have wanted Cressida to tell me I was crackers, but when I saw the look on her face I knew the same thought had just occurred to her. I was so flummoxed that I drove off, forgetting to fill the car with petrol.

'I could hardly manage the young one on my own. At one stage she grabbed hold of my mobile and took it apart, and before I could stop her she was flinging bits of it out the window. So I had no way of warning Evangeline that Cressida might say something to Sweeney and then God knows what might happen. You see, at the petrol station I suddenly saw the likeness between the two children. It was weird. Not alike but at the same time . . . Sweeney has a terrible temper. At that stage I was so confused I didn't know what to think. I was also very annoyed with Evangeline for stringing me along like that. Using me.

'I got to thinking that maybe her object was to humiliate, beggar Sweeney. Revenge is serious stuff, the way Evangeline went about it anyway. I didn't mind going along with the boat scam but the hotel was a different matter. For one thing I was deeply involved and for another I have a lot of respect for the Bleiberg family. I thought she had too, that she was serious about her commitment to Otto's dream. But it was a personal vendetta against Sweeney – the rest meant nothing to her.

'Up to then I thought of the pair of us as partners, making money, trying to build up her finances – at least that's what she told me. Now I saw that wasn't her motive at all. She'd made a right fool out of me, forgetting that I live here and will go on living here. People wouldn't tolerate that kind of vindictiveness, if it got out. Even if nobody much cared for Sweeney, Vangie made a few enemies hereabouts herself – specially among the women.' He smiled nervously.

'Tell us what happened after you got back that night,' Recaldo asked.

McBride wasn't so circumspect. 'The full story, this time. No beating about the bush,' he warned. 'I'm up to here with evasions.'

'As soon as I got home I phoned her and when I didn't get any answer, I went up to the attic to see if there were any lights on in her house. I thought I would go around if there were, and have it out with her. But while I was watching I saw Sweeney come into my line of vision from the direction of the river. He was carrying something – a cloth of some kind, I think. He disappeared into the house. When I opened the window to look out further, I heard music. Ella Fitzgerald singing "Manhattan", one of Vangie's favourites, so it came to me that maybe they had made up. Or that I might have got the story wrong. Or that she and Sweeney were laughing up their sleeves at me.' He hunched his shoulders. 'I was that confused and hurt, I didn't know what to think, so I went off to bed.'

'But you didn't seem surprised she was dead when you came around next morning,' Recaldo said.

'My first reaction was to assume she had collapsed naturally, as it were. If you'd seen her after we got off the boat, you wouldn't have been surprised either. The poor creature was nearly dead anyway. I knew she hadn't long. All that stuff about a holiday in Florida was only to keep her spirits up. She could hardly make it to

Duncreagh, never mind the airport. I took her to Duncreagh on Friday and she passed out on the way back. But then when I began to brood about it . . .'

'You really liked her, didn't you?' McBride was curiously subdued.

O'Dowd nodded. 'Yes,' he said simply. 'With her I could be myself. There aren't all that many like her, as you probably know,' he added slyly.

'But if she turned against you?' Recaldo asked. 'She was very capricious.'

'It was a risk,' O'Dowd smiled. He had a faraway look in his eye. 'But an exciting one. I reckon she had me infected with her conspiracies.' He grew serious. 'I'm sorry for my part in spreading those rumours about Spain. I can see now her information was probably unreliable. Though why she took so much against him, I don't know.'

'Recaldo here thinks it had something to do with her jealousy over the boy Gil. The way Spain was helping him while her daughter was left half-witted. How does that strike you?'

O'Dowd made a sour face. 'For pity's sake, she meant no harm – she was a great old tease.' He shook his head impatiently. 'I don't believe she would see it as harm.' *Would she?* hung in the air.

'You haven't seen Sweeney's car, have you?' Recaldo cut in.

'Yeah,' he drawled. 'I saw it in Daingean on Thursday evening, parked in the square. I waited by it for about an hour but there was no sign of him. Then I went off to collect a new phone and when I got back, the car wasn't there. I couldn't have been gone for more than ten minutes. I wanted a word with that bucko. Still do.' O'Dowd shook his head in frustration.

'Don't we all?' The two men stood up and were just at the door when Recaldo asked if Sweeney had been told about the proposed sale of the boat. It was then that O'Dowd pulled the detonator that stopped them in their tracks.

'Yeah. As we were getting off the boat on Tuesday, Evangeline told him to have it ready for Saturday morning. That was the plan at the time.' O'Dowd avoided looking at them. 'And as far as he's concerned, it still is.'

'*She* told him?' Recaldo said slowly. 'So he must have realized then, even if he hadn't before, that she was behind the purchase as well as the resale.'

'Did he not react?' McBride asked curiously. 'Was she not afraid he'd vamoose with it?'

O'Dowd shrugged. 'Well, it wasn't what we agreed and I felt a bit upset. But in the end I had faith in her. Evangeline usually knew what she was doing.' He rolled his eyes. 'Which goes to show you how wrong I was.' He paused for effect and gave them a lazy grin. 'I suppose you know the yacht's gone? No? Oh yes, indeed it has. A friend of mine rang me at half six this morning when he saw it motoring across the bay,' he said, with a hint of his old bravado. 'I was going to ring you about it, and then you turned up so I thought it was because you'd spotted it was missing.' He spread his hands elegantly. 'Don't worry, he won't get very far. How could he? He can't sail it single-handed and the engine guzzles up fuel so he'll have to pull in to fill her up somewhere along the coast.' He held up a miniature cellphone. 'This is the new one. I'll give you a tinkle if I hear anything. Otherwise if I were you I'd get those old admiralty charts out and figure out what's the most likely spot for him to put in. It won't be hard, half the marinas are already closed for the season. And there aren't that many to begin with.' He gave them a beatific smile as he showed them the door.

They drove away in silence, each of them locked into their thoughts. As they were passing the Spillanes' house Recaldo asked his companion to pull up. 'It'd be no harm to have another word with Mona Spillane,' he said. 'She might have remembered something else.'

The old lady was all dressed up to go out, with a sprightly little black hat tilted over one eye. 'You look bewitching, Miss Spillane,' Recaldo said. 'I've brought Inspector McBride to see you.'

'Howya Mona?' greeted McBride cheerily. 'Frank here's been telling me what a great help you were with the car movements.' He grinned when she blushed with pleasure. 'I have a bet with him that you can't remember what other cars went into Trianach late Tuesday night – round the time you saw Mr Sweeney's Lexus on the move.'

'I can, of course,' she protested. 'But Frank said not to bother with the residents.' She wheeled her chair to the window and pointed across to Trianach, where the road forked three ways at the top of the causeway. 'I thought you only wanted the cars going up the left fork?'

'Yes, we do, but what about Smiler's car?' Recaldo asked. 'You told me he went out at about half six or seven but you didn't mention the time he came home.'

'I've been thinking about that and, you know, I'm almost certain he hit the junction earlier, just coming up to one o'clock. I always keep the World Service on during the night and that comes on after the ten to one shipping news. Mr Sweeney had just gone in for the second time and Smiler's Mercedes crossed the causeway shortly after. There couldn't have been more than five minutes in it. "Lilliburlero" was playing. Smiler took the middle fork though, so they wouldn't have seen each other anyways. One o'clock,' she finished triumphantly. 'I didn't see anyone after that, except the lights on the ceiling I told Frank about – around three, was it?'

Recaldo held out his hand. 'Come on, pay up,' he said and McBride, going along with the charade, dropped a handful of coins into his outstretched palm, grinning broadly at the old lady.

'Mona Spillane, you are the best damn witness we've had the whole week, we owe you a few drinks,' he exclaimed just as a car drew up outside the house.

'That'll be Hannah Foley,' said Miss Spillane happily. 'She's taking me shopping in Duncreagh.' She looked as excited as a child.

'Won't it be very crowded on a Saturday?' Recaldo asked.

'Isn't that what I love?' she laughed. 'A bit of life. Now then, boys, would you like to give us a hand out to the car?'

McBride scooped her up in his burly arms. 'Over the threshold with you then,' he said.

'If that's a proposal, I'll say yes,' she giggled girlishly. He settled her into the front seat while Recaldo folded the chair and put it in the boot.

'You boys wouldn't like to come and help the other end, Frank?' asked Hannah Foley as she climbed back into the driving seat.

Recaldo leaned in the front window and handed Mona a small slip of paper. 'That's my mobile number and the registration of the Lexus,' he whispered. 'Just in case you happen to spot it. Give me a ring if you do. But keep it under your saucy hat. We don't want anyone else to know.'

'Right so and don't forget the drinks you owe me or I'll be ringing to remind ye.'

'What a charmer,' McBride said as they drove away. 'Quite a relief after that O'Dowd fella. It was like having your mouth washed out with fresh mint. Lively old bird, isn't she?'

'And sharp with it.'

'I can see that, but what makes you think she'll spot Sweeney's car? Bit of a long shot, isn't it?'

'Clutching at straws.' He coloured slightly. 'I only said it to make her feel involved,' he said sheepishly. 'Or maybe because I feel a bit superstitious about Mona. After all, she gave me the first real lead on Sweeney when things were at their blackest.' He rubbed his chin. 'Clocking that car into Trianach so precisely was the longest shot there was, so maybe she'll get lucky again?'

'Worth a go, eh?' McBride said. 'You're full of old shit, FX. You're just an old softie. I know what you were up to all right – you have her eating out of your hand.'

'Wasted effort, you think?' He smiled. 'Maybe. She's had an interesting life, I greatly admire the way she makes the best of things.' He huffed out his cheeks. 'And at the very least it can't do any harm. Anyway, as I said, I have a kind of hunch . . .'

'Don't you know that bally car is fine sure sitting in some marina or other waiting for your man to pull in and take off. Leastways that's what I'd say. You?'

Recaldo sat up straight. 'No. Somehow I wouldn't.' He spoke slowly. 'If Sweeney killed her then I think he's flying by the seat of his pants. With his drinking habits that might not be too clever. You heard what Smiler said, he's a conceited ass . . . and liable to underestimate us along with all the other peasants. The one thing I've learned about Smiler in the last few days is that he doesn't often tell you anything important straight out.'

'I have to give it to the man, he's a great sense of timing. But I don't suppose it strikes you that way, FX? What with you worrying about the lady Cressida and all. How are you going to break the news to her?'

Recaldo drew in his breath. 'You tell me.'

It was after ten thirty when they drew up at the hotel car park and McBride suggested a spot of breakfast before splitting up to search for Sweeney's car and boat. 'Me stomach thinks me throat is cut,' was how he put it. They had just begun to tuck in when he said, 'Now then, FX, seeing we're such pals and all, when am I to meet the delectable Mrs Sweeney?'

'Oh, give over, McBride. You've never laid eyes on her.'

'Ah now, Troilus,' McBride was back on form. 'I wouldn't be too sure. Tell you what, she could do with a visit to Grafton Street. Those old Barbour jackets are a disaster for a good-looking girl like that.'

Recaldo grinned but refused to be drawn. 'There's a few things I'd better fill you in on,' he said.

'That'll be a first,' McBride began, then held up his hands. 'I surrender. Fire away.'

As Recaldo recounted in detail what Cressida and John Spain had told him the day before, McBride became unusually subdued, shocked even. 'You're a master of understatement, FX,' he said. 'That was one wonderful bitch. She certainly seems to have made Spain's life a misery, but you know yourself it makes it look even worse for him, and I know exactly how Coffey will react. And if Spain goes down the tubes then so will your girlfriend. Things aren't looking too good for them, are they?'

'To say the least,' Recaldo agreed gloomily.

'Christ,' McBride exploded. 'I'm surprised that cow wasn't knocked off long before this. I don't think I ever said this about a woman victim before, but that one deserved what she got.'

'No-one deserves that. She was on her way out anyway.'

'Balls. Look what she could achieve in one day. Think what might have happened had she gone on another few weeks. Even old Smiler had me feeling a bit sorry for him this morning. We need,' he said thoughtfully, 'to get the link between Walter and Sweeney absolutely established. Pronto. Hearsay isn't enough.'

'The children's disability?'

'Come again?'

Recaldo put down his cup with such force it broke the saucer. 'Gil Sweeney is deaf,' he cried. 'I thought you knew that.'

'And how would I,' McBride flared, 'unless someone like you told me?'

'But you asked the nun if the girl's deafness was congenital.'

'No, I asked her if her disability was congenital. I was floundering around in the feckin' dark. As usual. So now, let me ask you another few questions. Why was she standing up?'

'What?' Recaldo shouted. McBride, unperturbed, repeated the question.

'I somehow assumed John Spain imagined it. He kept harping on about how she always stood there . . .'

292

'Yeah, but think – who else but the old man goes close enough to the bank to spot whether she was alive or dead? All that fancy stuff about the mist and the flaming light. It's my belief that he wasn't going a-fishing at all but went to see if she was OK after the previous night's cavorting.' He sucked his teeth and looked at his companion. But Recaldo's mind was racing along its own track.

'If Sweeney –' He held up his hand as McBride began to protest. 'If Sweeney propped her up, maybe it was because he knew Spain's routine. Knew he would go out in the morning and if he saw her standing in her usual place then he might have assumed she was OK and rowed on downriver. Maybe Sweeney didn't know how unusual it was for her to be there in the morning?'

McBride looked at him thoughtfully. 'You really are quite set on Sweeney's guilt, aren't you? Are you telling me the sex with Spain was just as a turn on for Sweeney?' His lip curled. 'Kinky.' He thought for a moment. 'That scenario doesn't take O'Dowd into account, does it? Too many loose ends, I think. Look, Frank, don't get me wrong, I know your reputation and I respect your hunches but honest to God man, we're going to have to come up with something better than that.' He stood up. 'Let's get moving.' As they left the hotel, McBride said, 'Tell you what, that Cressida's a bloody lucky woman, FX. Does she know that? Realize you feckin' nearly ended up on a charge for her? Would have, if old Coffey had his way,' he chuckled. 'You underestimated him as well, old son, in case you don't know it.'

Before he had time to reply Recaldo's mobile phone shrilled.

'Mr Recaldo? It's Hannah Foley. Mona asked me to ring. Look, I've only got a couple of coins on me so I may be cut off. She said you're to come to the supermarket car—' The line went dead.

'I think we might be in business, Phil,' Recaldo started when the phone rang again.

'Sorry about that,' Hannah continued. 'Mona says she thinks what you're looking for is in the car park. I don't know what she's talking about but she's very insistent that we're not to move till you get here. All the disabled spaces were full so we're stuck away at the very back, close to the fish market, behind the recycling bins. The stink is indescribable which may be why the space was free. The rest of the car park is packed.'

'We're on our way.' He slipped the phone in his pocket. 'That was Hannah. Can we use your car, Phil?' he was asking when Finbarr Spillane popped up out of nowhere, eager for a chat.

'Frank, Mr Sweeney's ketch went out this morning, did you know?' he asked. 'I tried to chase you earlier but ye got away on me.'

'We heard but thanks anyway, Finbarr. Sorry we can't stop now, we're in a bit of a hurry. We were talking to Mona earlier.'

Finbarr grinned. 'You had her in great humour altogether the last time. She was full of it. D'ye know the Sweeneys' launch went out as well?'

'What?' they chorused. 'When?'

'More or less at the same time,' he cackled gleefully. 'There wasn't but four or five minutes in it. 'Twas right behind.'

'What about John Spain? Seen his boat this morning?'

Finbarr shook his head and somehow they managed to extract themselves without further entanglement. 'We better talk to him again later,' said McBride as they shot off.

To say he was a fast driver would be to seriously understate the case. It took them precisely nineteen minutes to cover the twelve miles to Duncreagh, where they made for the supermarket. Mona was sitting in the front seat of Hannah's car with her beady eye fixed on a filthy vehicle squeezed into a tight space overhung by elder bushes and almost obscured by them. The back of it was so caked in mud that it was hard to tell its colour. But what had obviously caught the old woman's sharp eye was the British licence plate. Someone – Hannah by the look of her hand – had tried to rub the mud off it and when he glanced at it, Recaldo's heart sank. The registration was wrong.

'I'm sorry,' Mona said ruefully, catching his disappointment. 'I only just realized it's E 812 EER. You said L 812 FLR. I didn't notice at first, I was that sure it was the right car.'

'Hang on.' Recaldo and McBride exchanged glances. Acting as one, the two men bent over the licence plate and McBride began to scrape at certain of the letters. Black masking tape had altered the Ls and F to Es. He looked up and grinned. 'Bingo,' he breathed. Recaldo went over to Mona and kissed her cheek. 'You are a miracle, Miss Spillane. My lucky star,' he whispered in her ear. 'I'll be in to see you in a few days to tell you all about it. With a bottle of champagne – at the very least. Or maybe we'll have a meal together in Lia's?' He put his finger to his lips and stood up. 'Thank you very, very much, Hannah. Both of you. We'll take it from here,' he said and as if they had all the time in the world the two men waited until the women had driven out of the car park. They had no wish to draw attention to themselves or to the abandoned Lexus so they strolled over to McBride's car and got in.

'Any way of getting the keys for that yoke?' McBride asked. 'I don't suppose Sweeney would be stupid enough to leave a spare set at the house, would he?'

Recaldo was already dialling the Dillons' number. Cressie answered at the second ring. 'No,' she said. 'I don't have one but there is – or was – a second set in the study. Bottom left drawer of the desk.'

'Mind if I go and look?'

'No. Can you tell me—?'

'Later, Cress. I'll be with you as soon as I can.' He was just about to cut the line when Cressie let out a yelp.

'Hang on, Frank. Hang on. I've just remembered. Val was using the spare keys, something went wrong with the first lot a couple of weeks ago – the thingummy that operates the locks wasn't working properly. He ordered a replacement.'

'Where?'

'Malone's. The dealer on the—'

'I know where it is. I'm on my way. Thanks, love.'

'Frank, they close at twelve on Saturdays.'

It was five to. 'Jesus,' Recaldo exploded and cut the connection. 'Out,' he ordered McBride. 'I might just make it.' He jumped out of the car and sprinted around to the driver's side, leaving a bemused McBride standing in the middle of the car park and scattering a series of irate shoppers as he exited at speed.

Thady Malone was settling himself fatly into his car when Recaldo adroitly blocked off the exit of the forecourt. When he saw who it was Malone heaved himself out again. 'Something urgent?' he asked mildly.

Recaldo cooled down and forced a rueful smile. 'Urgent for me, anyway, Mr Malone,' he said. 'I promised Val Sweeney I'd collect his spare keys on the way over. I was halfway there when I remembered. I hope you don't mind, Mr Malone, but the blasted battery on the

295

spare has also gone phut,' he added with glaring unoriginality but Malone, who was an amiable type, didn't seem to notice.

'Just as well I ordered two then, isn't it?' he wheezed. 'I only did it because I was having a bit of trouble with my own, there must be some kind of fault on them. Come on in. It won't take a minute.' He didn't ask any questions but he made Recaldo sign for the keys before he handed them over.

By the time Recaldo got back to McBride, he'd organized the removal of the Lexus to the Duncreagh garda station and alerted Coffey. 'He's on his way,' he said. 'We're to wait till then before we open it up.' He held out his hand for the spare keys. 'The pick-up truck will be here in about twenty minutes. But Coffey will take another hour or so – he drives like an undertaker. You take the car, I'll get a lift to the station with the truck, or stroll over.'

'Thanks, Phil, I'll be straight back. Can you square Coffey?'

'Sure thing. I don't envy you telling Cressida all this.'

'Better me than anyone else,' Recaldo said grimly.

McBride cleared his throat. 'Coffey said you were to get her to Trianach and wait for us there. And you're to pick up John Spain as well.'

'Some hope,' Recaldo murmured.

McBride touched his arm. 'Keep the faith,' he said and gave him the thumbs up.

Chapter Twenty-eight

CRESSIDA WAS WAITING FOR RECALDO AT THE DILLONS' GATE. DRESSED carelessly in jeans and her Barbour jacket, she looked as though she hadn't slept for weeks. 'Mary took Gil and the twins swimming again,' she said distractedly. 'She said she'll look after him until we . . . I . . . get back. I don't know how I'm ever going to be able to thank her.' She was close to tears. Recaldo touched her cheek tenderly with his hand but said nothing.

He reversed the car and retraced his journey to Duncreagh. A few miles along the way he turned into a deserted lane and pulled up at an entrance to a meadow where two large Jersey cows were leaning over a five-bar gate. They watched with unflinching interest while Recaldo, as circumspectly as he could, filled Cressida in on all that had happened since he had last seen her. She sat bolt upright staring ahead, her pallor more deathly than he had ever seen it. She didn't turn to him for consolation, nor could he offer her any. How could he, when everything that helped her case further tightened the noose around her husband? Her whole concern now was how to protect her child. This seemed to involve airbrushing his father's image. Recaldo was overwhelmed by a curious sense of unreality and the futility of his belief that the Lexus would yield something important. He had pinned too much on finding it. Wasted too much precious time. 'He's taken the boat out, scarpered,' he said harshly.

'Val's a good sailor,' she said. 'He won't come to any harm.' She sounded as though she was talking about a harmless excursion. He wanted to take her by the shoulders and pitch her back into the reality of her life with, as he believed, a vicious murderer. Mercifully at that moment McBride rang and inadvertently did his dirty work for him.

'Frank? I've only got a minute, Coffey's taking a leak. You were right in every respect. We've got the bastard. Mrs Walter's Italian chest was in the boot of the Lexus with all the stuff including the missing laptop. They're being fingerprinted as we speak.'

'That all?' Recaldo murmured as Cressie grabbed his arm. She could hear McBride's booming voice clearly in the confined space of the car. Recaldo covered her hand with his and held tight.

'No, you sap, that's not all.' McBride couldn't keep the excitement out of his voice. 'Would you believe a bloody shawl buzzing with bluebottles? All wrapped up in Tuesday's newspaper? The guy's a clown. And, you'll love this, there was a dinky little dictating machine caught up in the crumpled pages. He can't have noticed it. It was switched on. Boy, oh boy. Out of juice of course but it may yield something useful when we get it rolling. Coffey looks like a cat with the gold top. The eejit thinks it's all down to him. Ha. Hell, he even allowed himself to mention your own small contribution.'

'Right.'

'One other thing, there's also a full set of gentleman's country gear, similarly soaked. The stink is desperate. Ask the lady what your man was wearing on Tuesday. Quick.'

'Buff cords and a navy sweater as far as she can remember,' Recaldo replied after a hurried consultation with Cressie, who looked as if she was about to throw up.

'Tell her she's a honey,' McBride said and cut off. Recaldo switched off the phone and slipped it in his pocket and took Cressie in his arms. He held her until she stopped sobbing, his face buried in her hair. It smelt of apples, he noted absently. His heart was racing at the thought of the ordeal awaiting her, and him. And the fragility of their future.

John Spain was not at home, nor was his boat when they went down to the spit. They sat on a rock, huddled together against the chill breeze and postponed going to the Old Corn Store for as long as they could. They didn't talk much. The atmosphere was loaded with a feeling of doom, as though the world had stopped and was waiting for something ominous to happen. It was after four when McBride rang again to say he was on his way. They trudged slowly along the riverbank to the Old Corn Store garden.

The French windows were standing open. 'I'll wait here,' Cressida said nervously and sat down at the picnic table. 'I couldn't bear to go inside.'

'I'll be right out,' he said. He found the Magraws in the kitchen. Murray was uncorking a bottle of wine while Grace unwrapped the cellophane from around a plate of sandwiches.

She looked up. 'We picked these up in the village,' she said. 'Would you like to join us?'

'Thanks, I would, but d'you mind if we go outside?' Recaldo asked.

'Isn't it a bit cold?' Murray said querulously, exchanging glances with Grace.

'No,' she said firmly, 'let's all go. We can wear our jackets and there's a rug on the sofa, if we're too cold.'

Recaldo coughed. 'Mrs Sweeney is in the garden. Inspector McBride will be along shortly.'

'And Superintendent Coffey?' Murray asked. 'He asked us to meet him here.'

'I'm not sure,' Recaldo said. 'There's been a development.'

The couple looked at him enquiringly but he shook his head. 'I'm sorry, but I'm afraid we'll have to wait until the others arrive.' He cleared his throat. 'You don't mind meeting Mrs Sweeney? I should tell you she knew nothing about your cousin's relationship with her husband. Until the last few days, that is.'

Murray stared at him stonily but Grace said firmly, 'We'll cope. It must be pretty terrible for her. To be played for a fool and then all this . . .'

They trooped outside and Recaldo introduced them to Cressida, then helped Murray move the picnic table into the shelter of the house, while Grace went back and forth to the kitchen to fetch plates and glasses. They dawdled, making time to break the ice, but eventually the two couples sat down facing each other, and surprisingly it was Cressida who spoke first.

'The police are looking for my husband,' she said starkly. 'For Evangeline Walter's murder.' She nervously brushed her hair from her face, inadvertently exposing the faded bruise on her cheek.

'For questioning about her death,' Recaldo corrected.

Cressida ignored the interruption and ploughed on. 'It wouldn't have happened if I hadn't seen the girl. If I hadn't told him . . .'

'Halcyon? You met her?' Murray asked, suddenly alert.

'I've seen her. She looks like my son Gil.' She bit her lip. 'Who is the image of his father.' She looked at Murray pleadingly. 'Is she Val's daughter?' she whispered.

Murray looked away. 'I believe she may be,' he answered evasively.

'Oh for pity's sake,' Grace exploded. 'You know damn well she is.'

'Nobody can be absolutely sure without DNA testing,' Murray started, then caught Cressida's eye. 'Yes,' he relented, looking on her with pity. His voice softened. 'Yes, as far as I know Halcyon is V.J. Sweeney's daughter.'

'When did he and Evangeline first meet? He always pretended he didn't like her,' Cressida said in bewilderment. 'I knew nothing, nothing.' She wiped the tears from her eyes impatiently.

'They met about twenty-five or -six years ago, when they were students. She was blonde then too. They were very beautiful together,' he said dreamily as if he were also part of the rosy image he portrayed. Then suddenly his tone changed and he sat bolt upright. 'She was wild about him. Not me. I only met him a few times but I guess I always thought he was a conceited jerk. Sorry, ma'am, but that's how I felt. Evangeline made all the running in that relationship.' He sniffed. 'They lived together in New York for five or six years. Until shortly after Halcyon was born.'

'He never mentioned her. Not once,' Cressida said faintly, her face flushed. It was unclear whether she meant Evangeline or her daughter. 'Maybe he didn't recognize her? Her hair was dark when she came here.'

'She changed the colour about . . . I guess about ten, twelve years ago,' he said vaguely. 'Said she was tired of being regarded as a dizzy blonde.'

Grace gave a derisory snort but didn't further the blonde discussion.

'Were they married?' Cressida asked and Recaldo thought how sad and pathetic it was that she could know so little of the man she had submitted herself to for a dozen years. How long would she continue to make excuses for him? How long would it take for her to come to terms with his reality, and the ordeal that still awaited her? I have to get out of this place, he thought desperately. I have to get off this case. I have to take her to where the air is clean and nobody knows her or him or their terrible story. Where she'll be safe. He damned Coffey to hell for demanding that they wait in that accursed house.

'Cressida.' He stood up and laid his hand on her shoulder. 'Cressida, I want you to come down to Passage South with me.'

'Yes,' she said but then turned back to Murray. 'Did they marry?' she repeated.

'Marry? Oh no, they were way too cool. Too cool for kids as well, I guess.' Murray remarked.

'Did he leave her because of Halcyon's disability?' Cressie asked. Her voice had hardened. Recaldo gripped her shoulder and she stared up at him as if to say – I know you think I'm bloody pathetic but I need to see this through.

'Yes, I believe the jerk blamed Evangeline for that,' Murray said.

Cressida winced. 'Yes, that makes sense. He could never bear Gil near him once he realized he couldn't hear. But he never harmed him until the night I mentioned seeing the girl. I went too far – it was a shot in the dark. I shouldn't have said what I did. I should have worked it out first . . . What will happen to her now?'

'We'll look out for her. Evangeline asked us to be her guardian,' Grace said and touched Murray on the back of his hand. He smiled at her.

'That's right,' he said. 'We will see to her, visit her in the convent. Evangeline didn't expect us to take her to live with us or anything like that. We just have to make sure she's OK.' Relief made him garrulous.

'Murray, please,' Grace said. 'Let's sort out the details later?'

'Do you mind me asking how long she's been in care?' Cressida enquired softly.

'Since she was two or three,' Murray replied. 'Since infancy. The nuns have always taken care of her. And probably will continue to do so.'

'Did Val support her in any way? Has he ever?'

'Not as far as I know,' Murray said reluctantly. 'No, almost certainly not.'

'I should go and see her,' Cressida said.

'But Cressie,' Recaldo started then stopped abruptly. What could he say? Your husband's going to jail? You're going to leave him for me? We're in this together? But he found he could say none of those things. Nor, in the end, did he want to. Cressida would do what she felt right because if she did not then there was no hope for

301

them as a couple. His waiting time wasn't over; maybe it had only begun.

As if he had spoken aloud, Cressie reached up for his hand and grasped it in hers. She turned to face him. 'Frank?' Her voice was sad. 'You know I can't leave him now? I have to stay.' She might have added, 'and see him through.'

'Cress,' he cried, but she had turned back to the Magraws.

'I will look after Halcyon,' she said firmly. 'Whatever Val felt about her, she needs a family. He is her closest relation.'

The Magraws looked at her, appalled. Grace stretched out her hand to Cressida. 'But my dear girl, don't you see . . .'

'She's happy in the convent,' Murray interrupted harshly. 'Evangeline did not neglect her, she cared about her, whatever you think.'

'Oh Murray, get real. Evangeline was driven by resentment and anger,' Grace said succinctly.

'Oh Grace, that's not like you . . .'

'I'm not going to sit here and let that young woman take responsibility for someone she never heard of until a few days ago,' Grace said angrily.

'Neither did you,' he said.

'Quite.'

Cressida's head swivelled from one to the other in bewilderment. 'I only meant I'd go and see her, make sure she had some sense of us, have her come and visit us as often as I could manage. I didn't mean that you shouldn't take care of her as well if you want to. But we live so near. I wouldn't take her away from the life she knows. If she's happy in the convent then she should be left with the nuns, but if her circumstances change . . .' She held out her hands. 'My son is deaf. I was never frightened by his disability.'

'But Halcyon is mentally handicapped as well,' Grace said.

'Yes, Frank told me.' She smiled. 'We are lucky having John Spain to help Gil. He'll help her too, I know he will, he's so kind and gentle. The more people helping her the better, don't you think?' she urged. And somehow this last desperate plea drew all of them into Cressida's reality. She was trying to protect the two children, shield them from the stigma of being the offspring of a murderous thug.

In the ensuing silence, something caught Recaldo's eye. He stared out over the estuary and was about to go inside the house to fetch Evangeline Walter's field glasses when McBride appeared. The two men walked down to the water's edge. 'I think that's Spain's boat moored at the Sweeneys' dock. D'you see?' Recaldo said. 'I have a sinking feeling he may have gone out in that launch.'

'Why?'

Recaldo hunched his shoulders, looking wretched. 'Somehow I don't feel the story is quite over yet, do you?'

'Indeed it is not. You never said a truer word.'

'Coffey not come?'

'No. He's buggered back to the forensic lab where the pathologist is at the ready, overjoyed at being hauled in from her weekend frolics.' He grinned. 'We've to consult him as the need arises,' he mimicked, then grew sober. 'She had the tape switched on. Forty-three minutes of mind-blowing horror. I don't know if there's an audio equivalent of snuff-movies. You don't want to know what sort of guy Cressida's been living with, but I think you want to keep her well clear of him. And if there is any nonsense about standing by her man, just you let me know. I'll soon put an end to it,' he said grimly. 'Jesus God. The press will lap it up. The mistress, the murderer, his wife, her lover. That's you, old son. Get them away from this place, her and the child. Yourself as well, Frank. You're finished here, the pair of you. This will never die down.' His lip curled. 'I'd burn this place down myself. That feckin' woman was off her rocker. Same as him. They were well met. They talked it all out while she waited for him to kill her. Lovely. Goaded him into it. She was high on it. It seems she's been on his case for nearly twenty years, since he abandoned her with the baby.' He shook his head from side to side. 'I should have told you. Doc Morrow said she was full of opiates, legal and otherwise. A whole blasted cocktail. All that was missing was a plastic bin-liner and an orange. If he hadn't done it she'd probably have managed it all by herself. But the bastard belted her one in the stomach.' He rubbed his cheek. 'We've put out a nationwide search for him. A too-dangerous-to-approach one. If he wasn't a monster before, he is now.' He looked around. 'And such a beautiful place too. You never know, do you? You just never know.' He sounded sickened.

For want of knowing what to do or say Recaldo clasped McBride's shoulder. As the two walked back up the garden to join the others, Recaldo stopped and held up his hand. 'Hear that?'

'What?'

'Come on. I think the lifeboat's going out.' He loped over the grass to the old slipway with McBride puffing after him. They couldn't see the lifeboat station, but could just hear the deep throbbing of the engines in the distance. Recaldo took his mobile phone from his pocket and dialled. 'Don't tell me you're on the crew?' McBride said. Recaldo shook his head. He held the receiver to his ear, identified himself then listened in silence. After a minute or two, he put the phone away.

'The *Halcyon*,' he said as calmly as he could. 'A Mayday call was received about five minutes ago. They've just called out the crew. Come on, we better get down there.'

They ran back to the others in the garden. The Magraws promised to give Cressida a lift to Recaldo's house. He gave her his keys. 'Wait for me there. Please. I'll be only five minutes.'

'We thought we'd go,' Murray said. He and Grace were standing hand in hand. 'If you like, we can stay with Mrs Sweeney until you get back then we'll check out of the hotel. We're going to stay with a friend in County Clare for a few days. We'll come back and sort this place out next week. If that's OK? We'll leave our contact address.'

Recaldo hopped into McBride's car and they drove away at high speed. At the approach to Passage South they were flagged down by one of the bar staff from Hussey's who wanted a lift to the lifeboat station. People were standing at their doorways looking solemn and watchful, as if they were already gearing themselves for bad news. A little group had gathered at the pier wall.

By the time they got to the boathouse four of the six men required, fully clad in yellow oilskins and rubber boots, were scrambling into the boat. 'The call came in a few minutes ago,' the coxswain shouted. 'There's a yacht in trouble off the Baltiboys Rocks.'

'How far is that?' McBride asked Recaldo.

'Oh, it's a good way out. It'll take a fair time – three or four hours, there and back. Charlie Curren will fill you in on what's going on. He's above in the Hon Sec's office. Up . . .' His voice was drowned as the huge twin engines roared into life and the lifeboat rushed down the slipway. Close to, the pristine, brightly painted vessel looked vast.

It was the first time McBride had seen it in action and he was astounded at how quickly it went from a standing start to full speed. He watched it spin round in a half-circle, making an enormous bow wave, but it looked much smaller in the water than it did close to and he found that he had crossed his fingers superstitiously as it roared out to sea.

Recaldo stood by the slipway and watched its progress while McBride climbed a metal ladder at the back of the building to the tiny office in the eaves where a young man in his early twenties was sitting at a desk in front of a panoramic window. He was wearing a set of headphones. When McBride waved his card in front of his nose, he pushed it aside and lifted one of the earpieces. 'It's OK. I know who you are, sir.' McBride postponed asking him how; he was getting used to the speed and accuracy of the local bush telegraph. He wondered laconically if they had yet acquired the full details of his pedigree and sexual preferences.

'Mind telling me how this works?'

Charlie Curren, one ear on the open phone line, quickly ran through the procedure. 'Mayday calls come into the IMES by radio, VHF channel sixteen.'

McBride held up his hand. 'What's IMES when it's at home?' he asked.

The boy gave him a withering look. 'The Irish Marine Emergency Services is what we call it around here, you can call it the coastguard if you like, 'tis all the one. They're very efficient. It all works like clockwork. When they have the position of the distressed vessel, they contact the nearest Marine Rescue Control Centre – in this case Valentia – which in turn controls the local transmitter.' He frowned. 'Hang on, we've lost contact with him. He's gone off air, but the call was automatically recorded so you can listen to it yourself.'

He flicked a switch and handed McBride the headphones. It was a male voice, slurred and indistinct. 'Mayday, Mayday, Mayday. Yacht *Halcyon* . . . Hotel Alpha Lima Charlie Yankee Oscar November. Ex *Azurra*. Repeat ex *Azurra*. One on board. Position north 51° 24′ west 9° 37′. Close Baltiboys Rocks . . .' Pause . . . 'Vessel drifting out of control. Out.'

'What does that mean, ex *Azurra*?' McBride asked.

'The boat used to be called *Azurra*. The name change was registered

305

a few months ago. But that's what it would still be known as, by many around here.'

'So you know who's on it?' McBride asked as he handed the headpiece back.

The other didn't answer for a moment. 'Yeah,' he said in a preoccupied voice. 'I saw him myself, going out this morning. I assumed he was just testing the engine or something because as far as I could see he was on his own. I didn't realize he was going out to sea or I would have warned him about the weather,' he said impatiently. 'We're still trying to raise him by radio but he seems to have let the microphone switch go. He's out of contact. Not good.' He looked dubious. 'Guy called Sweeney. He's a great sailor except for when he's drinking. Which is most of the time, these days. It's way too big a boat to be taking chances like that. I hope to God some other vessel out there picked up his distress call.'

'Was that his voice?'

Curren shrugged. 'Hard to say. Doesn't sound much like it. Too deep. Sounded familiar though. But it must be him all right. It says one on board.'

'How fast is the lifeboat?'

'She makes over seventeen knots – around twenty miles an hour.'

'That all? With those huge engines?' McBride expressed the astonishment of a true landlubber.

Curren smiled faintly. 'It takes some force to push through the weight of the sea. That's quite fast.'

'Right. So how long will it take to find the yacht?'

'About an hour or so to get there. They should find it easy enough – please God, unless the wind comes up and pushes her off position,' Charlie added, half to himself.

'Is that a possibility?'

'Anything's a possibility out there. Though it's calm enough at the moment, there's gales forecast for later on this evening. Then there's the problem of the light. The cloud cover is low, so it'll darken early. The greatest danger is Sweeney, if he's been drinking, then he would be, er, unpredictable. Might fall off or get too close to the Baltiboys. They're submerged most of the time. There's many a ship been wrecked on those old crags.'

McBride fell silent. 'Do you always alert the local garda?'

'Frank? We do. As a matter of routine. He has his own pager.'

306

'Does he usually come down for the call-out?'

'No-a but he's always down before the lifeboat gets back. He's very reliable.' Charlie's confident but scornful tone implied that Frank Recaldo had more sense than to be making a nuisance of himself in the middle of an emergency. McBride noted the criticism but his thoughts were drifting, with gathering concern, to the hours ahead and what trouble they might bring.

'How long will that be?'

Curren looked up. 'They should be at the Baltiboys in about three-quarters of an hour, maybe a bit more. Say an hour. Another to get the guy off the yacht. I'd begin to expect them back here after about three hours. So it's no use hanging around. Leave your mobile number and I'll call you as soon as they're close.' He spoke extremely politely but made it clear that the detective was a distraction he could do without. Nevertheless, McBride stayed for another ten minutes in the hope of some development. When there was none, he left the boathouse. It was a quarter to four. The lifeboat wouldn't be back till sometime between seven and eight – at the earliest. He went down to find Recaldo.

'What do you want to do?' McBride asked.

'Get back to Cressie. She'll probably want to have Gil with her. Then we'll go and look for John Spain. I need to keep her busy,' he said bleakly.

'Rather you than me. Let's hope the Sweeney bugger drowns. Save her and the rest of us a hell of a lot of trouble. One nice little anodyne statement to the press.'

'Chance would be . . .'

'A fine thing,' McBride finished. 'I wish. Look Frank, that feckin' car did for me, I'm knackered. I'm going up to the hotel to get this thing written up. I might even get in an hour's kip. The guy said he'd phone when the lifeboat is on its way back.' He took Recaldo's arm. 'Come on,' he said. 'I'll give you a lift home, old friend.'

Chapter Twenty-nine

IT WAS BLOWING A GALE AND DARK WHEN AT LAST THEY GOT WORD that the lifeboat was heading into port. McBride picked Recaldo up and they drove in silence to the boat station. They checked with Curren who remained in the office while they waited below on the jetty. Mercifully, all but the hardiest of the gawpers had long since retired even before the rain began to lash down.

'Did you get the boy?' McBride asked.

'No, he's better off where he is for now.'

'I don't suppose you found Spain?'

Recaldo shook his head. 'No sign. As sure as anything he's out in that blasted launch,' he added bleakly. 'Let's hope the lifeboat spotted him.'

'Shit. Cressida?'

'She's still at the house. Doctor McCarthy came around earlier and gave her some sedatives but she's in a terrible state. I'm taking her and Gil to Dingle as soon as you give me the word. I've arranged to borrow my brother's house. He's in the States for the next month or so, as it happens.'

'Good. So it all depends on what the lifeboat comes back with. I'll give you as much warning as I can before the press statement is issued. And do my best to sort Coffey. I'd like you to read my report before I give it to him. All packed?'

'Yeah.'

Curren came down from the office. 'She's coming in. They've towed back Sweeney's launch, that's what took them so long. It was out there as well. They're leaving it at the harbour.' His voice was accompanied by the low throb of the lifeboat engines as it neared the jetty.

The crew looked sombre and exhausted as they disembarked silently and trooped up to Hussey's bar. The cox climbed out last. Curren passed him a plate of sandwiches and flask of hot tea laced with brandy. He nodded to the Gardai and took several gulps before he said anything.

'Frank. We have John Spain's body below. I'm sorry, I know he was a friend of yours.'

Though he'd half expected it, it was like a punch in the solar plexus. 'Ah God.' Recaldo found his eyes welling. 'Did he drown?'

'No. I think he must have had a heart attack or something. He had Sweeney's body half in, half out of the launch and was slumped over him. Must have exerted himself too much – Sweeney was a big chap. We think it might have been Spain sent the Mayday. There was a radio on the launch.'

'You have Sweeney's body as well?' McBride intervened.

'No, the line went as we tried to haul him on board. We lost him, I'm afraid. It's a filthy night.' He looked shattered.

'We'll try not to keep you,' McBride said quietly. 'But could you tell us what happened?'

The cox took another gulp of tea. 'The storm closed in suddenly as we neared the Baltiboys. The conditions were atrocious, blowing hard, and the water was boiling up around the rocks. We could see the yacht lying on its side with the mast broken. It must have snapped at the base. We circled around, but could see no sign of life or anyone clinging to the rocks. It wasn't very likely, they were almost submerged. We were trying to work out a way of getting someone on board when suddenly one of the lads – young Paul Heron – spotted the launch drifting towards us. We nearly ran him down. I don't know how the hell he got out there in that stupid river boat, but there he was. He wouldn't have been seen except for his yellow overalls.'

The cox stopped and swallowed more tea thirstily and wolfed a couple of the sandwiches. 'God rest his troubled soul. I don't think it occurred to us that he might be dead. He's such a tough old fellow. Strong as a bull. Brave man.' In a despairing gesture, he put his hand to his beard. 'It took a long time to snag the boat with a grappling hook. We had to haul it in very, very slowly for fear it would break loose or run out of control and smash into us. It's not built for the sea at all, it was rolling and pitching like nobody's business. I don't know how he ever managed to keep it afloat. Then the hook let go and the boat went under a breaker; when it came up Sweeney – if it was Sweeney – was gone and Spain was hanging over the side. Paul volunteered to be lowered into the boat and attach the line. That young lad is a real hero. It was a risky manoeuvre and at first I wouldn't let him – it was bloody murder out there – but we couldn't leave the old man, he might have still been alive, though God knows there was little sign of it . . .' He stopped and ran his hand over his bald head. 'And that's what we did. Spain was dead though. We spent another half-hour trying to find the other body but had no luck. We'll go out tomorrow for another search, when the tide is low. He may wash up on the crags.'

It was another hour, and well past midnight, by the time Dr McCarthy had seen the body and pronounced John Spain dead. 'MI,' he said firmly. 'Myocardial infarction. I don't know how he's kept going so long. He had an attack about five years ago. And maybe since though he hasn't been to see me for some time. Tortured soul, wasn't he? But a sound man for all that. My wife will miss him. She always says his lobsters are the best in the world. God rest his soul.'

After the doctor left, McBride waited on his own for the Duncreagh undertaker while Recaldo went home. Cressida was in the kitchen, sitting at the table nursing a cold cup of tea. She looked up apprehensively when he let himself in the door. 'I woke up and heard the lifeboat coming in,' she said. 'I was waiting for you to call. Did they not find it?' She didn't look as if she could take much more.

Recaldo took off his coat and fetched the brandy before replying. He sat down beside her and took her hand. 'Yes, my love, they found the boat but . . .' he hesitated before gently outlining the cox's report verbatim. When she heard Spain was dead she put her head on the table and wept bitterly. Recaldo poured two stiff brandies and held one to her lips.

'Did you know he'd gone out after Val?' she asked.

'Finbarr saw the launch go out at the same time as the ketch.' He found he couldn't bring himself to pronounce Sweeney's name. 'When I saw John's boat at your dock, I guessed.'

'Why, why?' she sobbed. 'He must have known how dangerous it was.' She stopped short and lifted her head. 'How did he know where Val's boat was headed?' she whispered.

'I couldn't tell you, but I have a feeling he must have been watching the yacht. Maybe he even talked to him.'

'He destroyed himself, trying to save me,' she said fearfully. 'Poor John. Poor dear John. I'll miss him so much,' she sobbed. 'Oh Frank, what'll we do?'

He put his arms around her until she stopped crying and held her for a long time after that, with his face buried in her hair. They talked long into the small hours then stretched out on his bed together.

'Val's dead. Val's dead and all I feel is relief.' She swallowed hard. 'What'll happen now?'

'You're going to let me help you, that's what's going to happen. We're getting the hell out of here as soon as we possibly can. Later we'll decide what's best. For all of us. We'll pick up Gil first thing in the morning and go from there to Dingle,' he said. 'Phil has promised to cover for me.' Suddenly they were making love with a frenzy that took them beyond their fear. Afterwards Cressida slept but Recaldo only dozed fitfully, listening to the soft rise and fall of her breath.

The lifeboat did not go out again on Sunday morning. A trawler, fishing off the Baltiboys Rocks, picked up Valentine Sweeney's body at ten fifty-seven a.m. and delivered it up to the authorities, at Passage South, at ten minutes past noon. The captain reported that the *Halcyon* was completely broken up and not worth salvaging.

A shocked Cressida identified her husband with Dr McCarthy in attendance. Afterwards Recaldo drove Cressida to the Dillons' to collect Gil.

Passage South

THE PEOPLE OF PASSAGE SOUTH CAME DOWN TO THE SEA. THEY came singly or in small groups, in dribs and drabs, slowly gathering until a single file stretched from the harbour along the water's edge almost as far as the Glár estuary. Nobody bid them come. The knowledge of what was about to take place seemed simply to have osmosed into the collective consciousness. The need to mark the horror of what had happened was strong in them, as well as the need to mourn.

It was a soft evening, coming on to dusk, with rain so fine it was like a veil floating over the surface of the water. It gently shrouded Sweeney's motor launch and John Spain's small open fishing boat which were tied up at the pier. The crowd stood in expectant silence or else murmured amongst themselves until the church bell began to toll. A few minutes later a black-suited priest crossed the road and walked rapidly down the quay. He looked neither to right nor left.

A shiny black hearse gradually emerged from the mist with a straggle of mourners following behind on foot down the cobbled street. The funeral procession made its way slowly to the pier where the boats lay waiting, the lone helmsman standing amidships in the fishing boat, facing the shore. Four fishermen stepped forward and, as they lifted the coffin from its bier, the priest was seen to speak quietly over it. Those who had waited to pay their last respects bowed their heads and a low murmur rippled softly through the crowd as the coffin was carried down the narrow quay, the bearers keeping pace with the tolling bell. They stopped, then awkwardly lowered it into the fishing boat and laid it on the thwarts. There was so little space that the tall helmsman, Recaldo, looked in danger of being edged backwards over the transom.

Such a ceremony as this had never been seen. There was something strange and primitive about it, pagan almost, in the deepening gloom. The priest looked uncertain, unsure whether he should be taking part at all. It was perhaps as well that he had not been told how the disposal of the deceased was to be arranged. He passed among the mourners who had arrived on foot and spoke briefly to each of them. There were nine: Cressida and her son Gil, Halcyon, McBride, Grace and Murray, O'Dowd, Spain's sister and an accompanying nun. Strangely it was Cressida who was supporting Halcyon. The frail, childlike girl clung to one hand, Gil to the other. McBride stood behind them, shielding them protectively.

After a few minutes, the priest turned away and trudged back up the hill to the church. As if his departure was the signal, the little cluster of mourners walked to where the motor tender was tied up. Smiler O'Dowd got on board first. He put out his hand to steady the others as they climbed in then took his place at the wheel. The church bell stopped, the only sound now the water lapping against the sides of the boats and the quay wall.

Suddenly the silence was broken by the slow dull throb of the powerful engines of the lifeboat which burst out of the mist and eased into position in front of the harbour. Immediately the little engine of the *Consuela* sputtered into life and the fishing boat slipped its mooring. It arced slowly out into the bay, with the launch following at a short distance behind.

On cue, a flotilla of red-sailed Mermaids came around the point from the sailing school and scurried over to join the procession. From the marina a small fleet of fishing boats of all shapes and descriptions followed, then two or three sailing vessels, motor launches, and four or five rowing boats. The great armada stretched from the harbour to the mouth of the estuary, keeping some distance from the principal boats. When there was still draught and space enough, the lifeboat slowed down to a crawl and circled back into the bay while the funeral procession continued up the Glár.

At the ruined church by the water's edge the *Consuela* peeled off with the tender close behind. The remaining craft held back or else prowled slowly back and forth while the funeral boats were skilfully

313

navigated through the shallow waters to the bank where there was an ancient and long-disused graveyard. Cressida and Gil clambered on shore and, without ceremony, Gil laid a single lily on the grave of the famine children. His mother had her arm around him as they returned to the launch. They were both weeping.

The two boats regained the centre of the estuary by slow degrees and continued upstream until they had passed the Old Corn Store. Shortly after this they reached the spit of land which curled around to where John Spain's cottage lay. There, a small group of neighbours waited in silence at the little inlet and as the fishing boat made a deep circle, the children threw flowers on the water. After a moment or two Recaldo pointed the *Consuela* into midstream once more and with the launch in attendance passed back down the estuary.

The lifeboat was waiting to escort them as they came out into the bay. Night had begun to fall and pale light from a full moon shimmered on the surface of the water. By now the smaller boats were safely back in harbour, though a dozen or more bigger craft rejoined the flotilla which, led by the lifeboat, went far out into the bay. From the shore it was no longer possible to make out individual boats or to distinguish the *Consuela* in their midst. Yet the crowd on the shore continued to grow. Gradually the people inched further down the quayside to the water's edge and stood expectantly in the chilly night air. On the street above the harbour, people were watching from upper windows and a subdued group was gathered outside Hussey's bar.

Three flares, let off in rapid succession, exploded the silence, lighting the scene out in the bay. There was a sharp intake of breath from the waiting throng. They watched as the circle of boats widened further and further away from the *Consuela*, leaving it isolated in the centre. Recaldo cut the outboard motor and, undoing the brackets holding it to the transom, tipped it into the sea. The circle of ships continued to widen outwards as the mist miraculously cleared and the moon shone down on the frail little barque. The helmsman's dark figure pulled itself upright, one hand resting on the coffin. For a moment nothing moved, then the motor launch appeared out of the gloom and took Recaldo aboard.

As it moved away there was the sound of an explosion and simultaneously a light began to flicker beneath the coffin. The crowd grew even stiller. Two more explosions and now the fire took hold. Within seconds the boat was engulfed and, almost before the watchers realized what was happening, the burnt shell had disappeared from view behind a great pall of black, tar-laden smoke. The silence was tangible.

Epilogue

COUNTY KERRY – EIGHT MONTHS LATER

ON THE CLIFFS ABOVE THE BLASKET SOUND GIL WAS FLYING A KITE. HE ran back and forth over the wet grass with Finnegan and a much chastened Barker at his heels. Halcyon stood entranced, watching the kite swoop and rise in ever increasing circles into the clear blue sky. A little distance from the children, Frank and Cressie were walking arm in arm, their faces turned up to catch the frail warmth of the sun. 'Gil, don't go too near the edge,' Cressie called as the child dashed past. He turned and waved, then patted a small radio receiver clipped to the front of his dungarees. 'Can't 'ear,' he said cheekily and pointed skyward. 'Look, 'igh, 'igh,' he shouted in wild delight. When Halcyon set off in pursuit Cressie made to chase after her but Frank tightened his hold. 'Let her be, she'll be fine. Look how happy she is.'

It was a bright, chilly June morning with the sea an astonishing turquoise as it crested through the narrow rapids. 'This is perfect,' Cressie murmured. Frank pointed at a great mass of rain cloud gathering on the horizon. 'We better make the best of it then,' he said. 'I'm not sure it's going to last.'

'Oh you,' she laughed. 'It's bliss. The day. The cottage. Us, us, us. Just don't wake me.'

'Pleased?' he asked gently and stroked her cheek with the back of his hand. The strained anxious look she had carried for months was slowly fading. 'My darling girl,' he murmured. Cressie reached up, took his face in her hands and kissed him. They stood locked in each other's arms. The children circled around them. 'Yuk,' Gil cried – or at least something very like it. 'Oh yuk.' He grabbed hold of his half-sister's hand and pulled her away, giggling.

Coribeen was sold – inevitably – to Smiler O'Dowd. Frank and Cressie had just bought a holiday cottage on another estuary, near Castlebrion further north on the Dingle peninsula, and were due to move in for the summer after their wedding the following week. Meantime they were staying with Frank's brother near Dunquin. They had spent the previous eight months living quietly on the outskirts of Dublin where Gil was at last going to school – and loving it.

'Ahoy there,' a voice called. They turned in unison to see Phil McBride toiling up the slope towards them. He grinned broadly at their surprise. 'No, I'm not psychic, your brother told me where I'd find you.' As he enveloped Cressie in a huge bear hug, their protruding bellies collided. 'What's your excuse?' Cressie giggled.

'The good life, old love, the good life.' He grinned sheepishly and put his arm around her shoulders. 'I must say, it's great to see the pair of you looking so, looking so . . . well . . . great. Bloomin' marvellous.'

'As it were,' said Cressida, patting her seven-month bump.

'Is that Halcyon I see with Gil? I didn't realize she was living with you.'

'Only intermittently. She's been here for the past week. One of the nuns is collecting her tomorrow.'

'She and Gil seem to be getting on well.'

Frank and Cressie exchanged looks. 'We're trying to tire her out, otherwise she'll spend the night prowling around the house turning the telly on and off. Still, she's a lot better than she was, now that she's more used to us. But you're right, Gil is very good with her. He's even developed some sort of rudimentary sign language which he assumes she understands and somehow or other it seems to work. We just take it as it comes – visit by visit. Sometimes it's fine, sometimes not.'

Frank threw back his head and laughed. 'What she means is – sometimes it's absolute hell. By the way, any more fallout, Phil?' he asked.

McBride shrugged. 'Since my transfer? Nah. Oh all right, my new super had a bit of a go, but nothing I couldn't handle. Oddly enough, old man Coffey was quite decent in the end. He likes a tidy package and we certainly gave him one – even if our methods were a tad unconventional. Though mind you, if you hadn't resigned when you did, things might have been different.' He looked from one to the other then dropped a little kiss on Cressie's forehead. 'Enough of all that. We survived, didn't we? I'm back in Dublin where I belong and, well, let's say I've found a pal . . .' He coloured faintly.

'Love?' Frank put his arm around his friend. 'It's in the air.'

'Is that a fact?' McBride said lightly, but his colour deepened.

'It certainly is,' said Cressie. She held out her arms and when Gil jumped into them she twirled him around. As the kite swooped dangerously, Gil ran off again shouting: 'It's a girr-ul, it's a girr-ul.'

'Is it?' McBride asked.

'Gil seems to think so.' She linked his arm. 'It's wonderful you're here, we didn't expect to see you till the wedding next week. You are coming, aren't you?'

'Well you can't have it without me, can you? Amn't I your best man? But since Troilus here doesn't want a stag night, I thought we could have a nice couple of days together while you're still living in sin.' He laughed. 'All this respectability is threatening to do my head in.'